The Collected Supernatural and Weird Fiction of Charles Dickens Volume 2

The Collected Supernatural and Weird Fiction of Charles Dickens Volume 2

Contains two novellas 'The Haunted Man and the Ghost's Bargain' and 'The Cricket on the Hearth', two novelettes 'The Chimes' and 'The Haunted House' and ten short stories to chill the blood

Charles Dickens

The Collected
Supernatural and Weird
Fiction of Charles Dickens
Volume 2
Contains two novellas 'The Haunted Man and the Ghost's Bargain' and 'The Cricket on the Hearth', two novelettes 'The Chimes' and 'The Haunted House' and ten short stories to chill the blood
by Charles Dickens

FIRST EDITION

Leonaur is an imprint
of Oakpast Ltd

ISBN: 978-1-84677-848-3 (hardcover)
ISBN: 978-1-84677-847-6 (softcover)

http://www.leonaur.com

Publisher's Notes

In the interests of authenticity, the spellings, grammar and place names used have been retained from the original editions.

The opinions of the authors represent a view of events in which he was a participant related from his own perspective, as such the text is relevant as an historical document.

The views expressed in this book are not necessarily those of the publisher.

Contents

The Chimes

A.k.a. A Goblin Story of Some Bells That Rang an Old Year Out & a New Year In

First Quarter

There are not many people—and as it is desirable that a story-teller and a story-reader should establish a mutual understanding as soon as possible, I beg it to be noticed that I confine this observation neither to young people nor to little people, but extend it to all conditions of people: little and big, young and old: yet growing up, or already growing down again—there are not, I say, many people who would care to sleep in a church. I don't mean at sermon time in warm weather (when the thing has actually been done, once or twice), but in the night, and alone.

A great multitude of persons will be violently astonished, I know, by this position, in the broad bold Day. But it applies to Night. It must be argued by night. And I will undertake to maintain it successfully on any gusty winter's night appointed for the purpose, with any one opponent chosen from the rest, who will meet me singly in an old churchyard, before an old church door; and will previously empower me to lock him in, if needful to his satisfaction, until morning.

For the night-wind has a dismal trick of wandering round and round a building of that sort, and moaning as it goes; and of trying with its unseen hand, the windows and the doors; and seeking out some crevices by which to enter. And when it has got in; as one not finding what it seeks, whatever that may be, it wails and howls to issue forth again; and not content with stalking through the aisles, and gliding round and round the pillars, and tempting the deep organ, soars up to the roof, and strives to rend the rafters; then flings itself despairingly upon the stones below, and passes, muttering, into the vaults. Ugh! Heaven preserve us, sitting snugly round the fire! It has an awful voice, that wind at midnight, singing in a church!

But, high up in the steeple! There the foul blast roars and whistles! High up in the steeple, where it is free to come and go through many an airy arch and loophole, and to twist and twine itself about the giddy stair, and twirl the groaning weathercock, and make the very tower shake and shiver!

High up in the steeple of an old church, far above the light and murmur of the town and far below the flying clouds that shadow it, is the wild and dreary place at night: and high up in the steeple of an old church, dwelt the Chimes I tell of.

They were old Chimes, trust me. Centuries ago, these Bells had been baptized by bishops: so many centuries ago, that the register of their baptism was lost long, long before the memory of man, and no one knew their names. They had had their Godfathers and Godmothers, these Bells (for my part, by the way, I would rather incur the responsibility of being Godfather to a Bell than a Boy), and had had their silver mugs, no doubt, besides. But Time had mowed down their sponsors, and Henry the Eighth had melted down their mugs; and they now hung, nameless and mugless, in the church tower.

Not speechless, though. Far from it. They had clear, loud, lusty, sounding voices, had these Bells; and far and wide they might be heard upon the wind. Much too sturdy Chimes were they, to be dependent on the pleasure of the wind, moreover; for, fighting gallantly against it when it took an adverse whim, they would pour their cheerful notes into a listening ear right royally; and bent on being heard, on stormy nights, by some poor mother watching a sick child, or some lone wife whose husband was at sea, they had been sometimes known to beat a blustering Nor'Wester; ay, "all to fits," as Toby Veck said;—for though they chose to call him Trotty Veck, his name was Toby, and nobody could make it anything else either (except Tobias); he having been as lawfully christened in his day as the bells had been in theirs, though with not quite so much of solemnity or public rejoicing.

For my part, I confess myself of Toby Veck's belief, for I am sure he had opportunities enough of forming a correct one. And whatever Toby Veck said, I say. And I take my stand by Toby Veck, although he *did* stand all day long (and weary work it was) just outside the church-door. In fact he was a ticket-porter, Toby Veck, and waited there for jobs.

And a breezy, goose-skinned, blue-nosed, red-eyed, stony-toed, tooth-chattering place it was to wait in, in the winter-time, as Toby Veck well knew. The wind came tearing round the corner—especially the east wind—as if it had sallied forth, express, from the confines of the earth, to have a blow at Toby. And oftentimes it seemed to come upon him sooner than it had expected, for bouncing round the corner, and passing Toby, it would suddenly wheel round again, as if it cried "Why, here he is!"

Toby was curious about the Bells because there were points of resemblance between them and him. They hung there in all weathers, with the wind and rain driving in upon them; facing only the outsides of all the houses; never getting any nearer to the blazing fires that gleamed and shone upon the windows or came puffing out of the chimney tops; and incapable of participating in any of the good things that were constantly being handed through the street doors and iron railings to prodigious cooks. Being but a simple man, he invested the Bells with a strange and solemn character.

They were so mysterious, often heard and never seen; so high up, so far off, so full of such a deep, strong melody, that he regarded them with a species of awe; and sometimes when he looked up at the dark arched windows in the tower, he half expected to be beckoned to by something which was not a Bell, and yet was what he heard so often sounding in the Chimes. For all this Toby scouted with indignation a certain flying rumour that the Chimes were haunted, as implying the possibility of their being connected with any Evil thing. In short, they were very often in his ears, and very often in his thoughts, but always in his good opinion; and he very often got such a crick in his neck by staring with his mouth wide open, at the steeple where they hung, that he was fain to take an extra trot or two, afterward, to cure it.

The very thing he was in the act of doing one cold day, when the last drowsy sound of Twelve o'clock, just struck, was humming like a melodious monster of a Bee, and not by any means a busy Bee, all through the steeple?

"Dinner time, eh!" said Toby, trotting up and down before the church. "Ah!"

Toby's nose was very red, and his eyelids were very red, and he winked very much, and his shoulders were very near his ears, and his legs were very stiff, and altogether he was evidently a long way upon the frosty side of cool.

"Dinner time, eh!" repeated Toby, using his right hand muffler like an infantine boxing-glove, and punishing his chest for being cold. "Ah-h-h-h!"

He took a silent trot, after that, for a minute or two.

"There's nothing," said Toby, "more regular in its coming round than dinner time, and nothing less regular in its coming round than dinner. That's the great difference between 'em. It's took me a long time to find it out. I wonder whether it would be worth any gentleman's while, now, to buy that observation for the Papers; or the Parliament!"

Tony was only joking, for he gravely shook his head in self-depreciation.

"Why! Lord!" said Toby. "The Papers is full of observations as it is; and so's the Parliament. Here's last week's paper, now;" taking a very dirty one from his pocket, and holding it from him at arm's length; "full of observations! Full of observations! I like to know the news as well as any man," said Toby, slowly; folding it a little smaller, and putting it in his pocket again: "but it almost goes against the grain with me to read a paper now. It frightens me almost. I don't know what we poor people are coming to. Lord send we may be coming to something better in the New Year nigh upon us!"

"Why, father, father!" said a pleasant voice, hard by.

But Toby, not hearing it continued to trot backward and forward: musing as he went, and talking to himself.

"It seems as if we can't go right, or do right, or be righted," said Toby. "I hadn't much schooling, myself, when I was young; and I can't make out whether we have any business on the face of the earth, or not. Sometimes I think we must have—a little; and sometimes I think we must be intruding. I get so puzzled sometimes that I am not even able to make up my mind whether there is any good at all in us, or whether we are born bad. We seem to do dreadful things; we seem to give a deal of trouble; we are always being complained of and guarded against. One way or another, we fill the papers. Talk of a New Year!" said Toby, mournfully. "I can bear up as well as another man at most times; better than a good many, for I am as strong as a lion, and all men an't; but supposing it should really be that we have no right to a New Year—supposing we really *are* intruding——"

"Why, father, father!" said the pleasant voice again.

Toby heard it this time; started; stopped; and shortening his sight, which had been directed a long way off as seeking for enlightenment in the very heart of the approaching year, found himself face to face with his own child, and looking close into her eyes.

Bright eyes they were. Eyes that would bear a world of looking in, before their depth was fathomed. Dark eyes, that reflected back the eyes which searched them; not flashingly or at the owner's will, but with a clear, calm, honest, patient radiance, claiming kindred with that light which Heaven called into being. Eyes that were beautiful and true, and beaming with Hope. With Hope so young and fresh; with Hope so buoyant, vigorous and bright, despite the twenty years of work and poverty on which they had looked; that they became a voice to Trotty Veck, and said: "I think we have some business here—a little!"

Trotty kissed the lips belonging to the eyes, and squeezed the blooming face between his hands.

"Why, Pet," said Trotty. "What's to-do? I didn't expect you, today, Meg."

"Neither did I expect to come, father," cried the girl, nodding her head and smiling as she spoke. "But here I am! And not alone; not alone!"

"Why you don't mean to say," observed Trotty, looking curiously at a covered basket which she carried in her hand, "that you——"

"Smell it, father dear," said Meg, "Only smell it!"

Trotty was going to lift up the cover at once, in a great hurry, when she gayly interposed her hand.

"No, no, no," said Meg, with the glee of a child. "Lengthen it out a little. Let me just lift up the corner; just the lit-tle ti-ny cor-ner, you know," said Meg, suiting the action to the word with the utmost gentleness, and speaking very softly, as if she were afraid of being overheard by something inside the basket; "there. Now. What's that!"

Toby took the shortest possible sniff at the edge of the basket, and cried out in a rapture:

"Why, it's hot!"

"It is burning hot!" cried Meg. "Ha, ha, ha! It's scalding hot!"

"Ha, ha, ha!" roared Toby, with a sort of kick. "It's scalding hot!"

"But what is it father?" said Meg. "Come! you haven't guessed what it is. And you must guess what it is. I can't think of taking it out till you guess what it is. Don't be in such a hurry! Wait a minute! A little bit more of the cover. Now guess!"

Meg was in a perfect fright lest he should guess right too soon; shrinking away, as she held the basket toward him; curling up her pretty shoulders; stopping her ear with her hand, as if by so doing she could keep the right word out of Toby's lips; and laughing softly the whole time.

Meanwhile Toby, putting a hand on each knee, bent down his nose to the basket, and took a long inspiration at the lid; the grin upon his withered face expanded in the process, as if he were inhaling laughing gas.

"Ah! It's very nice," said Toby. "It ain't—I suppose it ain't Polonies?"

"No, no, no!" cried Meg, delighted. "Nothing like Polonies!"

"No," said Toby, after another sniff. "It's—it's mellower than Polonies. It's very nice. It improves every moment. It's too decided for Trotters. Ain't it?"

Meg was in ecstasy. He could *not* have gone wider of the mark than Trotters—except Polonies.

"Liver?" said Toby, communing with himself. "No. There's a mildness about it that don't answer to liver. Pettitoes? No. It an't faint enough for pettitoes. It wants the stringiness of Cocks' heads. And I know it an't sausages. I'll tell you what it is. It's chitterlings!"

"No, it an't!" cried Meg, in a burst of delight "No, it an't!"

"Why, what am I a thinking of!" said Toby, suddenly recovering a position as near the perpendicular as it was possible for him to assume. "I shall forget my own name next. It's tripe!"

Tripe it was; and Meg, in high joy, protested he should say, in half a minute more, it was the best tripe ever stewed.

"And so," said Meg, busying herself exultingly with her basket; "I'll lay the cloth at once, father; for I have brought the tripe in a basin, and tied the basin up in a pocket-handkerchief; and if I like to be proud for once, and spread that for a cloth, and call it a cloth, there's no law to prevent me; is there father?"

"Not that I know of, my dear," said Toby. "But they're always a bringing up some new law or other."

"And according to what I was reading you in the paper the other day, father; what the Judge said, you know; we poor people are supposed to know them all. Ha, ha! What a mistake! My goodness me, how clever they think us!"

"Yes, my dear," cried Trotty; "and they'd be very fond of any one of us that *did* know 'em all. He'd grow fat upon the work he'd get, that man, and be popular with the gentlefolks in his neighbourhood. Very much so!"

"He'd eat his dinner with an appetite, whoever he was, if it smelt like this," said Meg, cheerfully. "Make haste, for there's a potato besides. Where will you dine, father? On the Post, or on the Steps? Dear, dear, how grand we are. Two places to choose from!"

"The steps to day, my Pet," said Trotty. "Steps in dry weather. Post in wet. There's a great conveniency in the steps at all times, because of the sitting down; but they're rheumatic in the damp."

"Then here," said Meg, clapping her hands, after a moment's bustle; "here it is, all ready! And beautiful it looks! Come, father. Eat it while it's hot. Come!"

Since his discovery of the contents of the basket, Trotty had been standing looking at her—and had been speaking too—in an abstracted manner, which showed that though she was the object of his thoughts and eyes, to the exclusion even of tripe, he neither saw nor thought about her as she was at that moment, but had before him some imaginary rough sketch or drama of her future life. Roused, now, by her cheerful summons, he shook off a melancholy shake of the head which was just coming upon him, and trotted to her side. As he was stooping to sit down, the Chimes rang.

"Amen!" said Trotty, pulling off his hat and looking up toward them.

"Amen to the Bells, father?" cried Meg.

"They broke in like a grace, my dear," said Trotty, taking his seat. "They'd say a good one, I am sure, if they could. Many's the kind thing they say to me."

"The Bells do, father!" laughed Meg, as she set the basin, and a knife and fork before him. "Well!"

"Seem to, my Pet," said Trotty, falling to with great vigour. "And where's the difference? If I hear 'em, what does it matter whether they speak it or not? Why bless you, my dear," said Toby, pointing at the tower with his fork, and becoming more animated under the influence of dinner, "how often have I heard them bells say, 'Toby Veck, Toby Veck, keep a good heart Toby! Toby Veck, Toby Veck, keep a good heart Toby!' A million times? More!"

"Well, I never!" cried Meg.

She had, though—over and over again. For it was Toby's constant topic.

"When things is very bad," said Trotty; "very bad indeed, I mean; almost at the worst; then it's 'Toby Veck, Toby Veck, job coming soon, Toby! Toby Veck, Toby Veck, job coming soon, Toby!' That way."

"And it comes—at last, father," said Meg, with a touch of sadness in her pleasant voice.

"Always," answered the unconscious Toby. "Never fails."

While this discourse was holding, Trotty made no pause in his attack upon the savoury meat before him, but cut and ate, and cut and drank, and cut and chewed, and dodged about, from tripe to hot potato, and from hot potato back again to tripe, with an unctuous and unflagging relish. But happening now to look all round the street—in case anybody should be beckoning from any door or window, for a porter—his eyes, in coming back again, encountered Meg: sitting opposite to him, with her arms folded; and only busy in watching his progress with a smile of happiness.

"Why, Lord forgive me!" said Trotty, dropping his knife and fork. "My love! Meg! why didn't you tell me what a beast I was?"

"Father?"

"Sitting here," said Trotty, in penitent explanation, "cramming and stuffing, and gorging myself; and you before me there, never so much as breaking your precious fast, nor wanting to, when——"

"But I have broken it, father," interposed his daughter, laughing, "all to bits. I have had my dinner."

"Nonsense," said Trotty. "Two dinners in one day! It an't possible! You might as well tell me that two New Year's Days will come together, or that I have had a gold head all my life, and never changed it."

"I have had my dinner, father, for all that," said Meg, coming nearer to him. "And if you'll go on with yours, I'll tell you how and where; and how your dinner came to be brought; and-something else besides."

Toby still appeared incredulous; but she looked into his face with her clear eyes, and laying her hand upon his shoulder, motioned him to go on while the meat was hot. So Trotty took up his knife and fork again, and went to work. But much more slowly than before, and shaking his head, as if he were not at all pleased with himself.

"I had my dinner, father," said Meg, after a little hesitation, "with—with Richard. His dinner-time was early; and as he brought his dinner with him when he came to see me, we—we had it together, father."

Trotty said, "Oh!"—because she waited.

"And Richard says, father—" Meg resumed. Then stopped.

"What does Richard say, Meg?" asked Toby.

"Richard says, father—" Another stoppage.

"Richard's a long time saying it," said Toby.

"He says then, father," Meg continued, lifting up her eyes at last, and speaking in a tremble, but quite plainly; "another year is nearly gone, and where is the use of waiting on from year to year, when it is so unlikely we shall ever be better off than we are now? He says we are poor now, father, and we shall be poor then, but we are young now, and years will make us old before we know it. He says that if we wait, people in our condition, until we see our way quite clearly, the way will be a narrow one indeed—the common way—the Grave, father."

A bolder man than Trotty Veck must needs have drawn upon his boldness largely, to deny it. Trotty held his peace.

"And how hard, father, to grow old and die, and think we might have cheered and helped each other! How hard in all our lives to love each other; and to grieve, apart, to see each other working, changing, growing old and gray. Even if I got the better of it, and forgot him (which I never could), oh, father dear, how hard to have a heart so full as mine is now, and live to have it slowly drained out every drop, without the recollection of one happy moment of a woman's life, to stay behind and comfort me, and make me better!"

Trotty sat quite still, Meg dried her eyes, and said more gayly: that is to say, with here a laugh, and there a sob, and here a laugh and sob together:

"So Richard says, father; as his work was yesterday made certain for some time to come, and as I love him and have loved him fully three years—ah! longer than that, if he knew it!—will I marry him on New Year's Day; the best and happiest day, he says, in the whole year, and one that is almost sure to bring good fortune with it. It's a short notice, father—isn't it?—but I haven't my fortune to be settled, or my wedding dresses to be made, like the great ladies, father, have I? And he said so much, and said it in his way; so strong and earnest, and all the time so kind and gentle; that I said I'd come and talk to you, father. And as they paid the money for that work of mine this morning (unexpectedly, I am sure!), and as you have fared very poorly for a whole week, and as I couldn't help wishing there should be something to make this day a sort of holiday to you as well as a dear and happy day to me, father, I made a little treat and brought it to surprise you."

"And see how he leaves it cooling on the step!" said another voice.

It was the voice of the same Richard, who had come upon them unobserved, and stood before the father and daughter; looking down upon them with a face as glowing as the iron on which his stout sledge-hammer daily rung. A handsome, well-made, powerful youngster he was; with eyes that sparkled like the red-hot droppings from a furnace fire; black hair that curled about his swarthy temples rarely; and a smile—a smile that bore out Meg's eulogium on his style of conversation.

"See how he leaves it cooling on the step!" said Richard. "Meg don't know what he likes. Not she!"

Trotty, all action and enthusiasm, immediately reached up his hand to Richard, and was going to address him in a great hurry, when the house-door opened without any warning, and a footman very nearly put his foot in the tripe.

"Out of the ways here, will you! You must always go and be a-settin on our steps, must you! You can't go and give a turn to none of the neighbours never, can't you? *Will* you clear the road, or won't you?"

Strictly speaking, the last question was irrelevant, as they had already done it.

"What's the matter, what's the matter?" said the gentleman for whom the door was opened; coming out of the house at that kind of light, heavy pace—that peculiar compromise between a walk and jog-trot—with which a gentleman upon the smooth down-hill of life, wearing creaking boots, a watch-chain, and clean linen, *may* come out of his house: not only without any abatement of his dignity, but with an expression of having important and wealthy engagements elsewhere. "What's the matter? What's the matter?"

"You're always a-being begged, and prayed, upon your bended knees, you are," said the footman with great emphasis to Trotty Veck, "to let our door-steps be. Why don't you let 'em be? *Can't* you let 'em be?"

"There! That'll do, that'll do!" said the gentleman, "Halloa there! Porter!" beckoning with his head to Trotty Veck, "Come here. What's that? Your dinner?"

"Yes, sir," said Trotty, leaving it behind him in a corner.

"Don't leave it there!" exclaimed the gentleman. "Bring it here, bring it here! So! this is your dinner, is it?"

"Yes, sir," repeated Trotty, looking with a fixed eye and a watery mouth at the piece of tripe he had reserved for a last delicious tit-bit, which the gentleman was now turning over and over on the end of a fork.

Two other gentlemen had come out with him. One was a

low-spirited gentleman of middle age, of a meagre habit, and a disconsolate face; who kept his hands continually in the pockets of his scanty pepper-and-salt trousers, very large and dog's-eared from that custom; and was not particularly well brushed or washed. The other, a full sized, sleek, well-conditioned gentleman, in a blue coat, with bright buttons, and a white cravat. This gentleman had a very red face, as if an undue proportion of the blood in his body were squeezed up into his head, which perhaps accounted for his having also the appearance of being rather cold about the heart.

He who had Toby's meat upon the fork called to the first one by the name of Filer, and they both drew near together. Mr. Filer being exceedingly short sighted, was obliged to go so close to the remnant of Toby's dinner before he could make out what it was, that Toby's heart leaped up into his mouth. But Mr. Filer didn't eat it.

"This is a description of animal food, Alderman," said Filer, making little punches in it with a pencil-case, "commonly known to the labouring population of this country by the name of tripe."

The Alderman laughed, and winked; for he was a merry fellow. Alderman Cute. Oh, and a sly fellow too! A knowing fellow. Up to everything. Not to be imposed upon. Deep in the people's hearts! He knew them, Cute did. I believe you!

"But who eats tripe?" said Mr. Filer, looking round. "Tripe is without an exception the least economical, and the most wasteful article of consumption that the markets of this country can by possibility produce. The loss upon a pound of tripe has been found to be, in the boiling, seven-eighths of a fifth more than the loss upon a pound of any other animal substance whatever. Tripe is more expensive, properly understood, than the hothouse pineapple. Taking into account the number of animals slaughtered yearly within the bills of mortality alone; and forming a low estimate of the quantity of tripe which the carcases of these animals, reasonably well butchered, would yield—I find that the waste on that amount of tripe, if boiled, would victual a garrison of five hundred men for five months of thirty-one days each, and a February over. The Waste, the Waste!"

Trotty stood aghast, and his legs shook under him. He seemed to have starved a garrison of five hundred men with his own hand.

"Who eats tripe?" said Mr. Filer, warmly. "Who eats tripe?"

Trotty made a miserable bow.

"You do, do you?" said Mr. Filer. "Then I'll tell you something. You snatch your tripe, my friend, out of the mouths of widows and orphans."

"I hope not, sir," said Trotty, faintly. "I'd sooner die of want!"

"Divide the amount of tripe before-mentioned, Alderman," said Mr. Filer, "by the estimated number of existing widows and orphans, and the result will be one pennyweight of tripe to each. Not a grain is left for that man. Consequently, he's a robber."

Trotty was so shocked that it gave him no concern to see the Alderman finish the tripe himself. It was a relief to get rid of it, anyhow.

"And what do you say?" asked the Alderman, jocosely, of the red-faced gentleman in the blue coat. "You have heard friend Filer. What do *you* say?"

"What's it possible to say?" returned the gentleman. "What *is* to be said? Who can take any interest in a fellow like this," meaning Trotty, "in such degenerate times as these? Look at him! What an object! The good old times, the grand old times, the great old times! *Those* were the times for a bold peasantry, and all that sort of thing. Those were the times for every sort of thing, in fact. There's nothing now-a-days. Ah!" sighed the red-faced gentleman. "The good old times, the good old times!"

It is possible that poor Trotty's faith in these very vague Old Times was not entirely destroyed, for he felt vague enough, at that moment. One thing, however, was plain to him, in the midst of his distress; to wit, that however these gentlemen might differ in details, his misgivings of that morning, and of many other mornings, were well founded. "No, no. We can't go right or do right," thought Trotty in despair. "There is no good in us. We are born bad!"

But Trotty had a father's heart within him; which had somehow got into his breast in spite of this decree; and he could not bear that Meg, in the blush of her brief joy, should have her fortune read by these wise gentlemen. "God help her," thought poor Trotty. "She will know it soon enough."

He anxiously signed, therefore, to the young smith, to take her away. But he was so busy, talking to her softly at a little distance, that he only became conscious of this desire, simultaneously with Alderman Cute. Now, the Alderman had not yet had his say, but *he* was a philosopher, too—practical though! Oh, very practical!—and, as he had no idea of losing any portion of his audience, he cried "Stop!"

Trotty took Meg's hand and drew it through his arm. He didn't seem to know what he was doing though.

"Your daughter, eh?" said the Alderman, chucking her familiarly under the chin.

"And you're making love to her, are you?" said Cute to the young smith.

"Yes," returned Richard quickly, for he was nettled by the question. "And we are going to be married on New Year's Day."

"What do you mean?" cried Filer sharply. "Married!"

"Why, yes, we were thinking of it. Master," said Richard. "We're rather in a hurry you see, in case it should be Put Down first."

"Ah!" cried Filer, with a groan. "Put *that* down indeed. Alderman, and you'll do something. Married! Married!! The ignorance of the first principles of political economy on the part of these people; their improvidence; their wickedness is by Heavens! enough to—Now look at that couple, will you!"

Well! They were worth looking at. And marriage seemed as reasonable and fair a deed as they need have in contemplation.

"A man may live to be as old as Methuselah," said Mr. Filer, "and may labour all his life for the benefit of such people as those; and may heap up facts on figures, facts on figures, facts on figures, mountains high and dry; and he can no more hope to persuade 'em that they have no right or business to be married than he can hope to persuade 'em that they have no earthly right or business to be born. And *that* we know they haven't. We reduced that to a mathematical certainty long ago!"

"Come here, my girl!" said Alderman Cute.

The young blood of her lover had been mounting, wrathfully, within the last few minutes; and he was indisposed to let her come. But, setting a constraint upon himself, he came forward with a stride as Meg approached and stood beside her. Trotty kept her hand within his arm still, but looked from face to face as wildly as a sleeper in a dream.

"Now, I'm going to give you a word or two of good advice, my girl," said the Alderman, in his nice easy way. "It's my place to give advice, you know, because I'm a Justice. You know I'm a Justice, don't you?"

Meg timidly said, "Yes." But everybody knew Alderman Cute was a Justice! Oh dear, so active a Justice always! Who such a mote of brightness in the public eye, as Cute!

"You are going to be married, you say," pursued the Alderman. "Very unbecoming and indelicate in one of your sex! But never mind that. After you're married, you'll quarrel with your husband, and come to be a distressed wife. You may think not; but you will, because I tell you so. Now, I give you fair warning, that I have made up my mind to Put distressed wives Down. So, don't be brought before me. You'll have children—boys. Those boys will grow up bad, of course, and run wild in the streets without shoes or stockings.

"Mind, my young friend! I'll convict 'em summarily every one, for I am determined to Put boys without shoes or stockings, Down. Perhaps your husband will die young (most likely) and leave you with a baby. Then you'll be turned out of doors, and wander up and down the streets. Now don't wander near me, my dear, for I am resolved to Put all wandering mothers Down. All young mothers, of all sorts and kinds, it's my determination to Put Down. Don't think to plead illness as an excuse with me; or babies as an excuse with me; for all sick persons and young children (I hope you know the church-service, but I'm afraid not) I am determined to Put Down.

"And if you attempt, desperately and ungratefully, and impiously, and fraudulently attempt, to drown yourself, or hang yourself, I'll have no pity on you, for I have made up my mind to Put all suicide Down! If there is one thing," said the Alderman, with his self-satisfied smile, "on which I can be said to have made up my mind more than on another, it is to Put suicide Down. So don't try it on. That's the phrase, isn't it! Ha, ha! now we understand each other."

Toby knew not whether to be agonized or glad, to see that Meg had turned deadly white, and dropped her lover's hand.

"As for you, you dull dog," said the Alderman, turning with even increased cheerfulness and urbanity to the young smith, "what are you thinking of being married for? What do you want to be married for, you silly fellow? If I was a fine, young, strapping chap like you, I should be ashamed of being milksop enough to pin myself to a woman's apron-strings! Why, she'll be an old woman before you're a middle-aged man! And a pretty figure you'll cut then, with a draggle-tailed wife and a crowd of squalling children crying after you wherever you go!"

Oh, he knew how to banter the common people, Alderman Cute!

"There! Go along with you," said the Alderman, "and repent. Don't make such a fool of yourself as to get married on New Year's Day. You'll think very differently of it, long before next New Year's Day: a trim young fellow like you, with all the girls looking after you. There! Go along with you!"

They went along. Not arm in arm, or hand in hand, or interchanging bright glances; but she in tears; he gloomy and downlooking. Were these the hearts that had so lately made old Toby's leap up from its faintness? No, no. The Alderman (a blessing on his head!) had Put *them* down.

"As you happen to be here," said the Alderman to Toby, "you shall carry a letter for me. Can you be quick? You're an old man."

Toby, who had been looking after Meg, quite stupidly, made shift to murmur out that he was very quick, and very strong.

"How old are you?" inquired the Alderman.

"I am over sixty, sir," said Toby.

"Oh! This man's a great deal past the average age, you know," cried Mr. Filer, breaking in as if his patience would bear some trying, but this was really carrying matters a little too far.

"I feel I'm intruding, sir," said Toby. "I—I misdoubted it this morning. Oh dear me!"

The Alderman cut him short by giving him the letter from his pocket. Toby would have got a shilling too; but Mr. Filer clearly showing that in that case he would rob a certain given number of persons of ninepence-half-penny a-piece, he only got sixpence; and thought himself very well off to get that.

Then the Alderman gave an arm to each of his friends, and walked off in high feather; but, he immediately came hurrying back alone, as if he had forgotten something.

"Porter!" said the Alderman.

"Sir!" said Toby.

"Take care of that daughter of yours. She's much too handsome."

"Even her good looks are stolen from somebody or other I suppose," thought Toby, looking at the sixpence in his hand, and thinking of the tripe. "She's been and robbed five hundred ladies of a bloom a-piece, I shouldn't wonder. It's very dreadful!"

"She's much too handsome, my man," repeated the Alderman. "The chances are, that she'll come to no good, I clearly see. Observe what I say. Take care of her!" With which, he hurried off again.

"Wrong every way. Wrong every way!" said Trotty clasping his hands. "Born bad. No business here!"

The Chimes came clashing in upon him as he said the last words. Full, loud, and sounding—but with no encouragement. No, not a drop.

"The tune's changed," cried the old man, as he listened.

"There's not a word of all that fancy in it. Why should there be? I have no business with the New Year nor with the old one neither. Let me die!"

Still the Bells, pealing forth their changes, made the very air spin. Put 'em down. Put 'em down! Good old Times, Good old Times! Facts and Figures, Facts and Figures! Put 'em down, Put 'em down! If they said anything they said this, until the brain of Toby reeled.

He pressed his bewildered head between his hands as if to keep it from splitting asunder. A well-timed action, as it happened; for finding the letter in one of them, and being by that means reminded of his charge, he fell, mechanically, into his usual trot, and trotted off.

Second Quarter

The letter Toby had received from Alderman Cute, was addressed to a great man in the great district of the town. The greatest district of the town. It must have been the greatest district of the town, because it was commonly called "the world" by its inhabitants.

The Year was Old, that day. The patient Year had lived through the reproaches and misuses of its slanderers, and faithfully performed its work. Spring, summer, autumn, winter. It had laboured through the destined round, and now laid down its weary head to die.

Trotty had no portion, to his thinking, in the New Year or the Old.

"Put 'em down. Put 'em down! Facts and Figures, Facts and Figures! Good old Times, Good old Times! Put 'em down, Put 'em down!"—his trot went to that measure, and would fit itself to nothing else.

But, even that one, melancholy as it was, brought him, in due time, to the end of his journey. To the mansion of Sir Joseph Bowley, Member of Parliament.

The door was opened by a Porter. Such a Porter! Not of Toby's order. Quite another thing. His place was the ticket, though;

not Toby's.

This Porter underwent some hard panting before he could speak; having breathed himself by coming incautiously out of his chair, without first taking time to think about it and compose his mind. When he had found his voice—which it took him some time to do, for it was a long way off and hidden under a load of meat—he said in a fat whisper:

"Who's it from?"

Toby told him.

"You're to take it in yourself," said the Porter, pointing to a room at the end of a long passage, opening from the hall. "Everything goes straight in, on this day of the year. You're not a bit too soon; for the carriage is at the door now, and they have only come to town for a couple of hours, a'purpose."

Toby wiped his feet (which were quite dry already) with great care, and took the way pointed out to him, observing as he went that it was an awfully grand house, but hushed and covered up, as if the family were in the country. Knocking at the room door, he was told to enter from within; and doing so found himself in a spacious library, where, at a table strewn with files and papers, were a stately lady in a bonnet, and a not very stately gentleman in black, who wrote from her dictation; while another, and an older, and a much statelier gentleman, whose hat and cane were on the table, walked up and down, with one hand in his breast, and looked complacently from time to time at his own picture—a full length; a very full length—hanging over the fireplace.

"What is this?" said the last-named gentleman. "Mr. Fish, will you have the goodness to attend?"

Mr. Fish begged pardon, and taking the letter from Toby, handed it, with great respect.

"From Alderman Cute, Sir Joseph."

"Is this all? Have you nothing else, Porter?" inquired Sir Joseph.

Toby replied in the negative.

"You have no bill or demand upon me—my name is Bowley,

Sir Joseph Bowley—of any kind from anybody, have you?" said Sir Joseph. "If you have, present it. There is a cheque-book by the side of Mr. Fish. I allow nothing to be carried into the New Year. Every description of account is settled in this house at the close of the old one. So that if death was to—to—"

"To cut," suggested Mr. Fish.

"To sever, sir," returned Sir Joseph, with great asperity, "the cord of existence—my affairs would be found, I hope, in a state of preparation."

"My dear Sir Joseph!" said the lady, who was greatly younger than the gentleman. "How shocking!"

"My Lady Bowley," returned Sir Joseph, floundering now and then, as in the great depth of his observations, "at this season of the year we should think of—of—ourselves. We should look into our—our accounts. We should feel that every return of so eventful a period in human transactions involves matter of deep moment between a man and his—and his banker."

Sir Joseph delivered these words as if he felt the full morality of what he was saying, and desired that even Trotty should have an opportunity of being improved by such discourse. Possibly he had this end before him in still forbearing to break the seal of the letter, and in telling Trotty to wait where he was a minute.

"I *am* the Poor Man's Friend," observed Sir Joseph, glancing at the poor man present. "As such I may be taunted. As such I have been taunted. But I ask no other title."

"Bless him for a noble gentleman!" thought Trotty.

"I don't agree with Cute here, for instance," said Sir Joseph, holding out the letter. "I don't agree with the Filer party. I don't agree with any party. My friend, the Poor Man, has no business with anything of that sort, and nothing of that sort has any business with him. My friend, the Poor Man, in my district, is my business. No man or body of men has any right to interfere between my friend and me. That is the ground I take. I assume a—a paternal character toward my friend. I say, 'My good fellow, I will treat you paternally.'"

With that great sentiment, he opened the Alderman's letter,

and read it.

"Very polite and attentive, I am sure!" exclaimed Sir Joseph. "My lady, the Alderman is so obliging as to remind me that he has had 'the distinguished honour'—he is very good—of meeting me at the house of our mutual friend Deedles, the banker, and he does me the favour to inquire whether it will be agreeable to me to have Will Fern put down. He came up to London, it seems, to look for employment (trying to better himself—that's his story), and being found at night asleep in a shed, was taken into custody, and carried next morning before the Alderman. The Alderman observes (very properly) that he is determined to put this sort of thing down, and that if it will be agreeable to me to have Will Fern put down, he will be happy to begin with him."

"Let him be made an example of, by all means," returned the lady. "Last winter, when I introduced pinking and eyelet-holing among the men and boys in the village as a nice evening employment, and had the lines,

Oh let us love our occupations,
Bless the squire and his relations,
Live upon our daily rations,
And always know our proper stations,

set to music on the new system, for them to sing the while; this very Fern—I see him now—touched that hat of his, and said, 'I humbly ask your pardon, my lady, but *an't* I something different from a great girl?' I expected it, of course; who can expect anything but insolence and ingratitude from that class of people? That is not to the purpose, however. Sir Joseph! Make an example of him!"

Trotty, who had long ago relapsed, and was very low-spirited, stepped forward with a rueful face to take the letter Sir Joseph held out to him.

"You have heard, perhaps," said Sir Joseph, oracularly, "certain remarks into which I have been led respecting the solemn period of time at which we have arrived, and the duty imposed upon us of settling our affairs, and being prepared. Now, my friend, can you lay your hand upon your heart, and say that you also have made preparation for a New Year?"

"I am afraid, sir," stammered Trotty, looking meekly at him, "that I am a—a—little behind-hand with the world."

"Behind-hand with the world!" repeated Sir Joseph Bowley, in a tone of terrible distinctness.

"I am afraid, sir," faltered Trotty, "that there's a matter of ten or twelve shillings owing to Mrs. Chickenstalker."

"To Mrs. Chickenstalker!" repeated Sir Joseph, in the same tone as before.

"A shop, sir," exclaimed Toby, "in the general line. Also a—a little money on account of rent. A very little, sir. It oughtn't to be owing, I know, but we have been hard put to it, indeed!"

Sir Joseph looked at his lady, and at Mr. Fish, and at Trotty, one after another, twice all round. He then made a despondent gesture with both hands at once, as if he gave the thing up altogether.

"How a man, even among this improvident and impracticable race; an old man; a man grown grey; can look a New Year in the face with his affairs in this condition; how he can lie down on his bed at night, and get up again in the morning, and-There!" he said, turning his back on Trotty.

"Take the letter! Take the letter!"

"I heartily wish it was otherwise, sir," said Trotty, anxious to excuse himself. "We have been tried very hard."

Sir Joseph still repeating "Take the letter, take the letter!" and Mr. Fish not only saying the same thing, but giving additional force to the request by motioning the bearer to the door, he had nothing for it but to make his bow and leave the house. And in the street, poor Trotty pulled his worn old hat down on his head to hide the grief he felt at getting no hold on the New Year, anywhere.

He didn't even lift his hat to look up at the Bell tower when he came to the old church on his return. He halted there a moment, from habit; and knew that it was growing dark and that the steeple rose above him indistinct and faint in the murky air. He knew, too, that the Chimes would ring immediately, and that they sounded to his fancy, at such a time, like voices in the clouds. But he only made the more haste to deliver the Alderman's letter and get out of the way before they began; for he dreaded to hear them tagging "Friends and Fathers, Friends and Fathers," to the burden they had rung out last.

Toby discharged himself of his commission, therefore, with all possible speed and set off trotting homeward. But what with his pace, which was at best an awkward one in the street; and what with his hat, which didn't improve it; he trotted against somebody in less than no time and was sent staggering out into the road.

"I beg your pardon, I'm sure!" said Trotty, pulling up his hat in great confusion, and between the hat and the torn lining, fixing his head into a kind of beehive. "I hope I haven't hurt you."

As to hurting anybody, Toby was not such an absolute Samson, but that he was much more likely to be hurt himself; and indeed he had flown out into the road like a shuttle-cock. He had such an opinion of his own strength, however, that he was in real concern for the other party, and said again,

"I hope I haven't hurt you?"

The man against whom he had run, a sun-browned, sinewy, country-looking man, with grizzled hair and a rough chin, stared at him for a moment, as if he suspected him to be in jest. But, satisfied of his good faith, he answered:

"No, friend. You have not hurt me."

"Nor the child, I hope?" said Trotty.

"Nor the child," returned the man. "I thank you kindly."

As he said so, he glanced at a little girl he carried in his arms, asleep, and shading her face with the long end of the poor handkerchief he wore about his throat, went slowly on.

The tone in which he said "I thank you kindly," penetrated Trotty's heart. He was so jaded and foot sore, and so soiled with travel, and looked about him so forlorn and strange, that it was a comfort to him to be able to thank anyone, no matter for how little. Toby stood gazing after him as he plodded wearily away, with the child's arm clinging round his neck.

At the figure in the worn shoes—now the very shade and ghost of shoes—rough leather leggings, common frock and broad slouched hat, Trotty stood gazing, blind to the whole street. And at the child's arm, clinging round its neck.

Before he merged into the darkness the traveller stopped, and looking round and seeing Trotty standing there yet, seemed undecided whether to return or go on. After doing first the one and then the other, he came back, and Trotty went half way to meet him.

"You can tell me, perhaps," said the man with a faint smile, "and if you can I am sure will, and I'd rather ask you than another—where Alderman Cute lives."

"Close at hand," replied Toby, "I'll show you his house with pleasure."

"I was to have gone to him elsewhere tomorrow," said the man, accompanying Toby, "but I am uneasy under suspicion, and want to clear myself and to be free to go and seek my bread—I don't know where. So, maybe he'll forgive my going to his house tonight."

"It's impossible," cried Toby with a start, "that your name's Fern!"

"Eh!" cried the other, turning on him in astonishment.

"Fern! Will Fern!" said Trotty.

"That's my name," replied the other.

"Why, then," cried Trotty, seizing him by the arm and looking cautiously round, "for Heaven's sake don't go to him! Don't go to him! He'll put you down as sure as ever you were born. Here, come up this alley, and I'll tell you what I mean. Don't go to *him*."

His new acquaintance looked as if he thought him mad, but he bore him company, nevertheless. When they were shrouded from observation, Trotty told him what he knew, and what character he had received, and all about it.

The subject of his history listened to it with a calmness that surprised him. He did not contradict or interrupt it once. He nodded his head now and then—more in corroboration of an old and worn-out story, it appeared, than in refutation of it; and once or twice threw back his hat, and passed his freckled hand over a brow, where every furrow he had ploughed seemed to have set its image in little. But he did no more.

"It's true enough in the main," he said, "master, I could sift grain from the husk here and there, but let it be as 'tis. What odds? I have gone against his plans; to my misfortun'. I can't help it; I should do the like tomorrow. As to character, them gentlefolks will search and search, and pry and pry, and have it as free from spot or speck in us, afore they'll help us to a dry good word!—Well! I hope they don't lose good opinion as easy as we do, or their lives is strict indeed, and hardly worth the keeping. For myself, master, I never took with that hand"—holding it before him—"what wasn't my own; and never held it back from work, however hard, or poorly paid.

"Whoever can deny it, let him chop it off! But when work won't maintain me like a human creetur; when my living is so bad, that I am Hungry, out of doors and in; when I see a whole working life begin that way, go on that way, and end that way, without a chance or change; then I say to the gentlefolks 'Keep away from me! Let my cottage be. My doors is dark enough without your darkening of 'em more. Don't look for me to come up into the Park to help the show when there's a Birthday, or a fine Speechmaking, or what not. Act your Plays and Games without me, and be welcome to 'em and enjoy 'em. We've now to do with one another. I'm best let alone!'"

Seeing that the child in his arms had opened her eyes, and was looking about in wonder, he checked himself to say a word or two of foolish prattle in her ear, and stand her on the ground beside him. Then slowly winding one of her long tresses round and round his rough forefinger like a ring, while she hung about his dusty leg, he said to Trotty,

"I'm not a cross-grained man by natur', I believe; and easy satisfied, I'm sure. I bear no ill will against none of 'em. I only want to live like one of the Almighty's creeturs. I can't—I don't-and so there's a pit dug between me, and them that can and do. There's others like me. You might tell 'em off by hundreds and by thousands, sooner than by ones."

Trotty knew that he spoke the truth in this, and shook his head to signify as much.

"I've got a bad name this way," said Fern; "and I'm not likely, I'm afeared, to get a better. 'Tan't lawful to be out of sorts, and I AM out of sorts, though God knows, I'd sooner bear a cheerful spirit if I could. Well! I don't know as this Alderman could hurt *me* much by sending me to gaol; but without a friend to speak a word for me, he might do it; and you see—!" pointing downward with his finger, at the child.

He sunk his voice so low, and gazed upon her with an air so stern and strange, that Toby, to divert the current of his thoughts, inquired if his wife were living.

"I never had one," he returned, shaking his head. "She's my brother's child: a orphan. Nine year old, though you'd hardly think it; but she's tired and worn out now. They'd have taken care on her in the Union—eight and twenty mile away from where we live—between four walls (as they took care of my old father when he couldn't work no more, though he didn't trouble 'em long); but I took her instead, and she's lived with me ever since. Her mother had a friend once, in London here. We are trying to find her, and to find work too; but it's a large place. Never mind. More room for us to walk about in, Lilly!"

Meeting the child's eyes with a smile which melted Toby more than tears, he shook him by the hand.

"I don't so much as know your name," he said, "but I've opened my heart free to you, for I'm thankful to you; with good reason. I'll take your advice and keep clear of this—"

"Justice," suggested Toby.

"Ah!" he said. "If that's the name they give him. This Justice. And tomorrow will try whether there's better fortun' to be met with somewheres near London. Goodnight. A Happy New Year!"

"Stay!" cried Trotty, catching at his hand, as he relaxed his grip. "Stay! The New Year never can be happy to me, if we part like this. The New Year can never be happy to me, if I see the child and you go wandering away, you don't know where, without a shelter for your heads. Come home with me! I'm a poor man, living in a poor place; but I can give you lodging for one night and never miss it. Come home with me! Here! I'll take her!" cried Trotty, lifting up the child. "A pretty one! I'd carry twenty times her weight, and never know I'd got it. Tell me if I go too quick for you. I'm very fast. I always was!" Trotty said this, taking about six of his trotting paces to one stride of his fatigued companion; and with his thin legs quivering again, beneath the load he bore.

"Down the Mews here, Uncle Will, and step at the black door, with 'T. Veck, Ticket Porter,' wrote upon a board; and here we are, and here we go, and here we are indeed, my precious Meg, surprising you!"

With which words Trotty, in a breathless state, set the child down before his daughter in the middle of the floor. The little visitor looked once at Meg; and doubting nothing in that face, but trusting everything she saw there; ran into her arms.

"Here we are, and here we go!" cried Trotty, running round the room and choking audibly. "Here, Uncle Will, here's a fire you know! Why don't you come to the fire? Oh here we are and here we go! Meg, my precious darling, where's the kettle? Here it is and here it goes, and it'll bile in no time!"

Trotty really had picked up the kettle somewhere or other in the course of his wild career, and now put it on the fire; while Meg, seating the child in a warm corner, knelt down on the ground before her, and pulled off her shoes, and dried her wet feet on a cloth. Ay, and she laughed at Trotty too—so pleasantly, so cheerfully, that Trotty could have blessed her where she kneeled; for he had seen that, when they entered, she was sitting by the fire in tears.

"Why, father!" said Meg. "You're crazy tonight, I think. I don't know what the Bells would say to that."

Meg looked toward him and saw that he had elaborately stationed himself behind the chair of their male visitor, where with many mysterious gestures he was holding up the sixpence he had earned.

"I see, my dear," said Trotty, "as I was coming in, half an ounce of tea lying somewhere on the stairs; and I'm pretty sure there was a bit of bacon too. As I don't remember where it was exactly, I'll go myself and try to find 'em."

With this inscrutable artifice, Toby withdrew to purchase the viands he had spoken of, for ready money, at Mrs. Chickenstalker's; and presently came back, pretending that he had not been able to find them, at first in the dark.

"But here they are at last," said Trotty, setting out the tea things, "all correct! I was pretty sure it was tea and a rasher. So it is. Meg my pet, if you'll just make the tea, while your unworthy father toasts the bacon, we shall be ready immediate. It's a curious circumstance," said Trotty, proceeding in his cookery, with the assistance of the toasting-fork, "curious, but well known to my friends, that I never care, myself, for rashers, nor for tea. I like to see other people enjoy 'em," said Trotty, speaking very loud to impress the fact upon his guest, "but to me, as food, they are disagreeable."

Yet Trotty sniffed the savour of the hissing bacon—ah!—as if he liked it; and when he poured the boiling water in the tea-pot, looked lovingly down into the depths of that snug caldron, and suffering the fragrant steam to curl about his nose, and wreathe his head and face in a thick cloud. However, for all this, he neither ate nor drank, except at the very beginning, a mere morsel for form's sake, which he appeared to eat with infinite relish, but declared was perfectly uninteresting to him.

"Now, I'll tell you what," said Trotty after tea. "The little one, she sleeps with Meg, I know."

"With good Meg!" cried the child, caressing her. "With Meg."

"That's right," said Trotty. "And I shouldn't wonder if she'll kiss Meg's father, won't she? *I*'m Meg's father."

Mightily delighted Trotty was, when the child went timidly toward him, and having kissed him, fell back upon Meg again.

Meg looked toward their guest, who leaned upon her chair, and with his face turned from her, fondled the child's head, half hidden in her lap.

"To be sure," said Toby. "To be sure! I don't know what I am rambling on about, tonight. My wits are wool-gathering, I think. Will Fern, you come along with me. You're tired to death, and broken down for want of rest. You come along with me."

The hand released from the child's hair, had fallen, trembling, into Trotty's hand. So Trotty, talking without intermission, led him out as tenderly and easily as if he had been a child himself.

Returning before Meg, he listened for an instant at the door of her little chamber; an adjoining room. The child was murmuring a simple Prayer before lying down to sleep; and when she had remembered Meg's name, "Dearly, Dearly"—so her words ran—Trotty heard her stop and ask for his.

It was some short time before the foolish little old fellow could compose himself to mend the fire, and draw his chair to the warm hearth. But when he had done so, and had trimmed the light, he took his newspaper from his pocket and began to read. Carelessly at first, and skimming up and down the columns; but with an earnest and a sad attention, very soon.

For this same dreaded paper re-directed Trotty's thoughts into the channel they had taken all that day, and which the day's events had so marked out and shaped. His interest in the two wanderers had set him on another course of thinking, and a happier one, for the time; but being alone again, and reading of the crimes and violences of the people, he relapsed into his former train.

"It's too true, all I've heard today," Toby muttered; "too just, too full of proof. We're Bad!"

The Chimes took up the words so suddenly—burst out so loud, and clear, and sonorous—that the Bells seemed to strike him in his chair.

And what was that, they said?

"Toby Veck, Toby Veck, waiting for you Toby! Toby Veck, Toby Veck, waiting for you Toby! Come and see us, come and see us, Drag him to us, drag him to us, Haunt and hunt him, haunt and hunt him, Break his slumbers, break his slumbers! Toby Veck, Toby Veck, door open wide Toby, Toby Veck, Toby Veck, door open wide Toby—" then fiercely back to their impetuous strain again, and ringing in the very bricks and plaster on the walls.

Toby listened. Fancy, fancy! His remorse for having run away from them that afternoon! No, no. Nothing of the kind. Again, again, and yet a dozen times again. "Haunt and hunt him, haunt and hunt him, Drag him to us, drag him to us!" Deafening the whole town!

"Meg," said Trotty, softly; tapping at her door. "Do you hear anything?"

"I hear the Bells, father. Surely they're very loud tonight."

"Is she asleep?" said Toby, making an excuse for peeping in.

"So peacefully and happily! I can't leave her yet though, father. Look how she holds my hand!"

"Meg!" whispered Trotty. "Listen to the Bells!"

She listened, with her face toward him all the time. But it underwent no change. She didn't understand them.

Trotty withdrew, resumed his seat by the fire, and once more listened by himself. He remained here a little time.

It was impossible to bear it; their energy was dreadful.

"If the tower-door is really open," said Toby, hastily laying aside his apron, but never thinking of his hat, "what's to hinder me from going up in the steeple and satisfying myself? If it's shut, I don't want any other satisfaction. That's enough."

He was pretty certain as he slipped out quietly into the street that he should find it shut and locked, for he knew the door well, and had so rarely seen it open, that he couldn't reckon above three times in all. It was a low-arched portal outside the church, in a dark nook behind a column; and had such great iron hinges, and such a monstrous lock, that there was more hinge and lock than door.

But what was his astonishment when, coming bare-headed

to the church, and putting his hand into this dark nook, with a certain misgiving that it might be unexpectedly seized, and a shivering propensity to draw it back again, he found that the door, which opened outward, actually stood ajar!

He thought, on the first surprise, of going back; or of getting a light, or a companion; but his courage aided him immediately, and he determined to ascend alone.

"What have I to fear?" said Trotty. "It's a church! Besides the ringers may be there, and have forgotten to shut the door."

So he went in, feeling his way as he went, like a blind man; for it was very dark. And very quiet, for the Chimes were silent.

The dust from the street had blown into the recess; and lying there, heaped up, made it so soft and velvet-like to the foot, that there was something startling even in that. The narrow stair was so close to the door, too, that he stumbled at the very first; and shutting the door upon himself by striking it with his foot, and causing it to rebound back heavily, he couldn't open it again.

This was another reason, however, for going on. Trotty groped his way, and went on. Up, up, up, and round and round; and up, up, up, higher, higher, higher up!

Until, ascending through the floor, and pausing with his head just raised above its beams, he came among the Bells. It was barely possible to make out their great shapes in the gloom; but there they were. Shadowy, and dark, and dumb.

A heavy sense of dread and loneliness fell instantly upon him, as he climbed into this airy nest of stone and metal. His head went round and round. He listened and then raised a wild "Halloa!"

Halloa! was mournfully protracted by the echoes.

Giddy, confused, and out of breath, and frightened, Toby looked about him vacantly, and sunk down in a swoon.

Third Quarter

When and how the darkness of the night-black steeple changed to shining light; and how the solitary tower was peopled with a myriad figures; when and how the whispered "Haunt and hunt him," breathing monotonously through his sleep or swoon, became a voice exclaiming in the waking ears of Trotty, "Break his slumbers;" when and how he ceased to have a sluggish and confused idea that such things were, companioning a host of others that were not; there are no dates or means to tell. But, awake, and standing on his feet upon the boards where he had lately lain, he saw this Goblin Sight.

Then and not before, did Trotty see in every Bell a bearded figure of the bulk and stature of the Bell—incomprehensibly, a figure and the Bell itself. Gigantic, grave, and darkly watchful of him, as he stood rooted to the ground.

Mysterious and awful figures! Resting on nothing; poised in the night air of the tower, with their draped and hooded heads merged in the dim roof; motionless and shadowy. Shadowy and dark, although he saw them by some light belonging to themselves—none else was there—each with its muffled hand upon its goblin mouth.

He could not plunge down wildly through the opening in the floor; for, all power of motion had deserted him. Otherwise he would have done so—ay, would have thrown himself, head-foremost, from the steeple-top, rather than have seen them watching him with eyes that would have waked and watched, although the pupils had been taken out.

A blast of air—how cold and shrill!—came moaning through the tower. As it died away, the Great Bell, or the Goblin of the Great Bell, spoke.

"What visitor is this?" it said. The voice was low and deep, and Trotty fancied that it sounded in the other figures as well.

"I thought my name was called by the Chimes!" said Trotty, raising his hands in an attitude of supplication. "I hardly know why I am here, or how I came. I have listened to the Chimes these many years. They have cheered me often."

"And you have thanked them?" said the bell.

"A thousand times!" cried Trotty.

"How?"

"I am a poor man," faltered Trotty, "and could only thank

them in words."

"And always so?" inquired the Goblin of the Bell. "Have you never done us wrong in words?"

"No!" cried Trotty, eagerly.

"Never done us foul, and false, and wicked wrong, in words?" pursued the Goblin of the Bell.

Trotty was about to answer "Never!" But he stopped and was confused.

"The voice of Time," said the Phantom, "cries to man, Advance! Time is for his advancement and improvement; for his greater worth, his greater happiness, his better life; his progress onward to that goal within its knowledge and its view, and set there, in the period when Time and he began. Ages of darkness, wickedness, and violence, have come and gone—millions uncountable, have suffered, lived, and died—to point the way before him. Who seeks to turn him back, or stay him on his course, arrests a mighty engine which will strike the meddler dead; and be the fiercer and the wilder, ever, for its momentary check!"

"I never did so to my knowledge, sir," said Trotty. "It was quite by accident if I did. I wouldn't go to do it, I'm sure."

"Who puts into the mouth of Time, or of its servants," said the Goblin of the Bell, "a cry of lamentation for days which have had their trial and their failure, and have left deep traces of it which the blind may see—a cry that only serves the present time, by showing men how much it needs their help when any ears can listen to regrets for such a past—who does this, does a wrong. And you have done that wrong to us, the Chimes."

Trotty's first excess of fear was gone. But he had felt tenderly and gratefully toward the Bells, as you have seen; and when he heard himself arraigned as one who had offended them so weightily, his heart was touched with penitence and grief.

"If you knew," said Trotty, clasping his hands earnestly-"or perhaps you do know—if you know how often you have kept me company; how often you have cheered me up when I've been low; how you were quite the plaything of my little daughter Meg (almost the only one she ever had) when first her mother died, and she and me were left alone; you won't bear malice for a hasty word!"

"Who hears in us, the Chimes, one note bespeaking disregard, or stern regard, of any hope, or joy, or pain, or sorrow, of the many-sorrowed throng; who hears us make response to any creed that gauges human passions and affections, as it gauges the amount of miserable food on which humanity may pine and wither; does us wrong. That wrong you have done us!" said the Bell.

"I have!" said Trotty. "Oh, forgive me!"

"Spare me," cried Trotty, falling on his knees; "for Mercy's sake!"

"Listen!" said the Shadow.

"Listen!" cried the other Shadows.

"Listen!" said a clear and child-like voice, which Trotty thought he recognized as having heard before.

The organ sounded faintly in the church below. Swelling by degrees, the melody ascended to the roof, and filled the choir and nave. Expanding more and more, it rose up, up, up, up; higher, higher, higher up; awakening agitated hearts within the burly piles of oak, the hollow bells, the iron-bound doors, the stairs of solid stone; until the tower walls were insufficient to contain it, and it soared into the sky.

No wonder that an old man's breast could not contain a sound so vast and mighty. It broke from that weak prison in a rush of tears; and Trotty put his hands before his face.

"Listen!" said the Shadow.

"Listen!" said the other Shadows.

"Listen!" said the child's voice.

A solemn strain of blended voices rose into the tower.

It was a very low and mournful strain—a Dirge—and as he listened, Trotty heard his child among the singers.

"She is dead!" exclaimed the old man. "Meg is dead. Her spirit calls to me. I hear it!"

"The Spirit of your child bewails the dead, and mingles with the dead—dead hopes, dead fancies, dead imaginings of youth," returned the Bell, "but she is living. Learn from her life, a living truth. Learn from the creature dearest to your heart, how bad the bad are born. See every bud and leaf plucked one by one from off the fairest stem, and know how bare and wretched it may be. Follow her! To desperation!"

Each of the shadowy figures stretched its right arm forth, and pointed downward.

"The Spirit of the Chimes is your companion," said the figure. "Go! It stands behind you!"

Trotty turned, and saw—the child! The child Will Fern had carried in the street; the child whom Meg had watched, but now, asleep!

"I carried her myself, tonight," said Trotty. "In these arms!"

"Show him what he calls himself," said the dark figures, one and all.

The tower opened at his feet. He looked down, and beheld his own form, lying at the bottom, on the outside: crushed and motionless.

"No more a living man!" cried Trotty. "Dead!"

"Dead!" said the figures altogether.

"Gracious Heaven! And the New Year—'

"Past," said the figures.

"What!" he cried, shuddering, "I missed my way, and coming on the outside of this tower in the dark, fell down—a year ago?"

"Nine years ago!" replied the figures.

As they gave the answer, they recalled their outstretched hands; and where their figures had been, there the Bells were.

"What are these?" he asked his guide. "If I am not mad, what are these?"

"Spirits of the Bells. Their sound upon the air," returned the child. "They take such shapes and occupations as the hopes and thoughts of mortals, and the recollections they have stored up, give them."

"And you," said Trotty, wildly. "What are you?"

"Hush, hush!" returned the child. "Look here!"

In a poor, mean room; working at the same kind of embroidery, which he had often, often, seen before her; Meg, his own dear daughter, was presented to his view. He made no effort to imprint his kisses on her face; he did not strive to clasp her to his loving heart; he knew that such endearments were, for him, no more. But he held his trembling breath, and brushed away the blinding tears, that he might look upon her; that he might only see her.

Ah! Changed. Changed. The light of the clear eye, how dimmed. The bloom, how faded from the cheek. Beautiful she was, as she had ever been, but Hope, Hope, Hope, oh, where was the fresh Hope that had spoken to him like a voice!

She looked up from her work, at a companion. Following her eyes, the old man started back.

In the woman grown, he recognized her at a glance. In the long silken hair, he saw the self-same curls; around the lips, the child's expression lingering still. See! In the eyes, now turned inquiringly on Meg, there shone the very look that scanned those features when he brought her home!

Then what was this, beside him?

Looking with awe into its face, he saw a something reigning there: a lofty something, undefined and indistinct, which made it hardly more than a remembrance of that child—as yonder figure might be—yet it was the same: the same: and wore the dress.

Hark! They were speaking!

"Meg," said Lilian, hesitating. "How often you raise your head from your work to look at me!"

"Are my looks so altered, that they frighten you?" asked Meg.

"Nay, dear! But you smile at that yourself! Why not smile when you look at me, Meg?"

"I do so. Do I not?" she answered: smiling on her.

"Now you do," said Lilian, "but not usually. When you think I'm busy, and don't see you, you look so anxious and so doubtful, that I hardly like to raise my eyes. There is little cause for smiling in this hard and toilsome life, but you were once so cheerful."

"Am I not now?" cried Meg, speaking in a tone of strange alarm, and rising to embrace her. "Do *I* make our weary life more weary to you, Lilian?"

"You have been the only thing that made it life," said Lilian, fervently kissing her; "sometimes the only thing that made me care to live so, Meg. Such work, such work! So many hours, so many days, so many long, long nights of hopeless, cheerless, never-ending work—not to heap up riches, not to live grandly or gayly, not to live upon enough, however coarse; but to earn bare bread; to scrape together just enough to toil upon, and want upon, and keep alive in us the consciousness of our hard fate! Oh, Meg, Meg!" she raised her voice and twined her arms about her as she spoke, like one in pain. "How can the cruel world go round, and bear to look upon such lives!"

"Lilly!" said Meg, soothing her, and putting back her hair from her wet face. "Why, Lilly! You! So pretty and so young!"

"Oh, Meg!" she interrupted, holding her at arm's-length, and looking in her face imploringly. "The worst of all! The worst of all! Strike me old, Meg! Wither me and shrivel me, and free me from the dreadful thoughts that tempt me in my youth!"

Trotty turned to look upon his guide. But, the Spirit of the child had taken flight. Was gone.

Fourth Quarter

Some new remembrance of the ghostly figures in the Bells; some faint impression of the ringing of the Chimes; some giddy consciousness of having seen the swarm of phantoms reproduced and reproduced until the recollection of them lost itself in the confusion of their numbers; some hurried knowledge, how conveyed to him he knew not, that more years had passed; and Trotty, with the Spirit of the child attending him, stood looking on at mortal company.

Fat company, rosy-cheeked company, comfortable company. They were but two, but they were red enough for ten. They sat before a bright fire, with a small low table between them; and unless the fragrance of hot tea and muffins lingered longer in that room than in most others, the table had seen service very lately. But all the cups and saucers being clean, and in their proper places in the corner cupboard; and the brass toasting fork hanging in its usual nook, and spreading its four idle fingers out, as if it wanted to be measured for a glove; there remained no other visible tokens of the meal just finished, than such as purred and washed their whiskers in the person of the basking cat, and glistened in the gracious, not to say the greasy, faces of her patrons.

This cosy couple (married, evidently) had made a fair division of the fire between them, and sat looking at the glowing sparks that dropped into the grate; now nodding off into a doze; now waking up again when some hot fragment, larger than the rest, came rattling down, as if the fire were coming with it.

It was in no danger of sudden extinction, however; for it gleamed not only in the little room, and on the panes of window-glass in the door, and on the curtain half drawn across them, but in the little shop beyond. A little shop, quite crammed and choked with the abundance of its stock; a perfectly voracious little shop, with a maw as accommodating and full as any shark's. Cheese, butter, firewood, soap, pickles, matches, bacon, table-beer, peg-tops, sweetmeats, boys' kites, bird-seed, cold ham, birch brooms, hearth-stones, salt, vinegar, blacking, red herrings, stationery, lard, mushroom ketchup, stay-laces, loaves of bread, shuttlecocks, eggs, and slate-pencils; everything was fish that came to the net of this greedy little shop, and all articles were in its net.

Glancing at such of these items as were visible in the shining of the blaze, and the less cheerful radiance of two smoky lamps which burnt but dimly in the shop itself, as though its plethora sat heavy on their lungs; and glancing, then, at one of the two faces by the parlour-fire, Trotty had small difficulty in recognizing in the stout old lady, Mrs. Chickenstalker: always inclined to corpulency, even in the days when he had known her as established in the general line, and having a small balance against him in her books.

The features of her companion were less easy to him. The great broad chin, with creases in it large enough to hide a finger in; the astonished eyes, that seemed to expostulate with themselves for sinking deeper and deeper into the yielding fat of the soft face; the nose afflicted with that disordered action of its functions which is generally termed The Snuffles; the short thick throat and labouring chest, with other beauties of the like description, though calculated to impress the memory, Trotty could at first allot to nobody he had ever known: and yet he had some recollection of them too.

At length, in Mrs. Chickenstalker's partner in the general line, and in the crooked and eccentric line of life, he recognized the former porter of Sir Joseph Bowley; an apoplectic innocent, who had connected himself in Trotty's mind with Mrs. Chickenstalker years ago, by giving him admission to the mansion where he had confessed his obligations to that lady, and drawn on his unlucky head such grave reproach.

Trotty had little interest in a change like this, after the changes he had seen; but association is very strong sometimes; and he looked involuntarily behind the parlour-door, where the accounts of credit customers were usually kept in chalk. There was no record of his name. Some names were there, but they were strange to him, and infinitely fewer than of old; from which he argued that the porter was an advocate of ready money transactions, and on coming into the business had looked pretty sharp after the Chickenstalker defaulters.

So desolate was Trotty, and so mournful for the youth and promise of his blighted child, that it was a sorrow to him, even to have no place in Mrs. Chickenstalker's ledger.

"What sort of a night is it, Anne?" inquired the former porter of Sir Joseph Bowley, stretching out his legs before the fire, and rubbing as much of them as his short arms could reach; with an air that added, "Here I am if it's bad, and I don't want to go out if it's good."

"Hard weather indeed," returned his wife, shaking her head.

"Ay, ay! Years," said Mr. Tugby, "are like Christians in that respect. Some of 'em die hard; some of 'em die easy. This one hasn't many days to run, and is making a fight for it. I like him all the better. There's a customer, my love!"

Attentive to the rattling door, Mrs. Tugby had already risen.

"Now, then!" said that lady, passing out into the little shop. "What's wanted? Oh! I beg your pardon, sir, I'm sure. I didn't think it was you."

She made this apology to a gentleman in black, who, with his wristbands tucked up, and his hat cocked loungingly on one side, and his hand in his pocket, sat down astride on the table-beer barrel, and nodded in return.

"This is a bad business upstairs, Mrs. Tugby," said the gentleman. "The man can't live."

"Not the back-attic can't!" cried Tugby, coming out into the shop to join the conference.

"The back-attic, Mr. Tugby," said the gentleman, "is coming downstairs fast, and will be below the basement very soon."

Looking by turns at Tugby and his wife, he sounded the barrel with his knuckles for the depth of beer, and having found it, played a tune upon the empty part.

"The back-attic, Mr. Tugby," said the gentleman: Tugby having stood in silent consternation for some time; "is Going."

"Then," said Tugby, turning to his wife, "he must Go, you know, before he's Gone."

"I don't think you can move him," said the gentleman, shaking his head. "I wouldn't take the responsibility of saying it could be done, myself. You had better leave him where he is. He can't live long."

"It's the only subject," said Tugby, bringing the butter-scale down upon the counter with a crash, by weighing his fist on it, "that we've ever had a word upon; she and me; and look what it comes to! He's going to die here, after all. Going to die upon the premises. Going to die in our house!"

"And where should he have died, Tugby?" cried his wife.

"In the workhouse," he returned. "What are workhouses made for?"

"Not for that!" said Mrs. Tugby, with great energy. "Not for that! Neither did I marry you for that. Don't think it, Tugby. I won't have it. I won't allow it. I'd be separated first, and never see your face again. When my widow's name stood over that door, as it did for many, many years: the house being known as Mrs. Chickenstalker's far and wide, and never known but to its honest credit and its good report: when my widow's name stood over that door, Tugby, I knew him as a handsome, steady, manly, independent youth; I knew her as the sweetest looking, sweetest tempered girl, eyes ever saw; I knew her father (poor old creetur, he fell down from the steeple walking in his sleep, and killed himself), for the simplest, hardest working, childest-hearted man, that ever drew the breath of life; and when I turn them out of house and home, may angels turn me out of heaven. As they would! And serve me right!"

Her old face, which had been a plump and dimpled one before the changes which had come to pass, seemed to shine out of her as she said these words; and when she dried her eyes, and shook her head and her handkerchief at Tugby, with an expression of firmness which it was quite clear was not to be easily resisted, Trotty said, "Bless her! Bless her!"

Then he listened, with a panting heart, for what should follow. Knowing nothing yet, but that they spoke of Meg.

The gentleman upon the table-beer cask, who appeared to be some authorized medical attendant upon the poor, was far too well accustomed, evidently, to little differences of opinion between man and wife, to interpose any remark in this instance. He sat softly whistling, and turning little drops of beer out of the tap upon the ground, until there was a perfect calm: when he raised his head and said to Mrs. Tugby, late Chickenstalker:

"There's something interesting about the woman, even now. How did she come to marry him?"

"Why, that," said Mrs. Tugby, taking a seat near him, "is not the least cruel part of her story, sir. You see they kept company, she and Richard, many years ago. When they were a young and beautiful couple, everything was settled, and they were to have been married on a New Year's Day. But, somehow, Richard got it into his head, through what the gentleman told him, that he might do better, and that he'd soon repent it, and that she wasn't good enough for him, and that a young man of spirit had no business to be married. And the gentleman frightened her, and made her melancholy, and timid of his deserting her, and of her children coming to the gallows, and of its being wicked to be man and wife, and a good deal more of it.

"And in short, they lingered and lingered, and their trust in one another was broken, and so at last was the match. But the fault was his. She would have married him, sir, joyfully. I've seen her heart swell, many times afterwards, when he passed her in a proud and careless way; and never did a woman grieve more truly for a man, than she for Richard when he first went wrong."

"Oh! he went wrong, did he?" said the gentleman, pulling out the vent-peg of the table-beer, and trying to peep down into the barrel through the hole.

"Well, sir, I don't know that he rightly understood himself, you see. I think his mind was troubled by their having broke with one another; and that but for being ashamed before the gentlemen, and perhaps for being uncertain too, how she might take it, he'd have gone through any suffering or trial to have had Meg's promise, and Meg's hand again. That's my belief. He never said so; more's the pity! He took to drinking, idling, bad companions: all the fine resources that were to be so much better for him than the Home he might have had. He lost his looks, his character, his health, his strength, his friends, his work: everything!"

"He didn't lose everything, Mrs. Tugby," returned the gentleman, "because he gained a wife; and I want to know how he gained her."

"I'm coming to it, sir, in a moment. This went on for years and years; he sinking lower and lower; she enduring, poor thing, miseries enough to wear her life away. At last he was so cast down, and cast out, that no one would employ or notice him; and doors were shut upon him, go where he would. Applying from place to place, and door to door; and coming for the hundredth time to one gentleman, who had often and often tried him (he was a good workman to the very end); that gentleman, who knew his history, said, 'I believe you are incorrigible; there's only one person in the world who has a chance of reclaiming you; ask me to trust you no more, until she tries to do it.' Something like that, in his anger and vexation."

"Ah!" said the gentleman. "Well?"

"Well, sir, he went to her, and kneeled to her; said it was so; said it ever had been so; and made a prayer to her to save him."

"And she?—Don't distress yourself, Mrs. Tugby."

"She came to me that night to ask me about living here. 'What he was once to me,' she said, 'is buried in a grave, side by side with what I was to him. But I have thought of this; and I will make the trial. In the hope of saving him; for the love of the light-hearted girl (you remember her) who was to have been married on a New Year's Day; and for the love of her Richard.' And he said he had come to her from Lilian, and Lilian had trusted to him, and she never could forget that. So they were married; and when they came home here, and I saw them, I hoped that such prophecies as parted them when they were young, may not often fulfil themselves as they did in this case, or I wouldn't be the makers of them for a Mine of Gold."

The gentleman got off the cask, and stretched himself, observing:

"I suppose he used her ill, as soon as they were married?"

"I don't think he ever did that," said Mrs. Tugby, shaking her head and wiping her eyes. "He went on better for a short time; but, his habits were too old and strong to be got rid of; he soon fell back a little; and was falling fast back, when his illness came so strong upon him. I think he has always felt for her. I am sure he has. I've seen him in his crying fits and tremblings, try to kiss her hand; and I have heard him call her 'Meg,' and say it was her nineteenth birthday. There he has been lying, now, these weeks and months. Between him and her baby, she has not been able to do her old work; and by not being able to be regular, she has lost it, even if she could have done it. How they have lived, I hardly know!"

"*I* know," muttered Mr. Tugby, looking at the till, and round the shop, and at his wife; and rolling his head with immense intelligence.

He was interrupted by a cry—a sound of lamentation—from the upper story of the house. The gentleman moved hurriedly to the door.

"My friend," he said, looking back, "you needn't discuss whether he shall be removed or not. He has spared you that trouble, I believe."

Saying so, he ran upstairs, followed by Mrs. Tugby; while Mr. Tugby panted and grumbled after them at leisure: being rendered more than commonly short-winded by the weight of the till, in which there had been an inconvenient quantity of copper. Trotty, with the child beside him, floated up the staircase like mere air.

"Follow her! Follow her! Follow her!" He heard the ghostly voices in the Bells repeat their words as he ascended. "Learn it, from the creature dearest to your heart!"

It was over. It was over. And this was she, her father's pride and joy! This haggard, wretched woman, weeping by the bed, if it deserved that name, and pressing to her breast, and hanging down her head upon, an infant? Who can tell how spare, how sickly, and how poor an infant? Who can tell how dear?

"Thank God!" cried Trotty, holding up his folded hands. "O, God be thanked! She loves her child!"

Again Trotty heard the voices, saying, "Follow her!" He turned toward his guide, and saw it rising from him, passing through the air. "Follow her!" it said. And vanished.

He hovered round her; sat down at her feet; looked up into her face for one trace of her old self; listened for one note of her old pleasant voice. He flitted round the child: so wan, so prematurely old, so dreadful in its gravity, so plaintive in its feeble, mournful, miserable wail. He almost worshiped it. He clung to it as her only safeguard; as the last unbroken link that bound her to endurance. He set his father's hope and trust on the frail baby; watched her every look upon it as she held it in her arms; and cried a thousand times, "She loves it! God be thanked, she loves it!"

He saw the woman tend her in the night; return to her when her grudging husband was asleep, and all was still; encourage her, shed tears with her, set nourishment before her. He saw the day come, and the night again; the day, the night; the time go by; the house of death relieved of death; the room left to herself and to the child; he heard it moan and cry; he saw it harass her, and tire her out, and when she slumbered in exhaustion, drag her back to consciousness, and hold her with its little hands upon the rack; but she was constant to it, gentle with it, patient with it. Patient! Was its loving mother in her inmost heart and soul, and had its Being knitted up with hers as when she carried it unborn.

All this time, she was in want: languishing away, in dire and pining want. With the baby in her arms, she wandered here and there in quest of occupation; and with its thin face lying in her lap, and looking up in hers, did any work for any wretched sum: a day and night of labour for as many farthings as there were figures on the dial. If she had quarrelled with it; if she had neglected it; if she had looked upon it with a moment's hate! if, in the frenzy of an instant, she had struck it! No! His comfort was, She loved it always.

She told no one of her extremity, and wandered abroad in the day lest she should be questioned by her only friend: for any help she received from her hands, occasioned fresh disputes between the good woman and her husband; and it was new bitterness to be the daily cause of strife and discord, where she owed so much.

She loved it still. She loved it more and more. But a change fell on the aspect of her love.

One night she was singing faintly to it in its sleep and walking to and fro to hush it, when her door was softly opened, and a man looked in.

"For the last time," he said.

"William Fern!"

"For the last time."

He listened like a man pursued: and spoke in whispers.

"Margaret, my race is nearly run, I couldn't finish it, without a parting word with you. Without one grateful word."

"What have you done?" she asked: regarding him with terror.

He looked at her but gave no answer.

After a short silence, he made a gesture with his hand, as if he set her question by; as if he brushed it aside; and said:

"It's long ago, Margaret, now; but that night is as fresh in my memory as ever 'twas. We little thought then," he added, looking round, "that we should ever meet like this. Your child, Margaret? Let me have it in my arms. Let me hold your child."

He put his hat upon the floor, and took it. And he trembled as he took it, from head to foot.

"Is it a girl?"

"Yes."

He put his hand before its little face.

"See how weak I'm grown, Margaret, when I want the courage to look at it! Let her be, a moment. I won't hurt her. It's long ago, but—What's her name?"

"Margaret," she answered quickly.

"I'm glad of that," he said. "I'm glad of that!"

He seemed to breathe more freely; and after pausing for an instant, took away his hand, and looked upon the infant's face. But covered it again, immediately.

"Margaret!" he said; and gave her back the child. "It's Lilian's."

"Lilian's!"

"I held the same face in my arms when Lilian's mother died and left her."

"When Lilian's mother died and left her!" she repeated, wildly.

"How shrill you speak! Why do you fix your eyes upon me so? Margaret!"

She sunk down in a chair, and pressed the infant to her breast, and wept over it. Sometimes, she released it from her embrace, to look anxiously in its face: then strained it to her bosom again. At those times, when she gazed upon it, then it was that something fierce and terrible began to mingle with her love. Then it was that her old father quailed.

"Follow her!" was sounded through the house. "Learn it, from the creature dearest to your heart!"

"Margaret," said Fern, bending over her, and kissing her upon the brow: "I thank you for the last time. Good night. Good bye! Put your hand in mine, and tell me you'll forget me from this hour, and try to think the end of me was here."

She called to him; but he was gone. She sat down stupefied, until her infant roused her to a sense of hunger, cold, and darkness. She paced the room with it the livelong night, hushing it and soothing it. She said at intervals, "Like Lilian when her mother died and left her!" Why was her step so quick, her eyes so wild, her love so fierce and terrible, whenever she repeated those words?

"But, it is Love," said Trotty. "It is Love. She'll never cease to love it. My poor Meg!"

She dressed the child next morning with unusual care—ah, vain expenditure of care upon such squalid robes!—and once more tried to find some means of life. It was the last day of the Old Year. She tried till night, and never broke her fast. She tried in vain.

She mingled with an abject crowd, who tarried in the snow, until it pleased some officer appointed to dispense the public charity (the lawful charity; not that once preached upon a Mount), to call them in, and question them, and say to this one, "Go to such a place," to that one, "Come next week;" to make a foot-ball of another wretch, and pass him here and there, from hand to hand, from house to house, until he wearied and lay down to die; or started up and robbed, and so became a higher sort of criminal, whose claims allowed of no delay. Here, too, she failed.

She loved her child, and wished to have it lying on her breast. And that was quite enough.

It was night: a bleak, dark, cutting night: when pressing the child close to her for warmth, she arrived outside the house she called her home. She was so faint and giddy, that she saw no one standing in the doorway until she was close upon it, and about to enter. Then, she recognized the master of the house, who had so disposed himself—with his person it was not difficult—as to fill up the whole entry.

"Oh!" he said softly. "You have come back?"

She looked at the child and shook her head.

"Don't you think you have lived here long enough without paying any rent? Don't you think that, without any money, you've been a pretty constant customer at this shop, now?" said Mr. Tugby.

She repeated the same mute appeal.

"Suppose you try and deal somewhere else," he said. "And suppose you provide yourself with another lodging. Come! Don't you think you could manage it?"

She said, in a low voice, that it was very late. Tomorrow.

"Now I see what you want," said Tugby; "and what you mean. You know there are two parties in this house about you, and you delight in setting them by the ears. I don't want any quarrels; I'm speaking softly to avoid a quarrel; but if you don't go away, I'll speak out loud, and you shall cause words loud enough to please you. But you shan't come in, that I am determined."

She put her hair back with her hand, and looked in a sudden manner at the sky, and the dark lowering distance.

"This is the last night of an Old Year, and I won't carry ill-blood and quarrellings and disturbances into a New One, to please you nor anybody else," said Tugby, who was quite a retail Friend and Father. "I wonder you an't ashamed of yourself, to carry such practices into a New Year. If you haven't any business in the world, but to be always giving way, and always making disturbances between man and wife, you'd be better out of it. Go along with you!"

"Follow her! To desperation!"

Again the old man heard the voices. Looking up, he saw the figures hovering in the air, and pointing where she went, down the dark street.

"She loves it!" he exclaimed in agonized entreaty for her. "Chimes! she loves it still!"

"Follow her!" The shadows swept upon the track she had taken like a cloud.

Oh, for something to awaken her! For any sight or sound, or scent, to call up tender recollections in a brain on fire! For any gentle image of the Past, to rise up before her!

"I was her father! I was her father!" cried the old man, stretching out his hands to the dark shadows flying on above. "Have mercy on her, and on me! Where does she go? Turn her back! I was her father!"

But, they only pointed to her, as she hurried on; "To desperation! Learn it from the creature dearest to your heart!"

A hundred voices echoed it. The air was made of breath expended in those words. He seemed to take them in, at every gasp he drew. They were everywhere, and not to be escaped. And still she hurried on; the same light in her eyes.

All at once she stopped.

"Now, turn her back!" exclaimed the old man, tearing his white hair. "My child! Meg! Turn her back! Great Father, turn her back!"

In her own scanty shawl, she wrapped the baby warm. With her fevered hands, she smoothed its limbs, composed its face, arranged its mean attire. In her wasted arms she folded it, as though she never would resign it more. And with her dry lips, kissed it in a final pang, and last long agony of Love.

Putting its tiny hand up to her neck, and holding it there, within her dress, next to her distracted heart, she set its sleeping face against her: closely, steadily against her: and sped onward to the river.

To the rolling River, swift and dim, where Winter Night sat brooding like the last dark thoughts of many who had sought a refuge there before her. Where scattered lights upon the banks gleamed sullen, red and dull, as torches that were burning there to show the way to Death. Where no abode of living people cast its shadow, on the deep, impenetrable, melancholy shade.

To the River! To that portal of Eternity, her desperate footsteps tended with the swiftness of its rapid waters running to the sea. He tried to touch her as she passed him, going down to its dark level; but, the wild distempered form, the fierce and terrible love, the desperation that had left all human check or hold behind, swept by him like the wind.

He followed her. She paused a moment on the brink, before the dreadful plunge. He fell down on his knees, and in a shriek addressed the figures in the Bells now hovering above them.

"Have mercy on her!" he exclaimed, "as one in whom this dreadful crime has sprung from Love perverted; from the strongest, deepest Love we fallen creatures know! Think what her misery must have been, when such seed bears such fruit. Heaven meant her to be good. There is no loving mother on the earth who might not come to this, if such a life had gone before. Oh, have mercy on my child, who, even at this pass, means mercy to her own, and dies herself, and perils her immortal soul, to save it!"

She was in his arms. He held her now. His strength was like a giant's.

He might have said more; but the Bells, the old familiar Bells, his own dear, constant, steady friends, the Chimes, began to ring the joy-peals for a New Year; so lustily, so merrily, so happily, so gayly, that he leapt upon his feet, and broke the spell that bound him.

"And whatever you do, father," said Meg, "don't eat tripe again without asking some doctor whether it's likely to agree with you; for how you *have* been going on, Good gracious!"

She was working with her needle at the little table by the fire, dressing her simple gown with ribbons for her wedding. So quietly happy, so blooming and youthful, so full of beautiful promise, that he uttered a great cry as if it were an Angel in his house; then flew to clasp her in his arms.

But he caught his feet in the newspaper, which had fallen on the hearth, and somebody came rushing in between them.

"No!" cried the voice of this same somebody; a generous and jolly voice it was. "Not even you. Not even you. The first kiss of Meg in the New Year is mine. Mine! I have been waiting outside the house this hour to hear the Bells and claim it. Meg, my precious prize, a happy year! A life of happy years, my darling wife!"

And Richard smothered her with kisses.

You never in all your life saw anything like Trotty after this. I don't care where you have lived or what you have seen, you never in all your life saw anything at all approaching him! He sat down in his chair and beat his knees and cried; he sat down in his chair and beat his knees and laughed; he sat down in his chair and beat his knees and laughed and cried together; he got out of his chair and hugged Meg; he got out of his chair and hugged Richard; he got out of his chair and hugged them both at once; he kept running up to Meg and squeezing her fresh face between his hands and kissing it, going from her backward not to lose sight of it, and running up again like a figure in a magic lantern; and whatever he did, he was constantly sitting himself down in this chair, and never stopping in it for one single moment, being—that's the truth—beside himself with joy.

"And tomorrow's your wedding-day, my pet!" cried Trotty. "Your real, happy wedding-day!"

"Today!" cried Richard, shaking hands with him. "Today. The Chimes are ringing in the New Year. Hear them!"

They *were* ringing! Bless their sturdy hearts, they *were* ringing! Great Bells as they were; melodious, deep-mouthed, noble Bells; cast in no common metal; made by no common founder; when had they ever chimed like that before?

"But today, my pet," said Trotty. "You and Richard had some words today."

"Because he's such a bad fellow, father," said Meg. "An't you, Richard? Such a headstrong, violent man! He'd have made no more of speaking his mind to that great Alderman, and putting *him* down I don't know where, than he would of—"

"—Kissing Meg," suggested Richard. Doing it, too.

"No. Not a bit more," said Meg. "But I wouldn't let him, father. Where would have been the use?"

"Richard, my boy!" cried Trotty. "You was turned up Trumps originally, and Trumps you must be until you die! But you were crying by the fire tonight, my pet, when I came home. Why did you cry by the fire?"

"I was thinking of the years we've passed together, father. Only that. And thinking you might miss me, and be lonely."

Trotty was backing off to that extraordinary chair again, when the child, who had been awakened by the noise, came running in, half dressed.

"Why, here she is!" cried Trotty catching her up. "Here's little Lilian! Ha, ha, ha! Here we are and here we go! O, here we are and here we go again! And here we are and here we go! And Uncle Will, too!" Stopping in his trot to greet him heartily. "O, Uncle Will, the vision that I've had tonight, through lodging you! O, Uncle Will, the obligations that you've laid me under by your coming, my good friend!"

Before Will Fern could make the least reply, a band of music burst into the room, attended by a flock of neighbours, screaming: "A Happy New Year, Meg!" "A Happy Wedding!" "Many of 'em!" and other fragmentary good wishes of that sort. The Drum (who was a private friend of Trotty's) then stepped forward and said:

"Trotty Veck, my boy! It's got about that your daughter is going to be married tomorrow. There an't a soul that knows you that don't wish you well, or that knows her and don't wish her well. Or that knows you both and don't wish you both all the happiness the New Year can bring. And here we are, to play it in accordingly."

"What a happiness it is, I'm sure," said Trotty, "to be so esteemed. How kind and neighbourly you are! It's all along of my dear daughter. She deserves it."

At this moment a combination of prodigious sounds was heard outside, and a good-humoured, comely woman of some fifty years of age, or thereabouts, came running in, closely followed by the marrow-bones and cleavers and the bells—not *the* Bells, but a portable collection on a frame.

Trotty said: "It's Mrs. Chickenstalker!" And sat down and beat his knees again.

"Married, and not tell me, Meg!" cried the good woman. "Never! I couldn't rest on the last night of the Old Year without coming to wish you joy. I couldn't have done it, Meg. Not if I had been bed-ridden. So here I am."

"Mrs. Tugby," said Trotty, who had been going round and round her in an ecstasy—"I *should* say Chickenstalker—bless your heart and soul! A happy New Year, and many of 'em! Mrs. Tugby," said Trotty, when he had saluted her—"I *should* say Chickenstalker—this is William Fern and Lilian."

The worthy dame, to his surprise, turned very pale and very red.

"Not Lilian Fern, whose mother died in Dorsetshire?" said she.

Her uncle answered "Yes," and meeting hastily they exchanged some hurried words together, of which the upshot was that Mrs. Chickenstalker shook him by both hands, saluted Trotty on his cheek again of her own free will, and took the child to her capacious breast.

"Will Fern," said Trotty, pulling on his right-hand muffler. "Not the friend that you was hoping to find?"

"Ay," returned Will, putting a hand on each of Trotty's shoulders. "And like to prove a'most as good a friend, if that can be, as one I found."

"O!" said Trotty. "Please to play up there. Will you have the goodness?"

Had Trotty dreamed? Or are his joys and sorrows, and the actors in them, but a dream; himself a dream; the teller of this tale a dreamer, waking but now? If it be so, O listener, dear to him in all his visions, try to bear in mind the stern realities from which these shadows come; and in your sphere—none is too wide and none too limited for such an end—endeavour to correct, improve and soften them. So may the New Year be a happy one to you, happy to many more whose happiness depends on you! So may each year be happier than the last, and not the meanest of our brethren or sisterhood debarred their rightful share in what our great Creator formed them to enjoy.

The Ghost of the Bride's Chamber

A.k.a. The Ghost Chamber

The house was a genuine old house of a very quaint description, teeming with old carvings, and beams, and panels, and having an excellent old staircase, with a gallery or upper staircase, cut off from it by a curious fence-work of old oak, or of the old Honduras Mahogany wood. It was, and is, and will be, for many a long year to come, a remarkably picturesque house; and a certain grave mystery lurking in the depth of the old mahogany panels, as if they were so many deep pools of dark water—such, indeed, as they had been much among when they were trees-gave it a very mysterious character after nightfall.

When Mr. Goodchild and Mr. Idle had first alighted at the door, and stepped into the sombre, handsome old hall, they had been received by half-a-dozen noiseless old men in black, all dressed exactly alike, who glided up the stairs with the obliging landlord and waiter—but without appearing to get into their way, or to mind whether they did or no—and who had filed off to the right and left on the old staircase, as the guests entered their sitting-room. It was then broad, bright day. But, Mr. Goodchild had said, when their door was shut, 'Who on earth are those old men?' And afterwards, both on going out and coming in, he had noticed that there were no old men to be seen.

Neither, had the old men, or any one of the old men, reappeared since. The two friends had passed a night in the house, but had seen nothing more of the old men. Mr. Goodchild, in rambling about it, had looked along passages, and glanced in at doorways, but had encountered no old men; neither did it appear that any old men were, by any member of the establishment, missed or expected.

Another odd circumstance impressed itself on their attention. It was, that the door of their sitting-room was never left untouched for a quarter of an hour. It was opened with hesitation, opened with confidence, opened a little way, opened a good way,—always clapped-to again without a word of explanation. They were reading, they were writing, they were eating, they were drinking, they were talking, they were dozing; the door was always opened at an unexpected moment, and they looked towards it, and it was clapped- to again, and nobody was to be seen. When this had happened fifty times or so, Mr. Goodchild had said to his companion, jestingly: 'I begin to think, Tom, there was something wrong with those six old men.'

Night had come again, and they had been writing for two or three hours: writing, in short, a portion of the lazy notes from which these lazy sheets are taken. They had left off writing, and glasses were on the table between them. The house was closed and quiet. Around the head of Thomas Idle, as he lay upon his sofa, hovered light wreaths of fragrant smoke. The temples of Francis Goodchild, as he leaned back in his chair, with his two hands clasped behind his head, and his legs crossed, were similarly decorated.

They had been discussing several idle subjects of speculation, not omitting the strange old men, and were still so occupied, when Mr. Goodchild abruptly changed his attitude to wind up his watch. They were just becoming drowsy enough to be stopped in their talk by any such slight check. Thomas Idle, who was speaking at the moment, paused and said, 'How goes it?'

'One,' said Goodchild.

As if he had ordered One old man, and the order were promptly executed (truly, all orders were so, in that excellent hotel), the door opened, and One old man stood there.

He did not come in, but stood with the door in his hand.

'One of the six, Tom, at last!' said Mr. Goodchild, in a surprised whisper.—'Sir, your pleasure?'

'Sir, *your* pleasure?' said the One old man.

'I didn't ring.'

'The bell did,' said the One old man.

He said *bell*, in a deep, strong way, that would have expressed the church Bell.

'I had the pleasure, I believe, of seeing you, yesterday?' said Goodchild.

'I cannot undertake to say for certain,' was the grim reply of the One old man.

'I think you saw me? Did you not?'

'Saw *you*?' said the old man. 'O yes, I saw you. But, I see many who never see me.'

A chilled, slow, earthy, fixed old man. A cadaverous old man of measured speech. An old man who seemed as unable to wink, as if his eyelids had been nailed to his forehead. An old man whose eyes—two spots of fire—had no more motion than if they had been connected with the back of his skull by screws driven through it, and riveted and bolted outside, among his grey hair.

The night had turned so cold, to Mr. Goodchild's sensations, that he shivered. He remarked lightly, and half apologetically, 'I think somebody is walking over my grave.'

'No,' said the weird old man, 'there is no one there.'

Mr. Goodchild looked at Idle, but Idle lay with his head enwreathed in smoke.

'No one there?' said Goodchild.

'There is no one at your grave, I assure you,' said the old man.

He had come in and shut the door, and he now sat down. He did not bend himself to sit, as other people do, but seemed to sink bolt upright, as if in water, until the chair stopped him.

'My friend, Mr. Idle,' said Goodchild, extremely anxious to introduce a third person into the conversation.

'I am,' said the old man, without looking at him, 'at Mr. Idle's service.'

'If you are an old inhabitant of this place,' Francis Goodchild resumed.

'Yes.'

'Perhaps you can decide a point my friend and I were in doubt upon, this morning. They hang condemned criminals at the Castle, I believe?'

'*I* believe so,' said the old man.

'Are their faces turned towards that noble prospect?'

'Your face is turned,' replied the old man, 'to the Castle wall. When you are tied up, you see its stones expanding and contracting violently, and a similar expansion and contraction seem to take place in your own head and breast. Then, there is a rush of fire and an earthquake, and the Castle springs into the air, and you tumble down a precipice.'

His cravat appeared to trouble him. He put his hand to his throat, and moved his neck from side to side. He was an old man of a swollen character of face, and his nose was immoveably hitched up on one side, as if by a little hook inserted in that nostril. Mr. Goodchild felt exceedingly uncomfortable, and began to think the night was hot, and not cold.

'A strong description, sir,' he observed.

'A strong sensation,' the old man rejoined.

Again, Mr. Goodchild looked to Mr. Thomas Idle; but Thomas lay on his back with his face attentively turned towards the One old man, and made no sign. At this time Mr. Goodchild believed that he saw threads of fire stretch from the old man's eyes to his own, and there attach themselves. (Mr. Goodchild writes the present account of his experience, and, with the utmost solemnity, protests that he had the strongest sensation upon him of being forced to look at the old man along those two fiery films, from that moment.)

'I must tell it to you,' said the old man, with a ghastly and a stony stare.

'What?' asked Francis Goodchild.

'You know where it took place. Yonder!'

Whether he pointed to the room above, or to the room below, or to any room in that old house, or to a room in some other old house in that old town, Mr. Goodchild was not, nor is, nor ever can be, sure. He was confused by the circumstance that the right forefinger of the One old man seemed to dip itself in one of the threads of fire, light itself, and make a fiery start in the air, as it pointed somewhere. Having pointed somewhere, it went out.

'You know she was a Bride,' said the old man.

'I know they still send up Bride-cake,' Mr. Goodchild faltered. 'This is a very oppressive air.'

'She was a Bride,' said the old man. 'She was a fair, flaxen-haired, large-eyed girl, who had no character, no purpose. A weak, credulous, incapable, helpless nothing. Not like her mother. No, no. It was her father whose character she reflected.

'Her mother had taken care to secure everything to herself, for her own life, when the father of this girl (a child at that time) died—of sheer helplessness; no other disorder—and then He renewed the acquaintance that had once subsisted between the mother and Him. He had been put aside for the flaxen-haired, large-eyed man (or nonentity) with Money. He could overlook that for Money. He wanted compensation in Money.

'So, he returned to the side of that woman the mother, made love to her again, danced attendance on her, and submitted himself to her whims. She wreaked upon him every whim she had, or could invent. He bore it. And the more he bore, the more he wanted compensation in Money, and the more he was resolved to have it.

'But, lo! Before he got it, she cheated him. In one of her imperious states, she froze, and never thawed again. She put her hands to her head one night, uttered a cry, stiffened, lay in that attitude certain hours, and died. And he had got no compensation from her in Money, yet. Blight and Murrain on her! Not a penny.

'He had hated her throughout that second pursuit, and had longed for retaliation on her. He now counterfeited her signature to an instrument, leaving all she had to leave, to her daughter-ten years old then—to whom the property passed absolutely, and appointing himself the daughter's Guardian. When He slid it under the pillow of the bed on which she lay, He bent down in the deaf ear of Death, and whispered: "Mistress Pride, I have determined a long time that, dead or alive, you must make me compensation in Money.'

'So, now there were only two left. Which two were, He, and the fair flaxen-haired, large-eyed foolish daughter, who afterwards became the Bride.

'He put her to school. In a secret, dark, oppressive, ancient house, he put her to school with a watchful and unscrupulous woman. "My worthy lady," he said, "here is a mind to be formed; will you help me to form it?" She accepted the trust. For which she, too, wanted compensation in Money, and had it.

'The girl was formed in the fear of him, and in the conviction, that there was no escape from him. She was taught, from the first, to regard him as her future husband—the man who must marry her—the destiny that overshadowed her—the appointed certainty that could never be evaded. The poor fool was soft white wax in their hands, and took the impression that they put upon her. It hardened with time. It became a part of herself. Inseparable from herself, and only to be torn away from her, by tearing life away from her.

'Eleven years she had lived in the dark house and its gloomy garden. He was jealous of the very light and air getting to her, and they kept her close. He stopped the wide chimneys, shaded the little windows, left the strong-stemmed ivy to wander where it would over the house-front, the moss to accumulate on the untrimmed fruit-trees in the red-walled garden, the weeds to over-run its green and yellow walks. He surrounded her with images of sorrow and desolation. He caused her to be filled with fears of the place and of the stories that were told of it, and then on pretext of correcting them, to be left in it in solitude, or made to shrink about it in the dark. When her mind was most depressed and fullest of terrors, then, he would come out of one of the hiding-places from which he overlooked her, and present himself as her sole resource.

'Thus, by being from her childhood the one embodiment her life presented to her of power to coerce and power to relieve, power to bind and power to loose, the ascendency over her weakness was secured. She was twenty-one years and twenty-one days old, when he brought her home to the gloomy house, his half-witted, frightened, and submissive Bride of three weeks.

'He had dismissed the governess by that time—what he had left to do, he could best do alone—and they came back, upon a rain night, to the scene of her long preparation. She turned to him upon the threshold, as the rain was dripping from the porch, and said:

'"O sir, it is the Death-watch ticking for me!"

'"Well!" he answered. "And if it were?"

'"O sir!" she returned to him, "look kindly on me, and be merciful to me! I beg your pardon. I will do anything you wish, if you will only forgive me!"

'That had become the poor fool's constant song: "I beg your pardon," and "Forgive me!"

'She was not worth hating; he felt nothing but contempt for her. But, she had long been in the way, and he had long been weary, and the work was near its end, and had to be worked out.

'"You fool," he said. "Go up the stairs!"

'She obeyed very quickly, murmuring, "I will do anything you wish!" When he came into the Bride's Chamber, having been a little retarded by the heavy fastenings of the great door (for they were alone in the house, and he had arranged that the people who attended on them should come and go in the day), he found her withdrawn to the furthest corner, and there standing pressed against the panelling as if she would have shrunk through it: her flaxen hair all wild about her face, and her large eyes staring at him in vague terror.

'"What are you afraid of? Come and sit down by me."

'"I will do anything you wish. I beg your pardon, sir. Forgive me!" Her monotonous tune as usual.

'"Ellen, here is a writing that you must write out to-morrow, in your own hand. You may as well be seen by others, busily engaged upon it. When you have written it all fairly, and corrected all mistakes, call in any two people there may be about the house, and sign your name to it before them. Then, put it in your bosom to keep it safe, and when I sit here again tomorrow night, give it to me."

'"I will do it all, with the greatest care. I will do anything you wish."

'"Don't shake and tremble, then."

'"I will try my utmost not to do it—if you will only forgive me!"

'Next day, she sat down at her desk, and did as she had been told. He often passed in and out of the room, to observe her, and always saw her slowly and laboriously writing: repeating to herself the words she copied, in appearance quite mechanically, and without caring or endeavouring to comprehend them, so that she did her task. He saw her follow the directions she had received, in all particulars; and at night, when they were alone again in the same Bride's Chamber, and he drew his chair to the hearth, she timidly approached him from her distant seat, took the paper from her bosom, and gave it into his hand.

'It secured all her possessions to him, in the event of her death. He put her before him, face to face, that he might look at her steadily; and he asked her, in so many plain words, neither fewer nor more, did she know that?

'There were spots of ink upon the bosom of her white dress, and they made her face look whiter and her eyes look larger as she nodded her head. There were spots of ink upon the hand with which she stood before him, nervously plaiting and folding her white skirts.

'He took her by the arm, and looked her, yet more closely and steadily, in the face. "Now, die! I have done with you."

'She shrunk, and uttered a low, suppressed cry.

'"I am not going to kill you. I will not endanger my life for yours. Die!"

'He sat before her in the gloomy Bride's Chamber, day after day, night after night, looking the word at her when he did not utter it. As often as her large unmeaning eyes were raised from the hands in which she rocked her head, to the stern figure, sitting with crossed arms and knitted forehead, in the chair, they read in it, "Die!" When she dropped asleep in exhaustion, she was called back to shuddering consciousness, by the whisper, "Die!" When she fell upon her old entreaty to be pardoned, she was answered "Die!" When she had out-watched and out-suffered the long night, and the rising sun flamed into the sombre room, she heard it hailed with, "Another day and not dead?—Die!"

'Shut up in the deserted mansion, aloof from all mankind, and engaged alone in such a struggle without any respite, it came to this—that either he must die, or she. He knew it very well, and concentrated his strength against her feebleness. Hours upon hours he held her by the arm when her arm was black where he held it, and bade her Die!

'It was done, upon a windy morning, before sunrise. He computed the time to be half-past four; but, his forgotten watch had run down, and he could not be sure. She had broken away from him in the night, with loud and sudden cries—the first of that kind to which she had given vent—and he had had to put his hands over her mouth. Since then, she had been quiet in the corner of the panelling where she had sunk down; and he had left her, and had gone back with his folded arms and his knitted forehead to his chair.

'Paler in the pale light, more colourless than ever in the leaden dawn, he saw her coming, trailing herself along the floor towards him—a white wreck of hair, and dress, and wild eyes, pushing itself on by an irresolute and bending hand.

'"O, forgive me! I will do anything. O, sir, pray tell me I may live!"

'"Die!"

'"Are you so resolved? Is there no hope for me?"

'"Die!"

'Her large eyes strained themselves with wonder and fear;

wonder and fear changed to reproach; reproach to blank nothing. It was done. He was not at first so sure it was done, but that the morning sun was hanging jewels in her hair—he saw the diamond, emerald, and ruby, glittering among it in little points, as he stood looking down at her—when he lifted her and laid her on her bed.

'She was soon laid in the ground. And now they were all gone, and he had compensated himself well.

'He had a mind to travel. Not that he meant to waste his Money, for he was a pinching man and liked his Money dearly (liked nothing else, indeed), but, that he had grown tired of the desolate house and wished to turn his back upon it and have done with it. But, the house was worth Money, and Money must not be thrown away. He determined to sell it before he went. That it might look the less wretched and bring a better price, he hired some labourers to work in the overgrown garden; to cut out the dead wood, trim the ivy that drooped in heavy masses over the windows and gables, and clear the walks in which the weeds were growing mid-leg high.

'He worked, himself, along with them. He worked later than they did, and, one evening at dusk, was left working alone, with his bill-hook in his hand. One autumn evening, when the Bride was five weeks dead.

'"It grows too dark to work longer," he said to himself, "I must give over for the night."

'He detested the house, and was loath to enter it. He looked at the dark porch waiting for him like a tomb, and felt that it was an accursed house. Near to the porch, and near to where he stood, was a tree whose branches waved before the old bay-window of the Bride's Chamber, where it had been done. The tree swung suddenly, and made him start. It swung again, although the night was still. Looking up into it, he saw a figure among the branches.

'It was the figure of a young man. The face looked down, as his looked up; the branches cracked and swayed; the figure rapidly descended, and slid upon its feet before him. A slender youth of about her age, with long light brown hair.

'"What thief are you?" he said, seizing the youth by the collar.

'The young man, in shaking himself free, swung him a blow with his arm across the face and throat. They closed, but the young man got from him and stepped back, crying, with great eagerness and horror, "Don't touch me! I would as lieve be touched by the Devil!"

'He stood still, with his bill-hook in his hand, looking at the young man. For, the young man's look was the counterpart of her last look, and he had not expected ever to see that again.

'"I am no thief. Even if I were, I would not have a coin of your wealth, if it would buy me the Indies. You murderer!"

'"What!"

'"I climbed it," said the young man, pointing up into the tree, "for the first time, nigh four years ago. I climbed it, to look at her. I saw her. I spoke to her. I have climbed it, many a time, to watch and listen for her. I was a boy, hidden among its leaves, when from that bay-window she gave me this!"

'He showed a tress of flaxen hair, tied with a mourning ribbon.

'"Her life," said the young man, "was a life of mourning. She gave me this, as a token of it, and a sign that she was dead to everyone but you. If I had been older, if I had seen her sooner, I might have saved her from you. But, she was fast in the web when I first climbed the tree, and what could I do then to break it!"

'In saying those words, he burst into a fit of sobbing and crying: weakly at first, then passionately.

'"Murderer! I climbed the tree on the night when you brought her back. I heard her, from the tree, speak of the Death-watch at the door. I was three times in the tree while you were shut up with her, slowly killing her. I saw her, from the tree, lie dead upon her bed. I have watched you, from the tree, for proofs and traces of your guilt. The manner of it, is a mystery to me yet, but I will pursue you until you have rendered up your life to the hangman. You shall never, until then, be rid of me. I loved her! I can know no relenting towards you. Murderer, I loved her!"

'The youth was bare-headed, his hat having fluttered away in his descent from the tree. He moved towards the gate. He had to pass—Him—to get to it. There was breadth for two old-fashioned carriages abreast; and the youth's abhorrence, openly expressed in every feature of his face and limb of his body, and very hard to bear, had verge enough to keep itself at a distance in. He (by which I mean the other) had not stirred hand or foot, since he had stood still to look at the boy. He faced round, now, to follow him with his eyes. As the back of the bare light-brown head was turned to him, he saw a red curve stretch from his hand to it. He knew, before he threw the bill-hook, where it had alighted—I say, had alighted, and not, would alight; for, to his clear perception the thing was done before he did it. It cleft the head, and it remained there, and the boy lay on his face.

'He buried the body in the night, at the foot of the tree. As soon as it was light in the morning, he worked at turning up all the ground near the tree, and hacking and hewing at the neighbouring bushes and undergrowth. When the labourers came, there was nothing suspicious, and nothing suspected.

'But, he had, in a moment, defeated all his precautions, and destroyed the triumph of the scheme he had so long concerted, and so successfully worked out. He had got rid of the Bride, and had acquired her fortune without endangering his life; but now, for a death by which he had gained nothing, he had evermore to live with a rope around his neck.

'Beyond this, he was chained to the house of gloom and horror, which he could not endure. Being afraid to sell it or to quit it, lest discovery should be made, he was forced to live in it. He hired two old people, man and wife, for his servants; and dwelt in it, and dreaded it. His great difficulty, for a long time, was the garden. Whether he should keep it trim, whether he should suffer it to fall into its former state of neglect, what would be the least likely way of attracting attention to it?

'He took the middle course of gardening, himself, in his

evening leisure, and of then calling the old serving-man to help him; but, of never letting him work there alone. And he made himself an arbour over against the tree, where he could sit and see that it was safe.

'As the seasons changed, and the tree changed, his mind perceived dangers that were always changing. In the leafy time, he perceived that the upper boughs were growing into the form of the young man—that they made the shape of him exactly, sitting in a forked branch swinging in the wind. In the time of the falling leaves, he perceived that they came down from the tree, forming tell-tale letters on the path, or that they had a tendency to heap themselves into a churchyard mound above the grave. In the winter, when the tree was bare, he perceived that the boughs swung at him the ghost of the blow the young man had given, and that they threatened him openly. In the spring, when the sap was mounting in the trunk, he asked himself, were the dried-up particles of blood mounting with it: to make out more obviously this year than last, the leaf- screened figure of the young man, swinging in the wind?

'However, he turned his Money over and over, and still over. He was in the dark trade, the gold-dust trade, and most secret trades that yielded great returns. In ten years, he had turned his Money over, so many times, that the traders and shippers who had dealings with him, absolutely did not lie—for once—when they declared that he had increased his fortune, Twelve Hundred Per Cent.

'He possessed his riches one hundred years ago, when people could be lost easily. He had heard who the youth was, from hearing of the search that was made after him; but, it died away, and the youth was forgotten.

'The annual round of changes in the tree had been repeated ten times since the night of the burial at its foot, when there was a great thunder-storm over this place. It broke at midnight, and roared until morning. The first intelligence he heard from his old serving-man that morning, was, that the tree had been struck by Lightning.

'It had been riven down the stem, in a very surprising manner, and the stem lay in two blighted shafts: one resting against the house, and one against a portion of the old red garden-wall in which its fall had made a gap. The fissure went down the tree to a little above the earth, and there stopped. There was great curiosity to see the tree, and, with most of his former fears revived, he sat in his arbour—grown quite an old man—watching the people who came to see it.

'They quickly began to come, in such dangerous numbers, that he closed his garden-gate and refused to admit any more. But, there were certain men of science who travelled from a distance to examine the tree, and, in an evil hour, he let them in!—Blight and Murrain on them, let them in!

'They wanted to dig up the ruin by the roots, and closely examine it, and the earth about it. Never, while he lived! They offered money for it. They! Men of science, whom he could have bought by the gross, with a scratch of his pen! He showed them the garden-gate again, and locked and barred it.

'But they were bent on doing what they wanted to do, and they bribed the old serving-man—a thankless wretch who regularly complained when he received his wages, of being underpaid—and they stole into the garden by night with their lanterns, picks, and shovels, and fell to at the tree. He was lying in a turret-room on the other side of the house (the Bride's Chamber had been unoccupied ever since), but he soon dreamed of picks and shovels, and got up.

'He came to an upper window on that side, whence he could see their lanterns, and them, and the loose earth in a heap which he had himself disturbed and put back, when it was last turned to the air. It was found! They had that minute lighted on it. They were all bending over it. One of them said, "The skull is fractured;" and another, "See here the bones;" and another, "See here the clothes;" and then the first struck in again, and said, "A rusty bill-hook!"

'He became sensible, next day, that he was already put under a strict watch, and that he could go nowhere without being followed. Before a week was out, he was taken and laid in hold. The circumstances were gradually pieced together against him, with a desperate malignity, and an appalling ingenuity. But, see the justice of men, and how it was extended to him! He was further accused of having poisoned that girl in the Bride's Chamber. He, who had carefully and expressly avoided imperilling a hair of his head for her, and who had seen her die of her own incapacity!

'There was doubt for which of the two murders he should be first tried; but, the real one was chosen, and he was found Guilty, and cast for death. Bloodthirsty wretches! They would have made him Guilty of anything, so set they were upon having his life.

'His money could do nothing to save him, and he was hanged. *I* am He, and I was hanged at Lancaster Castle with my face to the wall, a hundred years ago!'

At this terrific announcement, Mr. Goodchild tried to rise and cry out. But, the two fiery lines extending from the old man's eyes to his own, kept him down, and he could not utter a sound. His sense of hearing, however, was acute, and he could hear the clock strike Two. No sooner had he heard the clock strike Two, than he saw before him Two old men!

Two.

The eyes of each, connected with his eyes by two films of fire: each, exactly like the other: each, addressing him at precisely one and the same instant: each, gnashing the same teeth in the same head, with the same twitched nostril above them, and the same suffused expression around it. Two old men. Differing in nothing, equally distinct to the sight, the copy no fainter than the original, the second as real as the first.

'At what time,' said the Two old men, 'did you arrive at the door below?'

'At Six.'

'And there were Six old men upon the stairs!'

Mr. Goodchild having wiped the perspiration from his brow, or tried to do it, the Two old men proceeded in one voice, and in the singular number:

'I had been anatomised, but had not yet had my skeleton put together and re-hung on an iron hook, when it began to be whispered that the Bride's Chamber was haunted. It *was* haunted, and I was there.

'WE were there. She and I were there. I, in the chair upon the hearth; she, a white wreck again, trailing itself towards me on the floor. But, I was the speaker no more, and the one word that she said to me from midnight until dawn was, 'Live!'

'The youth was there, likewise. In the tree outside the window. Coming and going in the moonlight, as the tree bent and gave. He has, ever since, been there, peeping in at me in my torment; revealing to me by snatches, in the pale lights and slatey shadows where he comes and goes, bare-headed—a bill-hook, standing edgewise in his hair.

'In the Bride's Chamber, every night from midnight until dawn—one month in the year excepted, as I am going to tell you—he hides in the tree, and she comes towards me on the floor; always approaching; never coming nearer; always visible as if by moonlight, whether the moon shines or no; always saying, from midnight until dawn, her one word, "Live!"

'But, in the month wherein I was forced out of this life—this present month of thirty days—the Bride's Chamber is empty and quiet. Not so my old dungeon. Not so the rooms where I was restless and afraid, ten years. Both are fitfully haunted then. At One in the morning. I am what you saw me when the clock struck that hour—One old man. At Two in the morning, I am Two old men. At Three, I am Three. By Twelve at noon, I am Twelve old men, One for every hundred *per cent.* of old gain. Every one of the Twelve, with Twelve times my old power of suffering and agony. From that hour until Twelve at night, I, Twelve old men in anguish and fearful foreboding, wait for the coming of the executioner. At Twelve at night, I, Twelve old men turned off, swing invisible outside Lancaster Castle, with Twelve faces to the wall!

'When the Bride's Chamber was first haunted, it was known to me that this punishment would never cease, until I could make its nature, and my story, known to two living men together. I waited for the coming of two living men together into the Bride's Chamber, years upon years. It was infused into my knowledge (of the means I am ignorant) that if two living men, with their eyes open, could be in the Bride's Chamber at One in the morning, they would see me sitting in my chair.

'At length, the whispers that the room was spiritually troubled, brought two men to try the adventure. I was scarcely struck upon the hearth at midnight (I come there as if the Lightning blasted me into being), when I heard them ascending the stairs. Next, I saw them enter. One of them was a bold, gay, active man, in the prime of life, some five and forty years of age; the other, a dozen years younger. They brought provisions with them in a basket, and bottles. A young woman accompanied them, with wood and coals for the lighting of the fire. When she had lighted it, the bold, gay, active man accompanied her along the gallery outside the room, to see her safely down the staircase, and came back laughing.

'He locked the door, examined the chamber, put out the contents of the basket on the table before the fire—little recking of me, in my appointed station on the hearth, close to him-and filled the glasses, and ate and drank. His companion did the same, and was as cheerful and confident as he: though he was the leader. When they had supped, they laid pistols on the table, turned to the fire, and began to smoke their pipes of foreign make.

'They had travelled together, and had been much together, and had an abundance of subjects in common. In the midst of their talking and laughing, the younger man made a reference to the leader's being always ready for any adventure; that one, or any other. He replied in these words:

'"Not quite so, Dick; if I am afraid of nothing else, I am afraid of myself."

'His companion seeming to grow a little dull, asked him, in what sense? How?

'"Why, thus," he returned. "Here is a Ghost to be disproved.

Well! I cannot answer for what my fancy might do if I were alone here, or what tricks my senses might play with me if they had me to themselves. But, in company with another man, and especially with Dick, I would consent to outface all the Ghosts that were ever of in the universe."

'"I had not the vanity to suppose that I was of so much importance tonight," said the other.

'"Of so much," rejoined the leader, more seriously than he had spoken yet, "that I would, for the reason I have given, on no account have undertaken to pass the night here alone."

'It was within a few minutes of One. The head of the younger man had drooped when he made his last remark, and it drooped lower now.

'"Keep awake, Dick!" said the leader, gaily. "The small hours are the worst."

'He tried, but his head drooped again.

'"Dick!" urged the leader. "Keep awake!"

'"I can't," he indistinctly muttered. "I don't know what strange influence is stealing over me. I can't."

'His companion looked at him with a sudden horror, and I, in my different way, felt a new horror also; for, it was on the stroke of One, and I felt that the second watcher was yielding to me, and that the curse was upon me that I must send him to sleep.

'"Get up and walk, Dick!" cried the leader. "Try!"

'It was in vain to go behind the slumber's chair and shake him. One o'clock sounded, and I was present to the elder man, and he stood transfixed before me.

'To him alone, I was obliged to relate my story, without hope of benefit. To him alone, I was an awful phantom making a quite useless confession. I foresee it will ever be the same. The two living men together will never come to release me. When I appear, the senses of one of the two will be locked in sleep; he will neither see nor hear me; my communication will ever be made to a solitary listener, and will ever be unserviceable. Woe! Woe! Woe!'

As the Two old men, with these words, wrung their hands, it shot into Mr. Goodchild's mind that he was in the terrible situation of being virtually alone with the spectre, and that Mr. Idle's immoveability was explained by his having been charmed asleep at One o'clock. In the terror of this sudden discovery which produced an indescribable dread, he struggled so hard to get free from the four fiery threads, that he snapped them, after he had pulled them out to a great width. Being then out of bonds, he caught up Mr. Idle from the sofa and rushed down-stairs with him.

'What are you about, Francis?' demanded Mr. Idle. 'My bedroom is not down here. What the deuce are you carrying me at all for? I can walk with a stick now. I don't want to be carried. Put me down.'

Mr. Goodchild put him down in the old hall, and looked about him wildly.

'What are you doing? Idiotically plunging at your own sex, and rescuing them or perishing in the attempt?' asked Mr. Idle, in a highly petulant state.

'The One old man!' cried Mr. Goodchild, distractedly,—'and the Two old men!'

Mr. Idle deigned no other reply than 'The One old woman, I think you mean,' as he began hobbling his way back up the staircase, with the assistance of its broad balustrade.

'I assure you, Tom,' began Mr. Goodchild, attending at his side, 'that since you fell asleep—'

'Come, I like that!' said Thomas Idle, 'I haven't closed an eye!'

With the peculiar sensitiveness on the subject of the disgraceful action of going to sleep out of bed, which is the lot of all mankind, Mr. Idle persisted in this declaration. The same peculiar sensitiveness impelled Mr. Goodchild, on being taxed with the same crime, to repudiate it with honourable resentment. The settlement of the question of The One old man and The Two old men was thus presently complicated, and soon made quite impracticable. Mr. Idle said it was all Bride-cake, and fragments, newly arranged, of things seen and thought about in the day. Mr. Goodchild said how could that be, when he hadn't been asleep, and what right could Mr. Idle have to say so, who had been asleep? Mr. Idle said he had never been asleep, and never did go to sleep, and that Mr. Goodchild, as a general rule, was always asleep. They consequently parted for the rest of the night, at their bedroom doors, a little ruffled. Mr. Goodchild's last words were, that he had had, in that real and tangible old sitting-room of that real and tangible old Inn (he supposed Mr. Idle denied its existence?), every sensation and experience, the present record of which is now within a line or two of completion; and that he would write it out and print it every word. Mr. Idle returned that he might if he liked—and he did like, and has now done it.

The Haunted Man and the Ghost's Bargain

CHAPTER 1
THE GIFT BESTOWED

Everybody said so.

Far be it from me to assert that what everybody says must be true. Everybody is, often, as likely to be wrong as right. In the general experience, everybody has been wrong so often, and it has taken, in most instances, such a weary while to find out how wrong, that the authority is proved to be fallible. Everybody may sometimes be right; "but *that's* no rule," as the ghost of Giles Scroggins says in the ballad.

The dread word, *Ghost*, recalls me.

Everybody said he looked like a haunted man. The extent of my present claim for everybody is, that they were so far right. He did.

Who could have seen his hollow cheek; his sunken brilliant eye; his black-attired figure, indefinably grim, although well-knit and well-proportioned; his grizzled hair hanging, like tangled seaweed, about his face,—as if he had been, through his whole life, a lonely mark for the chafing and beating of the great deep of humanity,—but might have said he looked like a haunted man?

Who could have observed his manner, taciturn, thoughtful, gloomy, shadowed by habitual reserve, retiring always and jocund never, with a distraught air of reverting to a bygone place and time, or of listening to some old echoes in his mind, but might have said it was the manner of a haunted man?

Who could have heard his voice, slow-speaking, deep, and grave, with a natural fullness and melody in it which he seemed to set himself against and stop, but might have said it was the voice of a haunted man?

Who that had seen him in his inner chamber, part library and part laboratory,—for he was, as the world knew, far and wide, a learned man in chemistry, and a teacher on whose lips and hands a crowd of aspiring ears and eyes hung daily,—who that had seen him there, upon a winter night, alone, surrounded by his drugs and instruments and books; the shadow of his shaded lamp a monstrous beetle on the wall, motionless among a crowd of spectral shapes raised there by the flickering of the fire upon the quaint objects around him; some of these phantoms (the reflection of glass vessels that held liquids), trembling at heart like things that knew his power to uncombine them, and to give back their component parts to fire and vapour;—who that had seen him then, his work done, and he pondering in his chair before the rusted grate and red flame, moving his thin mouth as if in speech, but silent as the dead, would not have said that the man seemed haunted and the chamber too?

Who might not, by a very easy flight of fancy, have believed that everything about him took this haunted tone, and that he lived on haunted ground?

His dwelling was so solitary and vault-like,—an old, retired part of an ancient endowment for students, once a brave edifice, planted in an open place, but now the obsolete whim of forgotten architects; smoke-age-and-weather-darkened, squeezed on every side by the overgrowing of the great city, and choked, like an old well, with stones and bricks; its small quadrangles, lying down in very pits formed by the streets and buildings, which, in course of time, had been constructed above its heavy chimney stalks; its old trees, insulted by the neighbouring smoke, which deigned to droop so low when it was very feeble and the weather very moody; its grass-plots, struggling with the mildewed earth to be grass, or to win any show of compromise; its silent pavements, unaccustomed to the tread of feet, and even to the observation of eyes, except when a stray face looked down from the upper world, wondering what nook it was; its sundial in a little bricked-up corner, where no sun had straggled for a hundred years, but where, in compensation for the sun's neglect, the snow would lie for weeks when it lay nowhere else, and the black east wind would spin like a huge humming-top, when in all other places it was silent and still.

His dwelling, at its heart and core—within doors—at his fireside—was so lowering and old, so crazy, yet so strong, with its worn-eaten beams of wood in the ceiling, and its sturdy floor shelving downward to the great oak chimney-piece; so environed and hemmed in by the pressure of the town yet so remote in fashion, age, and custom; so quiet, yet so thundering with echoes when a distant voice was raised or a door was shut,—echoes, not confined to the many low passages and empty rooms, but rumbling and grumbling till they were stifled in the heavy air of the forgotten Crypt where the Norman arches were half-buried in the earth.

You should have seen him in his dwelling about twilight, in the dead winter time.

When the wind was blowing, shrill and shrewd, with the going down of the blurred sun. When it was just so dark, as that the forms of things were indistinct and big—but not wholly lost. When sitters by the fire began to see wild faces and figures, mountains and abysses, ambuscades and armies, in the coals. When people in the streets bent down their heads and ran before the weather. When those who were obliged to meet it, were stopped at angry corners, stung by wandering snow-flakes alighting on the lashes of their eyes,—which fell too sparingly, and were blown away too quickly, to leave a trace upon the frozen ground. When windows of private houses closed up tight and warm. When lighted gas began to burst forth in the busy and the quiet streets, fast blackening otherwise. When stray pedestrians, shivering along the latter, looked down at the glowing fires in kitchens, and sharpened their sharp appetites by sniffing up the fragrance of whole miles of dinners.

When travellers by land were bitter cold, and looked wearily on gloomy landscapes, rustling and shuddering in the blast. When mariners at sea, outlying upon icy yards, were tossed and swung above the howling ocean dreadfully. When lighthouses, on rocks and headlands, showed solitary and watchful; and benighted sea-birds breasted on against their ponderous lanterns, and fell dead. When little readers of story-books, by the firelight, trembled to think of Cassim Baba cut into quarters, hanging in the Robbers' Cave, or had some small misgivings that the fierce little old woman, with the crutch, who used to start out of the box in the merchant Abudah's bedroom, might, one of these nights, be found upon the stairs, in the long, cold, dusky journey up to bed.

When, in rustic places, the last glimmering of daylight died away from the ends of avenues; and the trees, arching overhead, were sullen and black. When, in parks and woods, the high wet fern and sodden moss, and beds of fallen leaves, and trunks of trees, were lost to view, in masses of impenetrable shade. When mists arose from dyke, and fen, and river. When lights in old halls and in cottage windows, were a cheerful sight. When the mill stopped, the wheelwright and the blacksmith shut their workshops, the turnpike-gate closed, the plough and harrow were left lonely in the fields, the labourer and team went home, and the striking of the church clock had a deeper sound than at noon, and the churchyard wicket would be swung no more that night.

When twilight everywhere released the shadows, prisoned up all day, that now closed in and gathered like mustering swarms of ghosts. When they stood lowering, in corners of rooms, and frowned out from behind half-opened doors. When they had full possession of unoccupied apartments. When they danced upon the floors, and walls, and ceilings of inhabited chambers, while the fire was low, and withdrew like ebbing waters when it sprang into a blaze. When they fantastically mocked the shapes of household objects, making the nurse an ogress, the rocking-horse a monster, the wondering child, half-scared and half-amused, a stranger to itself,—the very tongs upon the hearth, a straddling giant with his arms *akimbo*, evidently smelling the blood of Englishmen, and wanting to grind people's bones to make his bread.

When these shadows brought into the minds of older people, other thoughts, and showed them different images. When they stole from their retreats, in the likenesses of forms and faces from the past, from the grave, from the deep, deep gulf, where the things that might have been, and never were, are always wandering.

When he sat, as already mentioned, gazing at the fire. When, as it rose and fell, the shadows went and came. When he took no heed of them, with his bodily eyes; but, let them come or let them go, looked fixedly at the fire. You should have seen him, then.

When the sounds that had arisen with the shadows, and come out of their lurking-places at the twilight summons, seemed to make a deeper stillness all about him. When the wind was rumbling in the chimney, and sometimes crooning, sometimes howling, in the house. When the old trees outside were so shaken and beaten, that one querulous old rook, unable to sleep, protested now and then, in a feeble, dozy, high-up "Caw!" When, at intervals, the window trembled, the rusty vane upon the turret-top complained, the clock beneath it recorded that another quarter of an hour was gone, or the fire collapsed and fell in with a rattle.

When a knock came at his door, in short, as he was sitting so, and roused him.

"Who's that?" said he. "Come in!"

Surely there had been no figure leaning on the back of his chair; no face looking over it. It is certain that no gliding footstep touched the floor, as he lifted up his head, with a start, and spoke. And yet there was no mirror in the room on whose surface his own form could have cast its shadow for a moment; and,

Something had passed darkly and gone!

"I'm humbly fearful, sir," said a fresh-coloured busy man, holding the door open with his foot for the admission of himself and a wooden tray he carried, and letting it go again by very gentle and careful degrees, when he and the tray had got in, lest it should close noisily, "that it's a good bit past the time tonight. But Mrs. William has been taken off her legs so often"

"By the wind? Ay! I have heard it rising."

"—By the wind, sir—that it's a mercy she got home at all. Oh dear, yes. Yes. It was by the wind, Mr. Redlaw. By the wind."

He had, by this time, put down the tray for dinner, and was employed in lighting the lamp, and spreading a cloth on the table. From this employment he desisted in a hurry, to stir and feed the fire, and then resumed it; the lamp he had lighted, and the blaze that rose under his hand, so quickly changing the appearance of the room, that it seemed as if the mere coming in of his fresh red face and active manner had made the pleasant alteration.

"Mrs. William is of course subject at any time, sir, to be taken off her balance by the elements. She is not formed superior to *that*."

"No," returned Mr. Redlaw good-naturedly, though abruptly.

"No, sir. Mrs. William may be taken off her balance by Earth; as for example, last Sunday week, when sloppy and greasy, and she going out to tea with her newest sister-in-law, and having a pride in herself, and wishing to appear perfectly spotless though pedestrian. Mrs. William may be taken off her balance by Air; as being once over-persuaded by a friend to try a swing at Peckham Fair, which acted on her constitution instantly like a steamboat. Mrs. William may be taken off her balance by Fire; as on a false alarm of engines at her mother's, when she went two miles in her nightcap. Mrs. William may be taken off her balance by Water; as at Battersea, when rowed into the piers by her young nephew, Charley Swidger junior, aged twelve, which had no idea of boats whatever. But these are elements. Mrs. William must be taken out of elements for the strength of *her* character to come into play."

As he stopped for a reply, the reply was "Yes," in the same tone as before.

"Yes, sir. Oh dear, yes!" said Mr. Swidger, still proceeding with his preparations, and checking them off as he made them. "That's where it is, sir. That's what I always say myself, sir. Such a many of us Swidgers!—Pepper. Why there's my father, sir, superannuated keeper and custodian of this Institution, eighty-seven year old. He's a Swidger!—Spoon."

"True, William," was the patient and abstracted answer, when he stopped again.

"Yes, sir," said Mr. Swidger. "That's what I always say, sir. You may call him the trunk of the tree!—Bread. Then you come to his successor, my unworthy self—Salt—and Mrs. William, Swidgers both.—Knife and fork. Then you come to all my brothers and their families, Swidgers, man and woman, boy and girl. Why, what with cousins, uncles, aunts, and relationships of this, that, and t'other degree, and whatnot degree, and marriages, and lyings-in, the Swidgers—Tumbler—might take hold of hands, and make a ring round England!"

Receiving no reply at all here, from the thoughtful man whom he addressed, Mr. William approached, him nearer, and made a feint of accidentally knocking the table with a decanter, to rouse him. The moment he succeeded, he went on, as if in great alacrity of acquiescence.

"Yes, sir! That's just what I say myself, sir. Mrs. William and me have often said so. 'There's Swidgers enough,' we say, 'without *our* voluntary contributions,'—Butter. In fact, sir, my father is a family in himself—Castors—to take care of; and it happens all for the best that we have no child of our own, though it's made Mrs. William rather quiet-like, too. Quite ready for the fowl and mashed potatoes, sir? Mrs. William said she'd dish in ten minutes when I left the Lodge."

"I am quite ready," said the other, waking as from a dream, and walking slowly to and fro.

"Mrs. William has been at it again, sir!" said the keeper, as he stood warming a plate at the fire, and pleasantly shading his face with it. Mr. Redlaw stopped in his walking, and an expression of interest appeared in him.

"What I always say myself, sir. She *will* do it! There's a motherly feeling in Mrs. William's breast that must and will have went."

"What has she done?"

"Why, sir, not satisfied with being a sort of mother to all the young gentlemen that come up from a variety of parts, to attend your courses of lectures at this ancient foundation—it's surprising how stone-chaney catches the heat this frosty weather, to be sure!" Here he turned the plate, and cooled his fingers.

"Well?" said Mr. Redlaw.

"That's just what I say myself, sir," returned Mr. William, speaking over his shoulder, as if in ready and delighted assent. "That's exactly where it is, sir! There ain't one of our students but appears to regard Mrs. William in that light. Every day, right through the course, they puts their heads into the Lodge, one after another, and have all got something to tell her, or something to ask her. 'Swidge' is the appellation by which they speak of Mrs. William in general, among themselves, I'm told; but that's what I say, sir. Better be called ever so far out of your name, if it's done in real liking, than have it made ever so much of, and not cared about! What's a name for? To know a person by. If Mrs. William is known by something better than her name—I allude to Mrs. William's qualities and disposition—never mind her name, though it *is* Swidger, by rights. Let 'em call her Swidge, Widge, Bridge—Lord! London Bridge, Blackfriars, Chelsea, Putney, Waterloo, or Hammersmith Suspension—if they like."

The close of this triumphant oration brought him and the plate to the table, upon which he half laid and half dropped it, with a lively sense of its being thoroughly heated, just as the subject of his praises entered the room, bearing another tray and a lantern, and followed by a venerable old man with long grey hair.

Mrs. William, like Mr. William, was a simple, innocent-looking person, in whose smooth cheeks the cheerful red of her husband's official waistcoat was very pleasantly repeated. But whereas Mr. William's light hair stood on end all over his head, and seemed to draw his eyes up with it in an excess of bustling readiness for anything, the dark brown hair of Mrs. William was carefully smoothed down, and waved away under a trim tidy cap, in the most exact and quiet manner imaginable. Whereas Mr. William's very trousers hitched themselves up at the ankles, as if it were not in their iron-grey nature to rest without looking about them, Mrs. William's neatly-flowered skirts—red and white, like her own pretty face—were as composed and orderly, as if the very wind that blew so hard out of doors could not disturb one of their folds.

Whereas his coat had something of a fly-away and half-off appearance about the collar and breast, her little bodice was so placid and neat, that there should have been protection for her, in it, had she needed any, with the roughest people. Who could have had the heart to make so calm a bosom swell with grief, or throb with fear, or flutter with a thought of shame! To whom would its repose and peace have not appealed against disturbance, like the innocent slumber of a child!

"Punctual, of course, Milly," said her husband, relieving her of the tray, "or it wouldn't be you. Here's Mrs. William, sir!—He looks lonelier than ever tonight," whispering to his wife, as he was taking the tray, "and ghostlier altogether."

Without any show of hurry or noise, or any show of herself even, she was so calm and quiet, Milly set the dishes she had brought upon the table,—Mr. William, after much clattering and running about, having only gained possession of a butter-boat of gravy, which he stood ready to serve.

"What is that the old man has in his arms?" asked Mr. Redlaw, as he sat down to his solitary meal.

"Holly, sir," replied the quiet voice of Milly.

"That's what I say myself, sir," interposed Mr. William, striking in with the butter-boat. "Berries is so seasonable to the time of year!—Brown gravy!"

"Another Christmas come, another year gone!" murmured the Chemist, with a gloomy sigh. "More figures in the lengthening sum of recollection that we work and work at to our torment, till Death idly jumbles all together, and rubs all out. So, Philip!" breaking off, and raising his voice as he addressed the old man, standing apart, with his glistening burden in his arms, from which the quiet Mrs. William took small branches, which she noiselessly trimmed with her scissors, and decorated the room with, while her aged father-in-law looked on much interested in the ceremony.

"My duty to you, sir," returned the old man. "Should have spoke before, sir, but know your ways, Mr. Redlaw—proud to say—and wait till spoke to! Merry Christmas, sir, and Happy New Year, and many of 'em. Have had a pretty many of 'em myself—ha, ha!—and may take the liberty of wishing 'em. I'm eighty-seven!"

"Have you had so many that were merry and happy?" asked the other.

"Ay, sir, ever so many," returned the old man.

"Is his memory impaired with age? It is to be expected now," said Mr. Redlaw, turning to the son, and speaking lower.

"Not a morsel of it, sir," replied Mr. William. "That's exactly what I say myself, sir. There never was such a memory as my father's. He's the most wonderful man in the world. He don't know what forgetting means. It's the very observation I'm always making to Mrs. William, sir, if you'll believe me!"

Mr. Swidger, in his polite desire to seem to acquiesce at all events, delivered this as if there were no iota of contradiction in it, and it were all said in unbounded and unqualified assent.

The Chemist pushed his plate away, and, rising from the table, walked across the room to where the old man stood looking at a little sprig of holly in his hand.

"It recalls the time when many of those years were old and new, then?" he said, observing him attentively, and touching him on the shoulder. "Does it?"

"Oh many, many!" said Philip, half awaking from his reverie. "I'm eighty-seven!"

"Merry and happy, was it?" asked the Chemist in a low voice. "Merry and happy, old man?"

"Maybe as high as that, no higher," said the old man, holding out his hand a little way above the level of his knee, and looking retrospectively at his questioner, "when I first remember 'em! Cold, sunshiny day it was, out a-walking, when someone—it was my mother as sure as you stand there, though I don't know what her blessed face was like, for she took ill and died that Christmas-time—told me they were food for birds. The pretty little fellow thought—that's me, you understand—that birds' eyes were so bright, perhaps, because the berries that they lived on in the winter were so bright. I recollect that. And I'm eighty-seven!"

"Merry and happy!" mused the other, bending his dark eyes upon the stooping figure, with a smile of compassion. "Merry and happy—and remember well?"

"Ay, ay, ay!" resumed the old man, catching the last words. "I remember 'em well in my school time, year after year, and all the merry-making that used to come along with them. I was a strong chap then, Mr. Redlaw; and, if you'll believe me, hadn't my match at football within ten mile. Where's my son William? Hadn't my match at football, William, within ten mile!"

"That's what I always say, father!" returned the son promptly, and with great respect. "You *are* a Swidger, if ever there was one of the family!"

"Dear!" said the old man, shaking his head as he again looked at the holly. "His mother—my son William's my youngest son—and I, have sat among 'em all, boys and girls, little children and babies, many a year, when the berries like these were not shining half so bright all round us, as their bright faces. Many of 'em are gone; she's gone; and my son George (our eldest, who was her pride more than all the rest!) is fallen very low: but I can see them, when I look here, alive and healthy, as they used to be in those days; and I can see him, thank God, in his innocence. It's a blessed thing to me, at eighty-seven."

The keen look that had been fixed upon him with so much earnestness, had gradually sought the ground.

"When my circumstances got to be not so good as formerly, through not being honestly dealt by, and I first come here to be custodian," said the old man, "—which was upwards of fifty years ago—where's my son William? More than half a century ago, William!"

"That's what I say, father," replied the son, as promptly and dutifully as before, "that's exactly where it is. Two times ought's an ought, and twice five ten, and there's a hundred of 'em."

"It was quite a pleasure to know that one of our founders-or more correctly speaking," said the old man, with a great glory in his subject and his knowledge of it, "one of the learned gentlemen that helped endow us in Queen Elizabeth's time, for we were founded afore her day—left in his will, among the other bequests he made us, so much to buy holly, for garnishing the walls and windows, come Christmas. There was something homely and friendly in it. Being but strange here, then, and coming at Christmas time, we took a liking for his very picter that hangs in what used to be, anciently, afore our ten poor gentlemen commuted for an annual stipend in money, our great Dinner Hall.—A sedate gentleman in a peaked beard, with a ruff round his neck, and a scroll below him, in old English letters, 'Lord! keep my memory green!' You know all about him, Mr. Redlaw?"

"I know the portrait hangs there, Philip."

"Yes, sure, it's the second on the right, above the panelling. I was going to say—he has helped to keep *my* memory green, I thank him; for going round the building every year, as I'm a doing now, and freshening up the bare rooms with these branches and berries, freshens up my bare old brain. One year brings back another, and that year another, and those others numbers! At last, it seems to me as if the birth-time of our Lord was the birth-time of all I have ever had affection for, or mourned for, or delighted in,—and they're a pretty many, for I'm eighty-seven!"

"Merry and happy," murmured Redlaw to himself.

The room began to darken strangely.

"So you see, sir," pursued old Philip, whose hale wintry cheek had warmed into a ruddier glow, and whose blue eyes had brightened while he spoke, "I have plenty to keep, when I keep this present season. Now, where's my quiet Mouse? Chattering's the sin of my time of life, and there's half the building to do yet, if the cold don't freeze us first, or the wind don't blow us away, or the darkness don't swallow us up."

The quiet Mouse had brought her calm face to his side, and silently taken his arm, before he finished speaking.

"Come away, my dear," said the old man. "Mr. Redlaw won't settle to his dinner, otherwise, till it's cold as the winter. I hope you'll excuse me rambling on, sir, and I wish you good night, and, once again, a merry—"

"Stay!" said Mr. Redlaw, resuming his place at the table, more, it would have seemed from his manner, to reassure the old keeper, than in any remembrance of his own appetite. "Spare me another moment, Philip. William, you were going to tell me something to your excellent wife's honour. It will not be disagreeable to her to hear you praise her. What was it?"

"Why, that's where it is, you see, sir," returned Mr. William Swidger, looking towards his wife in considerable embarrassment. "Mrs. William's got her eye upon me."

"But you're not afraid of Mrs. William's eye?"

"Why, no, sir," returned Mr. Swidger, "that's what I say myself. It wasn't made to be afraid of. It wouldn't have been made so mild, if that was the intention. But I wouldn't like to—Milly!—him, you know. Down in the Buildings."

Mr. William, standing behind the table, and rummaging disconcertedly among the objects upon it, directed persuasive glances at Mrs. William, and secret jerks of his head and thumb at Mr. Redlaw, as alluring her towards him.

"Him, you know, my love," said Mr. William. "Down in the Buildings. Tell, my dear! You're the works of Shakespeare in comparison with myself. Down in the Buildings, you know, my love.—Student."

"Student?" repeated Mr. Redlaw, raising his head.

"That's what I say, sir!" cried Mr. William, in the utmost animation of assent. "If it wasn't the poor student down in the Buildings, why should you wish to hear it from Mrs. William's lips? Mrs. William, my dear—Buildings."

"I didn't know," said Milly, with a quiet frankness, free from any haste or confusion, "that William had said anything about it, or I wouldn't have come. I asked him not to. It's a sick young gentleman, sir—and very poor, I am afraid—who is too ill to go home this holiday-time, and lives, unknown to any one, in but a common kind of lodging for a gentleman, down in Jerusalem Buildings. That's all, sir."

"Why have I never heard of him?" said the Chemist, rising hurriedly. "Why has he not made his situation known to me? Sick!—give me my hat and cloak. Poor!—what house?—what number?"

"Oh, you mustn't go there, sir," said Milly, leaving her father-in-law, and calmly confronting him with her collected little face and folded hands.

"Not go there?"

"Oh dear, no!" said Milly, shaking her head as at a most manifest and self-evident impossibility. "It couldn't be thought of!"

"What do you mean? Why not?"

"Why, you see, sir," said Mr. William Swidger, persuasively and confidentially, "that's what I say. Depend upon it, the young gentleman would never have made his situation known to one of his own sex. Mrs. Williams has got into his confidence, but that's quite different. They all confide in Mrs. William; they all trust *her*. A man, sir, couldn't have got a whisper out of him; but woman, sir, and Mrs. William combined—!"

"There is good sense and delicacy in what you say, William," returned Mr. Redlaw, observant of the gentle and composed face at his shoulder. And laying his finger on his lip, he secretly put his purse into her hand.

"Oh dear no, sir!" cried Milly, giving it back again. "Worse and worse! Couldn't be dreamed of!"

Such a staid matter-of-fact housewife she was, and so unruffled by the momentary haste of this rejection, that, an instant afterwards, she was tidily picking up a few leaves which had strayed from between her scissors and her apron, when she had arranged the holly.

Finding, when she rose from her stooping posture, that Mr. Redlaw was still regarding her with doubt and astonishment, she quietly repeated—looking about, the while, for any other fragments that might have escaped her observation:

"Oh dear no, sir! He said that of all the world he would not be known to you, or receive help from you—though he is a student in your class. I have made no terms of secrecy with you, but I trust to your honour completely."

"Why did he say so?"

"Indeed I can't tell, sir," said Milly, after thinking a little, "because I am not at all clever, you know; and I wanted to be useful to him in making things neat and comfortable about him, and employed myself that way. But I know he is poor, and lonely, and I think he is somehow neglected too.—How dark it is!"

The room had darkened more and more. There was a very heavy gloom and shadow gathering behind the Chemist's chair.

"What more about him?" he asked.

"He is engaged to be married when he can afford it," said Milly, "and is studying, I think, to qualify himself to earn a living. I have seen, a long time, that he has studied hard and denied himself much.—How very dark it is!"

"It's turned colder, too," said the old man, rubbing his hands. "There's a chill and dismal feeling in the room. Where's my son William? William, my boy, turn the lamp, and rouse the fire!"

Milly's voice resumed, like quiet music very softly played:

"He muttered in his broken sleep yesterday afternoon, after talking to me" (this was to herself) "about someone dead, and some great wrong done that could never be forgotten; but whether to him or to another person, I don't know. Not *by* him, I am sure."

"And, in short, Mrs. William, you see—which she wouldn't say herself, Mr. Redlaw, if she was to stop here till the new year after this next one—" said Mr. William, coming up to him to speak in his ear, "has done him worlds of good! Bless you, worlds of good! All at home just the same as ever—my father made as snug and comfortable—not a crumb of litter to be found in the house, if you were to offer fifty pound ready money for it-Mrs. William apparently never out of the way—yet Mrs. William backwards and forwards, backwards and forwards, up and down, up and down, a mother to him!"

The room turned darker and colder, and the gloom and shadow gathering behind the chair was heavier.

"Not content with this, sir, Mrs. William goes and finds, this very night, when she was coming home (why it's not above a couple of hours ago), a creature more like a young wild beast than a young child, shivering upon a door-step. What does Mrs. William do, but brings it home to dry it, and feed it, and keep it till our old Bounty of food and flannel is given away, on Christmas morning! If it ever felt a fire before, it's as much as ever it did; for it's sitting in the old Lodge chimney, staring at ours as if its ravenous eyes would never shut again. It's sitting there, at least," said Mr. William, correcting himself, on reflection, "unless it's bolted!"

"Heaven keep her happy!" said the Chemist aloud, "and you too, Philip! and you, William! I must consider what to do in this. I may desire to see this student, I'll not detain you any longer now. Goodnight!"

"I thank'ee, sir, I thank'ee!" said the old man, "for Mouse, and for my son William, and for myself. Where's my son William? William, you take the lantern and go on first, through them long dark passages, as you did last year and the year afore. Ha ha! *I* remember—though I'm eighty-seven! 'Lord, keep my memory green!' It's a very good prayer, Mr. Redlaw, that of the learned gentleman in the peaked beard, with a ruff round his neck-hangs up, second on the right above the panelling, in what used to be, afore our ten poor gentlemen commuted, our great Dinner Hall. 'Lord, keep my memory green!' It's very good and pious, sir. Amen! Amen!"

As they passed out and shut the heavy door, which, however carefully withheld, fired a long train of thundering reverberations when it shut at last, the room turned darker.

As he fell a musing in his chair alone, the healthy holly withered on the wall, and dropped—dead branches.

As the gloom and shadow thickened behind him, in that place where it had been gathering so darkly, it took, by slow degrees,—or out of it there came, by some unreal, unsubstantial process—not to be traced by any human sense,—an awful likeness of himself!

Ghastly and cold, colourless in its leaden face and hands, but with his features, and his bright eyes, and his grizzled hair, and dressed in the gloomy shadow of his dress, it came into his terrible appearance of existence, motionless, without a sound. As *he* leaned his arm upon the elbow of his chair, ruminating before the fire, *it* leaned upon the chair-back, close above him, with its appalling copy of his face looking where his face looked, and bearing the expression his face bore.

This, then, was the Something that had passed and gone already. This was the dread companion of the haunted man!

It took, for some moments, no more apparent heed of him, than he of it. The Christmas Waits were playing somewhere in the distance, and, through his thoughtfulness, he seemed to listen to the music. It seemed to listen too.

At length he spoke; without moving or lifting up his face.

"Here again!" he said.

"Here again," replied the Phantom.

"I see you in the fire," said the haunted man; "I hear you in music, in the wind, in the dead stillness of the night."

The Phantom moved its head, assenting.

"Why do you come, to haunt me thus?"

"I come as I am called," replied the Ghost.

"No. Unbidden," exclaimed the Chemist.

"Unbidden be it," said the Spectre. "It is enough. I am here."

Hitherto the light of the fire had shone on the two faces—if the dread lineaments behind the chair might be called a face-both addressed towards it, as at first, and neither looking at the other. But, now, the haunted man turned, suddenly, and stared upon the Ghost. The Ghost, as sudden in its motion, passed to before the chair, and stared on him.

The living man, and the animated image of himself dead, might so have looked, the one upon the other. An awful survey, in a lonely and remote part of an empty old pile of building, on a winter night, with the loud wind going by upon its journey of mystery—whence or whither, no man knowing since the world began—and the stars, in unimaginable millions, glittering through it, from eternal space, where the world's bulk is as a grain, and its hoary age is infancy.

"Look upon me!" said the Spectre. "I am he, neglected in my youth, and miserably poor, who strove and suffered, and still strove and suffered, until I hewed out knowledge from the mine where it was buried, and made rugged steps thereof, for my worn feet to rest and rise on."

"I *am* that man," returned the Chemist.

"No mother's self-denying love," pursued the Phantom, "no father's counsel, aided *me*. A stranger came into my father's place when I was but a child, and I was easily an alien from my mother's heart. My parents, at the best, were of that sort whose care soon ends, and whose duty is soon done; who cast their offspring loose, early, as birds do theirs; and, if they do well, claim the merit; and, if ill, the pity."

It paused, and seemed to tempt and goad him with its look, and with the manner of its speech, and with its smile.

"I am he," pursued the Phantom, "who, in this struggle upward, found a friend. I made him—won him—bound him to me! We worked together, side by side. All the love and confidence that in my earlier youth had had no outlet, and found no expression, I bestowed on him."

"Not all," said Redlaw, hoarsely.

"No, not all," returned the Phantom. "I had a sister."

The haunted man, with his head resting on his hands, replied "I had!" The Phantom, with an evil smile, drew closer to the chair, and resting its chin upon its folded hands, its folded hands upon the back, and looking down into his face with searching eyes, that seemed instinct with fire, went on:

"Such glimpses of the light of home as I had ever known, had streamed from her. How young she was, how fair, how loving! I took her to the first poor roof that I was master of, and made it rich. She came into the darkness of my life, and made it bright.—She is before me!"

"I saw her, in the fire, but now. I hear her in music, in the wind, in the dead stillness of the night," returned the haunted man.

"*Did* he love her?" said the Phantom, echoing his contemplative tone. "I think he did, once. I am sure he did. Better had she loved him less—less secretly, less dearly, from the shallower depths of a more divided heart!"

"Let me forget it!" said the Chemist, with an angry motion of his hand. "Let me blot it from my memory!"

The Spectre, without stirring, and with its unwinking, cruel eyes still fixed upon his face, went on:

"A dream, like hers, stole upon my own life."

"It did," said Redlaw.

"A love, as like hers," pursued the Phantom, "as my inferior nature might cherish, arose in my own heart. I was too poor to bind its object to my fortune then, by any thread of promise or entreaty. I loved her far too well, to seek to do it. But, more than ever I had striven in my life, I strove to climb! Only an inch gained, brought me something nearer to the height. I toiled up! In the late pauses of my labour at that time,—my sister (sweet companion!) still sharing with me the expiring embers and the cooling hearth,—when day was breaking, what pictures of the future did I see!"

"I saw them, in the fire, but now," he murmured. "They come back to me in music, in the wind, in the dead stillness of the night, in the revolving years."

"—Pictures of my own domestic life, in aftertime, with her who was the inspiration of my toil. Pictures of my sister, made the wife of my dear friend, on equal terms—for he had some inheritance, we none—pictures of our sobered age and mellowed happiness, and of the golden links, extending back so far, that should bind us, and our children, in a radiant garland," said the Phantom.

"Pictures," said the haunted man, "that were delusions. Why is it my doom to remember them too well!"

"Delusions," echoed the Phantom in its changeless voice, and glaring on him with its changeless eyes. "For my friend (in whose breast my confidence was locked as in my own), passing between me and the centre of the system of my hopes and struggles, won her to himself, and shattered my frail universe. My sister, doubly dear, doubly devoted, doubly cheerful in my home, lived on to see me famous, and my old ambition so rewarded when its spring was broken, and then—"

"Then died," he interposed. "Died, gentle as ever; happy; and with no concern but for her brother. Peace!"

The Phantom watched him silently.

"Remembered!" said the haunted man, after a pause. "Yes. So well remembered, that even now, when years have passed, and nothing is more idle or more visionary to me than the boyish love so long outlived, I think of it with sympathy, as if it were a younger brother's or a son's. Sometimes I even wonder when her heart first inclined to him, and how it had been affected towards me.—Not lightly, once, I think.—But that is nothing. Early unhappiness, a wound from a hand I loved and trusted, and a loss that nothing can replace, outlive such fancies."

"Thus," said the Phantom, "I bear within me a Sorrow and a Wrong. Thus I prey upon myself. Thus, memory is my curse; and, if I could forget my sorrow and my wrong, I would!"

"Mocker!" said the Chemist, leaping up, and making, with a wrathful hand, at the throat of his other self. "Why have I always that taunt in my ears?"

"Forbear!" exclaimed the Spectre in an awful voice. "Lay a

hand on Me, and die!"

He stopped midway, as if its words had paralysed him, and stood looking on it. It had glided from him; it had its arm raised high in warning; and a smile passed over its unearthly features, as it reared its dark figure in triumph.

"If I could forget my sorrow and wrong, I would," the Ghost repeated. "If I could forget my sorrow and my wrong, I would!"

"Evil spirit of myself," returned the haunted man, in a low, trembling tone, "my life is darkened by that incessant whisper."

"It is an echo," said the Phantom.

"If it be an echo of my thoughts—as now, indeed, I know it is," rejoined the haunted man, "why should I, therefore, be tormented? It is not a selfish thought. I suffer it to range beyond myself. All men and women have their sorrows,—most of them their wrongs; ingratitude, and sordid jealousy, and interest, besetting all degrees of life. Who would not forget their sorrows and their wrongs?"

"Who would not, truly, and be happier and better for it?" said the Phantom.

"These revolutions of years, which we commemorate," proceeded Redlaw, "what do *they* recall! Are there any minds in which they do not re-awaken some sorrow, or some trouble? What is the remembrance of the old man who was here to-night? A tissue of sorrow and trouble."

"But common natures," said the Phantom, with its evil smile upon its glassy face, "unenlightened minds and ordinary spirits, do not feel or reason on these things like men of higher cultivation and profounder thought."

"Tempter," answered Redlaw, "whose hollow look and voice I dread more than words can express, and from whom some dim foreshadowing of greater fear is stealing over me while I speak, I hear again an echo of my own mind."

"Receive it as a proof that I am powerful," returned the Ghost. "Hear what I offer! Forget the sorrow, wrong, and trouble you have known!"

"Forget them!" he repeated.

"I have the power to cancel their remembrance—to leave but very faint, confused traces of them, that will die out soon," returned the Spectre. "Say! Is it done?"

"Stay!" cried the haunted man, arresting by a terrified gesture the uplifted hand. "I tremble with distrust and doubt of you; and the dim fear you cast upon me deepens into a nameless horror I can hardly bear.—I would not deprive myself of any kindly recollection, or any sympathy that is good for me, or others. What shall I lose, if I assent to this? What else will pass from my remembrance?"

"No knowledge; no result of study; nothing but the intertwisted chain of feelings and associations, each in its turn dependent on, and nourished by, the banished recollections. Those will go."

"Are they so many?" said the haunted man, reflecting in alarm.

"They have been wont to show themselves in the fire, in music, in the wind, in the dead stillness of the night, in the revolving years," returned the Phantom scornfully.

"In nothing else?"

The Phantom held its peace.

But having stood before him, silent, for a little while, it moved towards the fire; then stopped.

"Decide!" it said, "before the opportunity is lost!"

"A moment! I call Heaven to witness," said the agitated man, "that I have never been a hater of any kind,—never morose, indifferent, or hard, to anything around me. If, living here alone, I have made too much of all that was and might have been, and too little of what is, the evil, I believe, has fallen on me, and not on others. But, if there were poison in my body, should I not, possessed of antidotes and knowledge how to use them, use them? If there be poison in my mind, and through this fearful shadow I can cast it out, shall I not cast it out?"

"Say," said the Spectre, "is it done?"

"A moment longer!" he answered hurriedly. "*I would forget it if I could*! Have *I* thought that, alone, or has it been the thought of thousands upon thousands, generation after generation? All human memory is fraught with sorrow and trouble. My memory is as the memory of other men, but other men have not this choice. Yes, I close the bargain. Yes! I *will* forget my sorrow, wrong, and trouble!"

"Say," said the Spectre, "is it done?"

"It is!"

"*It is.* And take this with you, man whom I here renounce! The gift that I have given, you shall give again, go where you will. Without recovering yourself the power that you have yielded up, you shall henceforth destroy its like in all whom you approach. Your wisdom has discovered that the memory of sorrow, wrong, and trouble is the lot of all mankind, and that mankind would be the happier, in its other memories, without it. Go! Be its benefactor! Freed from such remembrance, from this hour, carry involuntarily the blessing of such freedom with you. Its diffusion is inseparable and inalienable from you. Go! Be happy in the good you have won, and in the good you do!"

The Phantom, which had held its bloodless hand above him while it spoke, as if in some unholy invocation, or some ban; and which had gradually advanced its eyes so close to his, that he could see how they did not participate in the terrible smile upon its face, but were a fixed, unalterable, steady horror melted before him and was gone.

As he stood rooted to the spot, possessed by fear and wonder, and imagining he heard repeated in melancholy echoes, dying away fainter and fainter, the words, "Destroy its like in all whom you approach!" a shrill cry reached his ears. It came, not from the passages beyond the door, but from another part of the old building, and sounded like the cry of someone in the dark who had lost the way.

He looked confusedly upon his hands and limbs, as if to be assured of his identity, and then shouted in reply, loudly and wildly; for there was a strangeness and terror upon him, as if he too were lost.

The cry responding, and being nearer, he caught up the lamp, and raised a heavy curtain in the wall, by which he was accustomed to pass into and out of the theatre where he lectured,—which adjoined his room. Associated with youth and animation, and a high amphitheatre of faces which his entrance charmed to interest in a moment, it was a ghostly place when all this life was faded out of it, and stared upon him like an emblem of Death.

"Halloa!" he cried. "Halloa! This way! Come to the light!" When, as he held the curtain with one hand, and with the other raised the lamp and tried to pierce the gloom that filled the place, something rushed past him into the room like a wild-cat, and crouched down in a corner.

"What is it?" he said, hastily.

He might have asked "What is it?" even had he seen it well, as presently he did when he stood looking at it gathered up in its corner.

A bundle of tatters, held together by a hand, in size and form almost an infant's, but in its greedy, desperate little clutch, a bad old man's. A face rounded and smoothed by some half-dozen years, but pinched and twisted by the experiences of a life. Bright eyes, but not youthful. Naked feet, beautiful in their childish delicacy,—ugly in the blood and dirt that cracked upon them. A baby savage, a young monster, a child who had never been a child, a creature who might live to take the outward form of man, but who, within, would live and perish a mere beast.

Used, already, to be worried and hunted like a beast, the boy crouched down as he was looked at, and looked back again, and interposed his arm to ward off the expected blow.

"I'll bite," he said, "if you hit me!"

The time had been, and not many minutes since, when such a sight as this would have wrung the Chemist's heart. He looked upon it now, coldly; but with a heavy effort to remember something—he did not know what—he asked the boy what he did there, and whence he came.

"Where's the woman?" he replied. "I want to find the woman."

"Who?"

"The woman. Her that brought me here, and set me by the large fire. She was so long gone, that I went to look for her, and lost myself. I don't want you. I want the woman."

He made a spring, so suddenly, to get away, that the dull sound of his naked feet upon the floor was near the curtain, when Redlaw caught him by his rags.

"Come! you let me go!" muttered the boy, struggling, and clenching his teeth. "I've done nothing to you. Let me go, will you, to the woman!"

"That is not the way. There is a nearer one," said Redlaw, detaining him, in the same blank effort to remember some association that ought, of right, to bear upon this monstrous object. "What is your name?"

"Got none."

"Where do you live?"

"Live! What's that?"

The boy shook his hair from his eyes to look at him for a moment, and then, twisting round his legs and wrestling with him, broke again into his repetition of "You let me go, will you? I want to find the woman."

The Chemist led him to the door. "This way," he said, looking at him still confusedly, but with repugnance and avoidance, growing out of his coldness. "I'll take you to her."

The sharp eyes in the child's head, wandering round the room, lighted on the table where the remnants of the dinner were.

"Give me some of that!" he said, covetously.

"Has she not fed you?"

"I shall be hungry again tomorrow, sha'n't I? Ain't I hungry every day?"

Finding himself released, he bounded at the table like some small animal of prey, and hugging to his breast bread and meat, and his own rags, all together, said:

"There! Now take me to the woman!"

As the Chemist, with a new-born dislike to touch him, sternly motioned him to follow, and was going out of the door, he trembled and stopped.

"The gift that I have given, you shall give again, go where you will!"

The Phantom's words were blowing in the wind, and the wind blew chill upon him.

"I'll not go there, tonight," he murmured faintly. "I'll go nowhere tonight. Boy! straight down this long-arched passage, and past the great dark door into the yard,—you see the fire shining on the window there."

"The woman's fire?" inquired the boy.

He nodded, and the naked feet had sprung away. He came back with his lamp, locked his door hastily, and sat down in his chair, covering his face like one who was frightened at himself.

For now he was, indeed, alone. Alone, alone.

Chapter 2
The Gift Diffused

A small man sat in a small parlour, partitioned off from a small shop by a small screen, pasted all over with small scraps of newspapers. In company with the small man, was almost any amount of small children you may please to name—at least it seemed so; they made, in that very limited sphere of action, such an imposing effect, in point of numbers.

Of these small fry, two had, by some strong machinery, been got into bed in a corner, where they might have reposed snugly enough in the sleep of innocence, but for a constitutional propensity to keep awake, and also to scuffle in and out of bed. The immediate occasion of these predatory dashes at the waking world, was the construction of an oyster-shell wall in a corner, by two other youths of tender age; on which fortification the two in bed made harassing descents (like those accursed Picts and Scots who beleaguer the early historical studies of most young Britons), and then withdrew to their own territory.

In addition to the stir attendant on these inroads, and the retorts of the invaded, who pursued hotly, and made lunges at the bed-clothes under which the marauders took refuge, another little boy, in another little bed, contributed his mite of confusion to the family stock, by casting his boots upon the waters; in other words, by launching these and several small objects, inoffensive in themselves, though of a hard substance considered as missiles, at the disturbers of his repose,—who were not slow to return these compliments.

Besides which, another little boy—the biggest there, but still little—was tottering to and fro, bent on one side, and considerably affected in his knees by the weight of a large baby, which he was supposed by a fiction that obtains sometimes in sanguine families, to be hushing to sleep. But oh! the inexhaustible regions of contemplation and watchfulness into which this baby's eyes were then only beginning to compose themselves to stare, over his unconscious shoulder!

It was a very Moloch of a baby, on whose insatiate altar the whole existence of this particular young brother was offered up a daily sacrifice. Its personality may be said to have consisted in its never being quiet, in any one place, for five consecutive minutes, and never going to sleep when required. "Tetterby's baby" was as well known in the neighbourhood as the postman or the pot-boy. It roved from door-step to door-step, in the arms of little Johnny Tetterby, and lagged heavily at the rear of troops of juveniles who followed the Tumblers or the Monkey, and came up, all on one side, a little too late for everything that was attractive, from Monday morning until Saturday night.

Wherever childhood congregated to play, there was little Moloch making Johnny fag and toil. Wherever Johnny desired to stay, little Moloch became fractious, and would not remain. Whenever Johnny wanted to go out, Moloch was asleep, and must be watched. Whenever Johnny wanted to stay at home, Moloch was awake, and must be taken out. Yet Johnny was verily persuaded that it was a faultless baby, without its peer in the realm of England, and was quite content to catch meek glimpses of things in general from behind its skirts, or over its limp flapping bonnet, and to go staggering about with it like a very little porter with a very large parcel, which was not directed to anybody, and could never be delivered anywhere.

The small man who sat in the small parlour, making fruitless attempts to read his newspaper peaceably in the midst of this disturbance, was the father of the family, and the chief of the firm described in the inscription over the little shop front, by the name and title of *A. Tetterby and Co., Newsmen.* Indeed, strictly speaking, he was the only personage answering to that designation, as *Co.* was a mere poetical abstraction, altogether baseless and impersonal.

Tetterby's was the corner shop in Jerusalem Buildings. There was a good show of literature in the window, chiefly consisting of picture-newspapers out of date, and serial pirates, and footpads. Walking-sticks, likewise, and marbles, were included in the stock in trade. It had once extended into the light confectionery line; but it would seem that those elegancies of life were not in demand about Jerusalem Buildings, for nothing connected with that branch of commerce remained in the window, except a sort of small glass lantern containing a languishing mass of bull's-eyes, which had melted in the summer and congealed in the winter until all hope of ever getting them out, or of eating them without eating the lantern too, was gone forever.

Tetterby's had tried its hand at several things. It had once made a feeble little dart at the toy business; for, in another lantern, there was a heap of minute wax dolls, all sticking together upside down, in the direst confusion, with their feet on one another's heads, and a precipitate of broken arms and legs at the bottom. It had made a move in the millinery direction, which a few dry, wiry bonnet-shapes remained in a corner of the window to attest. It had fancied that a living might lie hidden in the tobacco trade, and had stuck up a representation of a native of each of the three integral portions of the British Empire, in the act of consuming that fragrant weed; with a poetic legend attached, importing that united in one cause they sat and joked, one chewed tobacco, one took snuff, one smoked: but nothing seemed to have come of it—except flies.

Time had been when it had put a forlorn trust in imitative

jewellery, for in one pane of glass there was a card of cheap seals, and another of pencil-cases, and a mysterious black amulet of inscrutable intention, labelled ninepence. But, to that hour, Jerusalem Buildings had bought none of them. In short, Tetterby's had tried so hard to get a livelihood out of Jerusalem Buildings in one way or other, and appeared to have done so indifferently in all, that the best position in the firm was too evidently Co.'s; Co., as a bodiless creation, being untroubled with the vulgar inconveniences of hunger and thirst, being chargeable neither to the poor's-rates nor the assessed taxes, and having no young family to provide for.

Tetterby himself, however, in his little parlour, as already mentioned, having the presence of a young family impressed upon his mind in a manner too clamorous to be disregarded, or to comport with the quiet perusal of a newspaper, laid down his paper, wheeled, in his distraction, a few times round the parlour, like an undecided carrier-pigeon, made an ineffectual rush at one or two flying little figures in bed-gowns that skimmed past him, and then, bearing suddenly down upon the only unoffending member of the family, boxed the ears of little Moloch's nurse.

"You bad boy!" said Mr. Tetterby, "haven't you any feeling for your poor father after the fatigues and anxieties of a hard winter's day, since five o'clock in the morning, but must you wither his rest, and corrode his latest intelligence, with *your* vicious tricks? Isn't it enough, sir, that your brother 'Dolphus is toiling and moiling in the fog and cold, and you rolling in the lap of luxury with a—with a baby, and everything you can wish for," said Mr. Tetterby, heaping this up as a great climax of blessings, "but must you make a wilderness of home, and maniacs of your parents? Must you, Johnny? Hey?" At each interrogation, Mr. Tetterby made a feint of boxing his ears again, but thought better of it, and held his hand.

"Oh, father!" whimpered Johnny, "when I wasn't doing anything, I'm sure, but taking such care of Sally, and getting her to sleep. Oh, father!"

"I wish my little woman would come home!" said Mr. Tetterby, relenting and repenting, "I only wish my little woman would come home! I ain't fit to deal with 'em. They make my head go round, and get the better of me. Oh, Johnny! Isn't it enough that your dear mother has provided you with that sweet sister?" indicating Moloch; "isn't it enough that you were seven boys before without a ray of gal, and that your dear mother went through what she *did* go through, on purpose that you might all of you have a little sister, but must you so behave yourself as to make my head swim?"

Softening more and more, as his own tender feelings and those of his injured son were worked on, Mr. Tetterby concluded by embracing him, and immediately breaking away to catch one of the real delinquents. A reasonably good start occurring, he succeeded, after a short but smart run, and some rather severe cross-country work under and over the bedsteads, and in and out among the intricacies of the chairs, in capturing this infant, whom he condignly punished, and bore to bed.

This example had a powerful, and apparently, mesmeric influence on him of the boots, who instantly fell into a deep sleep, though he had been, but a moment before, broad awake, and in the highest possible feather. Nor was it lost upon the two young architects, who retired to bed, in an adjoining closet, with great privacy and speed. The comrade of the Intercepted One also shrinking into his nest with similar discretion, Mr. Tetterby, when he paused for breath, found himself unexpectedly in a scene of peace.

"My little woman herself," said Mr. Tetterby, wiping his flushed face, "could hardly have done it better! I only wish my little woman had had it to do, I do indeed!"

Mr. Tetterby sought upon his screen for a passage appropriate to be impressed upon his children's minds on the occasion, and read the following.

"'It is an undoubted fact that all remarkable men have had remarkable mothers, and have respected them in after life as their best friends.' Think of your own remarkable mother, my boys," said Mr. Tetterby, "and know her value while she is still among you!"

He sat down again in his chair by the fire, and composed himself, cross-legged, over his newspaper.

"Let anybody, I don't care who it is, get out of bed again," said Tetterby, as a general proclamation, delivered in a very soft-hearted manner, "and astonishment will be the portion of that respected contemporary!"—which expression Mr. Tetterby selected from his screen. "Johnny, my child, take care of your only sister, Sally; for she's the brightest gem that ever sparkled on your early brow."

Johnny sat down on a little stool, and devotedly crushed himself beneath the weight of Moloch.

"Ah, what a gift that baby is to you, Johnny!" said his father, "and how thankful you ought to be! 'It is not generally known, Johnny,'" he was now referring to the screen again, "'but it is a fact ascertained, by accurate calculations, that the following immense percentage of babies never attain to two years old; that is to say—'"

"Oh, don't, father, please!" cried Johnny. "I can't bear it, when I think of Sally."

Mr. Tetterby desisting, Johnny, with a profound sense of his trust, wiped his eyes, and hushed his sister.

"Your brother 'Dolphus," said his father, poking the fire, "is late tonight, Johnny, and will come home like a lump of ice. What's got your precious mother?"

"Here's mother, and 'Dolphus too, father!" exclaimed Johnny, "I think."

"You're right!" returned his father, listening. "Yes, that's the footstep of my little woman."

The process of induction, by which Mr Tetterby had come to the conclusion that his wife was a little woman, was his own secret. She would have made two editions of himself, very easily. Considered as an individual, she was rather remarkable for being robust and portly; but considered with reference to her husband, her dimensions became magnificent. Nor did they assume a less imposing proportion, when studied with reference to the size of her seven sons, who were but diminutive. In the case of Sally, however, Mrs. Tetterby had asserted herself, at last; as nobody knew better than the victim Johnny, who weighed and measured that exacting idol every hour in the day.

Mrs. Tetterby, who had been marketing, and carried a basket, threw back her bonnet and shawl, and sitting down, fatigued, commanded Johnny to bring his sweet charge to her straightway, for a kiss. Johnny having complied, and gone back to his stool, and again crushed himself, Master Adolphus Tetterby, who had by this time unwound his torso out of a prismatic comforter, apparently interminable, requested the same favour. Johnny having again complied, and again gone back to his stool, and again crushed himself, Mr. Tetterby, struck by a sudden thought, preferred the same claim on his own parental part. The satisfaction of this third desire completely exhausted the sacrifice, who had hardly breath enough left to get back to his stool, crush himself again, and pant at his relations.

"Whatever you do, Johnny," said Mrs. Tetterby, shaking her head, "take care of her, or never look your mother in the face again."

"Nor your brother," said Adolphus.

"Nor your father, Johnny," added Mr. Tetterby.

Johnny, much affected by this conditional renunciation of him, looked down at Moloch's eyes to see that they were all right, so far, and skilfully patted her back (which was uppermost), and rocked her with his foot.

"Are you wet, 'Dolphus, my boy?" said his father. "Come and take my chair, and dry yourself."

"No, father, thank'ee," said Adolphus, smoothing himself down with his hands. "I an't very wet, I don't think. Does my face shine much, father?"

"Well, it *does* look waxy, my boy," returned Mr. Tetterby.

"It's the weather, father," said Adolphus, polishing his cheeks on the worn sleeve of his jacket. "What with rain, and sleet, and wind, and snow, and fog, my face gets quite brought out into a rash sometimes. And shines, it does—oh, don't it, though!"

Master Adolphus was also in the newspaper line of life, being employed, by a more thriving firm than his father and Co., to vend newspapers at a railway station, where his chubby little person, like a shabbily-disguised Cupid, and his shrill little voice (he was not much more than ten years old), were as well known as the hoarse panting of the locomotives, running in and out. His juvenility might have been at some loss for a harmless outlet, in this early application to traffic, but for a fortunate discovery he made of a means of entertaining himself, and of dividing the long day into stages of interest, without neglecting business.

This ingenious invention, remarkable, like many great discoveries, for its simplicity, consisted in varying the first vowel in the word "paper," and substituting, in its stead, at different periods of the day, all the other vowels in grammatical succession. Thus, before daylight in the winter-time, he went to and fro, in his little oilskin cap and cape, and his big comforter, piercing the heavy air with his cry of "Morn-ing Pa-per!" which, about an hour before noon, changed to "Morn-ing Pepper!" which, at about two, changed to "Morn-ing Pip-per!" which in a couple of hours changed to "Morn-ing Pop-per!" and so declined with the sun into "Eve-ning Pup-per!" to the great relief and comfort of this young gentleman's spirits.

Mrs. Tetterby, his lady-mother, who had been sitting with her bonnet and shawl thrown back, as aforesaid, thoughtfully turning her wedding-ring round and round upon her finger, now rose, and divesting herself of her out-of-door attire, began to lay the cloth for supper.

"Ah, dear me, dear me, dear me!" said Mrs. Tetterby. "That's the way the world goes!"

"Which is the way the world goes, my dear?" asked Mr. Tetterby, looking round.

"Oh, nothing," said Mrs. Tetterby.

Mr. Tetterby elevated his eyebrows, folded his newspaper afresh, and carried his eyes up it, and down it, and across it, but was wandering in his attention, and not reading it.

Mrs. Tetterby, at the same time, laid the cloth, but rather as if she were punishing the table than preparing the family supper; hitting it unnecessarily hard with the knives and forks, slapping it with the plates, dinting it with the salt-cellar, and coming heavily down upon it with the loaf.

"Ah, dear me, dear me, dear me!" said Mrs. Tetterby. "That's the way the world goes!"

"My duck," returned her husband, looking round again, "you said that before. Which is the way the world goes?"

"Oh, nothing!" said Mrs. Tetterby.

"Sophia!" remonstrated her husband, "you said *that* before, too."

"Well, I'll say it again if you like," returned Mrs. Tetterby. "Oh nothing—there! And again if you like, oh nothing—there! And again if you like, oh nothing—now then!"

Mr. Tetterby brought his eye to bear upon the partner of his bosom, and said, in mild astonishment:

"My little woman, what has put you out?"

"I'm sure *I* don't know," she retorted. "Don't ask me. Who said I was put out at all? *I* never did."

Mr. Tetterby gave up the perusal of his newspaper as a bad job, and, taking a slow walk across the room, with his hands behind him, and his shoulders raised—his gait according perfectly with the resignation of his manner—addressed himself to his two eldest offspring.

"Your supper will be ready in a minute, 'Dolphus," said Mr. Tetterby. "Your mother has been out in the wet, to the cook's shop, to buy it. It was very good of your mother so to do. *You* shall get some supper too, very soon, Johnny. Your mother's pleased with you, my man, for being so attentive to your precious sister."

Mrs. Tetterby, without any remark, but with a decided subsidence of her animosity towards the table, finished her preparations, and took, from her ample basket, a substantial slab of hot pease pudding wrapped in paper, and a basin covered with a saucer, which, on being uncovered, sent forth an odour so agreeable, that the three pair of eyes in the two beds opened wide and fixed themselves upon the banquet. Mr. Tetterby, without regarding this tacit invitation to be seated, stood repeating slowly, "Yes, yes, your supper will be ready in a minute, 'Dolphus—your mother went out in the wet, to the cook's shop, to buy it. It was very good of your mother so to do"—until Mrs. Tetterby, who had been exhibiting sundry tokens of contrition behind him, caught him round the neck, and wept.

"Oh, Dolphus!" said Mrs. Tetterby, "how could I go and behave so?"

This reconciliation affected Adolphus the younger and Johnny to that degree, that they both, as with one accord, raised a dismal cry, which had the effect of immediately shutting up the round eyes in the beds, and utterly routing the two remaining little Tetterbys, just then stealing in from the adjoining closet to see what was going on in the eating way.

"I am sure, 'Dolphus," sobbed Mrs. Tetterby, "coming home, I had no more idea than a child unborn—"

Mr. Tetterby seemed to dislike this figure of speech, and observed, "Say than the baby, my dear."

"—Had no more idea than the baby," said Mrs. Tetterby.- "Johnny, don't look at me, but look at her, or she'll fall out of your lap and be killed, and then you'll die in agonies of a broken heart, and serve you right.—No more idea I hadn't than that darling, of being cross when I came home; but somehow, 'Dolphus—" Mrs. Tetterby paused, and again turned her wedding-ring round and round upon her finger.

"I see!" said Mr. Tetterby. "I understand! My little woman was put out. Hard times, and hard weather, and hard work, make it trying now and then. I see, bless your soul! No wonder! Dolf, my man," continued Mr. Tetterby, exploring the basin with a fork, "here's your mother been and bought, at the cook's shop, besides pease pudding, a whole knuckle of a lovely roast leg of pork, with lots of crackling left upon it, and with seasoning gravy and mustard quite unlimited. Hand in your plate, my boy, and begin while it's simmering."

Master Adolphus, needing no second summons, received his portion with eyes rendered moist by appetite, and withdrawing to his particular stool, fell upon his supper tooth and nail. Johnny was not forgotten, but received his rations on bread, lest he should, in a flush of gravy, trickle any on the baby. He was required, for similar reasons, to keep his pudding, when not on active service, in his pocket.

There might have been more pork on the knucklebone,-which knucklebone the carver at the cook's shop had assuredly not forgotten in carving for previous customers—but there was no stint of seasoning, and that is an accessory dreamily suggesting pork, and pleasantly cheating the sense of taste. The pease pudding, too, the gravy and mustard, like the Eastern rose in respect of the nightingale, if they were not absolutely pork, had lived near it; so, upon the whole, there was the flavour of a middle-sized pig.

It was irresistible to the Tetterbys in bed, who, though professing to slumber peacefully, crawled out when unseen by their parents, and silently appealed to their brothers for any gastronomic token of fraternal affection. They, not hard of heart, presenting scraps in return, it resulted that a party of light skirmishers in nightgowns were careering about the parlour all through supper, which harassed Mr. Tetterby exceedingly, and once or twice imposed upon him the necessity of a charge, before which these guerrilla troops retired in all directions and in great confusion.

Mrs. Tetterby did not enjoy her supper. There seemed to be something on Mrs. Tetterby's mind. At one time she laughed without reason, and at another time she cried without reason, and at last she laughed and cried together in a manner so very unreasonable that her husband was confounded.

"My little woman," said Mr. Tetterby, "if the world goes that way, it appears to go the wrong way, and to choke you."

"Give me a drop of water," said Mrs. Tetterby, struggling with herself, "and don't speak to me for the present, or take any notice of me. Don't do it!"

Mr. Tetterby having administered the water, turned suddenly on the unlucky Johnny (who was full of sympathy), and demanded why he was wallowing there, in gluttony and idleness, instead of coming forward with the baby, that the sight of her might revive his mother. Johnny immediately approached, borne down by its weight; but Mrs. Tetterby holding out her hand to signify that she was not in a condition to bear that trying appeal to her feelings, he was interdicted from advancing another inch, on pain of perpetual hatred from all his dearest connections; and accordingly retired to his stool again, and crushed himself as before.

After a pause, Mrs. Tetterby said she was better now, and began to laugh.

"My little woman," said her husband, dubiously, "are you quite sure you're better? Or are you, Sophia, about to break out in a fresh direction?"

"No, 'Dolphus, no," replied his wife. "I'm quite myself." With that, settling her hair, and pressing the palms of her hands upon her eyes, she laughed again.

"What a wicked fool I was, to think so for a moment!" said Mrs. Tetterby. "Come nearer, 'Dolphus, and let me ease my mind, and tell you what I mean. Let me tell you all about it."

Mr. Tetterby bringing his chair closer, Mrs. Tetterby laughed again, gave him a hug, and wiped her eyes.

"You know, Dolphus, my dear," said Mrs. Tetterby, "that when I was single, I might have given myself away in several directions. At one time, four after me at once; two of them were sons of Mars."

"We're all sons of Ma's, my dear," said Mr. Tetterby, "jointly with Pa's."

"I don't mean that," replied his wife, "I mean soldiers—serjeants."

"Oh!" said Mr. Tetterby.

"Well, 'Dolphus, I'm sure I never think of such things now, to regret them; and I'm sure I've got as good a husband, and would do as much to prove that I was fond of him, as—"

"As any little woman in the world," said Mr. Tetterby. "Very good. *Very* good."

If Mr. Tetterby had been ten feet high, he could not have expressed a gentler consideration for Mrs. Tetterby's fairy-like stature; and if Mrs. Tetterby had been two feet high, she could not have felt it more appropriately her due.

"But you see, 'Dolphus," said Mrs. Tetterby, "this being Christmas-time, when all people who can, make holiday, and when all people who have got money, like to spend some, I did, somehow, get a little out of sorts when I was in the streets just now. There were so many things to be sold—such delicious things to eat, such fine things to look at, such delightful things to have—and there was so much calculating and calculating necessary, before I durst lay out a sixpence for the commonest thing; and the basket was so large, and wanted so much in it; and my stock of money was so small, and would go such a little way;—you hate me, don't you, 'Dolphus?"

"Not quite," said Mr. Tetterby, "as yet."

"Well! I'll tell you the whole truth," pursued his wife, penitently, "and then perhaps you will. I felt all this, so much, when I was trudging about in the cold, and when I saw a lot of other calculating faces and large baskets trudging about, too, that I began to think whether I mightn't have done better, and been happier, if—I—hadn't—" the wedding-ring went round again, and Mrs. Tetterby shook her downcast head as she turned it.

"I see," said her husband quietly; "if you hadn't married at all, or if you had married somebody else?"

"Yes," sobbed Mrs. Tetterby. "That's really what I thought. Do you hate me now, 'Dolphus?"

"Why no," said Mr. Tetterby. "I don't find that I do, as yet."

Mrs. Tetterby gave him a thankful kiss, and went on.

"I begin to hope you won't, now, 'Dolphus, though I'm afraid I haven't told you the worst. I can't think what came over me. I don't know whether I was ill, or mad, or what I was, but I couldn't call up anything that seemed to bind us to each other, or to reconcile me to my fortune. All the pleasures and enjoyments we had ever had—*they* seemed so poor and insignificant, I hated them. I could have trodden on them. And I could think of nothing else, except our being poor, and the number of mouths there were at home."

"Well, well, my dear," said Mr. Tetterby, shaking her hand encouragingly, "that's truth, after all. We *are* poor, and there *are* a number of mouths at home here."

"Ah! but, Dolf, Dolf!" cried his wife, laying her hands upon his neck, "my good, kind, patient fellow, when I had been at home a very little while—how different! Oh, Dolf, dear, how different it was! I felt as if there was a rush of recollection on me, all at once, that softened my hard heart, and filled it up till it was bursting.

"All our struggles for a livelihood, all our cares and wants since we have been married, all the times of sickness, all the hours of watching, we have ever had, by one another, or by the children, seemed to speak to me, and say that they had made us one, and that I never might have been, or could have been, or would have been, any other than the wife and mother I am. Then, the cheap enjoyments that I could have trodden on so cruelly, got to be so precious to me—Oh so priceless, and dear!—that I couldn't bear to think how much I had wronged them; and I said, and say again a hundred times, how could I ever behave so, 'Dolphus, how could I ever have the heart to do it!"

The good woman, quite carried away by her honest tenderness and remorse, was weeping with all her heart, when she started up with a scream, and ran behind her husband. Her cry was so terrified, that the children started from their sleep and from their beds, and clung about her. Nor did her gaze belie her voice, as she pointed to a pale man in a black cloak who had come into the room.

"Look at that man! Look there! What does he want?"

"My dear," returned her husband, "I'll ask him if you'll let me go. What's the matter! How you shake!"

"I saw him in the street, when I was out just now. He looked at me, and stood near me. I am afraid of him."

"Afraid of him! Why?"

"I don't know why—I—stop! husband!" for he was going towards the stranger.

She had one hand pressed upon her forehead, and one upon her breast; and there was a peculiar fluttering all over her, and a hurried unsteady motion of her eyes, as if she had lost something.

"Are you ill, my dear?"

"What is it that is going from me again?" she muttered, in a low voice. "What *is* this that is going away?"

Then she abruptly answered: "Ill? No, I am quite well," and stood looking vacantly at the floor.

Her husband, who had not been altogether free from the infection of her fear at first, and whom the present strangeness of her manner did not tend to reassure, addressed himself to the pale visitor in the black cloak, who stood still, and whose eyes were bent upon the ground.

"What may be your pleasure, sir," he asked, "with us?"

"I fear that my coming in unperceived," returned the visitor, "has alarmed you; but you were talking and did not hear me."

"My little woman says—perhaps you heard her say it," returned Mr. Tetterby, "that it's not the first time you have alarmed her tonight."

"I am sorry for it. I remember to have observed her, for a few moments only, in the street. I had no intention of frightening her."

As he raised his eyes in speaking, she raised hers. It was extraordinary to see what dread she had of him, and with what dread he observed it—and yet how narrowly and closely.

"My name," he said, "is Redlaw. I come from the old college hard by. A young gentleman who is a student there, lodges in your house, does he not?"

"Mr. Denham?" said Tetterby.

"Yes."

It was a natural action, and so slight as to be hardly noticeable; but the little man, before speaking again, passed his hand across his forehead, and looked quickly round the room, as though he were sensible of some change in its atmosphere. The Chemist, instantly transferring to him the look of dread he had directed towards the wife, stepped back, and his face turned paler.

"The gentleman's room," said Tetterby, "is upstairs, sir. There's a more convenient private entrance; but as you have come in here, it will save your going out into the cold, if you'll take this little staircase," showing one communicating directly with the parlour, "and go up to him that way, if you wish to see him."

"Yes, I wish to see him," said the Chemist. "Can you spare a light?"

The watchfulness of his haggard look, and the inexplicable distrust that darkened it, seemed to trouble Mr. Tetterby. He paused; and looking fixedly at him in return, stood for a minute or so, like a man stupefied, or fascinated.

At length he said, "I'll light you, sir, if you'll follow me."

"No," replied the Chemist, "I don't wish to be attended, or announced to him. He does not expect me. I would rather go alone. Please to give me the light, if you can spare it, and I'll find the way."

In the quickness of his expression of this desire, and in taking the candle from the newsman, he touched him on the breast. Withdrawing his hand hastily, almost as though he had wounded him by accident (for he did not know in what part of himself his new power resided, or how it was communicated, or how the manner of its reception varied in different persons), he turned and ascended the stair.

But when he reached the top, he stopped and looked down. The wife was standing in the same place, twisting her ring round and round upon her finger. The husband, with his head bent forward on his breast, was musing heavily and sullenly. The children, still clustering about the mother, gazed timidly after the visitor, and nestled together when they saw him looking down.

"Come!" said the father, roughly. "There's enough of this. Get to bed here!"

"The place is inconvenient and small enough," the mother

added, "without you. Get to bed!"

The whole brood, scared and sad, crept away; little Johnny and the baby lagging last. The mother, glancing contemptuously round the sordid room, and tossing from her the fragments of their meal, stopped on the threshold of her task of clearing the table, and sat down, pondering idly and dejectedly. The father betook himself to the chimney-corner, and impatiently raking the small fire together, bent over it as if he would monopolise it all. They did not interchange a word.

The Chemist, paler than before, stole upward like a thief; looking back upon the change below, and dreading equally to go on or return.

"What have I done!" he said, confusedly. "What am I going to do!"

"To be the benefactor of mankind," he thought he heard a voice reply.

He looked round, but there was nothing there; and a passage now shutting out the little parlour from his view, he went on, directing his eyes before him at the way he went.

"It is only since last night," he muttered gloomily, "that I have remained shut up, and yet all things are strange to me. I am strange to myself. I am here, as in a dream. What interest have I in this place, or in any place that I can bring to my remembrance? My mind is going blind!"

There was a door before him, and he knocked at it. Being invited, by a voice within, to enter, he complied.

"Is that my kind nurse?" said the voice. "But I need not ask her. There is no one else to come here."

It spoke cheerfully, though in a languid tone, and attracted his attention to a young man lying on a couch, drawn before the chimney-piece, with the back towards the door. A meagre scanty stove, pinched and hollowed like a sick man's cheeks, and bricked into the centre of a hearth that it could scarcely warm, contained the fire, to which his face was turned. Being so near the windy house-top, it wasted quickly, and with a busy sound, and the burning ashes dropped down fast.

"They chink when they shoot out here," said the student, smiling, "so, according to the gossips, they are not coffins, but purses. I shall be well and rich yet, some day, if it please God, and shall live perhaps to love a daughter Milly, in remembrance of the kindest nature and the gentlest heart in the world."

He put up his hand as if expecting her to take it, but, being weakened, he lay still, with his face resting on his other hand, and did not turn round.

The Chemist glanced about the room;—at the student's books and papers, piled upon a table in a corner, where they, and his extinguished reading-lamp, now prohibited and put away, told of the attentive hours that had gone before this illness, and perhaps caused it;—at such signs of his old health and freedom, as the out-of-door attire that hung idle on the wall;—at those remembrances of other and less solitary scenes, the little miniatures upon the chimney-piece, and the drawing of home;—at that token of his emulation, perhaps, in some sort, of his personal attachment too, the framed engraving of himself, the looker-on. The time had been, only yesterday, when not one of these objects, in its remotest association of interest with the living figure before him, would have been lost on Redlaw. Now, they were but objects; or, if any gleam of such connexion shot upon him, it perplexed, and not enlightened him, as he stood looking round with a dull wonder.

The student, recalling the thin hand which had remained so long untouched, raised himself on the couch, and turned his head.

"Mr. Redlaw!" he exclaimed, and started up.

Redlaw put out his arm.

"Don't come nearer to me. I will sit here. Remain you, where you are!"

He sat down on a chair near the door, and having glanced at the young man standing leaning with his hand upon the couch, spoke with his eyes averted towards the ground.

"I heard, by an accident, by what accident is no matter, that one of my class was ill and solitary. I received no other description of him, than that he lived in this street. Beginning my inquiries at the first house in it, I have found him."

"I have been ill, sir," returned the student, not merely with a modest hesitation, but with a kind of awe of him, "but am greatly better. An attack of fever—of the brain, I believe—has weakened me, but I am much better. I cannot say I have been solitary, in my illness, or I should forget the ministering hand that has been near me."

"You are speaking of the keeper's wife," said Redlaw.

"Yes." The student bent his head, as if he rendered her some silent homage.

The Chemist, in whom there was a cold, monotonous apathy, which rendered him more like a marble image on the tomb of the man who had started from his dinner yesterday at the first mention of this student's case, than the breathing man himself, glanced again at the student leaning with his hand upon the couch, and looked upon the ground, and in the air, as if for light for his blinded mind.

"I remembered your name," he said, "when it was mentioned to me down stairs, just now; and I recollect your face. We have held but very little personal communication together?"

"Very little."

"You have retired and withdrawn from me, more than any of the rest, I think?"

The student signified assent.

"And why?" said the Chemist; not with the least expression of interest, but with a moody, wayward kind of curiosity. "Why? How comes it that you have sought to keep especially from me, the knowledge of your remaining here, at this season, when all the rest have dispersed, and of your being ill? I want to know why this is?"

The young man, who had heard him with increasing agitation, raised his downcast eyes to his face, and clasping his hands together, cried with sudden earnestness and with trembling lips:

"Mr. Redlaw! You have discovered me. You know my secret!"

"Secret?" said the Chemist, harshly. "I know?"

"Yes! Your manner, so different from the interest and sympathy which endear you to so many hearts, your altered voice, the constraint there is in everything you say, and in your looks," replied the student, "warn me that you know me. That you would conceal it, even now, is but a proof to me (God knows I need none!) of your natural kindness and of the bar there is between us."

A vacant and contemptuous laugh, was all his answer.

"But, Mr. Redlaw," said the student, "as a just man, and a good man, think how innocent I am, except in name and descent, of participation in any wrong inflicted on you or in any sorrow you have borne."

"Sorrow!" said Redlaw, laughing. "Wrong! What are those to me?"

"For Heaven's sake," entreated the shrinking student, "do not let the mere interchange of a few words with me change you like this, sir! Let me pass again from your knowledge and notice. Let me occupy my old reserved and distant place among those whom you instruct. Know me only by the name I have assumed, and not by that of Longford—"

"Longford!" exclaimed the other.

He clasped his head with both his hands, and for a moment turned upon the young man his own intelligent and thoughtful face. But the light passed from it, like the sunbeam of an instant, and it clouded as before.

"The name my mother bears, sir," faltered the young man, "the name she took, when she might, perhaps, have taken one more honoured. Mr. Redlaw," hesitating, "I believe I know that history. Where my information halts, my guesses at what is wanting may supply something not remote from the truth. I am the child of a marriage that has not proved itself a well-assorted or a happy one. From infancy, I have heard you spoken of with honour and respect—with something that was almost reverence. I have heard of such devotion, of such fortitude and tenderness, of such rising up against the obstacles which press men down, that my fancy, since I learnt my little lesson from my mother, has shed a lustre on your name. At last, a poor student myself, from whom could I learn but you?"

Redlaw, unmoved, unchanged, and looking at him with a staring frown, answered by no word or sign.

"I cannot say," pursued the other, "I should try in vain to say, how much it has impressed me, and affected me, to find the gracious traces of the past, in that certain power of winning gratitude and confidence which is associated among us students (among the humblest of us, most) with Mr. Redlaw's generous name. Our ages and positions are so different, sir, and I am so accustomed to regard you from a distance, that I wonder at my own presumption when I touch, however lightly, on that theme. But to one who—I may say, who felt no common interest in my mother once—it may be something to hear, now that all is past, with what indescribable feelings of affection I have, in my obscurity, regarded him; with what pain and reluctance I have kept aloof from his encouragement, when a word of it would have made me rich; yet how I have felt it fit that I should hold my course, content to know him, and to be unknown. Mr. Redlaw," said the student, faintly, "what I would have said, I have said ill, for my strength is strange to me as yet; but for anything unworthy in this fraud of mine, forgive me, and for all the rest forget me!"

The staring frown remained on Redlaw's face, and yielded to no other expression until the student, with these words, advanced towards him, as if to touch his hand, when he drew back and cried to him:

"Don't come nearer to me!"

The young man stopped, shocked by the eagerness of his recoil, and by the sternness of his repulsion; and he passed his hand, thoughtfully, across his forehead.

"The past is past," said the Chemist. "It dies like the brutes. Who talks to me of its traces in my life? He raves or lies! What have I to do with your distempered dreams? If you want money, here it is. I came to offer it; and that is all I came for. There can be nothing else that brings me here," he muttered, holding his head again, with both his hands. "There *can* be nothing else, and yet—"

He had tossed his purse upon the table. As he fell into this dim cogitation with himself, the student took it up, and held it out to him.

"Take it back, sir," he said proudly, though not angrily. "I wish you could take from me, with it, the remembrance of your words and offer."

"You do?" he retorted, with a wild light in his eyes. "You do?"

"I do!"

The Chemist went close to him, for the first time, and took the purse, and turned him by the arm, and looked him in the face.

"There is sorrow and trouble in sickness, is there not?" he demanded, with a laugh.

The wondering student answered, "Yes."

"In its unrest, in its anxiety, in its suspense, in all its train of physical and mental miseries?" said the Chemist, with a wild unearthly exultation. "All best forgotten, are they not?"

The student did not answer, but again passed his hand, confusedly, across his forehead. Redlaw still held him by the sleeve, when Milly's voice was heard outside.

"I can see very well now," she said, "thank you, Dolf. Don't cry, dear. Father and mother will be comfortable again, tomorrow, and home will be comfortable too. A gentleman with him, is there!"

Redlaw released his hold, as he listened.

"I have feared, from the first moment," he murmured to himself, "to meet her. There is a steady quality of goodness in her, that I dread to influence. I may be the murderer of what is tenderest and best within her bosom."

She was knocking at the door.

"Shall I dismiss it as an idle foreboding, or still avoid her?" he muttered, looking uneasily around.

She was knocking at the door again.

"Of all the visitors who could come here," he said, in a hoarse alarmed voice, turning to his companion, "this is the one I should desire most to avoid. Hide me!"

The student opened a frail door in the wall, communicating where the garret-roof began to slope towards the floor, with a small inner room. Redlaw passed in hastily, and shut it after him.

The student then resumed his place upon the couch, and called to her to enter.

"Dear Mr. Edmund," said Milly, looking round, "they told me there was a gentleman here."

"There is no one here but I."

"There has been some one?"

"Yes, yes, there has been someone."

She put her little basket on the table, and went up to the back of the couch, as if to take the extended hand—but it was not there. A little surprised, in her quiet way, she leaned over to look at his face, and gently touched him on the brow.

"Are you quite as well tonight? Your head is not so cool as in the afternoon."

"Tut!" said the student, petulantly, "very little ails me."

A little more surprise, but no reproach, was expressed in her face, as she withdrew to the other side of the table, and took a small packet of needlework from her basket. But she laid it down again, on second thoughts, and going noiselessly about the room, set everything exactly in its place, and in the neatest order; even to the cushions on the couch, which she touched with so light a hand, that he hardly seemed to know it, as he lay looking at the fire. When all this was done, and she had swept the hearth, she sat down, in her modest little bonnet, to her work, and was quietly busy on it directly.

"It's the new muslin curtain for the window, Mr. Edmund," said Milly, stitching away as she talked. "It will look very clean and nice, though it costs very little, and will save your eyes, too, from the light. My William says the room should not be too light just now, when you are recovering so well, or the glare might make you giddy."

He said nothing; but there was something so fretful and impatient in his change of position, that her quick fingers stopped, and she looked at him anxiously.

"The pillows are not comfortable," she said, laying down her work and rising. "I will soon put them right."

"They are very well," he answered. "Leave them alone, pray. You make so much of everything."

He raised his head to say this, and looked at her so thanklessly, that, after he had thrown himself down again, she stood timidly pausing. However, she resumed her seat, and her needle, without having directed even a murmuring look towards him, and was soon as busy as before.

"I have been thinking, Mr. Edmund, that *you* have been often thinking of late, when I have been sitting by, how true the saying is, that adversity is a good teacher. Health will be more precious to you, after this illness, than it has ever been. And years hence, when this time of year comes round, and you remember the days when you lay here sick, alone, that the knowledge of your illness might not afflict those who are dearest to you, your home will be doubly dear and doubly blest. Now, isn't that a good, true thing?"

She was too intent upon her work, and too earnest in what she said, and too composed and quiet altogether, to be on the watch for any look he might direct towards her in reply; so the shaft of his ungrateful glance fell harmless, and did not wound her.

"Ah!" said Milly, with her pretty head inclining thoughtfully on one side, as she looked down, following her busy fingers with her eyes. "Even on me—and I am very different from you, Mr. Edmund, for I have no learning, and don't know how to think properly—this view of such things has made a great impression, since you have been lying ill. When I have seen you so touched by the kindness and attention of the poor people down stairs, I have felt that you thought even that experience some repayment for the loss of health, and I have read in your face, as plain as if it was a book, that but for some trouble and sorrow we should never know half the good there is about us."

His getting up from the couch, interrupted her, or she was going on to say more.

"We needn't magnify the merit, Mrs. William," he rejoined slightingly. "The people down stairs will be paid in good time I dare say, for any little extra service they may have rendered me; and perhaps they anticipate no less. I am much obliged to you, too."

Her fingers stopped, and she looked at him.

"I can't be made to feel the more obliged by your exaggerating the case," he said. "I am sensible that you have been interested in me, and I say I am much obliged to you. What more would you have?"

Her work fell on her lap, as she still looked at him walking to and fro with an intolerant air, and stopping now and then.

"I say again, I am much obliged to you. Why weaken my sense of what is your due in obligation, by preferring enormous claims upon me? Trouble, sorrow, affliction, adversity! One might suppose I had been dying a score of deaths here!"

"Do you believe, Mr. Edmund," she asked, rising and going nearer to him, "that I spoke of the poor people of the house, with any reference to myself? To me?" laying her hand upon her bosom with a simple and innocent smile of astonishment.

"Oh! I think nothing about it, my good creature," he returned. "I have had an indisposition, which your solicitude-observe! I say solicitude—makes a great deal more of, than it merits; and it's over, and we can't perpetuate it."

He coldly took a book, and sat down at the table.

She watched him for a little while, until her smile was quite gone, and then, returning to where her basket was, said gently:

"Mr. Edmund, would you rather be alone?"

"There is no reason why I should detain you here," he replied.

"Except—" said Milly, hesitating, and showing her work.

"Oh! the curtain," he answered, with a supercilious laugh. "That's not worth staying for."

She made up the little packet again, and put it in her basket. Then, standing before him with such an air of patient entreaty that he could not choose but look at her, she said:

"If you should want me, I will come back willingly. When you did want me, I was quite happy to come; there was no merit in it. I think you must be afraid, that, now you are getting well, I may be troublesome to you; but I should not have been, indeed. I should have come no longer than your weakness and confinement lasted. You owe me nothing; but it is right that you should deal as justly by me as if I was a lady—even the very lady that you love; and if you suspect me of meanly making much of the little I have tried to do to comfort your sick room, you do yourself more wrong than ever you can do me. That is why I am sorry. That is why I am very sorry."

If she had been as passionate as she was quiet, as indignant as she was calm, as angry in her look as she was gentle, as loud of tone as she was low and clear, she might have left no sense of her departure in the room, compared with that which fell upon the lonely student when she went away.

He was gazing drearily upon the place where she had been, when Redlaw came out of his concealment, and came to the door.

"When sickness lays its hand on you again," he said, looking fiercely back at him, "—may it be soon!—Die here! Rot here!"

"What have you done?" returned the other, catching at his cloak. "What change have you wrought in me? What curse have you brought upon me? Give me back *my*self!"

"Give me back myself!" exclaimed Redlaw like a madman. "I am infected! I am infectious! I am charged with poison for my own mind, and the minds of all mankind. Where I felt interest, compassion, sympathy, I am turning into stone. Selfishness and ingratitude spring up in my blighting footsteps.

I am only so much less base than the wretches whom I

make so, that in the moment of their transformation I can hate them."

As he spoke—the young man still holding to his cloak—he cast him off, and struck him: then, wildly hurried out into the night air where the wind was blowing, the snow falling, the cloud-drift sweeping on, the moon dimly shining; and where, blowing in the wind, falling with the snow, drifting with the clouds, shining in the moonlight, and heavily looming in the darkness, were the Phantom's words, "The gift that I have given, you shall give again, go where you will!"

Whither he went, he neither knew nor cared, so that he avoided company. The change he felt within him made the busy streets a desert, and himself a desert, and the multitude around him, in their manifold endurances and ways of life, a mighty waste of sand, which the winds tossed into unintelligible heaps and made a ruinous confusion of. Those traces in his breast which the Phantom had told him would "die out soon," were not, as yet, so far upon their way to death, but that he understood enough of what he was, and what he made of others, to desire to be alone.

This put it in his mind—he suddenly bethought himself, as he was going along, of the boy who had rushed into his room. And then he recollected, that of those with whom he had communicated since the Phantom's disappearance, that boy alone had shown no sign of being changed.

Monstrous and odious as the wild thing was to him, he determined to seek it out, and prove if this were really so; and also to seek it with another intention, which came into his thoughts at the same time.

So, resolving with some difficulty where he was, he directed his steps back to the old college, and to that part of it where the general porch was, and where, alone, the pavement was worn by the tread of the students' feet.

The keeper's house stood just within the iron gates, forming a part of the chief quadrangle. There was a little cloister outside, and from that sheltered place he knew he could look in at the window of their ordinary room, and see who was within. The iron gates were shut, but his hand was familiar with the fastening, and drawing it back by thrusting in his wrist between the bars, he passed through softly, shut it again, and crept up to the window, crumbling the thin crust of snow with his feet.

The fire, to which he had directed the boy last night, shining brightly through the glass, made an illuminated place upon the ground. Instinctively avoiding this, and going round it, he looked in at the window. At first, he thought that there was no one there, and that the blaze was reddening only the old beams in the ceiling and the dark walls; but peering in more narrowly, he saw the object of his search coiled asleep before it on the floor. He passed quickly to the door, opened it, and went in.

The creature lay in such a fiery heat, that, as the Chemist stooped to rouse him, it scorched his head. So soon as he was touched, the boy, not half awake, clutching his rags together with the instinct of flight upon him, half rolled and half ran into a distant corner of the room, where, heaped upon the ground, he struck his foot out to defend himself.

"Get up!" said the Chemist. "You have not forgotten me?"

"You let me alone!" returned the boy. "This is the woman's house—not yours."

The Chemist's steady eye controlled him somewhat, or inspired him with enough submission to be raised upon his feet, and looked at.

"Who washed them, and put those bandages where they were bruised and cracked?" asked the Chemist, pointing to their altered state.

"The woman did."

"And is it she who has made you cleaner in the face, too?"

"Yes, the woman."

Redlaw asked these questions to attract his eyes towards himself, and with the same intent now held him by the chin, and threw his wild hair back, though he loathed to touch him. The boy watched his eyes keenly, as if he thought it needful to his own defence, not knowing what he might do next; and Redlaw could see well that no change came over him.

"Where are they?" he inquired.

"The woman's out."

"I know she is. Where is the old man with the white hair, and his son?"

"The woman's husband, d'ye mean?" inquired the boy.

"Ay. Where are those two?"

"Out. Something's the matter, somewhere. They were fetched out in a hurry, and told me to stop here."

"Come with me," said the Chemist, "and I'll give you money."

"Come where? and how much will you give?"

"I'll give you more shillings than you ever saw, and bring you back soon. Do you know your way to where you came from?"

"You let me go," returned the boy, suddenly twisting out of his grasp. "I'm not a going to take you there. Let me be, or I'll heave some fire at you!"

He was down before it, and ready, with his savage little hand, to pluck the burning coals out.

What the Chemist had felt, in observing the effect of his charmed influence stealing over those with whom he came in contact, was not nearly equal to the cold vague terror with which he saw this baby-monster put it at defiance. It chilled his blood to look on the immovable impenetrable thing, in the likeness of a child, with its sharp malignant face turned up to his, and its almost infant hand, ready at the bars.

"Listen, boy!" he said. "You shall take me where you please, so that you take me where the people are very miserable or very wicked. I want to do them good, and not to harm them. You shall have money, as I have told you, and I will bring you back. Get up! Come quickly!" He made a hasty step towards the door, afraid of her returning.

"Will you let me walk by myself, and never hold me, nor yet touch me?" said the boy, slowly withdrawing the hand with which he threatened, and beginning to get up.

"I will!"

"And let me go, before, behind, or anyways I like?"

"I will!"

"Give me some money first, then, and go."

The Chemist laid a few shillings, one by one, in his extended hand. To count them was beyond the boy's knowledge, but he said "one," every time, and avariciously looked at each as it was given, and at the donor. He had nowhere to put them, out of his hand, but in his mouth; and he put them there.

Redlaw then wrote with his pencil on a leaf of his pocket-book, that the boy was with him; and laying it on the table, signed to him to follow. Keeping his rags together, as usual, the boy complied, and went out with his bare head and naked feet into the winter night.

Preferring not to depart by the iron gate by which he had entered, where they were in danger of meeting her whom he so anxiously avoided, the Chemist led the way, through some of those passages among which the boy had lost himself, and by that portion of the building where he lived, to a small door of which he had the key. When they got into the street, he stopped to ask his guide—who instantly retreated from him—if he knew where they were.

The savage thing looked here and there, and at length, nodding his head, pointed in the direction he designed to take. Redlaw going on at once, he followed, something less suspiciously; shifting his money from his mouth into his hand, and back again into his mouth, and stealthily rubbing it bright upon his shreds of dress, as he went along.

Three times, in their progress, they were side by side. Three times they stopped, being side by side. Three times the Chemist glanced down at his face, and shuddered as it forced upon him one reflection.

The first occasion was when they were crossing an old churchyard, and Redlaw stopped among the graves, utterly at a loss how to connect them with any tender, softening, or consolatory thought.

The second was, when the breaking forth of the moon induced him to look up at the Heavens, where he saw her in her glory, surrounded by a host of stars he still knew by the names and histories which human science has appended to them; but where he saw nothing else he had been wont to see, felt nothing he had been wont to feel, in looking up there, on a bright night.

The third was when he stopped to listen to a plaintive strain of music, but could only hear a tune, made manifest to him by the dry mechanism of the instruments and his own ears, with no address to any mystery within him, without a whisper in it of the past, or of the future, powerless upon him as the sound of last year's running water, or the rushing of last year's wind.

At each of these three times, he saw with horror that, in spite of the vast intellectual distance between them, and their being unlike each other in all physical respects, the expression on the boy's face was the expression on his own.

They journeyed on for some time—now through such crowded places, that he often looked over his shoulder thinking he had lost his guide, but generally finding him within his shadow on his other side; now by ways so quiet, that he could have counted his short, quick, naked footsteps coming on behind-until they arrived at a ruinous collection of houses, and the boy touched him and stopped.

"In there!" he said, pointing out one house where there were shattered lights in the windows, and a dim lantern in the doorway, with "Lodgings for Travellers" painted on it.

Redlaw looked about him; from the houses to the waste piece of ground on which the houses stood, or rather did not altogether tumble down, unfenced, undrained, unlighted, and bordered by a sluggish ditch; from that, to the sloping line of arches, part of some neighbouring viaduct or bridge with which it was surrounded, and which lessened gradually towards them, until the last but one was a mere kennel for a dog, the last a plundered little heap of bricks; from that, to the child, close to him, cowering and trembling with the cold, and limping on one little foot, while he coiled the other round his leg to warm it, yet staring at all these things with that frightful likeness of expression so apparent in his face, that Redlaw started from him.

"In there!" said the boy, pointing out the house again. "I'll wait."

"Will they let me in?" asked Redlaw.

"Say you're a doctor," he answered with a nod. "There's plenty ill here."

Looking back on his way to the house-door, Redlaw saw him trail himself upon the dust and crawl within the shelter of the smallest arch, as if he were a rat. He had no pity for the thing, but he was afraid of it; and when it looked out of its den at him, he hurried to the house as a retreat.

"Sorrow, wrong, and trouble," said the Chemist, with a painful effort at some more distinct remembrance, "at least haunt this place darkly. He can do no harm, who brings forgetfulness of such things here!"

With these words, he pushed the yielding door, and went in.

There was a woman sitting on the stairs, either asleep or forlorn, whose head was bent down on her hands and knees. As it was not easy to pass without treading on her, and as she was perfectly regardless of his near approach, he stopped, and touched her on the shoulder. Looking up, she showed him quite a young face, but one whose bloom and promise were all swept away, as if the haggard winter should unnaturally kill the spring.

With little or no show of concern on his account, she moved nearer to the wall to leave him a wider passage.

"What are you?" said Redlaw, pausing, with his hand upon the broken stair-rail.

"What do you think I am?" she answered, showing him her face again.

He looked upon the ruined Temple of God, so lately made, so soon disfigured; and something, which was not compassion-for the springs in which a true compassion for such miseries has its rise, were dried up in his breast—but which was nearer to it, for the moment, than any feeling that had lately struggled into the darkening, but not yet wholly darkened, night of his mind-mingled a touch of softness with his next words.

"I am come here to give relief, if I can," he said. "Are you thinking of any wrong?"

She frowned at him, and then laughed; and then her laugh prolonged itself into a shivering sigh, as she dropped her head again, and hid her fingers in her hair.

"Are you thinking of a wrong?" he asked once more.

"I am thinking of my life," she said, with a monetary look at him.

He had a perception that she was one of many, and that he saw the type of thousands, when he saw her, drooping at his feet.

"What are your parents?" he demanded.

"I had a good home once. My father was a gardener, far away, in the country."

"Is he dead?"

"He's dead to me. All such things are dead to me. You a gentleman, and not know that!" She raised her eyes again, and laughed at him.

"Girl!" said Redlaw, sternly, "before this death, of all such things, was brought about, was there no wrong done to you? In spite of all that you can do, does no remembrance of wrong cleave to you? Are there not times upon times when it is misery to you?"

So little of what was womanly was left in her appearance, that now, when she burst into tears, he stood amazed. But he was more amazed, and much disquieted, to note that in her awakened recollection of this wrong, the first trace of her old humanity and frozen tenderness appeared to show itself.

He drew a little off, and in doing so, observed that her arms were black, her face cut, and her bosom bruised.

"What brutal hand has hurt you so?" he asked.

"My own. I did it myself!" she answered quickly.

"It is impossible."

"I'll swear I did! He didn't touch me. I did it to myself in a passion, and threw myself down here. He wasn't near me. He never laid a hand upon me!"

In the white determination of her face, confronting him with this untruth, he saw enough of the last perversion and distortion of good surviving in that miserable breast, to be stricken with remorse that he had ever come near her.

"Sorrow, wrong, and trouble!" he muttered, turning his fearful gaze away. "All that connects her with the state from which she has fallen, has those roots! In the name of God, let me go by!"

Afraid to look at her again, afraid to touch her, afraid to think of having sundered the last thread by which she held upon the mercy of Heaven, he gathered his cloak about him, and glided swiftly up the stairs.

Opposite to him, on the landing, was a door, which stood partly open, and which, as he ascended, a man with a candle in his hand, came forward from within to shut. But this man, on seeing him, drew back, with much emotion in his manner, and, as if by a sudden impulse, mentioned his name aloud.

In the surprise of such a recognition there, he stopped, endeavouring to recollect the wan and startled face. He had no time to consider it, for, to his yet greater amazement, old Philip came out of the room, and took him by the hand.

"Mr. Redlaw," said the old man, "this is like you, this is like you, sir! you have heard of it, and have come after us to render any help you can. Ah, too late, too late!"

Redlaw, with a bewildered look, submitted to be led into the room. A man lay there, on a truckle-bed, and William Swidger stood at the bedside.

"Too late!" murmured the old man, looking wistfully into the Chemist's face; and the tears stole down his cheeks.

"That's what I say, father," interposed his son in a low voice. "That's where it is, exactly. To keep as quiet as ever we can while he's a dozing, is the only thing to do. You're right, father!"

Redlaw paused at the bedside, and looked down on the figure that was stretched upon the mattress. It was that of a man, who should have been in the vigour of his life, but on whom it was not likely the sun would ever shine again. The vices of his forty or fifty years' career had so branded him, that, in comparison with their effects upon his face, the heavy hand of Time upon the old man's face who watched him had been merciful and beautifying.

"Who is this?" asked the Chemist, looking round.

"My son George, Mr. Redlaw," said the old man, wringing his hands. "My eldest son, George, who was more his mother's pride than all the rest!"

Redlaw's eyes wandered from the old man's grey head, as he laid it down upon the bed, to the person who had recognised him, and who had kept aloof, in the remotest corner of the room. He seemed to be about his own age; and although he knew no such hopeless decay and broken man as he appeared to be, there was something in the turn of his figure, as he stood with his back towards him, and now went out at the door, that made him pass his hand uneasily across his brow.

"William," he said in a gloomy whisper, "who is that man?"

"Why you see, sir," returned Mr. William, "that's what I say, myself. Why should a man ever go and gamble, and the like of that, and let himself down inch by inch till he can't let himself down any lower!"

"Has *he* done so?" asked Redlaw, glancing after him with the same uneasy action as before.

"Just exactly that, sir," returned William Swidger, "as I'm told. He knows a little about medicine, sir, it seems; and having been wayfaring towards London with my unhappy brother that you see here," Mr. William passed his coat-sleeve across his eyes, "and being lodging up stairs for the night—what I say, you see, is that strange companions come together here sometimes—he looked in to attend upon him, and came for us at his request. What a mournful spectacle, sir! But that's where it is. It's enough to kill my father!"

Redlaw looked up, at these words, and, recalling where he was and with whom, and the spell he carried with him—which his surprise had obscured—retired a little, hurriedly, debating with himself whether to shun the house that moment, or remain.

Yielding to a certain sullen doggedness, which it seemed to be a part of his condition to struggle with, he argued for remaining.

"Was it only yesterday," he said, "when I observed the memory of this old man to be a tissue of sorrow and trouble, and shall I be afraid, tonight, to shake it? Are such remembrances as I can drive away, so precious to this dying man that I need fear for *him*? No! I'll stay here."

But he stayed in fear and trembling none the less for these words; and, shrouded in his black cloak with his face turned from them, stood away from the bedside, listening to what they said, as if he felt himself a demon in the place.

"Father!" murmured the sick man, rallying a little from stupor.

"My boy! My son George!" said old Philip.

"You spoke, just now, of my being mother's favourite, long ago. It's a dreadful thing to think now, of long ago!"

"No, no, no;" returned the old man. "Think of it. Don't say it's dreadful. It's not dreadful to me, my son."

"It cuts you to the heart, father." For the old man's tears were falling on him.

"Yes, yes," said Philip, "so it does; but it does me good. It's a heavy sorrow to think of that time, but it does me good, George. Oh, think of it too, think of it too, and your heart will be softened more and more! Where's my son William? William, my boy, your mother loved him dearly to the last, and with her latest breath said, 'Tell him I forgave him, blessed him, and prayed for him.' Those were her words to me. I have never forgotten them, and I'm eighty-seven!"

"Father!" said the man upon the bed, "I am dying, I know. I am so far gone, that I can hardly speak, even of what my mind most runs on. Is there any hope for me beyond this bed?"

"There is hope," returned the old man, "for all who are softened and penitent. There is hope for all such. Oh!" he exclaimed, clasping his hands and looking up, "I was thankful, only yesterday, that I could remember this unhappy son when he was an innocent child. But what a comfort it is, now, to think that even God himself has that remembrance of him!"

Redlaw spread his hands upon his face, and shrank, like a murderer.

"Ah!" feebly moaned the man upon the bed. "The waste since then, the waste of life since then!"

"But he was a child once," said the old man. "He played with children. Before he lay down on his bed at night, and fell into his guiltless rest, he said his prayers at his poor mother's knee. I have seen him do it, many a time; and seen her lay his head upon her breast, and kiss him. Sorrowful as it was to her and me, to think of this, when he went so wrong, and when our hopes and plans for him were all broken, this gave him still a hold upon us, that nothing else could have given. Oh, Father, so much better than the fathers upon earth! Oh, Father, so much more afflicted by the errors of Thy children! take this wanderer back! Not as he is, but as he was then, let him cry to Thee, as he has so often seemed to cry to us!"

As the old man lifted up his trembling hands, the son, for whom he made the supplication, laid his sinking head against him for support and comfort, as if he were indeed the child of whom he spoke.

When did man ever tremble, as Redlaw trembled, in the silence that ensued! He knew it must come upon them, knew that it was coming fast.

"My time is very short, my breath is shorter," said the sick man, supporting himself on one arm, and with the other groping in the air, "and I remember there is something on my mind concerning the man who was here just now, Father and William—wait!—is there really anything in black, out there?"

"Yes, yes, it is real," said his aged father.

"Is it a man?"

"What I say myself, George," interposed his brother, bending kindly over him. "It's Mr. Redlaw."

"I thought I had dreamed of him. Ask him to come here."

The Chemist, whiter than the dying man, appeared before him. Obedient to the motion of his hand, he sat upon the bed.

"It has been so ripped up, tonight, sir," said the sick man, laying his hand upon his heart, with a look in which the mute, imploring agony of his condition was concentrated, "by the sight of my poor old father, and the thought of all the trouble I have been the cause of, and all the wrong and sorrow lying at my door, that—"

Was it the extremity to which he had come, or was it the dawning of another change, that made him stop?

"—that what I *can* do right, with my mind running on so much, so fast, I'll try to do. There was another man here. Did you see him?"

Redlaw could not reply by any word; for when he saw that fatal sign he knew so well now, of the wandering hand upon the forehead, his voice died at his lips. But he made some indication of assent.

"He is penniless, hungry, and destitute. He is completely beaten down, and has no resource at all. Look after him! Lose no time! I know he has it in his mind to kill himself."

It was working. It was on his face. His face was changing, hardening, deepening in all its shades, and losing all its sorrow.

"Don't you remember? Don't you know him?" he pursued.

He shut his face out for a moment, with the hand that again wandered over his forehead, and then it lowered on Redlaw, reckless, ruffianly, and callous.

"Why, d-n you!" he said, scowling round, "what have you been doing to me here! I have lived bold, and I mean to die bold. To the Devil with you!"

And so lay down upon his bed, and put his arms up, over his head and ears, as resolute from that time to keep out all access, and to die in his indifference.

If Redlaw had been struck by lightning, it could not have struck him from the bedside with a more tremendous shock. But the old man, who had left the bed while his son was speaking to him, now returning, avoided it quickly likewise, and with abhorrence.

"Where's my boy William?" said the old man hurriedly. "William, come away from here. We'll go home."

"Home, father!" returned William. "Are you going to leave your own son?"

"Where's my own son?" replied the old man.

"Where? why, there!"

"That's no son of mine," said Philip, trembling with resentment. "No such wretch as that, has any claim on me. My children are pleasant to look at, and they wait upon me, and get my meat and drink ready, and are useful to me. I've a right to it! I'm eighty-seven!"

"You're old enough to be no older," muttered William, looking at him grudgingly, with his hands in his pockets. "I don't know what good you are, myself. We could have a deal more pleasure without you."

"*My* son, Mr. Redlaw!" said the old man. "*My* son, too! The boy talking to me of *my* son! Why, what has he ever done to give me any pleasure, I should like to know?"

"I don't know what you have ever done to give *me* any pleasure," said William, sulkily.

"Let me think," said the old man. "For how many Christmas times running, have I sat in my warm place, and never had to come out in the cold night air; and have made good cheer, without being disturbed by any such uncomfortable, wretched sight as him there? Is it twenty, William?"

"Nigher forty, it seems," he muttered. "Why, when I look at my father, sir, and come to think of it," addressing Redlaw, with an impatience and irritation that were quite new, "I'm whipped if I can see anything in him but a calendar of ever so many years of eating and drinking, and making himself comfortable, over and over again."

"I—I'm eighty-seven," said the old man, rambling on, childishly and weakly, "and I don't know as I ever was much put out by anything. I'm not going to begin now, because of what he calls my son. He's not my son. I've had a power of pleasant times. I recollect once—no I don't—no, it's broken off. It was something about a game of cricket and a friend of mine, but it's somehow broken off. I wonder who he was—I suppose I liked him? And I wonder what became of him—I suppose he died? But I don't know. And I don't care, neither; I don't care a bit."

In his drowsy chuckling, and the shaking of his head, he put his hands into his waistcoat pockets. In one of them he found a bit of holly (left there, probably last night), which he now took out, and looked at.

"Berries, eh?" said the old man. "Ah! It's a pity they're not good to eat. I recollect, when I was a little chap about as high as that, and out a walking with—let me see—who was I out a walking with?—no, I don't remember how that was. I don't remember as I ever walked with any one particular, or cared for any one, or any one for me. Berries, eh? There's good cheer when there's berries. Well; I ought to have my share of it, and to be waited on, and kept warm and comfortable; for I'm eighty-seven, and a poor old man. I'm eigh-ty-seven. Eigh-ty-seven!"

The drivelling, pitiable manner in which, as he repeated this, he nibbled at the leaves, and spat the morsels out; the cold, uninterested eye with which his youngest son (so changed) regarded him; the determined apathy with which his eldest son lay hardened in his sin; impressed themselves no more on Redlaw's observation,—for he broke his way from the spot to which his feet seemed to have been fixed, and ran out of the house.

His guide came crawling forth from his place of refuge, and was ready for him before he reached the arches.

"Back to the woman's?" he inquired.

"Back, quickly!" answered Redlaw. "Stop nowhere on the way!"

For a short distance the boy went on before; but their return was more like a flight than a walk, and it was as much as his bare feet could do, to keep pace with the Chemist's rapid strides. Shrinking from all who passed, shrouded in his cloak, and keeping it drawn closely about him, as though there were mortal contagion in any fluttering touch of his garments, he made no pause until they reached the door by which they had come out. He unlocked it with his key, went in, accompanied by the boy, and hastened through the dark passages to his own chamber.

The boy watched him as he made the door fast, and withdrew behind the table, when he looked round.

"Come!" he said. "Don't you touch me! You've not brought me here to take my money away."

Redlaw threw some more upon the ground. He flung his body on it immediately, as if to hide it from him, lest the sight of it should tempt him to reclaim it; and not until he saw him seated by his lamp, with his face hidden in his hands, began furtively to pick it up. When he had done so, he crept near the fire, and, sitting down in a great chair before it, took from his breast some broken scraps of food, and fell to munching, and to staring at the blaze, and now and then to glancing at his shillings, which he kept clenched up in a bunch, in one hand.

"And this," said Redlaw, gazing on him with increased repugnance and fear, "is the only one companion I have left on earth!"

How long it was before he was aroused from his contemplation of this creature, whom he dreaded so—whether half-an-hour, or half the night—he knew not. But the stillness of the room was broken by the boy (whom he had seen listening) starting up, and running towards the door.

"Here's the woman coming!" he exclaimed.

The Chemist stopped him on his way, at the moment when she knocked.

"Let me go to her, will you?" said the boy.

"Not now," returned the Chemist. "Stay here. Nobody must pass in or out of the room now. Who's that?"

"It's I, sir," cried Milly. "Pray, sir, let me in!"

"No! not for the world!" he said.

"Mr. Redlaw, Mr. Redlaw, pray, sir, let me in."

"What is the matter?" he said, holding the boy.

"The miserable man you saw, is worse, and nothing I can say

will wake him from his terrible infatuation. William's father has turned childish in a moment, William himself is changed. The shock has been too sudden for him; I cannot understand him; he is not like himself. Oh, Mr. Redlaw, pray advise me, help me!"

"No! No! No!" he answered.

"Mr. Redlaw! Dear sir! George has been muttering, in his doze, about the man you saw there, who, he fears, will kill himself."

"Better he should do it, than come near me!"

"He says, in his wandering, that you know him; that he was your friend once, long ago; that he is the ruined father of a student here—my mind misguides me, of the young gentleman who has been ill. What is to be done? How is he to be followed? How is he to be saved? Mr. Redlaw, pray, oh, pray, advise me! Help me!"

All this time he held the boy, who was half-mad to pass him, and let her in.

"Phantoms! Punishers of impious thoughts!" cried Redlaw, gazing round in anguish, "look upon me! From the darkness of my mind, let the glimmering of contrition that I know is there, shine up and show my misery! In the material world as I have long taught, nothing can be spared; no step or atom in the wondrous structure could be lost, without a blank being made in the great universe. I know, now, that it is the same with good and evil, happiness and sorrow, in the memories of men. Pity me! Relieve me!"

There was no response, but her "Help me, help me, let me in!" and the boy's struggling to get to her.

"Shadow of myself! Spirit of my darker hours!" cried Redlaw, in distraction, "come back, and haunt me day and night, but take this gift away! Or, if it must still rest with me, deprive me of the dreadful power of giving it to others. Undo what I have done. Leave me benighted, but restore the day to those whom I have cursed. As I have spared this woman from the first, and as I never will go forth again, but will die here, with no hand to tend me, save this creature's who is proof against me,—hear me!"

The only reply still was, the boy struggling to get to her, while he held him back; and the cry, increasing in its energy, "Help! let me in. He was your friend once, how shall he be followed, how shall he be saved? They are all changed, there is no one else to help me, pray, pray, let me in!"

Chapter 3
The Gift Reversed

Night was still heavy in the sky. On open plains, from hill-tops, and from the decks of solitary ships at sea, a distant low-lying line, that promised by-and-by to change to light, was visible in the dim horizon; but its promise was remote and doubtful, and the moon was striving with the night-clouds busily.

The shadows upon Redlaw's mind succeeded thick and fast to one another, and obscured its light as the night-clouds hovered between the moon and earth, and kept the latter veiled in darkness. Fitful and uncertain as the shadows which the night-clouds cast, were their concealments from him, and imperfect revelations to him; and, like the night-clouds still, if the clear light broke forth for a moment, it was only that they might sweep over it, and make the darkness deeper than before.

Without, there was a profound and solemn hush upon the ancient pile of building, and its buttresses and angles made dark shapes of mystery upon the ground, which now seemed to retire into the smooth white snow and now seemed to come out of it, as the moon's path was more or less beset. Within, the Chemist's room was indistinct and murky, by the light of the expiring lamp; a ghostly silence had succeeded to the knocking and the voice outside; nothing was audible but, now and then, a low sound among the whitened ashes of the fire, as of its yielding up its last breath. Before it on the ground the boy lay fast asleep. In his chair, the Chemist sat, as he had sat there since the calling at his door had ceased—like a man turned to stone.

At such a time, the Christmas music he had heard before, began to play. He listened to it at first, as he had listened in the church-yard; but presently—it playing still, and being borne towards him on the night air, in a low, sweet, melancholy strain-he rose, and stood stretching his hands about him, as if there were some friend approaching within his reach, on whom his desolate touch might rest, yet do no harm. As he did this, his face became less fixed and wondering; a gentle trembling came upon him; and at last his eyes filled with tears, and he put his hands before them, and bowed down his head.

His memory of sorrow, wrong, and trouble, had not come back to him; he knew that it was not restored; he had no passing belief or hope that it was. But some dumb stir within him made him capable, again, of being moved by what was hidden, afar off, in the music. If it were only that it told him sorrowfully the value of what he had lost, he thanked Heaven for it with a fervent gratitude.

As the last chord died upon his ear, he raised his head to listen to its lingering vibration. Beyond the boy, so that his sleeping figure lay at its feet, the Phantom stood, immovable and silent, with its eyes upon him.

Ghastly it was, as it had ever been, but not so cruel and relentless in its aspect—or he thought or hoped so, as he looked upon it trembling. It was not alone, but in its shadowy hand it held another hand.

And whose was that? Was the form that stood beside it indeed Milly's, or but her shade and picture? The quiet head was bent a little, as her manner was, and her eyes were looking down, as if in pity, on the sleeping child. A radiant light fell on her face, but did not touch the Phantom; for, though close beside her, it was dark and colourless as ever.

"Spectre!" said the Chemist, newly troubled as he looked, "I have not been stubborn or presumptuous in respect of her. Oh, do not bring her here. Spare me that!"

"This is but a shadow," said the Phantom; "when the morning shines seek out the reality whose image I present before you."

"Is it my inexorable doom to do so?" cried the Chemist.

"It is," replied the Phantom.

"To destroy her peace, her goodness; to make her what I am

myself, and what I have made of others!"

"I have said seek her out," returned the Phantom. "I have said no more."

"Oh, tell me," exclaimed Redlaw, catching at the hope which he fancied might lie hidden in the words. "Can I undo what I have done?"

"No," returned the Phantom.

"I do not ask for restoration to myself," said Redlaw. "What I abandoned, I abandoned of my own free will, and have justly lost. But for those to whom I have transferred the fatal gift; who never sought it; who unknowingly received a curse of which they had no warning, and which they had no power to shun; can I do nothing?"

"Nothing," said the Phantom.

"If I cannot, can anyone?"

The Phantom, standing like a statue, kept its gaze upon him for a while; then turned its head suddenly, and looked upon the shadow at its side.

"Ah! Can she?" cried Redlaw, still looking upon the shade.

The Phantom released the hand it had retained till now, and softly raised its own with a gesture of dismissal. Upon that, her shadow, still preserving the same attitude, began to move or melt away.

"Stay," cried Redlaw with an earnestness to which he could not give enough expression. "For a moment! As an act of mercy! I know that some change fell upon me, when those sounds were in the air just now. Tell me, have I lost the power of harming her? May I go near her without dread? Oh, let her give me any sign of hope!"

The Phantom looked upon the shade as he did—not at him—and gave no answer.

"At least, say this—has she, henceforth, the consciousness of any power to set right what I have done?"

"She has not," the Phantom answered.

"Has she the power bestowed on her without the consciousness?"

The phantom answered: "Seek her out."

And her shadow slowly vanished.

They were face to face again, and looking on each other, as intently and awfully as at the time of the bestowal of the gift, across the boy who still lay on the ground between them, at the Phantom's feet.

"Terrible instructor," said the Chemist, sinking on his knee before it, in an attitude of supplication, "by whom I was renounced, but by whom I am revisited (in which, and in whose milder aspect, I would fain believe I have a gleam of hope), I will obey without inquiry, praying that the cry I have sent up in the anguish of my soul has been, or will be, heard, in behalf of those whom I have injured beyond human reparation. But there is one thing—"

"You speak to me of what is lying here," the phantom interposed, and pointed with its finger to the boy.

"I do," returned the Chemist. "You know what I would ask. Why has this child alone been proof against my influence, and why, why, have I detected in its thoughts a terrible companionship with mine?"

"This," said the Phantom, pointing to the boy, "is the last, completest illustration of a human creature, utterly bereft of such remembrances as you have yielded up. No softening memory of sorrow, wrong, or trouble enters here, because this wretched mortal from his birth has been abandoned to a worse condition than the beasts, and has, within his knowledge, no one contrast, no humanising touch, to make a grain of such a memory spring up in his hardened breast. All within this desolate creature is barren wilderness. All within the man bereft of what you have resigned, is the same barren wilderness. Woe to such a man! Woe, tenfold, to the nation that shall count its monsters such as this, lying here, by hundreds and by thousands!"

Redlaw shrank, appalled, from what he heard.

"There is not," said the Phantom, "one of these—not one—but sows a harvest that mankind *must* reap. From every seed of evil in this boy, a field of ruin is grown that shall be gathered in, and garnered up, and sown again in many places in the world, until regions are overspread with wickedness enough to raise the waters of another Deluge. Open and unpunished murder in a city's streets would be less guilty in its daily toleration, than one such spectacle as this."

It seemed to look down upon the boy in his sleep. Redlaw, too, looked down upon him with a new emotion.

"There is not a father," said the Phantom, "by whose side in his daily or his nightly walk, these creatures pass; there is not a mother among all the ranks of loving mothers in this land; there is no one risen from the state of childhood, but shall be responsible in his or her degree for this enormity. There is not a country throughout the earth on which it would not bring a curse. There is no religion upon earth that it would not deny; there is no people upon earth it would not put to shame."

The Chemist clasped his hands, and looked, with trembling fear and pity, from the sleeping boy to the Phantom, standing above him with his finger pointing down.

"Behold, I say," pursued the Spectre, "the perfect type of what it was your choice to be. Your influence is powerless here, because from this child's bosom you can banish nothing. His thoughts have been in 'terrible companionship' with yours, because you have gone down to his unnatural level. He is the growth of man's indifference; you are the growth of man's presumption. The beneficent design of Heaven is, in each case, overthrown, and from the two poles of the immaterial world you come together."

The Chemist stooped upon the ground beside the boy, and, with the same kind of compassion for him that he now felt for himself, covered him as he slept, and no longer shrank from him with abhorrence or indifference.

Soon, now, the distant line on the horizon brightened, the darkness faded, the sun rose red and glorious, and the chimney stacks and gables of the ancient building gleamed in the clear air, which turned the smoke and vapour of the city into a cloud of gold. The very sundial in his shady corner, where the wind was used to spin with such unwindy constancy, shook off the finer particles of snow that had accumulated on his dull old face in the night, and looked out at the little white wreaths eddying round and round him. Doubtless some blind groping of the morning made its way down into the forgotten crypt so cold and earthy, where the Norman arches were half buried in the ground, and stirred the dull sap in the lazy vegetation hanging to the walls, and quickened the slow principle of life within the little world of wonderful and delicate creation which existed there, with some faint knowledge that the sun was up.

The Tetterbys were up, and doing. Mr. Tetterby took down the shutters of the shop, and, strip by strip, revealed the treasures of the window to the eyes, so proof against their seductions, of Jerusalem Buildings. Adolphus had been out so long already, that he was halfway on to "Morning Pepper." Five small Tetterbys, whose ten round eyes were much inflamed by soap and friction, were in the tortures of a cool wash in the back kitchen; Mrs. Tetterby presiding. Johnny, who was pushed and hustled through his toilet with great rapidity when Moloch chanced to be in an exacting frame of mind (which was always the case), staggered up and down with his charge before the shop door, under greater difficulties than usual; the weight of Moloch being much increased by a complication of defences against the cold, composed of knitted worsted-work, and forming a complete suit of chain-armour, with a head-piece and blue gaiters.

It was a peculiarity of this baby to be always cutting teeth. Whether they never came, or whether they came and went away again, is not in evidence; but it had certainly cut enough, on the showing of Mrs. Tetterby, to make a handsome dental provision for the sign of the Bull and Mouth. All sorts of objects were impressed for the rubbing of its gums, notwithstanding that it always carried, dangling at its waist (which was immediately under its chin), a bone ring, large enough to have represented the rosary of a young nun. Knife-handles, umbrella-tops, the heads of walking-sticks selected from the stock, the fingers of the family in general, but especially of Johnny, nutmeg-graters, crusts, the handles of doors, and the cool knobs on the tops of pokers, were among the commonest instruments indiscriminately applied for this baby's relief. The amount of electricity that must have been rubbed out of it in a week, is not to be calculated. Still Mrs. Tetterby always said "it was coming through, and then the child would be herself;" and still it never did come through, and the child continued to be somebody else.

The tempers of the little Tetterbys had sadly changed with a few hours. Mr. and Mrs. Tetterby themselves were not more altered than their offspring. Usually they were an unselfish, good-natured, yielding little race, sharing short commons when it happened (which was pretty often) contentedly and even generously, and taking a great deal of enjoyment out of a very little meat. But they were fighting now, not only for the soap and water, but even for the breakfast which was yet in perspective. The hand of every little Tetterby was against the other little Tetterbys; and even Johnny's hand—the patient, much-enduring, and devoted Johnny—rose against the baby! Yes, Mrs. Tetterby, going to the door by mere accident, saw him viciously pick out a weak place in the suit of armour where a slap would tell, and slap that blessed child.

Mrs. Tetterby had him into the parlour by the collar, in that same flash of time, and repaid him the assault with usury thereto.

"You brute, you murdering little boy," said Mrs. Tetterby. "Had you the heart to do it?"

"Why don't her teeth come through, then," retorted Johnny, in a loud rebellious voice, "instead of bothering me? How would you like it yourself?"

"Like it, sir!" said Mrs. Tetterby, relieving him of his dishonoured load.

"Yes, like it," said Johnny. "How would you? Not at all. If you was me, you'd go for a soldier. I will, too. There an't no babies in the Army."

Mr. Tetterby, who had arrived upon the scene of action, rubbed his chin thoughtfully, instead of correcting the rebel, and seemed rather struck by this view of a military life.

"I wish I was in the Army myself, if the child's in the right," said Mrs. Tetterby, looking at her husband, "for I have no peace of my life here. I'm a slave—a Virginia slave:" some indistinct association with their weak descent on the tobacco trade perhaps suggested this aggravated expression to Mrs. Tetterby. "I never have a holiday, or any pleasure at all, from year's end to year's end! Why, Lord bless and save the child," said Mrs. Tetterby, shaking the baby with an irritability hardly suited to so pious an aspiration, "what's the matter with her now?"

Not being able to discover, and not rendering the subject much clearer by shaking it, Mrs. Tetterby put the baby away in a cradle, and, folding her arms, sat rocking it angrily with her foot.

"How you stand there, 'Dolphus," said Mrs. Tetterby to her husband. "Why don't you do something?"

"Because I don't care about doing anything," Mr. Tetterby replied.

"I am sure *I* don't," said Mrs. Tetterby.

"I'll take my oath *I* don't," said Mr. Tetterby.

A diversion arose here among Johnny and his five younger brothers, who, in preparing the family breakfast table, had fallen to skirmishing for the temporary possession of the loaf, and were buffeting one another with great heartiness; the smallest boy of all, with precocious discretion, hovering outside the knot of combatants, and harassing their legs. Into the midst of this fray, Mr. and Mrs. Tetterby both precipitated themselves with great ardour, as if such ground were the only ground on which they could now agree; and having, with no visible remains of their late soft-heartedness, laid about them without any lenity, and done much execution, resumed their former relative positions.

"You had better read your paper than do nothing at all," said Mrs. Tetterby.

"What's there to read in a paper?" returned Mr. Tetterby, with excessive discontent.

"What?" said Mrs. Tetterby. "Police."

"It's nothing to me," said Tetterby. "What do I care what people do, or are done to?"

"Suicides," suggested Mrs. Tetterby.

"No business of mine," replied her husband.

"Births, deaths, and marriages, are those nothing to you?" said Mrs. Tetterby.

"If the births were all over for good, and all today; and the deaths were all to begin to come off tomorrow; I don't see why it should interest me, till I thought it was a coming to my turn," grumbled Tetterby. "As to marriages, I've done it myself. I know quite enough about *them*."

To judge from the dissatisfied expression of her face and manner, Mrs. Tetterby appeared to entertain the same opinions as her husband; but she opposed him, nevertheless, for the gratification of quarrelling with him.

"Oh, you're a consistent man," said Mrs. Tetterby, "an't you? You, with the screen of your own making there, made of nothing else but bits of newspapers, which you sit and read to the children by the half-hour together!"

"Say used to, if you please," returned her husband. "You won't find me doing so any more. I'm wiser now."

"Bah! wiser, indeed!" said Mrs. Tetterby. "Are you better?"

The question sounded some discordant note in Mr. Tetterby's breast. He ruminated dejectedly, and passed his hand across and across his forehead.

"Better!" murmured Mr. Tetterby. "I don't know as any of us are better, or happier either. Better, is it?"

He turned to the screen, and traced about it with his finger, until he found a certain paragraph of which he was in quest.

"This used to be one of the family favourites, I recollect," said Tetterby, in a forlorn and stupid way, "and used to draw tears from the children, and make 'em good, if there was any little bickering or discontent among 'em, next to the story of the robin redbreasts in the wood. 'Melancholy case of destitution. Yesterday a small man, with a baby in his arms, and surrounded by half-a-dozen ragged little ones, of various ages between ten and two, the whole of whom were evidently in a famishing condition, appeared before the worthy magistrate, and made the following recital:'—Ha! I don't understand it, I'm sure," said Tetterby; "I don't see what it has got to do with us."

"How old and shabby he looks," said Mrs. Tetterby, watching him. "I never saw such a change in a man. Ah! dear me, dear me, dear me, it was a sacrifice!"

"What was a sacrifice?" her husband sourly inquired.

Mrs. Tetterby shook her head; and without replying in words, raised a complete sea-storm about the baby, by her violent agitation of the cradle.

"If you mean your marriage was a sacrifice, my good woman—" said her husband.

"I *do* mean it" said his wife.

"Why, then I mean to say," pursued Mr. Tetterby, as sulkily and surlily as she, "that there are two sides to that affair; and that I was the sacrifice; and that I wish the sacrifice hadn't been accepted."

"I wish it hadn't, Tetterby, with all my heart and soul I do assure you," said his wife. "You can't wish it more than I do, Tetterby."

"I don't know what I saw in her," muttered the newsman, "I'm sure;—certainly, if I saw anything, it's not there now. I was thinking so, last night, after supper, by the fire. She's fat, she's ageing, she won't bear comparison with most other women."

"He's common-looking, he has no air with him, he's small, he's beginning to stoop and he's getting bald," muttered Mrs. Tetterby.

"I must have been half out of my mind when I did it," muttered Mr. Tetterby.

"My senses must have forsook me. That's the only way in which I can explain it to myself," said Mrs. Tetterby with elaboration.

In this mood they sat down to breakfast. The little Tetterbys were not habituated to regard that meal in the light of a sedentary occupation, but discussed it as a dance or trot; rather resembling a savage ceremony, in the occasionally shrill whoops, and brandishings of bread and butter, with which it was accompanied, as well as in the intricate filings off into the street and back again, and the hoppings up and down the door-steps, which were incidental to the performance.

In the present instance, the contentions between these Tetterby children for the milk-and-water jug, common to all, which stood upon the table, presented so lamentable an instance of angry passions risen very high indeed, that it was an outrage on the memory of Dr. Watts. It was not until Mr. Tetterby had driven the whole herd out at the front door, that a moment's peace was secured; and even that was broken by the discovery that Johnny had surreptitiously come back, and was at that instant choking in the jug like a ventriloquist, in his indecent and rapacious haste.

"These children will be the death of me at last!" said Mrs. Tetterby, after banishing the culprit. "And the sooner the better, I think."

"Poor people," said Mr. Tetterby, "ought not to have children at all. They give *us* no pleasure."

He was at that moment taking up the cup which Mrs. Tetterby had rudely pushed towards him, and Mrs. Tetterby was lifting her own cup to her lips, when they both stopped, as if they were transfixed.

"Here! Mother! Father!" cried Johnny, running into the room. "Here's Mrs. William coming down the street!"

And if ever, since the world began, a young boy took a baby from a cradle with the care of an old nurse, and hushed and soothed it tenderly, and tottered away with it cheerfully, Johnny was that boy, and Moloch was that baby, as they went out together!

Mr. Tetterby put down his cup; Mrs. Tetterby put down her cup. Mr. Tetterby rubbed his forehead; Mrs. Tetterby rubbed hers. Mr. Tetterby's face began to smooth and brighten; Mrs. Tetterby's began to smooth and brighten.

"Why, Lord forgive me," said Mr. Tetterby to himself, "what evil tempers have I been giving way to? What has been the matter here!"

"How could I ever treat him ill again, after all I said and felt last night!" sobbed Mrs. Tetterby, with her apron to her eyes.

"Am I a brute," said Mr. Tetterby, "or is there any good in me at all? Sophia! My little woman!"

"'Dolphus dear," returned his wife.

"I—I've been in a state of mind," said Mr. Tetterby, "that I can't abear to think of, Sophy."

"Oh! It's nothing to what I've been in, Dolf," cried his wife in a great burst of grief.

"My Sophia," said Mr. Tetterby, "don't take on. I never shall forgive myself. I must have nearly broke your heart, I know."

"No, Dolf, no. It was me! Me!" cried Mrs. Tetterby.

"My little woman," said her husband, "don't. You make me reproach myself dreadful, when you show such a noble spirit. Sophia, my dear, you don't know what I thought. I showed it bad enough, no doubt; but what I thought, my little woman!—"

"Oh, dear Dolf, don't! Don't!" cried his wife.

"Sophia," said Mr. Tetterby, "I must reveal it. I couldn't rest in my conscience unless I mentioned it. My little woman—"

"Mrs. William's very nearly here!" screamed Johnny at the door.

"My little woman, I wondered how," gasped Mr. Tetterby, supporting himself by his chair, "I wondered how I had ever admired you—I forgot the precious children you have brought about me, and thought you didn't look as slim as I could wish. I—I never gave a recollection," said Mr. Tetterby, with severe self-accusation, "to the cares you've had as my wife, and along of me and mine, when you might have had hardly any with another man, who got on better and was luckier than me (anybody might have found such a man easily I am sure); and I quarrelled with you for having aged a little in the rough years you have lightened for me. Can you believe it, my little woman? I hardly can myself."

Mrs. Tetterby, in a whirlwind of laughing and crying, caught his face within her hands, and held it there.

"Oh, Dolf!" she cried. "I am so happy that you thought so; I am so grateful that you thought so! For I thought that you were common-looking, Dolf; and so you are, my dear, and may you be the commonest of all sights in my eyes, till you close them with your own good hands. I thought that you were small; and so you are, and I'll make much of you because you are, and more of you because I love my husband. I thought that you began to stoop; and so you do, and you shall lean on me, and I'll do all I can to keep you up. I thought there was no air about you; but there is, and it's the air of home, and that's the purest and the best there is, and God bless home once more, and all belonging to it, Dolf!"

"Hurrah! Here's Mrs. William!" cried Johnny.

So she was, and all the children with her; and so she came in, they kissed her, and kissed one another, and kissed the baby, and kissed their father and mother, and then ran back and flocked and danced about her, trooping on with her in triumph.

Mr. and Mrs. Tetterby were not a bit behind-hand in the warmth of their reception. They were as much attracted to her as the children were; they ran towards her, kissed her hands, pressed round her, could not receive her ardently or enthusiastically enough. She came among them like the spirit of all goodness, affection, gentle consideration, love, and domesticity.

"What! are *you* all so glad to see me, too, this bright Christmas morning?" said Milly, clapping her hands in a pleasant wonder. "Oh dear, how delightful this is!"

More shouting from the children, more kissing, more trooping round her, more happiness, more love, more joy, more honour, on all sides, than she could bear.

"Oh dear!" said Milly, "what delicious tears you make me shed. How can I ever have deserved this! What have I done to be so loved?"

"Who can help it!" cried Mr. Tetterby.

"Who can help it!" cried Mrs. Tetterby.

"Who can help it!" echoed the children, in a joyful chorus. And they danced and trooped about her again, and clung to her, and laid their rosy faces against her dress, and kissed and fondled it, and could not fondle it, or her, enough.

"I never was so moved," said Milly, drying her eyes, "as I have been this morning. I must tell you, as soon as I can speak.—Mr. Redlaw came to me at sunrise, and with a tenderness in his manner, more as if I had been his darling daughter than myself, implored me to go with him to where William's brother George is lying ill. We went together, and all the way along he was so kind, and so subdued, and seemed to put such trust and hope in me, that I could not help trying with pleasure. When we got to the house, we met a woman at the door (somebody had bruised and hurt her, I am afraid), who caught me by the hand, and blessed me as I passed."

"She was right!" said Mr. Tetterby. Mrs. Tetterby said she was right. All the children cried out that she was right.

"Ah, but there's more than that," said Milly. "When we got up stairs, into the room, the sick man who had lain for hours in a state from which no effort could rouse him, rose up in his bed, and, bursting into tears, stretched out his arms to me, and said that he had led a misspent life, but that he was truly repentant now, in his sorrow for the past, which was all as plain to him as a great prospect, from which a dense black cloud had cleared away, and that he entreated me to ask his poor old father for his pardon and his blessing, and to say a prayer beside his bed.

"And when I did so, Mr. Redlaw joined in it so fervently, and then so thanked and thanked me, and thanked Heaven, that my heart quite overflowed, and I could have done nothing but sob and cry, if the sick man had not begged me to sit down by him,—which made me quiet of course. As I sat there, he held my hand in his until he sank in a doze; and even then, when I withdrew my hand to leave him to come here (which Mr. Redlaw was very earnest indeed in wishing me to do), his hand felt for mine, so that someone else was obliged to take my place and make believe to give him my hand back. Oh dear, oh dear," said Milly, sobbing. "How thankful and how happy I should feel, and do feel, for all this!"

While she was speaking, Redlaw had come in, and, after pausing for a moment to observe the group of which she was the centre, had silently ascended the stairs. Upon those stairs he now appeared again; remaining there, while the young student passed him, and came running down.

"Kind nurse, gentlest, best of creatures," he said, falling on his knee to her, and catching at her hand, "forgive my cruel ingratitude!"

"Oh dear, oh dear!" cried Milly innocently, "here's another of them! Oh dear, here's somebody else who likes me. What shall I ever do!"

The guileless, simple way in which she said it, and in which she put her hands before her eyes and wept for very happiness, was as touching as it was delightful.

"I was not myself," he said. "I don't know what it was—it was some consequence of my disorder perhaps—I was mad. But I am so no longer. Almost as I speak, I am restored. I heard the children crying out your name, and the shade passed from me at the very sound of it. Oh, don't weep! Dear Milly, if you could read my heart, and only knew with what affection and what grateful homage it is glowing, you would not let me see you weep. It is such deep reproach."

"No, no," said Milly, "it's not that. It's not indeed. It's joy. It's wonder that you should think it necessary to ask me to forgive so little, and yet it's pleasure that you do."

"And will you come again? and will you finish the little curtain?"

"No," said Milly, drying her eyes, and shaking her head. "You won't care for my needlework now."

"Is it forgiving me, to say that?"

She beckoned him aside, and whispered in his ear.

"There is news from your home, Mr. Edmund."

"News? How?"

"Either your not writing when you were very ill, or the change in your handwriting when you began to be better, created some suspicion of the truth; however that is—but you're sure you'll not be the worse for any news, if it's not bad news?"

"Sure."

"Then there's someone come!" said Milly.

"My mother?" asked the student, glancing round involuntarily towards Redlaw, who had come down from the stairs.

"Hush! No," said Milly.

"It can be no one else."

"Indeed?" said Milly, "are you sure?"

"It is not—" Before he could say more, she put her hand upon his mouth.

"Yes it is!" said Milly. "The young lady (she is very like the miniature, Mr. Edmund, but she is prettier) was too unhappy to rest without satisfying her doubts, and came up, last night, with a little servant-maid. As you always dated your letters from the college, she came there; and before I saw Mr. Redlaw this morning, I saw her. *She* likes me too!" said Milly. "Oh dear, that's another!"

"This morning! Where is she now?"

"Why, she is now," said Milly, advancing her lips to his ear, "in my little parlour in the Lodge, and waiting to see you."

He pressed her hand, and was darting off, but she detained him.

"Mr. Redlaw is much altered, and has told me this morning that his memory is impaired. Be very considerate to him, Mr. Edmund; he needs that from us all."

The young man assured her, by a look, that her caution was not ill-bestowed; and as he passed the Chemist on his way out, bent respectfully and with an obvious interest before him.

Redlaw returned the salutation courteously and even humbly, and looked after him as he passed on. He dropped his head upon his hand too, as trying to reawaken something he had lost. But it was gone.

The abiding change that had come upon him since the influence of the music, and the Phantom's reappearance, was, that now he truly felt how much he had lost, and could compassionate his own condition, and contrast it, clearly, with the natural state of those who were around him. In this, an interest in those who were around him was revived, and a meek, submissive sense of his calamity was bred, resembling that which sometimes obtains in age, when its mental powers are weakened, without insensibility or sullenness being added to the list of its infirmities.

He was conscious that, as he redeemed, through Milly, more and more of the evil he had done, and as he was more and more with her, this change ripened itself within him. Therefore, and because of the attachment she inspired him with (but without other hope), he felt that he was quite dependent on her, and that she was his staff in his affliction.

So, when she asked him whether they should go home now, to where the old man and her husband were, and he readily replied "yes"—being anxious in that regard—he put his arm through hers, and walked beside her; not as if he were the wise and learned man to whom the wonders of Nature were an open book, and hers were the uninstructed mind, but as if their two positions were reversed, and he knew nothing, and she all.

He saw the children throng about her, and caress her, as he and she went away together thus, out of the house; he heard the ringing of their laughter, and their merry voices; he saw their bright faces, clustering around him like flowers; he witnessed the renewed contentment and affection of their parents; he breathed the simple air of their poor home, restored to its tranquillity; he thought of the unwholesome blight he had shed upon it, and might, but for her, have been diffusing then; and perhaps it is no wonder that he walked submissively beside her, and drew her gentle bosom nearer to his own.

When they arrived at the Lodge, the old man was sitting in his chair in the chimney-corner, with his eyes fixed on the ground, and his son was leaning against the opposite side of the fireplace, looking at him. As she came in at the door, both started, and turned round towards her, and a radiant change came upon their faces.

"Oh dear, dear, dear, they are all pleased to see me like the rest!" cried Milly, clapping her hands in an ecstasy, and stopping short. "Here are two more!"

Pleased to see her! Pleasure was no word for it. She ran into her husband's arms, thrown wide open to receive her, and he would have been glad to have her there, with her head lying on his shoulder, through the short winter's day. But the old man couldn't spare her. He had arms for her too, and he locked her in them.

"Why, where has my quiet Mouse been all this time?" said the old man. "She has been a long while away. I find that it's impossible for me to get on without Mouse. I—where's my son William?—I fancy I have been dreaming, William."

"That's what I say myself, father," returned his son. "I have been in an ugly sort of dream, I think.—How are you, father? Are you pretty well?"

"Strong and brave, my boy," returned the old man.

It was quite a sight to see Mr. William shaking hands with his father, and patting him on the back, and rubbing him gently down with his hand, as if he could not possibly do enough to show an interest in him.

"What a wonderful man you are, father!—How are you, father? Are you really pretty hearty, though?" said William, shaking hands with him again, and patting him again, and rubbing him gently down again.

"I never was fresher or stouter in my life, my boy."

"What a wonderful man you are, father! But that's exactly where it is," said Mr. William, with enthusiasm. "When I think of all that my father's gone through, and all the chances and changes, and sorrows and troubles, that have happened to him in the course of his long life, and under which his head has grown grey, and years upon years have gathered on it, I feel as if we couldn't do enough to honour the old gentleman, and make his old age easy.—How are you, father? Are you really pretty well, though?"

Mr. William might never have left off repeating this inquiry, and shaking hands with him again, and patting him again, and rubbing him down again, if the old man had not espied the

Chemist, whom until now he had not seen.

"I ask your pardon, Mr. Redlaw," said Philip, "but didn't know you were here, sir, or should have made less free. It reminds me, Mr. Redlaw, seeing you here on a Christmas morning, of the time when you was a student yourself, and worked so hard that you were backwards and forwards in our Library even at Christmas time. Ha! ha! I'm old enough to remember that; and I remember it right well, I do, though I am eight-seven. It was after you left here that my poor wife died. You remember my poor wife, Mr. Redlaw?"

The Chemist answered yes.

"Yes," said the old man. "She was a dear creetur.—I recollect you come here one Christmas morning with a young lady—I ask your pardon, Mr. Redlaw, but I think it was a sister you was very much attached to?"

The Chemist looked at him, and shook his head. "I had a sister," he said vacantly. He knew no more.

"One Christmas morning," pursued the old man, "that you come here with her—and it began to snow, and my wife invited the lady to walk in, and sit by the fire that is always a burning on Christmas Day in what used to be, before our ten poor gentlemen commuted, our great Dinner Hall. I was there; and I recollect, as I was stirring up the blaze for the young lady to warm her pretty feet by, she read the scroll out loud, that is underneath that picture, 'Lord, keep my memory green!'

"She and my poor wife fell a talking about it; and it's a strange thing to think of, now, that they both said (both being so unlike to die) that it was a good prayer, and that it was one they would put up very earnestly, if they were called away young, with reference to those who were dearest to them. 'My brother,' says the young lady—'My husband,' says my poor wife.—'Lord, keep his memory of me, green, and do not let me be forgotten!'"

Tears more painful, and more bitter than he had ever shed in all his life, coursed down Redlaw's face. Philip, fully occupied in recalling his story, had not observed him until now, nor Milly's anxiety that he should not proceed.

"Philip!" said Redlaw, laying his hand upon his arm, "I am a stricken man, on whom the hand of Providence has fallen heavily, although deservedly. You speak to me, my friend, of what I cannot follow; my memory is gone."

"Merciful power!" cried the old man.

"I have lost my memory of sorrow, wrong, and trouble," said the Chemist, "and with that I have lost all man would remember!"

To see old Philip's pity for him, to see him wheel his own great chair for him to rest in, and look down upon him with a solemn sense of his bereavement, was to know, in some degree, how precious to old age such recollections are.

The boy came running in, and ran to Milly.

"Here's the man," he said, "in the other room. I don't want *him*."

"What man does he mean?" asked Mr. William.

"Hush!" said Milly.

Obedient to a sign from her, he and his old father softly withdrew. As they went out, unnoticed, Redlaw beckoned to the boy to come to him.

"I like the woman best," he answered, holding to her skirts.

"You are right," said Redlaw, with a faint smile. "But you needn't fear to come to me. I am gentler than I was. Of all the world, to you, poor child!"

The boy still held back at first, but yielding little by little to her urging, he consented to approach, and even to sit down at his feet. As Redlaw laid his hand upon the shoulder of the child, looking on him with compassion and a fellow-feeling, he put out his other hand to Milly. She stooped down on that side of him, so that she could look into his face, and after silence, said:

"Mr. Redlaw, may I speak to you?"

"Yes," he answered, fixing his eyes upon her. "Your voice and music are the same to me."

"May I ask you something?"

"What you will."

"Do you remember what I said, when I knocked at your

door last night? About one who was your friend once, and who stood on the verge of destruction?"

"Yes. I remember," he said, with some hesitation.

"Do you understand it?"

He smoothed the boy's hair—looking at her fixedly the while, and shook his head.

"This person," said Milly, in her clear, soft voice, which her mild eyes, looking at him, made clearer and softer, "I found soon afterwards. I went back to the house, and, with Heaven's help, traced him. I was not too soon. A very little and I should have been too late."

He took his hand from the boy, and laying it on the back of that hand of hers, whose timid and yet earnest touch addressed him no less appealingly than her voice and eyes, looked more intently on her.

"He *is* the father of Mr. Edmund, the young gentleman we saw just now. His real name is Longford.—You recollect the name?"

"I recollect the name."

"And the man?"

"No, not the man. Did he ever wrong me?"

"Yes!"

"Ah! Then it's hopeless—hopeless."

He shook his head, and softly beat upon the hand he held, as though mutely asking her commiseration.

"I did not go to Mr. Edmund last night," said Milly,—"You will listen to me just the same as if you did remember all?"

"To every syllable you say."

"Both, because I did not know, then, that this really was his father, and because I was fearful of the effect of such intelligence upon him, after his illness, if it should be. Since I have known who this person is, I have not gone either; but that is for another reason. He has long been separated from his wife and son-has been a stranger to his home almost from this son's infancy, I learn from him—and has abandoned and deserted what he should have held most dear. In all that time he has been falling from the state of a gentleman, more and more, until—" she rose up, hastily, and going out for a moment, returned, accompanied by the wreck that Redlaw had beheld last night.

"Do you know me?" asked the Chemist.

"I should be glad," returned the other, "and that is an unwonted word for me to use, if I could answer no."

The Chemist looked at the man, standing in self-abasement and degradation before him, and would have looked longer, in an ineffectual struggle for enlightenment, but that Milly resumed her late position by his side, and attracted his attentive gaze to her own face.

"See how low he is sunk, how lost he is!" she whispered, stretching out her arm towards him, without looking from the Chemist's face. "If you could remember all that is connected with him, do you not think it would move your pity to reflect that one you ever loved (do not let us mind how long ago, or in what belief that he has forfeited), should come to this?"

"I hope it would," he answered. "I believe it would."

His eyes wandered to the figure standing near the door, but came back speedily to her, on whom he gazed intently, as if he strove to learn some lesson from every tone of her voice, and every beam of her eyes.

"I have no learning, and you have much," said Milly; "I am not used to think, and you are always thinking. May I tell you why it seems to me a good thing for us, to remember wrong that has been done us?"

"Yes."

"That we may forgive it."

"Pardon me, great Heaven!" said Redlaw, lifting up his eyes, "for having thrown away thine own high attribute!"

"And if," said Milly, "if your memory should one day be restored, as we will hope and pray it may be, would it not be a blessing to you to recall at once a wrong and its forgiveness?"

He looked at the figure by the door, and fastened his attentive eyes on her again; a ray of clearer light appeared to him to shine into his mind, from her bright face.

"He cannot go to his abandoned home. He does not seek to go there. He knows that he could only carry shame and trouble to those he has so cruelly neglected; and that the best reparation he can make them now, is to avoid them. A very little money carefully bestowed, would remove him to some distant place, where he might live and do no wrong, and make such atonement as is left within his power for the wrong he has done. To the unfortunate lady who is his wife, and to his son, this would be the best and kindest boon that their best friend could give them—one too that they need never know of; and to him, shattered in reputation, mind, and body, it might be salvation."

He took her head between her hands, and kissed it, and said: "It shall be done. I trust to you to do it for me, now and secretly; and to tell him that I would forgive him, if I were so happy as to know for what."

As she rose, and turned her beaming face towards the fallen man, implying that her mediation had been successful, he advanced a step, and without raising his eyes, addressed himself to Redlaw.

"You are so generous," he said, "—you ever were—that you will try to banish your rising sense of retribution in the spectacle that is before you. I do not try to banish it from myself, Redlaw. If you can, believe me."

The Chemist entreated Milly, by a gesture, to come nearer to him; and, as he listened looked in her face, as if to find in it the clue to what he heard.

"I am too decayed a wretch to make professions; I recollect my own career too well, to array any such before you. But from the day on which I made my first step downward, in dealing falsely by you, I have gone down with a certain, steady, doomed progression. That, I say."

Redlaw, keeping her close at his side, turned his face towards the speaker, and there was sorrow in it. Something like mournful recognition too.

"I might have been another man, my life might have been another life, if I had avoided that first fatal step. I don't know that it would have been. I claim nothing for the possibility. Your sister is at rest, and better than she could have been with me, if I had continued even what you thought me: even what I once supposed myself to be."

Redlaw made a hasty motion with his hand, as if he would have put that subject on one side.

"I speak," the other went on, "like a man taken from the grave. I should have made my own grave, last night, had it not been for this blessed hand."

"Oh dear, he likes me too!" sobbed Milly, under her breath. "That's another!"

"I could not have put myself in your way, last night, even for bread. But, today, my recollection of what has been is so strongly stirred, and is presented to me, I don't know how, so vividly, that I have dared to come at her suggestion, and to take your bounty, and to thank you for it, and to beg you, Redlaw, in your dying hour, to be as merciful to me in your thoughts, as you are in your deeds."

He turned towards the door, and stopped a moment on his way forth.

"I hope my son may interest you, for his mother's sake. I hope he may deserve to do so. Unless my life should be preserved a long time, and I should know that I have not misused your aid, I shall never look upon him more."

Going out, he raised his eyes to Redlaw for the first time. Redlaw, whose steadfast gaze was fixed upon him, dreamily held out his hand. He returned and touched it—little more—with both his own; and bending down his head, went slowly out.

In the few moments that elapsed, while Milly silently took him to the gate, the Chemist dropped into his chair, and covered his face with his hands. Seeing him thus, when she came back, accompanied by her husband and his father (who were both greatly concerned for him), she avoided disturbing him, or permitting him to be disturbed; and kneeled down near the chair to put some warm clothing on the boy.

"That's exactly where it is. That's what I always say, father!"

exclaimed her admiring husband. "There's a motherly feeling in Mrs. William's breast that must and will have went!"

"Ay, ay," said the old man; "you're right. My son William's right!"

"It happens all for the best, Milly dear, no doubt," said Mr. William, tenderly, "that we have no children of our own; and yet I sometimes wish you had one to love and cherish. Our little dead child that you built such hopes upon, and that never breathed the breath of life—it has made you quiet-like, Milly."

"I am very happy in the recollection of it, William dear," she answered. "I think of it every day."

"I was afraid you thought of it a good deal."

"Don't say, afraid; it is a comfort to me; it speaks to me in so many ways. The innocent thing that never lived on earth, is like an angel to me, William."

"You are like an angel to father and me," said Mr. William, softly. "I know that."

"When I think of all those hopes I built upon it, and the many times I sat and pictured to myself the little smiling face upon my bosom that never lay there, and the sweet eyes turned up to mine that never opened to the light," said Milly, "I can feel a greater tenderness, I think, for all the disappointed hopes in which there is no harm. When I see a beautiful child in its fond mother's arms, I love it all the better, thinking that my child might have been like that, and might have made my heart as proud and happy."

Redlaw raised his head, and looked towards her.

"All through life, it seems by me," she continued, "to tell me something. For poor neglected children, my little child pleads as if it were alive, and had a voice I knew, with which to speak to me. When I hear of youth in suffering or shame, I think that my child might have come to that, perhaps, and that God took it from me in His mercy. Even in age and grey hair, such as father's, it is present: saying that it too might have lived to be old, long and long after you and I were gone, and to have needed the respect and love of younger people."

Her quiet voice was quieter than ever, as she took her husband's arm, and laid her head against it.

"Children love me so, that sometimes I half fancy—it's a silly fancy, William—they have some way I don't know of, of feeling for my little child, and me, and understanding why their love is precious to me. If I have been quiet since, I have been more happy, William, in a hundred ways. Not least happy, dear, in this—that even when my little child was born and dead but a few days, and I was weak and sorrowful, and could not help grieving a little, the thought arose, that if I tried to lead a good life, I should meet in Heaven a bright creature, who would call me, Mother!"

Redlaw fell upon his knees, with a loud cry.

"O Thou, he said, "who through the teaching of pure love, hast graciously restored me to the memory which was the memory of Christ upon the Cross, and of all the good who perished in His cause, receive my thanks, and bless her!"

Then, he folded her to his heart; and Milly, sobbing more than ever, cried, as she laughed, "He is come back to himself! He likes me very much indeed, too! Oh, dear, dear, dear me, here's another!"

Then, the student entered, leading by the hand a lovely girl, who was afraid to come. And Redlaw so changed towards him, seeing in him and his youthful choice, the softened shadow of that chastening passage in his own life, to which, as to a shady tree, the dove so long imprisoned in his solitary ark might fly for rest and company, fell upon his neck, entreating them to be his children.

Then, as Christmas is a time in which, of all times in the year, the memory of every remediable sorrow, wrong, and trouble in the world around us, should be active with us, not less than our own experiences, for all good, he laid his hand upon the boy, and, silently calling Him to witness who laid His hand on children in old time, rebuking, in the majesty of His prophetic knowledge, those who kept them from Him, vowed to protect him, teach him, and reclaim him.

Then, he gave his right hand cheerily to Philip, and said that they would that day hold a Christmas dinner in what used to be, before the ten poor gentlemen commuted, their great Dinner Hall; and that they would bid to it as many of that Swidger family, who, his son had told him, were so numerous that they might join hands and make a ring round England, as could be brought together on so short a notice.

And it was that day done. There were so many Swidgers there, grown up and children, that an attempt to state them in round numbers might engender doubts, in the distrustful, of the veracity of this history. Therefore the attempt shall not be made. But there they were, by dozens and scores—and there was good news and good hope there, ready for them, of George, who had been visited again by his father and brother, and by Milly, and again left in a quiet sleep. There, present at the dinner, too, were the Tetterbys, including young Adolphus, who arrived in his prismatic comforter, in good time for the beef. Johnny and the baby were too late, of course, and came in all on one side, the one exhausted, the other in a supposed state of double-tooth; but that was customary, and not alarming.

It was sad to see the child who had no name or lineage, watching the other children as they played, not knowing how to talk with them, or sport with them, and more strange to the ways of childhood than a rough dog. It was sad, though in a different way, to see what an instinctive knowledge the youngest children there had of his being different from all the rest, and how they made timid approaches to him with soft words and touches, and with little presents, that he might not be unhappy. But he kept by Milly, and began to love her—that was another, as she said!—and, as they all liked her dearly, they were glad of that, and when they saw him peeping at them from behind her chair, they were pleased that he was so close to it.

All this, the Chemist, sitting with the student and his bride that was to be, Philip, and the rest, saw.

Some people have said since, that he only thought what has

been herein set down; others, that he read it in the fire, one winter night about the twilight time; others, that the Ghost was but the representation of his gloomy thoughts, and Milly the embodiment of his better wisdom. *I* say nothing.

—Except this. That as they were assembled in the old Hall, by no other light than that of a great fire (having dined early), the shadows once more stole out of their hiding-places, and danced about the room, showing the children marvellous shapes and faces on the walls, and gradually changing what was real and familiar there, to what was wild and magical. But that there was one thing in the Hall, to which the eyes of Redlaw, and of Milly and her husband, and of the old man, and of the student, and his bride that was to be, were often turned, which the shadows did not obscure or change. Deepened in its gravity by the firelight, and gazing from the darkness of the panelled wall like life, the sedate face in the portrait, with the beard and ruff, looked down at them from under its verdant wreath of holly, as they looked up at it; and, clear and plain below, as if a voice had uttered them, were the words.

Lord keep my Memory green.

The Lawyer and the Ghost

I knew a man—forty years ago now—who took an old, damp, rotten set of chambers, in one of the most ancient inns, that had been shut up and empty for years and years before. There were lots of old women's stories about the place, and it certainly was very far from being a cheerful one; but he was poor, and the rooms were cheap, and that would have been quite a sufficient reason for him, if they had been ten times worse than they really were.

He was obliged to take some mouldering fixtures that were on the place, and, among the rest, was a great lumbering wooden press for papers, with large glass doors, and a green curtain inside; a pretty useless thing for him, for he had no papers to put in it; and as to his clothes, he carried them about with him, and that wasn't very hard work, either. Well, he had moved in all his furniture—it wasn't quite a truck-full—and had sprinkled it about the room, so as to make the four chairs look as much like a dozen as possible, and was sitting down before the fire at night, drinking the first glass of two gallons of whisky he had ordered on credit, wondering whether it would ever be paid for, and if so, in how many years' time, when his eyes encountered the glass doors of the wooden press.

"Ah," says he, "if I hadn't been obliged to take that ugly article at the old broker's valuation, I might have got something comfortable for the money. I'll tell you what it is, old fellow," he said, speaking aloud to the press, having nothing else to speak to, "if it wouldn't cost more to break up your old carcass, than it would ever be worth afterward, I'd have a fire out of you in less than no time."

He had hardly spoken the words, when a sound resembling a faint groan, appeared to issue from the interior of the case. It startled him at first, but thinking, on a moment's reflection, that it must be some young fellow in the next chamber, who had been dining out, he put his feet on the fender, and raised the poker to stir the fire.

At that moment, the sound was repeated; and one of the glass doors slowly opening, disclosed a pale and emaciated figure in soiled and worn apparel, standing erect in the press. The figure was tall and thin, and the countenance expressive of care and anxiety; but there was something in the hue of the skin, and gaunt and unearthly appearance of the whole form, which no being of this world was ever seen to wear. "Who are you?" said the new tenant, turning very pale; poising the poker in his hand, however, and taking a very decent aim at the countenance of the figure. "Who are you?"

"Don't throw that poker at me," replied the form; "if you hurled it with ever so sure an aim, it would pass through me, without resistance, and expend its force on the wood behind. I am a spirit."

"And pray, what do you want here?" faltered the tenant.

"In this room," replied the apparition, "my worldly ruin was worked, and I and my children beggared. In this press, the papers in a long, long suit, which accumulated for years, were deposited. In this room, when I had died of grief, and long-deferred hope, two wily harpies divided the wealth for which I had contested during a wretched existence, and of which, at last, not one farthing was left for my unhappy descendants. I terrified them from the spot, and since that day have prowled by night—the only period at which I can revisit the earth—about the scenes of my long-protracted misery. This apartment is mine: leave it to me."

"If you insist upon making your appearance here," said the tenant, who had had time to collect his presence of mind, "I shall give up possession with the greatest pleasure; but I should like to ask you one question, if you will allow me."

"Say on," said the apparition sternly.

"Well," said the tenant, "I don't apply the observation personally to you, because it is equally applicable to most of the ghosts I ever heard of; but it does appear to me somewhat inconsistent, that when you have an opportunity of visiting the fairest spots of earth—for I suppose space is nothing to you—you should always return exactly to the very places where you have been most miserable."

"Egad, that's very true; I never thought of that before," said the ghost.

"You see, Sir," pursued the tenant, "this is a very uncomfortable room. From the appearance of that press, I should be disposed to say that it is not wholly free from bugs; and I really think you might find much more comfortable quarters: to say nothing of the climate of London, which is extremely disagreeable."

"You are very right, Sir," said the ghost politely, "it never struck me till now; I'll try change of air directly"—and, in fact, he began to vanish as he spoke; his legs, indeed, had quite disappeared.

"And if, Sir," said the tenant, calling after him, "if you *would* have the goodness to suggest to the other ladies and gentlemen who are now engaged in haunting old empty houses, that they might be much more comfortable elsewhere, you will confer a very great benefit on society." "I will," replied the ghost; "we must be dull fellows—very dull fellows, indeed; I can't imagine how we can have been so stupid." With these words, the spirit disappeared; and what is rather remarkable, he never came back again.

The Ghosts of the Mail

A.k.a The Story of the Bagman's Uncle or The Mail Coach Ghosts

'My uncle, gentlemen,' said the bagman, 'was one of the merriest, pleasantest, cleverest fellows, that ever lived. I wish you had known him, gentlemen. On second thoughts, gentlemen, I don't wish you had known him, for if you had, you would have been all, by this time, in the ordinary course of nature, if not dead, at all events so near it, as to have taken to stopping at home and giving up company, which would have deprived me of the inestimable pleasure of addressing you at this moment. Gentlemen, I wish your fathers and mothers had known my uncle. They would have been amazingly fond of him, especially your respectable mothers; I know they would. If any two of his numerous virtues predominated over the many that adorned his character, I should say they were his mixed punch and his after-supper song. Excuse my dwelling on these melancholy recollections of departed worth; you won't see a man like my uncle every day in the week.

'I have always considered it a great point in my uncle's character, gentlemen, that he was the intimate friend and companion of Tom Smart, of the great house of Bilson and Slum, Cateaton Street, City. My uncle collected for Tiggin and Welps, but for a long time he went pretty near the same journey as Tom; and the very first night they met, my uncle took a fancy for Tom, and Tom took a fancy for my uncle. They made a bet of a new hat before they had known each other half an hour, who should brew the best quart of punch and drink it the quickest. My uncle was judged to have won the making, but Tom Smart beat him in the drinking by about half a salt-spoonful. They took another quart apiece to drink each other's health in, and were staunch friends ever afterwards. There's a destiny in these things, gentlemen; we can't help it.

'In personal appearance, my uncle was a trifle shorter than the middle size; he was a thought stouter too, than the ordinary run of people, and perhaps his face might be a shade redder. He had the jolliest face you ever saw, gentleman: something like Punch, with a handsome nose and chin; his eyes were always twinkling and sparkling with good-humour; and a smile—not one of your unmeaning wooden grins, but a real, merry, hearty, good-tempered smile—was perpetually on his countenance. He was pitched out of his gig once, and knocked, head first, against a milestone.

'There he lay, stunned, and so cut about the face with some gravel which had been heaped up alongside it, that, to use my uncle's own strong expression, if his mother could have revisited the earth, she wouldn't have known him. Indeed, when I come to think of the matter, gentlemen, I feel pretty sure she wouldn't. for she died when my uncle was two years and seven months old, and I think it's very likely that, even without the gravel, his top-boots would have puzzled the good lady not a little; to say nothing of his jolly red face.

'However, there he lay, and I have heard my uncle say, many a time, that the man said who picked him up that he was smiling as merrily as if he had tumbled out for a treat, and that after they had bled him, the first faint glimmerings of returning animation, were his jumping up in bed, bursting out into a loud laugh, kissing the young woman who held the basin, and demanding a mutton chop and a pickled walnut. He was very fond of pickled walnuts, gentlemen. He said he always found that, taken without vinegar, they relished the beer.

'My uncle's great journey was in the fall of the leaf, at which time he collected debts, and took orders, in the north; going from London to Edinburgh, from Edinburgh to Glasgow, from Glasgow back to Edinburgh, and thence to London by the smack. You are to understand that his second visit to Edinburgh was for his own pleasure. He used to go back for a week, just to look up his old friends; and what with breakfasting with this one, lunching with that, dining with the third, and supping with another, a pretty tight week he used to make of it. I don't know whether any of you, gentlemen, ever partook of a real substantial hospitable Scotch breakfast, and then went out to a slight lunch of a bushel of oysters, a dozen or so of bottled ale, and a noggin or two of whiskey to close up with. If you ever did, you will agree with me that it requires a pretty strong head to go out to dinner and supper afterwards.

'But bless your hearts and eyebrows, all this sort of thing was nothing to my uncle! He was so well seasoned, that it was mere child's play. I have heard him say that he could see the Dundee people out, any day, and walk home afterwards without staggering; and yet the Dundee people have as strong heads and as strong punch, gentlemen, as you are likely to meet with, between the poles. I have heard of a Glasgow man and a Dundee man drinking against each other for fifteen hours at a sitting. They were both suffocated, as nearly as could be ascertained, at the same moment, but with this trifling exception, gentlemen, they were not a bit the worse for it.

'One night, within four-and-twenty hours of the time when he had settled to take shipping for London, my uncle supped at the house of a very old friend of his, a Bailie Mac something and four syllables after it, who lived in the old town of Edinburgh. There were the bailie's wife, and the bailie's three daughters, and the bailie's grown-up son, and three or four stout, bushy eyebrowed, canny, old Scotch fellows, that the bailie had got together to do honour to my uncle, and help to make merry. It was a glorious supper.

'There was kippered salmon, and Finnan haddocks, and a lamb's head, and a haggis—a celebrated Scotch dish, gentlemen, which my uncle used to say always looked to him, when it came to table, very much like a Cupid's stomach—and a great many other things besides, that I forget the names of, but very good things, notwithstanding. The lassies were pretty and agreeable; the bailie's wife was one of the best creatures that ever lived; and my uncle was in thoroughly good cue. The consequence of which was, that the young ladies tittered and giggled, and the old lady laughed out loud, and the bailie and the other old fellows roared till they were red in the face, the whole mortal time.

'I don't quite recollect how many tumblers of whiskey-toddy each man drank after supper; but this I know, that about one o'clock in the morning, the bailie's grown-up son became insensible while attempting the first verse of "Willie brewed a peck o' maut"; and he having been, for half an hour before, the only other man visible above the mahogany, it occurred to my uncle that it was almost time to think about going, especially as drinking had set in at seven o'clock, in order that he might get home at a decent hour. But, thinking it might not be quite polite to go just then, my uncle voted himself into the chair, mixed another glass, rose to propose his own health, addressed himself in a neat and complimentary speech, and drank the toast with great enthusiasm. Still nobody woke; so my uncle took a little drop more—neat this time, to prevent the toddy from disagreeing with him—and, laying violent hands on his hat, sallied forth into the street.

'It was a wild, gusty night when my uncle closed the bailie's door, and settling his hat firmly on his head to prevent the wind from taking it, thrust his hands into his pockets, and looking upward, took a short survey of the state of the weather. The clouds were drifting over the moon at their giddiest speed; at one time wholly obscuring her; at another, suffering her to burst forth in full splendour and shed her light on all the objects around; anon, driving over her again, with increased velocity, and shrouding everything in darkness.

'"Really, this won't do," said my uncle, addressing himself to the weather, as if he felt himself personally offended. "This is not at all the kind of thing for my voyage. It will not do at any price," said my uncle, very impressively. Having repeated this, several times, he recovered his balance with some difficulty—for he was rather giddy with looking up into the sky so long—and walked merrily on.

'The bailie's house was in the Canongate, and my uncle was going to the other end of Leith Walk, rather better than a mile's journey. On either side of him, there shot up against the dark sky, tall, gaunt, straggling houses, with time-stained fronts, and windows that seemed to have shared the lot of eyes in mortals, and to have grown dim and sunken with age. Six, seven, eight Storey high, were the houses; storey piled upon storey, as children build with cards—throwing their dark shadows over the roughly paved road, and making the dark night darker. A few oil lamps were scattered at long distances, but they only served to mark the dirty entrance to some narrow close, or to show where a common stair communicated, by steep and intricate windings, with the various flats above.

'Glancing at all these things with the air of a man who had seen them too often before, to think them worthy of much notice now, my uncle walked up the middle of the street, with a thumb in each waistcoat pocket, indulging from time to time in various snatches of song, chanted forth with such good-will and spirit, that the quiet honest folk started from their first sleep and lay trembling in bed till the sound died away in the distance; when, satisfying themselves that it was only some drunken ne'er-do-weel finding his way home, they covered themselves up warm and fell asleep again.

'I am particular in describing how my uncle walked up the middle of the street, with his thumbs in his waistcoat pockets, gentlemen, because, as he often used to say (and with great reason too) there is nothing at all extraordinary in this story, unless you distinctly understand at the beginning, that he was not by any means of a marvellous or romantic turn.

'Gentlemen, my uncle walked on with his thumbs in his waistcoat pockets, taking the middle of the street to himself, and singing, now a verse of a love song, and then a verse of a drinking one, and when he was tired of both, whistling melodiously, until he reached the North Bridge, which, at this point, connects the old and new towns of Edinburgh. Here he stopped for a minute, to look at the strange, irregular clusters of lights piled one above the other, and twinkling afar off so high, that they looked like stars, gleaming from the castle walls on the one side and the Calton Hill on the other, as if they illuminated veritable castles in the air; while the old picturesque town slept heavily on, in gloom and darkness below: its palace and chapel of Holyrood, guarded day and night, as a friend of my uncle's used to say, by old Arthur's Seat, towering, surly and dark, like some gruff genius, over the ancient city he has watched so long.

'I say, gentlemen, my uncle stopped here, for a minute, to look about him; and then, paying a compliment to the weather, which had a little cleared up, though the moon was sinking, walked on again, as royally as before; keeping the middle of the road with great dignity, and looking as if he would very much like to meet with somebody who would dispute possession of it with him. There was nobody at all disposed to contest the point, as it happened; and so, on he went, with his thumbs in his waistcoat pockets, like a lamb.

'When my uncle reached the end of Leith Walk, he had to cross a pretty large piece of waste ground which separated him from a short street which he had to turn down to go direct to his lodging. Now, in this piece of waste ground, there was, at that time, an enclosure belonging to some wheelwright who contracted with the Post Office for the purchase of old, worn-out mail coaches; and my uncle, being very fond of coaches, old, young, or middle-aged, all at once took it into his head to step out of his road for no other purpose than to peep between the palings at these mails—about a dozen of which he remembered to have seen, crowded together in a very forlorn and dismantled state, inside.

'My uncle was a very enthusiastic, emphatic sort of person, gentlemen; so, finding that he could not obtain a good peep between the palings he got over them, and sitting himself quietly down on an old axle-tree, began to contemplate the mail coaches with a deal of gravity.

'There might be a dozen of them, or there might be more—my uncle was never quite certain on this point, and being a man of very scrupulous veracity about numbers, didn't like to say—but there they stood, all huddled together in the most desolate condition imaginable. The doors had been torn from their hinges and removed; the linings had been stripped off, only a shred hanging here and there by a rusty nail; the lamps were gone, the poles had long since vanished, the ironwork was rusty, the paint was worn away; the wind whistled through the chinks in the bare woodwork; and the rain, which had collected on the roofs, fell, drop by drop, into the insides with a hollow and melancholy sound. They were the decaying skeletons of departed mails, and in that lonely place, at that time of night, they looked chill and dismal.

'My uncle rested his head upon his hands, and thought of the busy, bustling people who had rattled about, years before, in the old coaches, and were now as silent and changed; he thought of the numbers of people to whom one of these crazy, mouldering vehicles had borne, night after night, for many years, and through all weathers, the anxiously expected intelligence, the eagerly looked-for remittance, the promised assurance of health and safety, the sudden announcement of sickness and death. The merchant, the lover, the wife, the widow, the mother, the schoolboy, the very child who tottered to the door at the postman's knock—how had they all looked forward to the arrival of the old coach. And where were they all now?

'Gentlemen, my uncle used to *say* that he thought all this at the time, but I rather suspect he learned it out of some book afterwards, for he distinctly stated that he fell into a kind of doze, as he sat on the old axle-tree looking at the decayed mail coaches, and that he was suddenly awakened by some deep church bell striking two. Now, my uncle was never a fast thinker, and if he had thought all these things, I am quite certain it would have taken him till full half-past two o'clock at the very least. I am, therefore, decidedly of opinion, gentlemen, that my uncle fell into a kind of doze, without having thought about anything at all.

'Be this as it may, a church bell struck two. My uncle woke, rubbed his eyes, and jumped up in astonishment.

'In one instant, after the clock struck two, the whole of this deserted and quiet spot had become a scene of most extraordinary life and animation. The mail coach doors were on their hinges, the lining was replaced, the ironwork was as good as new, the paint was restored, the lamps were alight; cushions and greatcoats were on every coach-box, porters were thrusting parcels into every boot, guards were stowing away letter-bags, hostlers were dashing pails of water against the renovated wheels; numbers of men were pushing about, fixing poles into every coach; passengers arrived, portmanteaus were handed up, horses were put to; in short, it was perfectly clear that every mail there, was to be off directly. Gentlemen, my uncle opened his eyes so wide at all this, that, to the very last moment of his life, he used to wonder how it fell out that he had ever been able to shut 'em again.

'"Now then!" said a voice, as my uncle felt a hand on his shoulder, "you're booked for one inside. You'd better get in."

'"I booked!" said my uncle, turning round.

'"Yes, certainly."

'My uncle, gentlemen, could say nothing, he was so very much astonished. The queerest thing of all was that although there was such a crowd of persons, and although fresh faces were pouring in, every moment, there was no telling where they came from. They seemed to start up, in some strange manner, from the ground, or the air, and disappear in the same way. When a porter had put his luggage in the coach, and received his fare, he turned round and was gone; and before my uncle had well begun to wonder what had become of him, half a dozen fresh ones started up, and staggered along under the weight of parcels, which seemed big enough to crush them.

'The passengers were all dressed so oddly too! Large, broad-skirted laced coats, with great cuffs and no collars; and wigs, gentlemen—great formal wigs with a tie behind. My uncle could make nothing of it.

'"Now, are you going to get in?" said the person who had addressed my uncle before. He was dressed as a mail guard, with a wig on his head and most enormous cuffs to his coat, and had a lantern in one hand, and a huge blunderbuss in the other, which he was going to stow away in his little arm-chest. "*Are* you going to get in, Jack Martin?" said the guard, holding the lantern to my uncle's face.

'"Hollo!" said my uncle, falling back a step or two. "That's familiar!"

'"It's so on the way-bill," said the guard.

'"Isn't there a 'Mister' before it?" said my uncle. For he felt, gentlemen, that for a guard he didn't know, to call him Jack Martin, was a liberty which the Post Office wouldn't have sanctioned if they had known it.

'"No, there is not," rejoined the guard coolly.

'"Is the fare paid?" inquired my uncle.

'"Of course it is," rejoined the guard.

'"it is, is it?" said my uncle. "Then here goes! Which coach?"

'"This," said the guard, pointing to an old-fashioned Edinburgh and London mail, which had the steps down and the door open. "Stop! Here are the other passengers. Let them get in first."

'As the guard spoke, there all at once appeared, right in front of my uncle, a young gentleman in a powdered wig, and a sky-blue coat trimmed with silver, made very full and broad in the skirts, which were lined with buckram. Tiggin and Welps were in the printed calico and waistcoat piece line, gentlemen, so my uncle knew all the materials at once. He wore knee breeches, and a kind of leggings rolled up over his silk stockings, and shoes with buckles; he had ruffles at his wrists, a three-cornered hat on his head, and a long taper sword by his side. The flaps of his waist-coat came half-way down his thighs, and the ends of his cravat reached to his waist.

'He stalked gravely to the coach door, pulled off his hat, and held it above his head at arm's length, cocking his little finger in the air at the same time, as some affected people do, when they take a cup of tea. Then he drew his feet together, and made a low, grave bow, and then put out his left hand. My uncle was just going to step forward, and shake it heartily, when he perceived that these attentions were directed, not towards him, but to a young lady who just then appeared at the foot of the steps, attired in an old-fashioned green velvet dress with a long waist and stomacher.

'She had no bonnet on her head, gentlemen, which was muffled in a black silk hood, but she looked round for an instant as she prepared to get into the coach, and such a beautiful face as she disclosed, my uncle had never seen—not even in a picture. She got into the coach, holding up her dress with one hand; and as my uncle always said with a round oath, when he told the story, he wouldn't have believed it possible that legs and feet could have been brought to such a state of perfection unless he had seen them with his own eyes.

'But, in this one glimpse of the beautiful face, my uncle saw that the young lady cast an imploring look upon him, and that she appeared terrified and distressed. He noticed, too, that the young fellow in the powdered wig, notwithstanding his show of gallantry, which was all very fine and grand, clasped her tight by the wrist when she got in, and followed himself immediately afterwards. An uncommonly ill-looking fellow, in a close brown wig, and a plum-coloured suit, wearing a very large sword, and boots up to his hips, belonged to the party; and when he sat himself down next to the young lady, who shrank into a corner at his approach, my uncle was confirmed in his original impression that something dark and mysterious was going forward, or, as he always said himself, that "there was a screw loose somewhere." It's quite surprising how quickly he made up his mind to help the lady at any peril, if she needed any help.

'"Death and lightning!" exclaimed the young gentleman, laying his hand upon his sword as my uncle entered the coach.

'"Blood and thunder!" roared the other gentleman. With this, he whipped his sword out, and made a lunge at my uncle without further ceremony. My uncle had no weapon about him, but with great dexterity he snatched the ill-looking gentleman's three-cornered hat from his head, and, receiving the point of his sword right through the crown, squeezed the sides together, and held it tight.

'"Pink him behind!" cried the ill-looking gentleman to his companion, as he struggled to regain his sword.

'"He had better not," cried my uncle, displaying the heel of one of his shoes, in a threatening manner. "I'll kick his brains out, if he has any—, or fracture his skull if he hasn't." Exerting all his strength, at this moment, my uncle wrenched the ill-looking man's sword from his grasp, and flung it clean out of the coach window, upon which the younger gentleman vociferated, "Death and lightning!" again, and laid his hand upon the hilt of his sword, in a very fierce manner, but didn't draw it. Perhaps, gentlemen, as my uncle used to say with a smile, perhaps he was afraid of alarming the lady.

'"Now, gentlemen," said my uncle, taking his seat deliberately, "I don't want to have any death, with or without lightning, in a lady's presence, and we have had quite blood and thundering enough for one journey; so, if you please, we'll sit in our places like quiet insides. Here, guard, pick up that gentleman's carving-knife."

'As quickly as my uncle said the words, the guard appeared at the coach window, with the gentleman's sword in his hand. He held up his lantern, and looked earnestly in my uncle's face, as he handed it in, when, by its light, my uncle saw, to his great surprise, that an immense crowd of mail-coach guards swarmed round the window, every one of whom had his eyes earnestly fixed upon him too. He had never seen such a sea of white faces, red bodies, and earnest eyes, in all his born days.

'"This is the strangest sort of thing I ever had anything to do with," thought my uncle; "allow me to return you your hat, sir."

'The ill-looking gentleman received his three-cornered hat in silence, looked at the hole in the middle with an inquiring air, and finally stuck it on the top of his wig with a solemnity the effect of which was a trifle impaired by his sneezing violently at the moment, and jerking it off again.

'"All right!" cried the guard with the lantern, mounting into his little seat behind. Away they went. My uncle peeped out of the coach window as they emerged from the yard, and observed that the other mails, with coachmen, guards, horses, and passengers, complete, were driving round and round in circles, at a slow trot of about five miles an hour. My uncle burned with indignation, gentlemen. As a commercial man, he felt that the mail-bags were not to be trifled with, and he resolved to memorialise the Post Office on the subject, the very instant he reached London.

'At present, however, his thoughts were occupied with the young lady who sat in the farthest corner of the coach, with her face muffled closely in her hood; the gentleman with the sky-blue coat sitting opposite to her; the other man in the plum-coloured suit, by her side; and both watching her intently. If she so much as rustled the folds of her hood, he could hear the ill-looking man clap his hand upon his sword, and could tell by the other's breathing (it was so dark he couldn't see his face) that he was looking as big as if he were going to devour her at a mouthful. This roused my uncle more and more, and he resolved, come what might, to see the end of it. He had a great admiration for bright eyes, and sweet faces, and pretty legs and feet; in short, he was fond of the whole sex. It runs in our family, gentleman—so am I.

'Many were the devices which my uncle practised, to attract the lady's attention, or at all events, to engage the mysterious gentlemen in conversation. They were all in vain; the gentlemen wouldn't talk, and the lady didn't dare. He thrust his head out of the coach window at intervals, and bawled out to know why they didn't go faster. But he called till he was hoarse; nobody paid the least attention to him. He leaned back in the coach, and thought of the beautiful face, and the feet and legs. This answered better; it whiled away the time, and kept him from wondering where he was going, and how it was that he found himself in such an odd situation. Not that this would have worried him much, anyway —he was a mighty free and easy, roving, devil-may-care sort of person, was my uncle, gentlemen.

'All of a sudden the coach stopped. "Hollo!" said my uncle, "what's in the wind now?"

'"Alight here," said the guard, letting down the steps.

'"Here!" cried my uncle.

'"Here," rejoined the guard.

'"I'll do nothing of the sort," said my uncle.

'"Very well, then stop where you are," said the guard.

'"I will," said my uncle.

'"Do," said the guard.

'The passengers had regarded this colloquy with great attention, and, finding that my uncle was determined not to alight, the younger man squeezed past him, to hand the lady out. At this moment, the ill-looking man was inspecting the hole in the crown of his three-cornered hat. As the young lady brushed past, she dropped one of her gloves into my uncle's hand, and softly whispered, with her lips so close to his face that he felt her warm breath on his nose, the single word "Help!" Gentlemen, my uncle leaped out of the coach at once, with such violence that it rocked on the springs again.

'"Oh! you've thought better of it, have you?" said the guard, when he saw my uncle standing on the ground.

'My uncle looked at the guard for a few seconds, in some doubt whether it wouldn't be better to wrench his blunderbuss from him, fire it in the face of the man with the big sword, knock the rest of the company over the head with the stock, snatch up the young lady, and go off in the smoke. On second thoughts, however, he abandoned this plan, as being a shade too melodramatic in the execution, and followed the two mysterious men, who, keeping the lady between them, were now entering an old house in front of which the coach had stopped. They turned into the passage, and my uncle followed.

'Of all the ruinous and desolate places my uncle had ever beheld, this was the most so. It looked as if it had once been a large house of entertainment; but the roof had fallen in, in many places, and the stairs were steep, rugged, and broken. There was a huge fireplace in the room into which they walked, and the chimney was blackened with smoke; but no warm blaze lighted it up now. The white feathery dust of burned wood was still strewed over the hearth, but the stove was cold, and all was dark and gloomy.

'"Well," said my uncle, as he looked about him, "a mail travelling at the rate of six miles and a half an hour, and stopping for an indefinite time at such a hole as this, is rather an irregular sort of proceeding, I fancy. This shall be made known. I'll write to the papers."

'My uncle said this in a pretty loud voice, and in an open, unreserved sort of manner, with the view of engaging the two strangers in conversation if he could. But, neither of them took any more notice of him than whispering to each other, and scowling at him as they did so. The lady was at the farther end of the room, and once she ventured to wave her hand, as if beseeching my uncle's assistance.

'At length the two strangers advanced a little, and the conversation began in earnest.

'"You don't know this is a private room, I suppose, fellow?" said the gentleman in sky-blue.

'"No, I do not, fellow," rejoined my uncle. "Only, if this is a private room specially ordered for the occasion, I should think the public room must be a *very* comfortable one;" with this, my uncle sat himself down in a high-backed chair, and took such an accurate measure of the gentleman, with his eyes, that Tiggin and Welps could have supplied him with printed calico for a suit, and not an inch too much or too little, from that estimate alone.

'"Quit this room," said both men together, grasping their

swords.

'"Eh?" said my uncle, not at all appearing to comprehend their meaning.

'"Quit the room, or you are a dead man," said the ill-looking fellow with the large sword, drawing it at the same time and flourishing it in the air.

'"Down with him!" cried the gentleman in sky-blue, drawing his sword also, and falling back two or three yards. "Down with him!" The lady gave a loud scream.

'Now, my uncle was always remarkable for great boldness, and great presence of mind. All the time that he had appeared so indifferent to what was going on, he had been looking slily about for some missile or weapon of defence, and at the very instant when the swords were drawn, he espied, standing in the chimney-corner, an old basket-hilted rapier in a rusty scabbard. At one bound, my uncle caught it in his hand, drew it, flourished it gallantly above his head, called aloud to the lady to keep out of the way, hurled the chair at the man in sky-blue, and the scabbard at the man in plum-colour, and taking advantage of the confusion, fell upon them both, pell-mell.

'Gentlemen, there is an old story—none the worse for being true—regarding a fine young Irish gentleman, who being asked if he could play the fiddle, replied he had no doubt he could, but he couldn't exactly say, for certain, because he had never tried. This is not inapplicable to my uncle and his fencing. He had never had a sword in his hand before, except once when he played Richard the Third at a private theatre, upon which occasion it was arranged with Richmond that he was to be run through, from behind, without showing fight at all. But here he was, cutting and slashing with two experienced swordsman, thrusting, and guarding, and poking, and slicing, and acquitting himself in the most manful and dexterous manner possible, although up to that time he had never been aware that he had the least notion of the science. It only shows how true the old saying is, that a man never knows what he can do till he tries, gentlemen.

'The noise of the combat was terrific; each of the three combatants swearing like troopers, and their swords clashing with as much noise as if all the knives and steels in Newport market were rattling together, at the same time. When it was at its very height, the lady (to encourage my uncle most probably) withdrew her hood entirely from her face, and disclosed a countenance of such dazzling beauty, that he would have fought against fifty men, to win one smile from it and die. He had done wonders before, but now he began to powder away like a raving mad giant.

'At this very moment, the gentleman in sky-blue turning round, and seeing the young lady with her face uncovered, vented an exclamation of rage and jealousy, and, turning his weapon against her beautiful bosom, pointed a thrust at her heart, which caused my uncle to utter a cry of apprehension that made the building ring. The lady stepped lightly aside, and snatching the young man's sword from his hand, before he had recovered his balance, drove him to the wall, and running it through him, and the panelling, up to the very hilt, pinned him there, hard and fast. It was a splendid example.

'My uncle, with a loud shout of triumph, and a strength that was irresistible, made his adversary retreat in the same direction, and plunging the old rapier into the very centre of a large red flower in the pattern of his waistcoat, nailed him beside his friend; there they both stood, gentlemen, jerking their arms and legs about in agony, like the toy-shop figures that are moved by a piece of pack-thread. My uncle always said, afterwards, that this was one of the surest means he knew of, for disposing of an enemy; but it was liable to one objection on the ground of expense, inasmuch as it involved the loss of a sword for every man disabled.

'"The mail, the mail!" cried the lady, running up to my uncle and throwing her beautiful arms round his neck; "we may yet escape."

'"May!" cried my uncle; "why, my dear, there's nobody else to kill, is there?" My uncle was rather disappointed, gentlemen, for he thought a little quiet bit of love-making would be agreeable after the slaughtering, if it were only to change the subject.

'"We have not an instant to lose here," said the young lady. "He (pointing to the young gentleman in sky-blue) is the only son of the powerful Marquess of Filletoville." '"Well then, my dear, I'm afraid he'll never come to the title," said my uncle, looking coolly at the young gentleman as he stood fixed up against the wall, in the cockchafer fashion that I have described. "You have cut off the entail, my love."

'"I have been torn from my home and my friends by these villains," said the young lady, her features glowing with indignation. "That wretch would have married me by violence in another hour."

'"Confound his impudence!" said my uncle, bestowing a very contemptuous look on the dying heir of Filletoville.

'"As you may guess from what you have seen," said the young lady, "the party were prepared to murder me if I appealed to any one for assistance. If their accomplices find us here, we are lost. Two minutes hence may be too late. The mail!" With these words, overpowered by her feelings, and the exertion of sticking the young Marquess of Filletoville, she sank into my uncle's arms. My uncle caught her up, and bore her to the house door. There stood the mail, with four long-tailed, flowing-maned, black horses, ready harnessed; but no coachman, no guard, no hostler even, at the horses' heads.

'Gentlemen, I hope I do no injustice to my uncle's memory, when I express my opinion, that although he was a bachelor, he had held some ladies in his arms before this time; I believe, indeed, that he had rather a habit of kissing barmaids; and I know, that in one or two instances, he had been seen by credible witnesses, to hug a landlady in a very perceptible manner. I mention the circumstance, to show what a very uncommon sort of person this beautiful young lady must have been, to have affected my uncle in the way she did; he used to say, that as her long dark hair trailed over his arm, and her beautiful dark eyes fixed themselves upon his face when she recovered, he felt so strange and nervous that his legs trembled beneath him. But who can look in a sweet, soft pair of dark eyes, without feeling queer? I can't, gentlemen. I am afraid to look at some eyes I know, and that's the truth of it.

'"You will never leave me," murmured the young lady.

'"Never," said my uncle. And he meant it too.

'"My dear preserver!" exclaimed the young lady. "My dear, kind, brave preserver!"

'"Don't," said my uncle, interrupting her.

'"Why?" inquired the young lady.

'"Because your mouth looks so beautiful when you speak," rejoined my uncle, "that I'm afraid I shall be rude enough to kiss it."

'The young lady put up her hand as if to caution my uncle not to do so, and said—No, she didn't say anything—she smiled. When you are looking at a pair of the most delicious lips in the world, and see them gently break into a roguish smile—if you are very near them, and nobody else by—you cannot better testify your admiration of their beautiful form and colour than by kissing them at once. My uncle did so, and I honour him for it.

'"Hark!" cried the young lady, starting. "The noise of wheels, and horses!"

'"So it is," said my uncle, listening. He had a good ear for wheels, and the trampling of hoofs; but there appeared to be so many horses and carriages rattling towards them, from a distance, that it was impossible to form a guess at their number. The sound was like that of fifty brakes, with six blood cattle in each.

'"We are pursued!" cried the young lady, clasping her hands. "We are pursued. I have no hope but in you!"

'There was such an expression of terror in her beautiful face, that my uncle made up his mind at once. He lifted her into the coach, told her not to be frightened, pressed his lips to hers once more, and then advising her to draw up the window to keep the cold air out, mounted to the box.

'"Stay, love," cried the young lady.

'"What's the matter?" said my uncle, from the coach-box.

'"I want to speak to you," said the young lady; "only a word. Only one word, dearest."

'"Must I get down?" inquired my uncle. The lady made no answer, but she smiled again. Such a smile, gentlemen! It beat the other one, all to nothing. My uncle descended from his perch in a twinkling.

'"What is it, my dear?" said my uncle, looking in at the coach window. The lady happened to bend forward at the same time, and my uncle thought she looked more beautiful than she had done yet. He was very close to her just then, gentlemen, so he really ought to know.

'"What is it, my dear?" said my uncle.

'"Will you never love anyone but me—never marry any one beside?" said the young lady.

'My uncle swore a great oath that he never would marry anybody else, and the young lady drew in her head, and pulled up the window. He jumped upon the box, squared his elbows, adjusted the ribands, seized the whip which lay on the roof, gave one flick to the off leader, and away went the four long-tailed, flowing-maned black horses, at fifteen good English miles an hour, with the old mail-coach behind them. Whew! How they tore along!

'The noise behind grew louder. The faster the old mail went, the faster came the pursuers—men, horses, dogs, were leagued in the pursuit. The noise was frightful, but, above all, rose the voice of the young lady, urging my uncle on, and shrieking, "Faster! Faster!"

'They whirled past the dark trees, as feathers would be swept before a hurricane. Houses, gates, churches, haystacks, objects of every kind they shot by, with a velocity and noise like roaring waters suddenly let loose. But still the noise of pursuit grew louder, and still my uncle could hear the young lady wildly screaming, "Faster! Faster!"

'My uncle plied whip and rein, and the horses flew onward till they were white with foam; and yet the noise behind increased; and yet the young lady cried, "Faster! Faster!" My uncle gave a loud stamp on the boot in the energy of the moment, and—found that it was gray morning, and he was sitting in the wheelwright's yard, on the box of an old Edinburgh mail, shivering with the cold and wet and stamping his feet to warm them! He got down, and looked eagerly inside for the beautiful young lady. Alas! There was neither door nor seat to the coach. It was a mere shell.

'Of course, my uncle knew very well that there was some mystery in the matter, and that everything had passed exactly as he used to relate it. He remained staunch to the great oath he had sworn to the beautiful young lady, refusing several eligible landladies on her account, and dying a bachelor at last. He always said what a curious thing it was that he should have found out, by such a mere accident as his clambering over the palings, that the ghosts of mail-coaches and horses, guards, coachmen, and passengers, were in the habit of making journeys regularly every night. He used to add, that he believed he was the only living person who had ever been taken as a passenger on one of these excursions. And I think he was right, gentlemen—at least I never heard of any other.'

'I wonder what these ghosts of mail-coaches carry in their bags,' said the landlord, who had listened to the whole story with profound attention.

'The dead letters, of course,' said the bagman.

'Oh, ah! To be sure,' rejoined the landlord. 'I never thought of that.'

The Story of the Goblins who stole a Sexton

A.k.a The Christmas Goblins or
The Goblin and the Gravedigger

In an old abbey town, a long, long while ago there officiated as sexton and gravedigger in the churchyard one Gabriel Grubb. He was an ill conditioned cross-grained, surly fellow, who consorted with nobody but himself and an old wicker-bottle which fitted into his large, deep waistcoat pocket.

A little before twilight one Christmas Eve, Gabriel shouldered his spade, lighted his lantern, and betook himself toward the old churchyard, for he had a grave to finish by next morning, and feeling very low, he thought it might raise his spirits, perhaps, if he went on with his work at once.

He strode along until he turned into the dark lane which led to the churchyard—a nice, gloomy, mournful place into which the towns-people did not care to go except in broad daylight, consequently he was not a little indignant to hear a young urchin roaring out some jolly song about a Merry Christmas. Gabriel waited until the boy came up, then rapped him over the head with his lantern five or six times to teach him to modulate his voice. And as the boy hurried away, with his hand to his head, Gabriel Grubb chuckled to himself and entered the churchyard, locking the gate behind him.

He took off his coat, put down his lantern, and getting into an unfinished grave, worked at it for an hour or so with right good will. But the earth was hardened with the frost, and it was no easy matter to break it up and shovel it out. At any other time this would have made Gabriel very miserable, but he was so pleased at having stopped the small boy's singing that he took little heed of the scanty progress he had made when he had finished work for the night, and looked down into the grave with grim satisfaction, murmuring as he gathered up his things:

Brave lodgings for one, brave lodgings for one,
A few feet of cold earth when life is done.

"Ho! ho!" he laughed, as he set himself down on a flat tombstone, which was a favourite resting-place of his, and drew forth his wicker-bottle. "A coffin at Christmas! A Christmas box. Ho! ho! ho!"

"Ho! ho! ho!" repeated a voice close beside him.

"It was the echoes," said he, raising the bottle to his lips again.

"It was not," said a deep voice.

Gabriel started up and stood rooted to the spot with terror, for his eyes rested on a form that made his blood run cold.

Seated on an upright tombstone close to him was a strange, unearthly figure. He was sitting perfectly still, grinning at Gabriel Grubb with such a grin as only a goblin could call up.

"What do you here on Christmas Eve?" said the goblin, sternly.

"I came to dig a grave, sir," stammered Gabriel.

"What man wanders among graves on such a night as this?" cried the goblin.

"Gabriel Grubb! Gabriel Grubb!" screamed a wild chorus of voices that seemed to fill the churchyard.

"What have you got in that bottle?" said the goblin.

"Hollands, sir," replied the sexton, trembling more than ever, for he had bought it of the smugglers, and he thought his questioner might be in the excise department of the goblins.

"Who drinks Hollands alone, and in a churchyard on such a night as this?"

"Gabriel Grubb! Gabriel Grubb!" exclaimed the wild voices

again.

"And who, then, is our lawful prize?" exclaimed the goblin, raising his voice.

The invisible chorus replied, "Gabriel Grubb! Gabriel Grubb!"

"Well, Gabriel, what do you say to this?" said the goblin, as he grinned a broader grin than before.

The sexton gasped for breath.

"What do you think of this, Gabriel?"

"It's—it's very curious, sir, very curious, sir, and very pretty," replied the sexton, half-dead with fright. "But I think I'll go back and finish my work, sir, if you please."

"Work!" said the goblin, "what work?"

"The grave, sir."

"Oh! the grave, eh? Who makes graves at a time when other men are merry, and takes a pleasure in it?"

Again the voices replied, "Gabriel Grubb! Gabriel Grubb!"

"I'm afraid my friends want you, Gabriel," said the goblin.

"Under favour, sir," replied the horror-stricken sexton, "I don't think they can; they don't know me, sir; I don't think the gentlemen have ever seen me."

"Oh! yes, they have. We know the man who struck the boy in the envious malice of his heart because the boy could be merry and he could not."

Here the goblin gave a loud, shrill laugh which the echoes returned twenty-fold.

"I—I am afraid I must leave you, sir," said the sexton, making an effort to move.

"Leave us!" said the goblin; "ho! ho! ho!"

As the goblin laughed he suddenly darted toward Gabriel, laid his hand upon his collar, and sank with him through the earth. And when he had had time to fetch his breath he found himself in what appeared to be a large cavern, surrounded on all sides by goblins ugly and grim.

"And now," said the king of the goblins, seated in the centre of the room on an elevated seat—his friend of the churchyard-

"show the man of misery and gloom a few of the pictures from our great storehouses."

As the goblin said this a cloud rolled gradually away and disclosed a small and scantily furnished but neat apartment. Little children were gathered round a bright fire, clinging to their mother's gown, or gambolling round her chair. A frugal meal was spread upon the table and an elbow-chair was placed near the fire. Soon the father entered and the children ran to meet him. As he sat down to his meal the mother sat by his side and all seemed happiness and comfort.

"What do you think of that?" said the goblin.

Gabriel murmured something about its being very pretty.

"Show him some more," said the goblin.

At these words, the cloud was dispelled, and a rich and beautiful landscape was disclosed to view—there is just such another, to this day, within half a mile of the old abbey town. The sun shone from out the clear blue sky, the water sparkled beneath his rays, and the trees looked greener, and the flowers more gay, beneath his cheering influence. The water rippled on, with a pleasant sound; the trees rustled In the light wind that murmured among their leaves; the birds sang upon the boughs; and the lark carolled on high her welcome to the morning.

Yes, it was morning; the bright, balmy morning of summer; the minutest leaf, the smallest blade of grass, was instinct with life. The ant crept forth to her daily toil, the butterfly fluttered and basked in the warm rays of the sun; myriads of insects spread their transparent wings, and revelled in their brief but happy existence. Man walked forth, elated with the scene; and all was brightness and splendour.

'You a miserable man!' said the king of the goblins, in I more contemptuous tone than before. And again the king of the goblins gave his leg a flourish; again it descended on the shoulders of the sexton; and again the attendant goblins imitated the example of their chief.

Many a time the cloud went and came, and many a lesson it taught to Gabriel Grub, who, although his shoulders smarted with pain from the frequent applications of the goblins' feet, looked on with an interest that nothing could diminish. He saw that men who worked hard, and earned their scanty bread with lives of labour, were cheerful and happy; and that to the most ignorant, the sweet face of nature was a never-failing source of cheerfulness and joy. He saw those who had been delicately nurtured, and tenderly brought up, cheerful under privations, and superior to suffering that would have crushed many of a rougher grain, because they bore within their own bosoms the materials of happiness, contentment, and peace. He saw that women, the tenderest and most fragile of all God's creatures, were the oftenest superior to sorrow, adversity, and distress; and he saw that it was because they bore, in their own hearts, an inexhaustible well-spring of affection and devotion.

Above all, he saw that men like himself, who snarled at the mirth and cheerfulness of others, were the foulest weeds on the fair surface of the earth; and setting all the good of the world against the evil, he came to the conclusion that it was a very decent and respectable sort of world after all. No sooner had he formed it, than the cloud which closed over the last picture, seemed to settle on his senses, and lull him to repose. One by one, the goblins faded from his sight; and as the last one disappeared, he sunk to sleep.

The day had broken when Gabriel Grub awoke, and found himself lying, at full length on the flat gravestone in the churchyard, with the wicker bottle lying empty by his side, and his coat, spade, and lantern, all well whitened by the last night's frost, scattered on the ground. The stone on which he had first seen the goblin seated, stood bolt upright before him, and the grave at which he had worked, the night before, was not far off.

At first, he began to doubt the reality of his adventures, but the acute pain in his shoulders when he attempted to rise, assured him that the kicking of the goblins was certainly not ideal. He was staggered again, by observing no traces of footsteps in the snow on which the goblins had played at leap-frog with the gravestones, but he speedily accounted for this circumstance when he remembered that, being spirits, they would leave no visible impression behind them.

So, Gabriel Grub got on his feet as well as he could, for the pain in his back; and brushing the frost off his coat, put it on, and turned his face towards the town. But he was an altered man, and he could not bear the thought of returning to a place where his repentance would be scoffed at, and his reformation disbelieved. He hesitated for a few moments; and then turned away to wander where he might, and seek his bread elsewhere.

The lantern, the spade, and the wicker bottle, were found, that day, in the churchyard. There were a great many speculations about the sexton's fate, at first, but it was speedily determined that he had been carried away by the goblins; and there were not wanting some very credible witnesses who had distinctly seen him whisked through the air on the back of a chestnut horse blind of one eye, with the hind-quarters of a lion, and the tail of a bear. At length all this was devoutly believed; and the new sexton used to exhibit to the curious, for a trifling emolument, a good-sized piece of the church weathercock which had been accidentally picked up by himself in the churchyard, a year or two afterwards.

Unfortunately, these stories were somewhat disturbed by the unlooked-for reappearance of Gabriel Grub himself, some ten years afterwards, a ragged, contented, rheumatic old man. He told his story to the clergyman, and also to the mayor; and in course of time it began to be received, as a matter of history, in which form it has continued down to this very day. The believers in the weathercock tale, having misplaced their confidence once, were not easily prevailed upon to part with it again, so they looked as wise as they could, shrugged their shoulders, touched their foreheads, and murmured something about Gabriel Grub having drunk all the Hollands, and then fallen asleep on the flat tombstone; and they affected to explain what he supposed he had witnessed in the goblin's cavern, by saying that he had seen the world, and grown wiser.

But this opinion, which was by no means a popular one at

any time, gradually died off; and be the matter how it may, as Gabriel Grub was afflicted with rheumatism to the end of his days, this story has at least one moral, if it teach no better one—and that is, that if a man turn sulky and drink by himself at Christmas time, he may make up his mind to be not a bit the better for it: let the spirits be never so good, or let them be even at many degrees beyond proof, as those which Gabriel Grub saw in the goblin's cavern.

The True Legend of Prince Bladud

Less than two hundred years ago, on one of the public baths in this city, there appeared an inscription in honour of its mighty founder, the renowned Prince Bladud. That inscription is now erased.

For many hundred years before that time, there had been handed down, from age to age, an old legend, that the illustrious prince being afflicted with leprosy, on his return from reaping a rich harvest of knowledge in Athens, shunned the court of his royal father, and consorted moodily with husbandman and pigs. Among the herd (so said the legend) was a pig of grave and solemn countenance, with whom the prince had a fellow-feeling —for he too was wise—a pig of thoughtful and reserved demeanour; an animal superior to his fellows, whose grunt was terrible, and whose bite was sharp. The young prince sighed deeply as he looked upon the countenance of the majestic swine; he thought of his royal father, and his eyes were bedewed with tears.

This sagacious pig was fond of bathing in rich, moist mud. Not in summer, as common pigs do now, to cool themselves, and did even in those distant ages (which is a proof that the light of civilisation had already begun to dawn, though feebly), but in the cold, sharp days of winter. His coat was ever so sleek, and his complexion so clear, that the prince resolved to essay the purifying qualities of the same water that his friend resorted to. He made the trial. Beneath that black mud, bubbled the hot springs of Bath. He washed, and was cured. Hastening to his father's court, he paid his best respects, and returning quickly hither, founded this city and its famous baths.

He sought the pig with all the ardour of their early friendship —but, alas! the waters had been his death. He had imprudently taken a bath at too high a temperature, and the natural philosopher was no more! He was succeeded by Pliny, who also fell a victim to his thirst for knowledge.

This was the legend. Listen to the true one.

A great many centuries since, there flourished, in great state, the famous and renowned Lud Hudibras, king of Britain. He was a mighty monarch. The earth shook when he walked—he was so very stout. His people basked in the light of his countenance—it was so red and glowing. He was, indeed, every inch a king. And there were a good many inches of him, too, for although he was not very tall, he was a remarkable size round, and the inches that he wanted in height, he made up in circumference. If any degenerate monarch of modern times could be in any way compared with him, I should say the venerable King Cole would be that illustrious potentate.

This good king had a queen, who eighteen years before, had had a son, who was called Bladud. He was sent to a preparatory seminary in his father's dominions until he was ten years old, and was then despatched, in charge of a trusty messenger, to a finishing school at Athens; and as there was no extra charge for remaining during the holidays, and no notice required previous to the removal of a pupil, there he remained for eight long years, at the expiration of which time, the king his father sent the lord chamberlain over, to settle the bill, and to bring him home; which, the lord chamberlain doing, was received with shouts, and pensioned immediately.

When King Lud saw the prince his son, and found he had grown up such a fine young man, he perceived what a grand thing it would be to have him married without delay, so that his children might be the means of perpetuating the glorious race of Lud, down to the very latest ages of the world. With this view, he sent a special embassy, composed of great noblemen who had nothing particular to do, and wanted lucrative employment, to a neighbouring king, and demanded his fair daughter in marriage for his son; stating at the same time that he was anxious to be on the most affectionate terms with his brother and friend, but that if they couldn't agree in arranging this marriage, he should be under the unpleasant necessity of invading his kingdom and putting his eyes out. To this, the other king (who was the weaker of the two) replied that he was very much obliged to his friend and brother for all his goodness and magnanimity, and that his daughter was quite ready to be married, whenever Prince Bladud liked to come and fetch her.

This answer no sooner reached Britain, than the whole nation was transported with joy. Nothing was heard, on all sides, but the sounds of feasting and revelry—except the chinking of money as it was paid in by the people to the collector of the royal treasures, to defray the expenses of the happy ceremony. It was upon this occasion that King Lud, seated on the top of his throne in full council, rose, in the exuberance of his feelings, and commanded the lord chief justice to order in the richest wines and the court minstrels—an act of graciousness which has been, through the ignorance of traditionary historians, attributed to King Cole, in those celebrated lines in which his Majesty is represented as

Calling for his pipe, and calling for his pot,
And calling for his fiddlers three.

Which is an obvious injustice to the memory of King Lud, and a dishonest exaltation of the virtues of King Cole.

But, in the midst of all this festivity and rejoicing, there was one individual present, who tasted not when the sparkling wines were poured forth, and who danced not, when the minstrels played. This was no other than Prince Bladud himself, in honour of whose happiness a whole people were, at that very moment, straining alike their throats and purse-strings. The truth was, that the prince, forgetting the undoubted right of the minister for foreign affairs to fall in love on his behalf, had, contrary to every precedent of policy and diplomacy, already fallen in love on his own account, and privately contracted himself unto the fair daughter of a noble Athenian.

Here we have a striking example of one of the manifold advantages of civilisation and refinement. If the prince had lived in later days, he might at once have married the object of his father's choice, and then set himself seriously to work, to relieve himself of the burden which rested heavily upon him. He might have endeavoured to break her heart by a systematic course of insult and neglect; or, if the spirit of her sex, and a proud consciousness of her many wrongs had upheld her under this ill-treatment, he might have sought to take her life, and so get rid of her effectually. But neither mode of relief suggested itself to Prince Bladud; so he solicited a private audience, and told his father.

It is an old prerogative of kings to govern everything but their passions. King Lud flew into a frightful rage, tossed his crown up to the ceiling, and caught it again—for in those days kings kept their crowns on their heads, and not in the Tower—stamped the ground, rapped his forehead, wondered why his own flesh and blood rebelled against him, and, finally, calling in his guards, ordered the prince away to instant Confinement in a lofty turret; a course of treatment which the kings of old very generally pursued towards their sons, when their matrimonial inclinations did not happen to point to the same quarter as their own.

When Prince Bladud had been shut up in the lofty turret for the greater part of a year, with no better prospect before his bodily eyes than a stone wall, or before his mental vision than prolonged imprisonment, he naturally began to ruminate on a plan of escape, which, after months of preparation, he managed to accomplish; considerately leaving his dinner-knife in the heart of his jailer, lest the poor fellow (who had a family) should be considered privy to his flight, and punished accordingly by the infuriated king.

The monarch was frantic at the loss of his son. He knew not on whom to vent his grief and wrath, until fortunately bethinking himself of the lord chamberlain who had brought him home, he struck off his pension and his head together.

Meanwhile, the young prince, effectually disguised, wandered on foot through his father's dominions, cheered and supported in all his hardships by sweet thoughts of the Athenian maid, who was the innocent cause of his weary trials. One day he stopped to rest in a country village; and seeing that there were gay dances going forward on the green, and gay faces passing to and fro, ventured to inquire of a reveller who stood near him, the reason for this rejoicing.

"Know you not, O stranger," was the reply, "of the recent proclamation of our gracious king?"

"Proclamation! No. What proclamation?" rejoined the prince—for he had travelled along the by and little-frequented ways, and knew nothing of what had passed upon the public roads, such as they were.

"Why," replied the peasant, "the foreign lady that our prince wished to wed, is married to a foreign noble of her own country, and the king proclaims the fact, and a great public festival besides; for now, of course, Prince Bladud will come back and marry the lady his father chose, who they say is as beautiful as the noonday sun. Your health, sir. God save the king!"

'The prince remained to hear no more. He fled from the spot, and plunged into the thickest recesses of a neighbouring wood. On, on, he wandered, night and day; beneath the blazing sun, and the cold pale moon; through the dry heat of noon, and the damp cold of night; in the gray light of morn, and the red glare of eve. So heedless was he of time or object, that being bound for Athens, he wandered as far out of his way as Bath.

There was no city where Bath stands, then. There was no vestige of human habitation, or sign of man's resort, to bear the name; but there was the same noble country, the same broad expanse of hill and dale, the same beautiful channel stealing on, far away, the same lofty mountains which, like the troubles of life, viewed at a distance, and partially obscured by the bright mist of its morning, lose their ruggedness and asperity, and seem all ease and softness. Moved by the gentle beauty of the scene, the prince sank upon the green turf, and bathed his swollen feet in his tears.

"Oh!" said the unhappy Bladud, clasping his hands, and mournfully raising his eyes towards the sky, "would that my wanderings might end here! Would that these grateful tears with which I now mourn hope misplaced, and love despised, might flow in peace for ever!"

The wish was heard. It was in the time of the heathen deities, who used occasionally to take people at their words, with a promptness, in some cases, extremely awkward. The ground opened beneath the prince's feet; he sank into the chasm; and instantaneously it closed upon his head for ever, save where his hot tears welled up through the earth, and where they have continued to gush forth ever since.

It is observable that, to this day, large numbers of elderly ladies and gentlemen who have been disappointed in procuring partners, and almost as many young ones who are anxious to obtain them, repair annually to Bath to drink the waters, from which they derive much strength and comfort. This is most complimentary to the virtue of Prince Bladud's tears, and strongly corroborative of the veracity of this legend.

To be Read at Dusk

One, two, three, four, five. There were five of them.

Five couriers, sitting on a bench outside the convent on the summit of the Great St. Bernard in Switzerland, looking at the remote heights, stained by the setting sun as if a mighty quantity of red wine had been broached upon the mountain top, and had not yet had time to sink into the snow.

This is not my simile. It was made for the occasion by the stoutest courier, who was a German. None of the others took any more notice of it than they took of me, sitting on another bench on the other side of the convent door, smoking my cigar, like them, and—also like them—looking at the reddened snow, and at the lonely shed hard by, where the bodies of belated travellers, dug out of it, slowly wither away, knowing no corruption in that cold region.

The wine upon the mountain top soaked in as we looked; the mountain became white; the sky, a very dark blue; the wind rose; and the air turned piercing cold. The five couriers buttoned their rough coats. There being no safer man to imitate in all such proceedings than a courier, I buttoned mine.

The mountain in the sunset had stopped the five couriers in a conversation. It is a sublime sight, likely to stop conversation. The mountain being now out of the sunset, they resumed. Not that I had heard any part of their previous discourse; for indeed, I had not then broken away from the American gentleman, in the travellers' parlour of the convent, who, sitting with his face to the fire, had undertaken to realise to me the whole progress of events which had led to the accumulation by the Honourable Ananias Dodger of one of the largest acquisitions of dollars ever made in our country.

'My God!' said the Swiss courier, speaking in French, which I do not hold (as some authors appear to do) to be such an all-sufficient excuse for a naughty word, that I have only to write it in that language to make it innocent; 'if you talk of ghosts—'

'But I *don't* talk of ghosts,' said the German.

'Of what then?' asked the Swiss.

'If I knew of what then,' said the German, 'I should probably know a great deal more.'

It was a good answer, I thought, and it made me curious. So, I moved my position to that corner of my bench which was nearest to them, and leaning my back against the convent wall, heard perfectly, without appearing to attend.

'Thunder and lightning!' said the German, warming, 'when a certain man is coming to see you, unexpectedly; and, without his own knowledge, sends some invisible messenger, to put the idea of him into your head all day, what do you call that? When you walk along a crowded street—at Frankfort, Milan, London, Paris—and think that a passing stranger is like your friend Heinrich, and then that another passing stranger is like your friend Heinrich, and so begin to have a strange foreknowledge that presently you'll meet your friend Heinrich—which you do, though you believed him at Trieste—what do you call *that*?'

'It's not uncommon, either,' murmured the Swiss and the other three.

'Uncommon!' said the German. 'It's as common as cherries in the Black Forest. It's as common as maccaroni at Naples. And Naples reminds me! When the old Marchesa Senzanima shrieks at a card-party on the Chiaja—as I heard and saw her, for it happened in a Bavarian family of mine, and I was overlooking the service that evening—I say, when the old Marchesa starts up at the card-table, white through her rouge, and cries, "My sister in Spain is dead! I felt her cold touch on my back!"—and when that sister IS dead at the moment—what do you call that?'

'Or when the blood of San Gennaro liquefies at the request of the clergy—as all the world knows that it does regularly once a-year, in my native city,' said the Neapolitan courier after a pause, with a comical look, 'what do you call that?'

'*That*!' cried the German. 'Well, I think I know a name for that.'

'Miracle?' said the Neapolitan, with the same sly face.

The German merely smoked and laughed; and they all smoked and laughed.

'Bah!' said the German, presently. 'I speak of things that really do happen. When I want to see the conjurer, I pay to see a professed one, and have my money's worth. Very strange things do happen without ghosts. Ghosts! Giovanni Baptista, tell your story of the English bride. There's no ghost in that, but something full as strange. Will any man tell me what?'

As there was a silence among them, I glanced around. He whom I took to be Baptista was lighting a fresh cigar. He presently went on to speak. He was a Genoese, as I judged.

'The story of the English bride?' said he. 'Basta! one ought not to call so slight a thing a story. Well, it's all one. But it's true. Observe me well, gentlemen, it's true. That which glitters is not always gold; but what I am going to tell, is true.'

He repeated this more than once.

Ten years ago, I took my credentials to an English gentleman at Long's Hotel, in Bond Street, London, who was about to travel—it might be for one year, it might be for two. He approved of them; likewise of me. He was pleased to make inquiry. The testimony that he received was favourable. He engaged me by the six months, and my entertainment was generous.

He was young, handsome, very happy. He was enamoured of a fair young English lady, with a sufficient fortune, and they were going to be married. It was the wedding-trip, in short, that we were going to take. For three months' rest in the hot weather (it was early summer then) he had hired an old place on the Riviera, at an easy distance from my city, Genoa, on the road to Nice. Did I know that place? Yes; I told him I knew it well. It was an old palace with great gardens. It was a little bare, and it was a little dark and gloomy, being close surrounded by trees; but it was spacious, ancient, grand, and on the seashore. He said it had been so described to him exactly, and he was well pleased that I knew it. For its being a little bare of furniture, all such places were. For its being a little gloomy, he had hired it principally for the gardens, and he and my mistress would pass the summer weather in their shade.

'So all goes well, Baptista?' said he.

'Indubitably, *signore*; very well.'

We had a travelling chariot for our journey, newly built for us, and in all respects complete. All we had was complete; we wanted for nothing. The marriage took place. They were happy. I was happy, seeing all so bright, being so well situated, going to my own city, teaching my language in the rumble to the maid, *la bella* Carolina, whose heart was gay with laughter: who was young and rosy.

The time flew. But I observed—listen to this, I pray! (and here the courier dropped his voice)—I observed my mistress sometimes brooding in a manner very strange; in a frightened manner; in an unhappy manner; with a cloudy, uncertain alarm upon her. I think that I began to notice this when I was walking up hills by the carriage side, and master had gone on in front. At any rate, I remember that it impressed itself upon my mind one evening in the South of France, when she called to me to call master back; and when he came back, and walked for a long way, talking encouragingly and affectionately to her, with his hand upon the open window, and hers in it. Now and then, he laughed in a merry way, as if he were bantering her out of something. By-and-by, she laughed, and then all went well again.

It was curious. I asked *la bella* Carolina, the pretty little one, Was mistress unwell?—No.—Out of spirits?—No.—Fearful of bad roads, or brigands?—No. And what made it more mysterious was, the pretty little one would not look at me in giving answer, but *would* look at the view.

But, one day she told me the secret.

'If you must know,' said Carolina, 'I find, from what I have overheard, that mistress is haunted.'

'How haunted?'

'By a dream.'

'What dream?'

'By a dream of a face. For three nights before her marriage, she saw a face in a dream—always the same face, and only One.'

'A terrible face?'

'No. The face of a dark, remarkable-looking man, in black, with black hair and a grey moustache—a handsome man except for a reserved and secret air. Not a face she ever saw, or at all like a face she ever saw. Doing nothing in the dream but looking at her fixedly, out of darkness.'

'Does the dream come back?'

'Never. The recollection of it is all her trouble.'

'And why does it trouble her?'

Carolina shook her head.

'That's master's question,' said *la bella*. 'She don't know. She wonders why, herself. But I heard her tell him, only last night, that if she was to find a picture of that face in our Italian house (which she is afraid she will) she did not know how she could ever bear it.'

Upon my word I was fearful after this (said the Genoese courier) of our coming to the old *palazzo*, lest some such ill-starred picture should happen to be there. I knew there were many there; and, as we got nearer and nearer to the place, I wished the whole gallery in the crater of Vesuvius. To mend the matter, it was a stormy dismal evening when we, at last, approached that part of the Riviera. It thundered; and the thunder of my city and its environs, rolling among the high hills, is very loud. The lizards ran in and out of the chinks in the broken stone wall of the garden, as if they were frightened; the frogs bubbled and croaked their loudest; the sea-wind moaned, and the wet trees dripped; and the lightning—body of San Lorenzo, how it lightened!

We all know what an old palace in or near Genoa is—how time and the sea air have blotted it—how the drapery painted on the outer walls has peeled off in great flakes of plaster—how the lower windows are darkened with rusty bars of iron—how the courtyard is overgrown with grass—how the outer buildings are dilapidated—how the whole pile seems devoted to ruin. Our *palazzo* was one of the true kind. It had been shut up close for months. Months?—years!—it had an earthy smell, like a tomb.

The scent of the orange trees on the broad back terrace, and of the lemons ripening on the wall, and of some shrubs that grew around a broken fountain, had got into the house somehow, and had never been able to get out again. There was, in every room, an aged smell, grown faint with confinement. It pined in all the cupboards and drawers. In the little rooms of communication between great rooms, it was stifling. If you turned a picture—to come back to the pictures—there it still was, clinging to the wall behind the frame, like a sort of bat.

The lattice-blinds were close shut, all over the house. There were two ugly, grey old women in the house, to take care of it; one of them with a spindle, who stood winding and mumbling in the doorway, and who would as soon have let in the devil as the air. Master, mistress, *la bella* Carolina, and I, went all through the *palazzo*. I went first, though I have named myself last, opening the windows and the lattice-blinds, and shaking down on myself splashes of rain, and scraps of mortar, and now and then a dozing mosquito, or a monstrous, fat, blotchy, Genoese spider.

When I had let the evening light into a room, master, mistress, and *la bella* Carolina, entered. Then, we looked round at all the pictures, and I went forward again into another room. Mistress secretly had great fear of meeting with the likeness of that face—we all had; but there was no such thing. The Madonna and Bambino, San Francisco, San Sebastiano, Venus, Santa Caterina, Angels, Brigands, Friars, Temples at Sunset, Battles, White Horses, Forests, Apostles, Doges, all my old acquaintances many times repeated?—yes. Dark, handsome man in black, reserved and secret, with black hair and grey moustache, looking fixedly at mistress out of darkness?—no.

At last we got through all the rooms and all the pictures, and came out into the gardens. They were pretty well kept, being rented by a gardener, and were large and shady. In one place there was a rustic theatre, open to the sky; the stage a green slope; the coulisses, three entrances upon a side, sweet-smelling leafy screens. Mistress moved her bright eyes, even there, as if she looked to see the face come in upon the scene; but all was well.

'Now, Clara,' master said, in a low voice, 'you see that it is nothing? You are happy.'

Mistress was much encouraged. She soon accustomed herself to that grim *palazzo*, and would sing, and play the harp, and copy the old pictures, and stroll with master under the green trees and vines all day. She was beautiful. He was happy. He would laugh and say to me, mounting his horse for his morning ride before the heat:

'All goes well, Baptista!'

'Yes, *signore*, thank God, very well.'

We kept no company. I took *la bella* to the Duomo and Annunciata, to the Cafe, to the Opera, to the village Festa, to the Public Garden, to the Day Theatre, to the Marionetti. The pretty little one was charmed with all she saw. She learnt Italian—heavens! miraculously! Was mistress quite forgetful of that dream? I asked Carolina sometimes. Nearly, said *la bella*—almost. It was wearing out.

One day master received a letter, and called me.

'Baptista!'

'*Signore*!'

'A gentleman who is presented to me will dine here today. He is called the Signor Dellombra. Let me dine like a prince.'

It was an odd name. I did not know that name. But, there had been many noblemen and gentlemen pursued by Austria on political suspicions, lately, and some names had changed. Perhaps this was one. *Altro*! Dellombra was as good a name to me as another.

When the Signor Dellombra came to dinner (said the Genoese courier in the low voice, into which he had subsided once before), I showed him into the reception-room, the great *sala* of the old *palazzo*. Master received him with cordiality, and presented him to mistress. As she rose, her face changed, she gave a cry, and fell upon the marble floor.

Then, I turned my head to the Signor Dellombra, and saw that he was dressed in black, and had a reserved and secret air, and was a dark, remarkable-looking man, with black hair and a grey moustache.

Master raised mistress in his arms, and carried her to her own room, where I sent *la bella* Carolina straight. *La bella* told me afterwards that mistress was nearly terrified to death, and that she wandered in her mind about her dream, all night.

Master was vexed and anxious—almost angry, and yet full of solicitude. The Signor Dellombra was a courtly gentleman, and spoke with great respect and sympathy of mistress's being so ill. The African wind had been blowing for some days (they had told him at his hotel of the Maltese Cross), and he knew that it was often hurtful. He hoped the beautiful lady would recover soon. He begged permission to retire, and to renew his visit when he should have the happiness of hearing that she was better. Master would not allow of this, and they dined alone.

He withdrew early. Next day he called at the gate, on horseback, to inquire for mistress. He did so two or three times in that week.

What I observed myself, and what *la bella* Carolina told me, united to explain to me that master had now set his mind on curing mistress of her fanciful terror. He was all kindness, but he was sensible and firm. He reasoned with her, that to encourage such fancies was to invite melancholy, if not madness. That it rested with herself to be herself. That if she once resisted her strange weakness, so successfully as to receive the Signor Dellombra as an English lady would receive any other guest, it was forever conquered. To make an end, the *signore* came again, and mistress received him without marked distress (though with constraint and apprehension still), and the evening passed serenely. Master was so delighted with this change, and so anxious to confirm it, that the Signor Dellombra became a constant guest. He was accomplished in pictures, books, and music; and his society, in any grim *palazzo*, would have been welcome.

I used to notice, many times, that mistress was not quite recovered. She would cast down her eyes and droop her head, before the Signor Dellombra, or would look at him with a terrified and fascinated glance, as if his presence had some evil influence or power upon her. Turning from her to him, I used to see him in the shaded gardens, or the large half-lighted *sala*, looking, as I might say, 'fixedly upon her out of darkness.' But, truly, I had not forgotten *la bella* Carolina's words describing the face in the dream.

After his second visit I heard master say:

'Now, see, my dear Clara, it's over! Dellombra has come and gone, and your apprehension is broken like glass.'

'Will he—will he ever come again?' asked mistress.

'Again? Why, surely, over and over again! Are you cold?' (she shivered).

'No, dear—but—he terrifies me: are you sure that he need come again?'

'The surer for the question, Clara!' replied master, cheerfully.

But, he was very hopeful of her complete recovery now, and grew more and more so every day. She was beautiful. He was happy.

'All goes well, Baptista?' he would say to me again.

'Yes, *signore*, thank God; very well.'

We were all (said the Genoese courier, constraining himself to speak a little louder), we were all at Rome for the Carnival. I had been out, all day, with a Sicilian, a friend of mine, and a courier, who was there with an English family. As I returned at night to our hotel, I met the little Carolina, who never stirred from home alone, running distractedly along the Corso.

'Carolina! What's the matter?'

'O Baptista! O, for the Lord's sake! where is my mistress?'

'Mistress, Carolina?'

'Gone since morning—told me, when master went out on

his day's journey, not to call her, for she was tired with not resting in the night (having been in pain), and would lie in bed until the evening; then get up refreshed. She is gone!—she is gone! Master has come back, broken down the door, and she is gone! My beautiful, my good, my innocent mistress!'

The pretty little one so cried, and raved, and tore herself that I could not have held her, but for her swooning on my arm as if she had been shot. Master came up—in manner, face, or voice, no more the master that I knew, than I was he. He took me (I laid the little one upon her bed in the hotel, and left her with the chamber-women), in a carriage, furiously through the darkness, across the desolate Campagna. When it was day, and we stopped at a miserable post-house, all the horses had been hired twelve hours ago, and sent away in different directions. Mark me! by the Signor Dellombra, who had passed there in a carriage, with a frightened English lady crouching in one corner.

I never heard (said the Genoese courier, drawing a long breath) that she was ever traced beyond that spot. All I know is, that she vanished into infamous oblivion, with the dreaded face beside her that she had seen in her dream.

'What do you call *that*?' said the German courier, triumphantly. 'Ghosts! There are no ghosts *there*! What do you call this, that I am going to tell you? Ghosts! There are no ghosts *here*!'

I took an engagement once (pursued the German courier) with an English gentleman, elderly and a bachelor, to travel through my country, my Fatherland. He was a merchant who traded with my country and knew the language, but who had never been there since he was a boy—as I judge, some sixty years before.

His name was James, and he had a twin-brother John, also a bachelor. Between these brothers there was a great affection. They were in business together, at Goodman's Fields, but they did not live together. Mr. James dwelt in Poland Street, turning out of Oxford Street, London; Mr. John resided by Epping Forest.

Mr. James and I were to start for Germany in about a week.

The exact day depended on business. Mr. John came to Poland Street (where I was staying in the house), to pass that week with Mr. James. But, he said to his brother on the second day, 'I don't feel very well, James. There's not much the matter with me; but I think I am a little gouty. I'll go home and put myself under the care of my old housekeeper, who understands my ways. If I get quite better, I'll come back and see you before you go. If I don't feel well enough to resume my visit where I leave it off, why *you* will come and see me before you go.' Mr. James, of course, said he would, and they shook hands—both hands, as they always did—and Mr. John ordered out his old-fashioned chariot and rumbled home.

It was on the second night after that—that is to say, the fourth in the week—when I was awoke out of my sound sleep by Mr. James coming into my bedroom in his flannel-gown, with a lighted candle. He sat upon the side of my bed, and looking at me, said:

'Wilhelm, I have reason to think I have got some strange illness upon me.'

I then perceived that there was a very unusual expression in his face.

'Wilhelm,' said he, 'I am not afraid or ashamed to tell you what I might be afraid or ashamed to tell another man. You come from a sensible country, where mysterious things are inquired into and are not settled to have been weighed and measured—or to have been unweighable and unmeasurable—or in either case to have been completely disposed of, for all time-ever so many years ago. I have just now seen the phantom of my brother.'

I confess (said the German courier) that it gave me a little tingling of the blood to hear it.

'I have just now seen,' Mr. James repeated, looking full at me, that I might see how collected he was, 'the phantom of my brother John. I was sitting up in bed, unable to sleep, when it came into my room, in a white dress, and regarding me earnestly, passed up to the end of the room, glanced at some papers on my writing-desk, turned, and, still looking earnestly at me as it passed the bed, went out at the door. Now, I am not in the least mad, and am not in the least disposed to invest that phantom with any external existence out of myself. I think it is a warning to me that I am ill; and I think I had better be bled.'

I got out of bed directly (said the German courier) and began to get on my clothes, begging him not to be alarmed, and telling him that I would go myself to the doctor. I was just ready, when we heard a loud knocking and ringing at the street door. My room being an attic at the back, and Mr. James's being the second-floor room in the front, we went down to his room, and put up the window, to see what was the matter.

'Is that Mr. James?' said a man below, falling back to the opposite side of the way to look up.

'It is,' said Mr. James, 'and you are my brother's man, Robert.'

'Yes, Sir. I am sorry to say, Sir, that Mr. John is ill. He is very bad, Sir. It is even feared that he may be lying at the point of death. He wants to see you, Sir. I have a chaise here. Pray come to him. Pray lose no time.'

Mr. James and I looked at one another. 'Wilhelm,' said he, 'this is strange. I wish you to come with me!' I helped him to dress, partly there and partly in the chaise; and no grass grew under the horses' iron shoes between Poland Street and the Forest.

Now, mind! (said the German courier) I went with Mr. James into his brother's room, and I saw and heard myself what follows.

His brother lay upon his bed, at the upper end of a long bedchamber. His old housekeeper was there, and others were there: I think three others were there, if not four, and they had been with him since early in the afternoon. He was in white, like the figure—necessarily so, because he had his night-dress on. He looked like the figure—necessarily so, because he looked earnestly at his brother when he saw him come into the room.

But, when his brother reached the bedside, he slowly raised himself in bed, and looking full upon him, said these words:

'James, you have seen me before, Tonight—and you know it!'

And so died!

I waited, when the German courier ceased, to hear something said of this strange story. The silence was unbroken. I looked round, and the five couriers were gone: so noiselessly that the ghostly mountain might have absorbed them into its eternal snows. By this time, I was by no means in a mood to sit alone in that awful scene, with the chill air coming solemnly upon me—or, if I may tell the truth, to sit alone anywhere. So I went back into the convent-parlour, and, finding the American gentleman still disposed to relate the biography of the Honourable Ananias Dodger, heard it all out.

Trial for Murder

A.k.a. To be Taken With a Pinch of Salt

I have always noticed a prevalent want of courage, even among persons of superior intelligence and culture, as to imparting their own psychological experiences when those have been of a strange sort. Almost all men are afraid that what they could relate in such wise would find no parallel or response in a listener's internal life, and might be suspected or laughed at. A truthful traveller, who should have seen some extraordinary creature in the likeness of a sea-serpent, would have no fear of mentioning it; but the same traveller, having had some singular presentiment, impulse, vagary of thought, vision (so-called), dream, or other remarkable mental impression, would hesitate considerably before he would own to it.

To this reticence I attribute much of the obscurity in which such subjects are involved. We do not habitually communicate our experiences of these subjective things as we do our experiences of objective creation. The consequence is, that the general stock of experience in this regard appears exceptional, and really is so, in respect of being miserably imperfect.

In what I am going to relate, I have no intention of setting up, opposing, or supporting, any theory whatever. I know the history of the Bookseller of Berlin, I have studied the case of the wife of a late Astronomer Royal as related by Sir David Brewster, and I have followed the minutest details of a much more remarkable case of Spectral Illusion occurring within my private circle of friends. It may be necessary to state as to this last, that the sufferer (a lady) was in no degree, however distant, related to me. A mistaken assumption on that head might suggest an explanation of a part of my own case,—but only a part,—which would be wholly without foundation. It cannot be referred to my inheritance of any developed peculiarity, nor had I ever before any at all similar experience, nor have I ever had any at all similar experience since.

It does not signify how many years ago, or how few, a certain murder was committed in England, which attracted great attention. We hear more than enough of murderers as they rise in succession to their atrocious eminence, and I would bury the memory of this particular brute, if I could, as his body was buried, in Newgate Jail. I purposely abstain from giving any direct clue to the criminal's individuality.

When the murder was first discovered, no suspicion fell—or I ought rather to say, for I cannot be too precise in my facts, it was nowhere publicly hinted that any suspicion fell—on the man who was afterwards brought to trial. As no reference was at that time made to him in the newspapers, it is obviously impossible that any description of him can at that time have been given in the newspapers. It is essential that this fact be remembered.

Unfolding at breakfast my morning paper, containing the account of that first discovery, I found it to be deeply interesting, and I read it with close attention. I read it twice, if not three times. The discovery had been made in a bedroom, and, when I laid down the paper, I was aware of a flash—rush—flow—I do not know what to call it,—no word I can find is satisfactorily descriptive,—in which I seemed to see that bedroom passing through my room, like a picture impossibly painted on a running river. Though almost instantaneous in its passing, it was perfectly clear; so clear that I distinctly, and with a sense of relief, observed the absence of the dead body from the bed.

It was in no romantic place that I had this curious sensation, but in chambers in Piccadilly, very near to the corner of St. James's Street. It was entirely new to me. I was in my easy-chair at the moment, and the sensation was accompanied with a peculiar shiver which started the chair from its position. (But it is to be noted that the chair ran easily on castors.) I went to one of the windows (there are two in the room, and the room is on the second floor) to refresh my eyes with the moving objects down in Piccadilly. It was a bright autumn morning, and the street was sparkling and cheerful. The wind was high. As I looked out, it brought down from the Park a quantity of fallen leaves, which a gust took, and whirled into a spiral pillar.

As the pillar fell and the leaves dispersed, I saw two men on the opposite side of the way, going from West to East. They were one behind the other. The foremost man often looked back over his shoulder. The second man followed him, at a distance of some thirty paces, with his right hand menacingly raised. First, the singularity and steadiness of this threatening gesture in so public a thoroughfare attracted my attention; and next, the more remarkable circumstance that nobody heeded it. Both men threaded their way among the other passengers with a smoothness hardly consistent even with the action of walking on a pavement; and no single creature, that I could see, gave them place, touched them, or looked after them.

In passing before my windows, they both stared up at me. I saw their two faces very distinctly, and I knew that I could recognise them anywhere. Not that I had consciously noticed anything very remarkable in either face, except that the man who went first had an unusually lowering appearance, and that the face of the man who followed him was of the colour of impure wax.

I am a bachelor, and my valet and his wife constitute my whole establishment. My occupation is in a certain Branch Bank, and I wish that my duties as head of a Department were as light as they are popularly supposed to be. They kept me in town that autumn, when I stood in need of change. I was not ill, but I was not well. My reader is to make the most that can be reasonably made of my feeling jaded, having a depressing sense upon me of a monotonous life, and being "slightly dyspeptic." I am assured by my renowned doctor that my real state of health at that time justifies no stronger description, and I quote his own from his written answer to my request for it.

As the circumstances of the murder, gradually unravelling, took stronger and stronger possession of the public mind, I kept them away from mine by knowing as little about them as was possible in the midst of the universal excitement. But I knew that a verdict of Wilful Murder had been found against the suspected murderer, and that he had been committed to Newgate for trial. I also knew that his trial had been postponed over one Sessions of the Central Criminal Court, on the ground of general prejudice and want of time for the preparation of the defence. I may further have known, but I believe I did not, when, or about when, the Sessions to which his trial stood postponed would come on.

My sitting-room, bedroom, and dressing-room, are all on one floor. With the last there is no communication but through the bedroom. True, there is a door in it, once communicating with the staircase; but a part of the fitting of my bath has been—and had then been for some years—fixed across it. At the same period, and as a part of the same arrangement,—the door had been nailed up and canvased over.

I was standing in my bedroom late one night, giving some directions to my servant before he went to bed. My face was towards the only available door of communication with the dressing-room, and it was closed. My servant's back was towards that door. While I was speaking to him, I saw it open, and a man look in, who very earnestly and mysteriously beckoned to me. That man was the man who had gone second of the two along Piccadilly, and whose face was of the colour of impure wax.

The figure, having beckoned, drew back, and closed the door. With no longer pause than was made by my crossing the bedroom, I opened the dressing-room door, and looked in. I had a lighted candle already in my hand. I felt no inward expectation of seeing the figure in the dressing-room, and I did not see it there.

Conscious that my servant stood amazed, I turned round to

him, and said: "Derrick, could you believe that in my cool senses I fancied I saw a—" As I there laid my hand upon his breast, with a sudden start he trembled violently, and said, "O Lord, yes, sir! A dead man beckoning!"

Now I do not believe that this John Derrick, my trusty and attached servant for more than twenty years, had any impression whatever of having seen any such figure, until I touched him. The change in him was so startling, when I touched him, that I fully believe he derived his impression in some occult manner from me at that instant.

I bade John Derrick bring some brandy, and I gave him a dram, and was glad to take one myself. Of what had preceded that night's phenomenon, I told him not a single word. Reflecting on it, I was absolutely certain that I had never seen that face before, except on the one occasion in Piccadilly. Comparing its expression when beckoning at the door with its expression when it had stared up at me as I stood at my window, I came to the conclusion that on the first occasion it had sought to fasten itself upon my memory, and that on the second occasion it had made sure of being immediately remembered.

I was not very comfortable that night, though I felt a certainty, difficult to explain, that the figure would not return. At daylight I fell into a heavy sleep, from which I was awakened by John Derrick's coming to my bedside with a paper in his hand.

This paper, it appeared, had been the subject of an altercation at the door between its bearer and my servant. It was a summons to me to serve upon a Jury at the forthcoming Sessions of the Central Criminal Court at the Old Bailey. I had never before been summoned on such a Jury, as John Derrick well knew. He believed—I am not certain at this hour whether with reason or otherwise—that that class of Jurors were customarily chosen on a lower qualification than mine, and he had at first refused to accept the summons. The man who served it had taken the matter very coolly. He had said that my attendance or non-attendance was nothing to him; there the summons was; and I should deal with it at my own peril, and not at his.

For a day or two I was undecided whether to respond to this call, or take no notice of it. I was not conscious of the slightest mysterious bias, influence, or attraction, one way or other. Of that I am as strictly sure as of every other statement that I make here. Ultimately I decided, as a break in the monotony of my life, that I would go.

The appointed morning was a raw morning in the month of November. There was a dense brown fog in Piccadilly, and it became positively black and in the last degree oppressive East of Temple Bar. I found the passages and staircases of the Court-House flaringly lighted with gas, and the Court itself similarly illuminated. I *think* that, until I was conducted by officers into the Old Court and saw its crowded state, I did not know that the Murderer was to be tried that day. I *think* that, until I was so helped into the Old Court with considerable difficulty, I did not know into which of the two Courts sitting my summons would take me. But this must not be received as a positive assertion, for I am not completely satisfied in my mind on either point.

I took my seat in the place appropriated to Jurors in waiting, and I looked about the Court as well as I could through the cloud of fog and breath that was heavy in it. I noticed the black vapour hanging like a murky curtain outside the great windows, and I noticed the stifled sound of wheels on the straw or tan that was littered in the street; also, the hum of the people gathered there, which a shrill whistle, or a louder song or hail than the rest, occasionally pierced.

Soon afterwards the Judges, two in number, entered, and took their seats. The buzz in the Court was awfully hushed. The direction was given to put the Murderer to the bar. He appeared there. And in that same instant I recognised in him the first of the two men who had gone down Piccadilly.

If my name had been called then, I doubt if I could have answered to it audibly. But it was called about sixth or eighth in the panel, and I was by that time able to say, "Here!" Now, observe. As I stepped into the box, the prisoner, who had been looking on attentively, but with no sign of concern, became violently agitated, and beckoned to his attorney. The prisoner's wish to challenge me was so manifest, that it occasioned a pause, during which the attorney, with his hand upon the dock, whispered with his client, and shook his head. I afterwards had it from that gentleman, that the prisoner's first affrighted words to him were, "*At all hazards, challenge that man*!" But that, as he would give no reason for it, and admitted that he had not even known my name until he heard it called and I appeared, it was not done.

Both on the ground already explained, that I wish to avoid reviving the unwholesome memory of that Murderer, and also because a detailed account of his long trial is by no means indispensable to my narrative, I shall confine myself closely to such incidents in the ten days and nights during which we, the Jury, were kept together, as directly bear on my own curious personal experience. It is in that, and not in the Murderer, that I seek to interest my reader. It is to that, and not to a page of the Newgate Calendar, that I beg attention.

I was chosen Foreman of the Jury. On the second morning of the trial, after evidence had been taken for two hours (I heard the church clocks strike), happening to cast my eyes over my brother jurymen, I found an inexplicable difficulty in counting them. I counted them several times, yet always with the same difficulty. In short, I made them one too many.

I touched the brother jurymen whose place was next me, and I whispered to him, "Oblige me by counting us." He looked surprised by the request, but turned his head and counted. "Why," says he, suddenly, "we are Thirt-; but no, it's not possible. No. We are twelve."

According to my counting that day, we were always right in detail, but in the gross we were always one too many. There was no appearance—no figure—to account for it; but I had now an inward foreshadowing of the figure that was surely coming.

The Jury were housed at the London Tavern. We all slept in one large room on separate tables, and we were constantly in the charge and under the eye of the officer sworn to hold us in safe-keeping. I see no reason for suppressing the real name of that officer. He was intelligent, highly polite, and obliging, and (I was glad to hear) much respected in the City. He had an agreeable presence, good eyes, enviable black whiskers, and a fine sonorous voice. His name was Mr. Harker.

When we turned into our twelve beds at night, Mr. Harker's bed was drawn across the door. On the night of the second day, not being disposed to lie down, and seeing Mr. Harker sitting on his bed, I went and sat beside him, and offered him a pinch of snuff. As Mr. Harker's hand touched mine in taking it from my box, a peculiar shiver crossed him, and he said, "Who is this?"

Following Mr. Harker's eyes, and looking along the room, I saw again the figure I expected,—the second of the two men who had gone down Piccadilly. I rose, and advanced a few steps; then stopped, and looked round at Mr. Harker. He was quite unconcerned, laughed, and said in a pleasant way, "I thought for a moment we had a thirteenth juryman, without a bed. But I see it is the moonlight."

Making no revelation to Mr. Harker, but inviting him to take a walk with me to the end of the room, I watched what the figure did. It stood for a few moments by the bedside of each of my eleven brother jurymen, close to the pillow. It always went to the right-hand side of the bed, and always passed out crossing the foot of the next bed. It seemed, from the action of the head, merely to look down pensively at each recumbent figure. It took no notice of me, or of my bed, which was that nearest to Mr. Harker's. It seemed to go out where the moonlight came in, through a high window, as by an aerial flight of stairs.

Next morning at breakfast, it appeared that everybody present had dreamed of the murdered man last night, except myself and Mr. Harker.

I now felt as convinced that the second man who had gone down Piccadilly was the murdered man (so to speak), as if it had been borne into my comprehension by his immediate testimony. But even this took place, and in a manner for which I was not at all prepared.

On the fifth day of the trial, when the case for the prosecution was drawing to a close, a miniature of the murdered man, missing from his bedroom upon the discovery of the deed, and afterwards found in a hiding-place where the Murderer had been seen digging, was put in evidence. Having been identified by the witness under examination, it was handed up to the Bench, and thence handed down to be inspected by the Jury. As an officer in a black gown was making his way with it across to me, the figure of the second man who had gone down Piccadilly impetuously started from the crowd, caught the miniature from the officer, and gave it to me with his own hands, at the same time saying, in a low and hollow tone,—before I saw the miniature, which was in a locket,—"*I was younger then, and my face was not then drained of blood.*"

It also came between me and the brother juryman to whom I would have given the miniature, and between him and the brother juryman to whom he would have given it, and so passed it on through the whole of our number, and back into my possession. Not one of them, however, detected this.

At table, and generally when we were shut up together in Mr. Harker's custody, we had from the first naturally discussed the day's proceedings a good deal. On that fifth day, the case for the prosecution being closed, and we having that side of the question in a completed shape before us, our discussion was more animated and serious. Among our number was a vestryman,—the densest idiot I have ever seen at large,—who met the plainest evidence with the most preposterous objections, and who was sided with by two flabby parochial parasites; all the three impanelled from a district so delivered over to Fever that they ought to have been upon their own trial for five hundred Murders.

When these mischievous blockheads were at their loudest, which was towards midnight, while some of us were already preparing for bed, I again saw the murdered man. He stood grimly behind them, beckoning to me. On my going towards them, and striking into the conversation, he immediately retired. This was the beginning of a separate series of appearances, confined to that long room in which we were confined. Whenever a knot of my brother jurymen laid their heads together, I saw the head of the murdered man among theirs. Whenever their comparison of notes was going against him, he would solemnly and irresistibly beckon to me.

It will be borne in mind that down to the production of the miniature, on the fifth day of the trial, I had never seen the Appearance in Court. Three changes occurred now that we entered on the case for the defence. Two of them I will mention together, first. The figure was now in Court continually, and it never there addressed itself to me, but always to the person who was speaking at the time. For instance: the throat of the murdered man had been cut straight across.

In the opening speech for the defence, it was suggested that the deceased might have cut his own throat. At that very moment, the figure, with its throat in the dreadful condition referred to (this it had concealed before), stood at the speaker's elbow, motioning across and across its windpipe, now with the right hand, now with the left, vigorously suggesting to the speaker himself the impossibility of such a wound having been self-inflicted by either hand. For another instance: a witness to character, a woman, deposed to the prisoner's being the most amiable of mankind. The figure at that instant stood on the floor before her, looking her full in the face, and pointing out the prisoner's evil countenance with an extended arm and an outstretched finger.

The third change now to be added impressed me strongly as the most marked and striking of all. I do not theorise upon it; I accurately state it, and there leave it. Although the Appearance was not itself perceived by those whom it addressed, its coming close to such persons was invariably attended by some trepidation or disturbance on their part. It seemed to me as if it were prevented, by laws to which I was not amenable, from fully revealing itself to others, and yet as if it could invisibly, dumbly, and darkly overshadow their minds.

When the leading counsel for the defence suggested that hypothesis of suicide, and the figure stood at the learned gentleman's elbow, frightfully sawing at its severed throat, it is undeniable that the counsel faltered in his speech, lost for a few seconds the thread of his ingenious discourse, wiped his forehead with his handkerchief, and turned extremely pale. When the witness to character was confronted by the Appearance, her eyes most certainly did follow the direction of its pointed finger, and rest in great hesitation and trouble upon the prisoner's face. Two additional illustrations will suffice. On the eighth day of the trial, after the pause which was every day made early in the afternoon for a few minutes' rest and refreshment, I came back into Court with the rest of the Jury some little time before the return of the Judges.

Standing up in the box and looking about me, I thought the figure was not there, until, chancing to raise my eyes to the gallery, I saw it bending forward, and leaning over a very decent woman, as if to assure itself whether the Judges had resumed their seats or not. Immediately afterwards that woman screamed, fainted, and was carried out. So with the venerable, sagacious, and patient Judge who conducted the trial.

When the case was over, and he settled himself and his papers to sum up, the murdered man, entering by the Judges' door, advanced to his Lordship's desk, and looked eagerly over his shoulder at the pages of his notes which he was turning. A change came over his Lordship's face; his hand stopped; the peculiar shiver, that I knew so well, passed over him; he faltered, "Excuse me, gentlemen, for a few moments. I am somewhat oppressed by the vitiated air;" and did not recover until he had drunk a glass of water.

Through all the monotony of six of those interminable ten days,—the same Judges and others on the bench, the same Murderer in the dock, the same lawyers at the table, the same tones of question and answer rising to the roof of the court, the same scratching of the Judge's pen, the same ushers going in and out, the same lights kindled at the same hour when there had been any natural light of day, the same foggy curtain outside the great windows when it was foggy, the same rain pattering and dripping when it was rainy, the same footmarks of turnkeys and prisoner day after day on the same sawdust, the same keys locking and unlocking the same heavy doors,—through all the wearisome monotony which made me feel as if I had been Foreman of the Jury for a vast cried of time, and Piccadilly had flourished coevally with Babylon, the murdered man never lost one trace of his distinctness in my eyes, nor was he at any moment less distinct than anybody else.

I must not omit, as a matter of fact, that I never once saw the Appearance which I call by the name of the murdered man look at the Murderer. Again and again I wondered, "Why does he not?" But he never did.

Nor did he look at me, after the production of the miniature, until the last closing minutes of the trial arrived. We retired to consider, at seven minutes before ten at night. The idiotic vestryman and his two parochial parasites gave us so much trouble that we twice returned into Court to beg to have certain extracts from the Judge's notes re-read. Nine of us had not the smallest doubt about those passages, neither, I believe, had any one in the Court; the dunder-headed *triumvirate*, having no idea but obstruction, disputed them for that very reason. At length we prevailed, and finally the Jury returned into Court at ten minutes past twelve.

The murdered man at that time stood directly opposite the Jury-box, on the other side of the Court. As I took my place, his eyes rested on me with great attention; he seemed satisfied, and slowly shook a great gray veil, which he carried on his arm for the first time, over his head and whole form. As I gave in our verdict, "Guilty," the veil collapsed, all was gone, and his place was empty.

The Murderer, being asked by the Judge, according to usage, whether he had anything to say before sentence of Death should be passed upon him, indistinctly muttered something which was described in the leading newspapers of the following day as "a few rambling, incoherent, and half-audible words, in which he was understood to complain that he had not had a fair trial, because the Foreman of the Jury was prepossessed against him." The remarkable declaration that he really made was this:

My Lord, I knew I was a doomed man, when the foreman of my jury came into the box. my lord, I knew he would never let me off, because, before I was taken, he somehow got to my bedside in the night, woke me, and put a rope round my neck.

The Ghost of Art

I *am* a bachelor, residing in rather a dreary set of chambers in the Temple. They are situated in a square court of high houses, which would be a complete well, but for the want of water and the absence of a bucket. I live at the top of the house, among the tiles and sparrows. Like the little man in the nursery-story, I live by myself, and all the bread and cheese I get—which is not much—I put upon a shelf. I need scarcely add, perhaps, that I am in love, and that the father of my charming Julia objects to our union.

I mention these little particulars as I might deliver a letter of introduction. The reader is now acquainted with me, and perhaps will condescend to listen to my narrative.

I am naturally of a dreamy turn of mind; and my abundant leisure—for I am called to the Bar—coupled with much lonely listening to the twittering of sparrows, and the pattering of rain, has encouraged that disposition. In my 'top set' I hear the wind howl on a winter night, when the man on the ground floor believes it is perfectly still weather. The dim lamps with which our Honourable Society (supposed to be as yet unconscious of the new discovery called Gas) make the horrors of the staircase visible, deepen the gloom which generally settles on my soul when I go home at night.

I am in the Law, but not of it. I can't exactly make out what it means. I sit in Westminster Hall sometimes (in character) from ten to four; and when I go out of Court, I don't know whether I am standing on my wig or my boots.

It appears to me (I mention this in confidence) as if there were too much talk and too much law—as if some grains of truth were started overboard into a tempestuous sea of chaff.

All this may make me mystical. Still, I am confident that what I am going to describe myself as having seen and heard, I actually did see and hear.

It is necessary that I should observe that I have a great delight in pictures. I am no painter myself, but I have studied pictures and written about them. I have seen all the most famous pictures in the world; my education and reading have been sufficiently general to possess me beforehand with a knowledge of most of the subjects to which a Painter is likely to have recourse; and, although I might be in some doubt as to the rightful fashion of the scabbard of King Lear's sword, for instance, I think I should know King Lear tolerably well, if I happened to meet with him.

I go to all the Modern Exhibitions every season, and of course I revere the Royal Academy. I stand by its forty Academical articles almost as firmly as I stand by the thirty-nine Articles of the Church of England. I am convinced that in neither case could there be, by any rightful possibility, one article more or less.

It is now exactly three years—three years ago, this very month—since I went from Westminster to the Temple, one Thursday afternoon, in a cheap steamboat. The sky was black, when I imprudently walked on board. It began to thunder and lighten immediately afterwards, and the rain poured down in torrents. The deck seeming to smoke with the wet, I went below; but so many passengers were there, smoking too, that I came up again, and buttoning my pea-coat, and standing in the shadow of the paddle-box, stood as upright as I could, and made the best of it.

It was at this moment that I first beheld the terrible Being, who is the subject of my present recollections.

Standing against the funnel, apparently with the intention of drying himself by the heat as fast as he got wet, was a shabby man in threadbare black, and with his hands in his pockets, who fascinated me from the memorable instant when I caught his eye.

Where had I caught that eye before? Who was he? Why did I connect him, all at once, with the Vicar of Wakefield, Alfred the Great, Gil Blas, Charles the Second, Joseph and his Brethren, the Fairy Queen, Tom Jones, the Decameron of Boccaccio, Tam O'Shanter, the Marriage of the Doge of Venice with the Adriatic, and the Great Plague of London? Why, when he bent one leg, and placed one hand upon the back of the seat near him, did my mind associate him wildly with the words, 'Number one hundred and forty-two, Portrait of a gentleman'? Could it be that I was going mad?

I looked at him again, and now I could have taken my affidavit that he belonged to the Vicar of Wakefield's family. Whether he was the Vicar, or Moses, or Mr. Burchill, or the Squire, or a conglomeration of all four, I knew not; but I was impelled to seize him by the throat, and charge him with being, in some fell way, connected with the Primrose blood. He looked up at the rain, and then—oh Heaven!—he became Saint John. He folded his arms, resigning himself to the weather, and I was frantically inclined to address him as the Spectator, and firmly demand to know what he had done with Sir Roger de Coverley.

The frightful suspicion that I was becoming deranged, returned upon me with redoubled force. Meantime, this awful stranger, inexplicably linked to my distress, stood drying himself at the funnel; and ever, as the steam rose from his clothes, diffusing a mist around him, I saw through the ghostly medium all the people I have mentioned, and a score more, sacred and profane.

I am conscious of a dreadful inclination that stole upon me, as it thundered and lightened, to grapple with this man, or demon, and plunge him over the side. But, I constrained myself—I know not how—to speak to him, and in a pause of the storm, I crossed the deck, and said:

'What are you?'

He replied, hoarsely, 'A Model.'

'A what?' said I.

'A Model,' he replied. 'I sets to the profession for a bob a-hour.' (All through this narrative I give his own words, which are indelibly imprinted on my memory.)

The relief which this disclosure gave me, the exquisite delight of the restoration of my confidence in my own sanity, I cannot describe. I should have fallen on his neck, but for the consciousness of being observed by the man at the wheel.

'You then,' said I, shaking him so warmly by the hand, that I wrung the rain out of his coat-cuff, 'are the gentleman whom I have so frequently contemplated, in connection with a high-backed chair with a red cushion, and a table with twisted legs.'

'I am that Model,' he rejoined moodily, 'and I wish I was anything else.'

'Say not so,' I returned. 'I have seen you in the society of many beautiful young women;' as in truth I had, and always (I now remember) in the act of making the most of his legs.

'No doubt,' said he. 'And you've seen me along with varses of flowers, and any number of table-kivers, and antique cabinets, and various gammon.'

'Sir?' said I.

'And various gammon,' he repeated, in a louder voice. 'You might have seen me in armour, too, if you had looked sharp. Blessed if I ha'n't stood in half the suits of armour as ever came out of Pratt's shop: and sat, for weeks together, a-eating nothing, out of half the gold and silver dishes as has ever been lent for the purpose out of Storrses, and Mortimerses, or Garrardses, and Davenportseseses.'

Excited, as it appeared, by a sense of injury, I thought he would never have found an end for the last word. But, at length it rolled sullenly away with the thunder.

'Pardon me,' said I, 'you are a well-favoured, well-made man, and yet—forgive me—I find, on examining my mind, that I associate you with—that my recollection indistinctly makes you, in short—excuse me—a kind of powerful monster.'

'It would be a wonder if it didn't,' he said. 'Do you know what my points are?'

'No,' said I.

'My throat and my legs,' said he. 'When I don't set for a head, I mostly sets for a throat and a pair of legs. Now, granted you was a painter, and was to work at my throat for a week together, I suppose you'd see a lot of lumps and bumps there, that would never be there at all, if you looked at me, complete, instead of only my throat. Wouldn't you?'

'Probably,' said I, surveying him.

'Why, it stands to reason,' said the Model. 'Work another week at my legs, and it'll be the same thing. You'll make 'em out as knotty and as knobby, at last, as if they was the trunks of two old trees. Then, take and stick my legs and throat on to another man's body, and you'll make a reg'lar monster. And that's the way the public gets their reg'lar monsters, every first Monday in May, when the Royal Academy Exhibition opens.'

'You are a critic,' said I, with an air of deference.

'I'm in an uncommon ill humour, if that's it,' rejoined the Model, with great indignation. 'As if it warn't bad enough for a bob a-hour, for a man to be mixing himself up with that there jolly old furniter that one 'ud think the public know'd the very nails in by this time—or to be putting on greasy old 'ats and cloaks, and playing tambourines in the Bay o' Naples, with Vesuvius a smokin' according to pattern in the background, and the wines a bearing wonderful in the middle distance—or to be unpolitely kicking up his legs among a lot o' gals, with no reason whatever in his mind but to show 'em—as if this warn't bad enough, I'm to go and be thrown out of employment too!'

'Surely no!' said I.

'Surely yes,' said the indignant Model. '*But I'll grow one.*'

The gloomy and threatening manner in which he muttered the last words, can never be effaced from my remembrance. My blood ran cold.

I asked of myself, what was it that this desperate Being was resolved to grow. My breast made no response.

I ventured to implore him to explain his meaning. With a scornful laugh, he uttered this dark prophecy:

'*I'll grow one. and, mark my words, it shall haunt you!*'

We parted in the storm, after I had forced half-a-crown on his acceptance, with a trembling hand. I conclude that something supernatural happened to the steamboat, as it bore his reeking figure down the river; but it never got into the papers.

Two years elapsed, during which I followed my profession without any vicissitudes; never holding so much as a motion, of course. At the expiration of that period, I found myself making my way home to the Temple, one night, in precisely such another storm of thunder and lightning as that by which I had been overtaken on board the steamboat—except that this storm, bursting over the town at midnight, was rendered much more awful by the darkness and the hour.

As I turned into my court, I really thought a thunderbolt would fall, and plough the pavement up. Every brick and stone in the place seemed to have an echo of its own for the thunder. The waterspouts were overcharged, and the rain came tearing down from the housetops as if they had been mountain-tops.

Mrs. Parkins, my laundress—wife of Parkins the porter, then newly dead of a dropsy—had particular instructions to place a bedroom candle and a match under the staircase lamp on my landing, in order that I might light my candle there, whenever I came home. Mrs. Parkins invariably disregarding all instructions, they were never there. Thus it happened that on this occasion I groped my way into my sitting-room to find the candle, and came out to light it.

What were my emotions when, underneath the staircase lamp, shining with wet as if he had never been dry since our last meeting, stood the mysterious Being whom I had encountered on the steamboat in a thunderstorm, two years before! His prediction rushed upon my mind, and I turned faint.

'I said I'd do it,' he observed, in a hollow voice, 'and I have done it. May I come in?'

'Misguided creature, what have you done?' I returned.

'I'll let you know,' was his reply, 'if you'll let me in.'

Could it be murder that he had done? And had he been so

successful that he wanted to do it again, at my expense?

I hesitated.

'May I come in?' said he.

I inclined my head, with as much presence of mind as I could command, and he followed me into my chambers. There, I saw that the lower part of his face was tied up, in what is commonly called a Belcher handkerchief. He slowly removed this bandage, and exposed to view a long dark beard, curling over his upper lip, twisting about the corners of his mouth, and hanging down upon his breast.

'What is this?' I exclaimed involuntarily, 'and what have you become?'

'I am the Ghost of Art!' said he.

The effect of these words, slowly uttered in the thunderstorm at midnight, was appalling in the last degree. More dead than alive, I surveyed him in silence.

'The German taste came up,' said he, 'and threw me out of bread. I am ready for the taste now.'

He made his beard a little jagged with his hands, folded his arms, and said,

'Severity!'

I shuddered. It was so severe.

He made his beard flowing on his breast, and, leaning both hands on the staff of a carpet-broom which Mrs. Parkins had left among my books, said:

'Benevolence.'

I stood transfixed. The change of sentiment was entirely in the beard. The man might have left his face alone, or had no face.

The beard did everything.

He lay down, on his back, on my table, and with that action of his head threw up his beard at the chin.

'That's death!' said he.

He got off my table and, looking up at the ceiling, cocked his beard a little awry; at the same time making it stick out before him.

'Adoration, or a vow of vengeance,' he observed.

He turned his profile to me, making his upper lip very bulky with the upper part of his beard.

'Romantic character,' said he.

He looked sideways out of his beard, as if it were an ivy-bush. 'Jealousy,' said he. He gave it an ingenious twist in the air, and informed me that he was carousing. He made it shaggy with his fingers—and it was Despair; lank—and it was avarice: tossed it all kinds of ways—and it was rage. The beard did everything.

'I am the Ghost of Art,' said he. 'Two bob a-day now, and more when it's longer! Hair's the true expression. There is no other. *I said I'd grow it, and I've grown it, and it shall haunt you!'*

He may have tumbled downstairs in the dark, but he never walked down or ran down. I looked over the banisters, and I was alone with the thunder.

Need I add more of my terrific fate? *It has* haunted me ever since. It glares upon me from the walls of the Royal Academy, (except when *Maclise* subdues it to his genius,) it fills my soul with terror at the British Institution, it lures young artists on to their destruction. Go where I will, the Ghost of Art, eternally working the passions in hair, and expressing everything by beard, pursues me. The prediction is accomplished, and the victim has no rest.

The Haunted House

Chapter 1

The Mortals in the House

Under none of the accredited ghostly circumstances, and environed by none of the conventional ghostly surroundings, did I first make acquaintance with the house which is the subject of this Christmas piece. I saw it in the daylight, with the sun upon it. There was no wind, no rain, no lightning, no thunder, no awful or unwonted circumstance, of any kind, to heighten its effect. More than that: I had come to it direct from a railway station: it was not more than a mile distant from the railway station; and, as I stood outside the house, looking back upon the way I had come, I could see the goods train running smoothly along the embankment in the valley. I will not say that everything was utterly commonplace, because I doubt if anything can be that, except to utterly commonplace people—and there my vanity steps in; but, I will take it on myself to say that anybody might see the house as I saw it, any fine autumn morning.

The manner of my lighting on it was this.

I was travelling towards London out of the North, intending to stop by the way, to look at the house. My health required a temporary residence in the country; and a friend of mine who knew that, and who had happened to drive past the house, had written to me to suggest it as a likely place. I had got into the train at midnight, and had fallen asleep, and had woke up and had sat looking out of window at the brilliant Northern Lights in the sky, and had fallen asleep again, and had woke up again to find the night gone, with the usual discontented conviction on me that I hadn't been to sleep at all;—upon which question, in the first imbecility of that condition, I am ashamed to believe that I would have done wager by battle with the man who sat opposite me.

That opposite man had had, through the night—as that opposite man always has—several legs too many, and all of them too long. In addition to this unreasonable conduct (which was only to be expected of him), he had had a pencil and a pocket-book, and had been perpetually listening and taking notes. It had appeared to me that these aggravating notes related to the jolts and bumps of the carriage, and I should have resigned myself to his taking them, under a general supposition that he was in the civil-engineering way of life, if he had not sat staring straight over my head whenever he listened. He was a goggle-eyed gentleman of a perplexed aspect, and his demeanour became unbearable.

It was a cold, dead morning (the sun not being up yet), and when I had out-watched the paling light of the fires of the iron country, and the curtain of heavy smoke that hung at once between me and the stars and between me and the day, I turned to my fellow-traveller and said:

"I BEG your pardon, sir, but do you observe anything particular in me"? For, really, he appeared to be taking down, either my travelling-cap or my hair, with a minuteness that was a liberty.

The goggle-eyed gentleman withdrew his eyes from behind me, as if the back of the carriage were a hundred miles off, and said, with a lofty look of compassion for my insignificance:

"In you, sir?—B."

"B, sir?" said I, growing warm.

"I have nothing to do with you, sir," returned the gentleman; "pray let me listen—O."

He enunciated this vowel after a pause, and noted it down.

At first I was alarmed, for an Express lunatic and no communication with the guard is a serious position. The thought came to my relief that the gentleman might be what is popularly called a Rapper: one of a sect for (some of) whom I have the highest respect, but whom I don't believe in. I was going to ask him the question, when he took the bread out of my mouth.

"You will excuse me," said the gentleman contemptuously, "if I am too much in advance of common humanity to trouble myself at all about it. I have passed the night—as indeed I pass the whole of my time now—in spiritual intercourse."

"O!" said I, somewhat snappishly.

"The conferences of the night began," continued the gentleman, turning several leaves of his note-book, "with this message: 'Evil communications corrupt good manners.'"

"Sound," said I; "but, absolutely new?"

"New from spirits," returned the gentleman.

I could only repeat my rather snappish "O!" and ask if I might be favoured with the last communication.

"*A bird in the hand*," said the gentleman, reading his last entry with great solemnity, "*is worth two in the Bosh*."

"Truly I am of the same opinion," said I; "but shouldn't it be Bush?"

"It came to me, Bosh," returned the gentleman.

The gentleman then informed me that the spirit of Socrates had delivered this special revelation in the course of the night. "My friend, I hope you are pretty well. There are two in this railway carriage. How do you do? There are seventeen thousand four hundred and seventy-nine spirits here, but you cannot see them. Pythagoras is here. He is not at liberty to mention it, but hopes you like travelling." Galileo likewise had dropped in, with this scientific intelligence. "I am glad to see you, *AMICO. COME STA*? Water will freeze when it is cold enough. *ADDIO*!" In the course of the night, also, the following phenomena had occurred.

Bishop Butler had insisted on spelling his name, "Bubler," for which offence against orthography and good manners he had been dismissed as out of temper. John Milton (suspected of wilful mystification) had repudiated the authorship of Paradise

Lost, and had introduced, as joint authors of that poem, two Unknown gentlemen, respectively named Grungers and Scadgingtone. And Prince Arthur, nephew of King John of England, had described himself as tolerably comfortable in the seventh circle, where he was learning to paint on velvet, under the direction of Mrs. Trimmer and Mary Queen of Scots.

If this should meet the eye of the gentleman who favoured me with these disclosures, I trust he will excuse my confessing that the sight of the rising sun, and the contemplation of the magnificent Order of the vast Universe, made me impatient of them. In a word, I was so impatient of them, that I was mightily glad to get out at the next station, and to exchange these clouds and vapours for the free air of Heaven.

By that time it was a beautiful morning. As I walked away among such leaves as had already fallen from the golden, brown, and russet trees; and as I looked around me on the wonders of Creation, and thought of the steady, unchanging, and harmonious laws by which they are sustained; the gentleman's spiritual intercourse seemed to me as poor a piece of journey-work as ever this world saw. In which heathen state of mind, I came within view of the house, and stopped to examine it attentively.

It was a solitary house, standing in a sadly neglected garden: a pretty even square of some two acres. It was a house of about the time of George the Second; as stiff, as cold, as formal, and in as bad taste, as could possibly be desired by the most loyal admirer of the whole quartet of Georges. It was uninhabited, but had, within a year or two, been cheaply repaired to render it habitable; I say cheaply, because the work had been done in a surface manner, and was already decaying as to the paint and plaster, though the colours were fresh. A lop-sided board drooped over the garden wall, announcing that it was "to let on very reasonable terms, well furnished." It was much too closely and heavily shadowed by trees, and, in particular, there were six tall poplars before the front windows, which were excessively melancholy, and the site of which had been extremely ill chosen.

It was easy to see that it was an avoided house—a house that was shunned by the village, to which my eye was guided by a church spire some half a mile off—a house that nobody would take. And the natural inference was, that it had the reputation of being a haunted house.

No period within the four-and-twenty hours of day and night is so solemn to me, as the early morning. In the summer-time, I often rise very early, and repair to my room to do a day's work before breakfast, and I am always on those occasions deeply impressed by the stillness and solitude around me. Besides that there is something awful in the being surrounded by familiar faces asleep—in the knowledge that those who are dearest to us and to whom we are dearest, are profoundly unconscious of us, in an impassive state, anticipative of that mysterious condition to which we are all tending—the stopped life, the broken threads of yesterday, the deserted seat, the closed book, the unfinished but abandoned occupation, all are images of Death. The tranquillity of the hour is the tranquillity of Death. The colour and the chill have the same association.

Even a certain air that familiar household objects take upon them when they first emerge from the shadows of the night into the morning, of being newer, and as they used to be long ago, has its counterpart in the subsidence of the worn face of maturity or age, in death, into the old youthful look. Moreover, I once saw the apparition of my father, at this hour. He was alive and well, and nothing ever came of it, but I saw him in the daylight, sitting with his back towards me, on a seat that stood beside my bed. His head was resting on his hand, and whether he was slumbering or grieving, I could not discern. Amazed to see him there, I sat up, moved my position, leaned out of bed, and watched him. As he did not move, I spoke to him more than once. As he did not move then, I became alarmed and laid my hand upon his shoulder, as I thought—and there was no such thing.

For all these reasons, and for others less easily and briefly statable, I find the early morning to be my most ghostly time. Any house would be more or less haunted, to me, in the early morning; and a haunted house could scarcely address me to greater advantage than then.

I walked on into the village, with the desertion of this house upon my mind, and I found the landlord of the little inn, sanding his doorstep. I bespoke breakfast, and broached the subject of the house.

"Is it haunted?" I asked.

The landlord looked at me, shook his head, and answered, "I say nothing."

"Then it IS haunted?"

"Well!" cried the landlord, in an outburst of frankness that had the appearance of desperation—"I wouldn't sleep in it."

"Why not?"

"If I wanted to have all the bells in a house ring, with nobody to ring 'em; and all the doors in a house bang, with nobody to bang 'em; and all sorts of feet treading about, with no feet there; why, then," said the landlord, "I'd sleep in that house."

"Is anything seen there?"

The landlord looked at me again, and then, with his former appearance of desperation, called down his stable-yard for "Ikey!"

The call produced a high-shouldered young fellow, with a round red face, a short crop of sandy hair, a very broad humorous mouth, a turned-up nose, and a great sleeved waistcoat of purple bars, with mother-of-pearl buttons, that seemed to be growing upon him, and to be in a fair way—if it were not pruned—of covering his head and overunning his boots.

"This gentleman wants to know," said the landlord, "if anything's seen at the Poplars."

"'Ooded woman with a howl," said Ikey, in a state of great freshness.

"Do you mean a cry?"

"I mean a bird, sir."

"A hooded woman with an owl. Dear me! Did you ever see her?"

"I seen the howl."

"Never the woman?"

"Not so plain as the howl, but they always keeps together."

"Has anybody ever seen the woman as plainly as the owl?"

"Lord bless you, sir! Lots."

"Who?"

"Lord bless you, sir! Lots."

"The general-dealer opposite, for instance, who is opening his shop?"

"Perkins? Bless you, Perkins wouldn't go a-nigh the place. No!" observed the young man, with considerable feeling; "he an't overwise, an't Perkins, but he an't such a fool as THAT."

(Here, the landlord murmured his confidence in Perkins's knowing better.)

"Who is—or who was—the hooded woman with the owl? Do you know?"

"Well!" said Ikey, holding up his cap with one hand while he scratched his head with the other, "they say, in general, that she was murdered, and the howl he 'ooted the while."

This very concise summary of the facts was all I could learn, except that a young man, as hearty and likely a young man as ever I see, had been took with fits and held down in 'em, after seeing the hooded woman. Also, that a personage, dimly described as "a hold chap, a sort of one-eyed tramp, answering to the name of Joby, unless you challenged him as Greenwood, and then he said, 'Why not? And even if so, mind your own business,'" had encountered the hooded woman, a matter of five or six times. But, I was not materially assisted by these witnesses: inasmuch as the first was in California, and the last was, as Ikey said (and he was confirmed by the landlord), Anywheres.

Now, although I regard with a hushed and solemn fear, the mysteries, between which and this state of existence is interposed the barrier of the great trial and change that fall on all the things that live; and although I have not the audacity to pretend that I know anything of them; I can no more reconcile the mere banging of doors, ringing of bells, creaking of boards, and such-like insignificances, with the majestic beauty and pervading analogy of all the Divine rules that I am permitted to understand, than I had been able, a little while before, to yoke the spiritual intercourse of my fellow-traveller to the chariot of the rising sun. Moreover, I had lived in two haunted houses—both abroad. In one of these, an old Italian palace, which bore the reputation of being very badly haunted indeed, and which had recently been twice abandoned on that account, I lived eight months, most tranquilly and pleasantly: notwithstanding that the house had a score of mysterious bedrooms, which were never used, and possessed, in one large room in which I sat reading, times out of number at all hours, and next to which I slept, a haunted chamber of the first pretensions.

I gently hinted these considerations to the landlord. And as to this particular house having a bad name, I reasoned with him, Why, how many things had bad names undeservedly, and how easy it was to give bad names, and did he not think that if he and I were persistently to whisper in the village that any weird-looking old drunken tinker of the neighbourhood had sold himself to the Devil, he would come in time to be suspected of that commercial venture! All this wise talk was perfectly ineffective with the landlord, I am bound to confess, and was as dead a failure as ever I made in my life.

To cut this part of the story short, I was piqued about the haunted house, and was already half resolved to take it. So, after breakfast, I got the keys from Perkins's brother-in-law (a whip and harness maker, who keeps the Post Office, and is under submission to a most rigorous wife of the Doubly Seceding Little Emmanuel persuasion), and went up to the house, attended by my landlord and by Ikey.

Within, I found it, as I had expected, transcendently dismal. The slowly changing shadows waved on it from the heavy trees, were doleful in the last degree; the house was ill-placed, ill-built, ill-planned, and ill-fitted. It was damp, it was not free from dry rot, there was a flavour of rats in it, and it was the gloomy victim of that indescribable decay which settles on all the work of man's hands whenever it's not turned to man's account. The kitchens and offices were too large, and too remote from each other. Above stairs and below, waste tracts of passage intervened between patches of fertility represented by rooms; and there was a mouldy old well with a green growth upon it, hiding like a murderous trap, near the bottom of the back-stairs, under the double row of bells. One of these bells was labelled, on a black ground in faded white letters, MASTER B. This, they told me, was the bell that rang the most.

"Who was Master B.?" I asked. "Is it known what he did while the owl hooted?"

"Rang the bell," said Ikey.

I was rather struck by the prompt dexterity with which this young man pitched his fur cap at the bell, and rang it himself. It was a loud, unpleasant bell, and made a very disagreeable sound. The other bells were inscribed according to the names of the rooms to which their wires were conducted: as "Picture Room," "Double Room," "Clock Room," and the like. Following Master B.'s bell to its source I found that young gentleman to have had but indifferent third-class accommodation in a triangular cabin under the cock-loft, with a corner fireplace which Master B. must have been exceedingly small if he were ever able to warm himself at, and a corner chimney-piece like a pyramidal staircase to the ceiling for Tom Thumb. The papering of one side of the room had dropped down bodily, with fragments of plaster adhering to it, and almost blocked up the door. It appeared that Master B., in his spiritual condition, always made a point of pulling the paper down. Neither the landlord nor Ikey could suggest why he made such a fool of himself.

Except that the house had an immensely large rambling loft at top, I made no other discoveries. It was moderately well furnished, but sparely. Some of the furniture—say, a third—was as old as the house; the rest was of various periods within the last half-century. I was referred to a corn-chandler in the market-place of the county town to treat for the house. I went that day, and I took it for six months.

It was just the middle of October when I moved in with my

maiden sister (I venture to call her eight-and-thirty, she is so very handsome, sensible, and engaging). We took with us, a deaf stable-man, my bloodhound Turk, two women servants, and a young person called an Odd Girl. I have reason to record of the attendant last enumerated, who was one of the Saint Lawrence's Union Female Orphans, that she was a fatal mistake and a disastrous engagement.

The year was dying early, the leaves were falling fast, it was a raw cold day when we took possession, and the gloom of the house was most depressing. The cook (an amiable woman, but of a weak turn of intellect) burst into tears on beholding the kitchen, and requested that her silver watch might be delivered over to her sister (2 Tuppintock's Gardens, Liggs's Walk, Clapham Rise), in the event of anything happening to her from the damp. Streaker, the housemaid, feigned cheerfulness, but was the greater martyr. The Odd Girl, who had never been in the country, alone was pleased, and made arrangements for sowing an acorn in the garden outside the scullery window, and rearing an oak.

We went, before dark, through all the natural—as opposed to supernatural—miseries incidental to our state. Dispiriting reports ascended (like the smoke) from the basement in volumes, and descended from the upper rooms. There was no rolling-pin, there was no salamander (which failed to surprise me, for I don't know what it is), there was nothing in the house, what there was, was broken, the last people must have lived like pigs, what could the meaning of the landlord be? Through these distresses, the Odd Girl was cheerful and exemplary. But within four hours after dark we had got into a supernatural groove, and the Odd Girl had seen "Eyes," and was in hysterics.

My sister and I had agreed to keep the haunting strictly to ourselves, and my impression was, and still is, that I had not left Ikey, when he helped to unload the cart, alone with the women, or any one of them, for one minute. Nevertheless, as I say, the Odd Girl had "seen Eyes" (no other explanation could ever be drawn from her), before nine, and by ten o'clock had

had as much vinegar applied to her as would pickle a handsome salmon.

I leave a discerning public to judge of my feelings, when, under these untoward circumstances, at about half-past ten o'clock Master B.'s bell began to ring in a most infuriated manner, and Turk howled until the house resounded with his lamentations!

I hope I may never again be in a state of mind so unchristian as the mental frame in which I lived for some weeks, respecting the memory of Master B. Whether his bell was rung by rats, or mice, or bats, or wind, or what other accidental vibration, or sometimes by one cause, sometimes another, and sometimes by collusion, I don't know; but, certain it is, that it did ring two nights out of three, until I conceived the happy idea of twisting Master B.'s neck—in other words, breaking his bell short off—and silencing that young gentleman, as to my experience and belief, forever.

But, by that time, the Odd Girl had developed such improving powers of catalepsy, that she had become a shining example of that very inconvenient disorder. She would stiffen, like a Guy Fawkes endowed with unreason, on the most irrelevant occasions. I would address the servants in a lucid manner, pointing out to them that I had painted Master B.'s room and balked the paper, and taken Master B.'s bell away and balked the ringing, and if they could suppose that that confounded boy had lived and died, to clothe himself with no better behaviour than would most unquestionably have brought him and the sharpest particles of a birch-broom into close acquaintance in the present imperfect state of existence, could they also suppose a mere poor human being, such as I was, capable by those contemptible means of counteracting and limiting the powers of the disembodied spirits of the dead, or of any spirits?—I say I would become emphatic and cogent, not to say rather complacent, in such an address, when it would all go for nothing by reason of the Odd Girl's suddenly stiffening from the toes upward, and glaring among us like a parochial petrifaction.

Streaker, the housemaid, too, had an attribute of a most discomfiting nature. I am unable to say whether she was of an usually lymphatic temperament, or what else was the matter with her, but this young woman became a mere Distillery for the production of the largest and most transparent tears I ever met with. Combined with these characteristics, was a peculiar tenacity of hold in those specimens, so that they didn't fall, but hung upon her face and nose. In this condition, and mildly and deplorably shaking her head, her silence would throw me more heavily than the Admirable Crichton could have done in a verbal disputation for a purse of money. Cook, likewise, always covered me with confusion as with a garment, by neatly winding up the session with the protest that the Ouse was wearing her out, and by meekly repeating her last wishes regarding her silver watch.

As to our nightly life, the contagion of suspicion and fear was among us, and there is no such contagion under the sky. Hooded woman? According to the accounts, we were in a perfect Convent of hooded women. Noises? With that contagion downstairs, I myself have sat in the dismal parlour, listening, until I have heard so many and such strange noises, that they would have chilled my blood if I had not warmed it by dashing out to make discoveries. Try this in bed, in the dead of the night: try this at your own comfortable fireside, in the life of the night. You can fill any house with noises, if you will, until you have a noise for every nerve in your nervous system.

I repeat; the contagion of suspicion and fear was among us, and there is no such contagion under the sky. The women (their noses in a chronic state of excoriation from smelling-salts) were always primed and loaded for a swoon, and ready to go off with hair-triggers. The two elder detached the Odd Girl on all expeditions that were considered doubly hazardous, and she always established the reputation of such adventures by coming back cataleptic. If Cook or Streaker went overhead after dark, we knew we should presently hear a bump on the ceiling; and this took place so constantly, that it was as if a fighting man were engaged to go about the house, administering a touch of his art which I believe is called The Auctioneer, to every domestic he met with.

It was in vain to do anything. It was in vain to be frightened, for the moment in one's own person, by a real owl, and then to show the owl. It was in vain to discover, by striking an accidental discord on the piano, that Turk always howled at particular notes and combinations. It was in vain to be a Rhadamanthus with the bells, and if an unfortunate bell rang without leave, to have it down inexorably and silence it. It was in vain to fire up chimneys, let torches down the well, charge furiously into suspected rooms and recesses. We changed servants, and it was no better. The new set ran away, and a third set came, and it was no better. At last, our comfortable housekeeping got to be so disorganised and wretched, that I one night dejectedly said to my sister: "Patty, I begin to despair of our getting people to go on with us here, and I think we must give this up."

My sister, who is a woman of immense spirit, replied, "No, John, don't give it up. Don't be beaten, John. There is another way."

"And what is that?" said I.

"John," returned my sister, "if we are not to be driven out of this house, and that for no reason whatever, that is apparent to you or me, we must help ourselves and take the house wholly and solely into our own hands."

"But, the servants," said I.

"Have no servants," said my sister, boldly.

Like most people in my grade of life, I had never thought of the possibility of going on without those faithful obstructions. The notion was so new to me when suggested, that I looked very doubtful. "We know they come here to be frightened and infect one another, and we know they are frightened and do infect one another," said my sister.

"With the exception of Bottles," I observed, in a meditative tone.

(The deaf stable-man. I kept him in my service, and still keep him, as a phenomenon of moroseness not to be matched in

England.)

"To be sure, John," assented my sister; "except Bottles. And what does that go to prove? Bottles talks to nobody, and hears nobody unless he is absolutely roared at, and what alarm has Bottles ever given, or taken! None."

This was perfectly true; the individual in question having retired, every night at ten o'clock, to his bed over the coach-house, with no other company than a pitchfork and a pail of water. That the pail of water would have been over me, and the pitchfork through me, if I had put myself without announcement in Bottles's way after that minute, I had deposited in my own mind as a fact worth remembering. Neither had Bottles ever taken the least notice of any of our many uproars. An imperturbable and speechless man, he had sat at his supper, with Streaker present in a swoon, and the Odd Girl marble, and had only put another potato in his cheek, or profited by the general misery to help himself to beefsteak pie.

"And so," continued my sister, "I exempt Bottles. And considering, John, that the house is too large, and perhaps too lonely, to be kept well in hand by Bottles, you, and me, I propose that we cast about among our friends for a certain selected number of the most reliable and willing—form a Society here for three months—wait upon ourselves and one another—live cheerfully and socially—and see what happens."

I was so charmed with my sister, that I embraced her on the spot, and went into her plan with the greatest ardour.

We were then in the third week of November; but, we took our measures so vigorously, and were so well seconded by the friends in whom we confided, that there was still a week of the month unexpired, when our party all came down together merrily, and mustered in the haunted house.

I will mention, in this place, two small changes that I made while my sister and I were yet alone. It occurring to me as not improbable that Turk howled in the house at night, partly because he wanted to get out of it, I stationed him in his kennel outside, but unchained; and I seriously warned the village that any man who came in his way must not expect to leave him without a rip in his own throat. I then casually asked Ikey if he were a judge of a gun? On his saying, "Yes, sir, I knows a good gun when I sees her," I begged the favour of his stepping up to the house and looking at mine.

"SHE'S a true one, sir," said Ikey, after inspecting a double-barrelled rifle that I bought in New York a few years ago. "No mistake about HER, sir."

"Ikey," said I, "don't mention it; I have seen something in this house."

"No, sir?" he whispered, greedily opening his eyes. "'Ooded lady, sir?"

"Don't be frightened," said I. "It was a figure rather like you."

"Lord, sir?"

"Ikey!" said I, shaking hands with him warmly: I may say affectionately; "if there is any truth in these ghost-stories, the greatest service I can do you, is, to fire at that figure. And I promise you, by Heaven and earth, I will do it with this gun if I see it again!"

The young man thanked me, and took his leave with some little precipitation, after declining a glass of liquor. I imparted my secret to him, because I had never quite forgotten his throwing his cap at the bell; because I had, on another occasion, noticed something very like a fur cap, lying not far from the bell, one night when it had burst out ringing; and because I had remarked that we were at our ghostliest whenever he came up in the evening to comfort the servants. Let me do Ikey no injustice. He was afraid of the house, and believed in its being haunted; and yet he would play false on the haunting side, so surely as he got an opportunity.

The Odd Girl's case was exactly similar. She went about the house in a state of real terror, and yet lied monstrously and wilfully, and invented many of the alarms she spread, and made many of the sounds we heard. I had had my eye on the two, and I know it. It is not necessary for me, here, to account for this preposterous state of mind; I content myself with remarking that it is familiarly known to every intelligent man who has had fair medical, legal, or other watchful experience; that it is as well established and as common a state of mind as any with which observers are acquainted; and that it is one of the first elements, above all others, rationally to be suspected in, and strictly looked for, and separated from, any question of this kind.

To return to our party. The first thing we did when we were all assembled, was, to draw lots for bedrooms. That done, and every bedroom, and, indeed, the whole house, having been minutely examined by the whole body, we allotted the various household duties, as if we had been on a gipsy party, or a yachting party, or a hunting party, or were shipwrecked. I then recounted the floating rumours concerning the hooded lady, the owl, and Master B.: with others, still more filmy, which had floated about during our occupation, relative to some ridiculous old ghost of the female gender who went up and down, carrying the ghost of a round table; and also to an impalpable Jackass, whom nobody was ever able to catch.

Some of these ideas I really believe our people below had communicated to one another in some diseased way, without conveying them in words. We then gravely called one another to witness, that we were not there to be deceived, or to deceive—which we considered pretty much the same thing—and that, with a serious sense of responsibility, we would be strictly true to one another, and would strictly follow out the truth. The understanding was established, that anyone who heard unusual noises in the night, and who wished to trace them, should knock at my door; lastly, that on Twelfth Night, the last night of holy Christmas, all our individual experiences since that then present hour of our coming together in the haunted house, should be brought to light for the good of all; and that we would hold our peace on the subject till then, unless on some remarkable provocation to break silence.

We were, in number and in character, as follows:

First—to get my sister and myself out of the way—there were

we two. In the drawing of lots, my sister drew her own room, and I drew Master B.'s. Next, there was our first cousin John Herschel, so called after the great astronomer: than whom I suppose a better man at a telescope does not breathe. With him, was his wife: a charming creature to whom he had been married in the previous spring. I thought it (under the circumstances) rather imprudent to bring her, because there is no knowing what even a false alarm may do at such a time; but I suppose he knew his own business best, and I must say that if she had been MY wife, I never could have left her endearing and bright face behind.

They drew the Clock Room. Alfred Starling, an uncommonly agreeable young fellow of eight-and-twenty for whom I have the greatest liking, was in the Double Room; mine, usually, and designated by that name from having a dressing-room within it, with two large and cumbersome windows, which no wedges I was ever able to make, would keep from shaking, in any weather, wind or no wind. Alfred is a young fellow who pretends to be "fast" (another word for loose, as I understand the term), but who is much too good and sensible for that nonsense, and who would have distinguished himself before now, if his father had not unfortunately left him a small independence of two hundred a year, on the strength of which his only occupation in life has been to spend six. I am in hopes, however, that his Banker may break, or that he may enter into some speculation guaranteed to pay twenty *per cent.*; for, I am convinced that if he could only be ruined, his fortune is made.

Belinda Bates, bosom friend of my sister, and a most intellectual, amiable, and delightful girl, got the Picture Room. She has a fine genius for poetry, combined with real business earnestness, and "goes in"—to use an expression of Alfred's—for Woman's mission, Woman's rights, Woman's wrongs, and everything that is woman's with a capital W, or is not and ought to be, or is and ought not to be. "Most praiseworthy, my dear, and Heaven prosper you!"

I whispered to her on the first night of my taking leave of her at the Picture-Room door, "but don't overdo it. And in respect of the great necessity there is, my darling, for more employments being within the reach of Woman than our civilisation has as yet assigned to her, don't fly at the unfortunate men, even those men who are at first sight in your way, as if they were the natural oppressors of your sex; for, trust me, Belinda, they do sometimes spend their wages among wives and daughters, sisters, mothers, aunts, and grandmothers; and the play is, really, not ALL Wolf and Red Riding-Hood, but has other parts in it." However, I digress.

Belinda, as I have mentioned, occupied the Picture Room. We had but three other chambers: the Corner Room, the Cupboard Room, and the Garden Room. My old friend, Jack Governor, "slung his hammock," as he called it, in the Corner Room. I have always regarded Jack as the finest-looking sailor that ever sailed. He is gray now, but as handsome as he was a quarter of a century ago—nay, handsomer. A portly, cheery, well-built figure of a broad-shouldered man, with a frank smile, a brilliant dark eye, and a rich dark eyebrow.

I remember those under darker hair, and they look all the better for their silver setting. He has been wherever his Union namesake flies, has Jack, and I have met old shipmates of his, away in the Mediterranean and on the other side of the Atlantic, who have beamed and brightened at the casual mention of his name, and have cried, "You know Jack Governor? Then you know a prince of men!" That he is! And so unmistakably a naval officer, that if you were to meet him coming out of an Esquimaux snow-hut in seal's skin, you would be vaguely persuaded he was in full naval uniform.

Jack once had that bright clear eye of his on my sister; but, it fell out that he married another lady and took her to South America, where she died. This was a dozen years ago or more. He brought down with him to our haunted house a little cask of salt beef; for, he is always convinced that all salt beef not of his own pickling, is mere carrion, and invariably, when he goes to London, packs a piece in his portmanteau. He had also volunteered to bring with him one "Nat Beaver," an old comrade of his, captain of a merchantman.

Mr. Beaver, with a thick-set wooden face and figure, and apparently as hard as a block all over, proved to be an intelligent man, with a world of watery experiences in him, and great practical knowledge. At times, there was a curious nervousness about him, apparently the lingering result of some old illness; but, it seldom lasted many minutes. He got the Cupboard Room, and lay there next to Mr. Undery, my friend and solicitor: who came down, in an amateur capacity, "to go through with it," as he said, and who plays whist better than the whole Law List, from the red cover at the beginning to the red cover at the end.

I never was happier in my life, and I believe it was the universal feeling among us. Jack Governor, always a man of wonderful resources, was Chief Cook, and made some of the best dishes I ever ate, including unapproachable curries. My sister was pastrycook and confectioner. Starling and I were Cook's Mate, turn and turn about, and on special occasions the chief cook "pressed" Mr. Beaver. We had a great deal of outdoor sport and exercise, but nothing was neglected within, and there was no ill-humour or misunderstanding among us, and our evenings were so delightful that we had at least one good reason for being reluctant to go to bed.

We had a few night alarms in the beginning. On the first night, I was knocked up by Jack with a most wonderful ship's lantern in his hand, like the gills of some monster of the deep, who informed me that he "was going aloft to the main truck," to have the weathercock down. It was a stormy night and I remonstrated; but Jack called my attention to its making a sound like a cry of despair, and said somebody would be "hailing a ghost" presently, if it wasn't done.

So, up to the top of the house, where I could hardly stand for the wind, we went, accompanied by Mr. Beaver; and there Jack, lantern and all, with Mr. Beaver after him, swarmed up to the top of a cupola, some two dozen feet above the chimneys, and stood upon nothing particular, coolly knocking the weathercock off, until they both got into such good spirits with the wind and the height, that I thought they would never come down.

Another night, they turned out again, and had a chimney-cowl off. Another night, they cut a sobbing and gulping water-pipe away. Another night, they found out something else. On several occasions, they both, in the coolest manner, simultaneously dropped out of their respective bedroom windows, hand over hand by their counterpanes, to "overhaul" something mysterious in the garden.

The engagement among us was faithfully kept, and nobody revealed anything. All we knew was, if any one's room were haunted, no one looked the worse for it.

Chapter 2

The Ghost in Master B.'s Room

When I established myself in the triangular garret which had gained so distinguished a reputation, my thoughts naturally turned to Master B. My speculations about him were uneasy and manifold. Whether his Christian name was Benjamin, Bissextile (from his having been born in Leap Year), Bartholomew, or Bill. Whether the initial letter belonged to his family name, and that was Baxter, Black, Brown, Barker, Buggins, Baker, or Bird. Whether he was a foundling, and had been baptized B. Whether he was a lion-hearted boy, and B. was short for Briton, or for Bull. Whether he could possibly have been kith and kin to an illustrious lady who brightened my own childhood, and had come of the blood of the brilliant Mother Bunch?

With these profitless meditations I tormented myself much. I also carried the mysterious letter into the appearance and pursuits of the deceased; wondering whether he dressed in Blue, wore Boots (he couldn't have been Bald), was a boy of Brains, liked Books, was good at Bowling, had any skill as a Boxer, even in his Buoyant Boyhood Bathed from a Bathing-machine at Bognor, Bangor, Bournemouth, Brighton, or Broadstairs, like a Bounding Billiard Ball?

So, from the first, I was haunted by the letter B.

It was not long before I remarked that I never by any hazard had a dream of Master B., or of anything belonging to him. But, the instant I awoke from sleep, at whatever hour of the night, my thoughts took him up, and roamed away, trying to attach his initial letter to something that would fit it and keep it quiet.

For six nights, I had been worried this in Master B.'s room, when I began to perceive that things were going wrong.

The first appearance that presented itself was early in the morning when it was but just daylight and no more. I was standing shaving at my glass, when I suddenly discovered, to my consternation and amazement, that I was shaving—not myself—I am fifty—but a boy. Apparently Master B.!

I trembled and looked over my shoulder; nothing there. I looked again in the glass, and distinctly saw the features and expression of a boy, who was shaving, not to get rid of a beard, but to get one. Extremely troubled in my mind, I took a few turns in the room, and went back to the looking-glass, resolved to steady my hand and complete the operation in which I had been disturbed. Opening my eyes, which I had shut while recovering my firmness, I now met in the glass, looking straight at me, the eyes of a young man of four or five and twenty. Terrified by this new ghost, I closed my eyes, and made a strong effort to recover myself. Opening them again, I saw, shaving his cheek in the glass, my father, who has long been dead. Nay, I even saw my grandfather too, whom I never did see in my life.

Although naturally much affected by these remarkable visitations, I determined to keep my secret, until the time agreed upon for the present general disclosure. Agitated by a multitude of curious thoughts, I retired to my room, that night, prepared to encounter some new experience of a spectral character. Nor was my preparation needless, for, waking from an uneasy sleep at exactly two o'clock in the morning, what were my feelings to find that I was sharing my bed with the skeleton of Master B.!

I sprang up, and the skeleton sprang up also. I then heard a plaintive voice saying, "Where am I? What is become of me?" and, looking hard in that direction, perceived the ghost of Master B.

The young spectre was dressed in an obsolete fashion: or rather, was not so much dressed as put into a case of inferior pepper-and-salt cloth, made horrible by means of shining buttons. I observed that these buttons went, in a double row, over each shoulder of the young ghost, and appeared to descend his back. He wore a frill round his neck. His right hand (which I distinctly noticed to be inky) was laid upon his stomach; connecting this action with some feeble pimples on his countenance, and his general air of nausea, I concluded this ghost to be the ghost of a boy who had habitually taken a great deal too much medicine.

"Where am I?" said the little spectre, in a pathetic voice. "And why was I born in the Calomel days, and why did I have all that Calomel given me?"

I replied, with sincere earnestness, that upon my soul I couldn't tell him.

"Where is my little sister," said the ghost, "and where my angelic little wife, and where is the boy I went to school with?"

I entreated the phantom to be comforted, and above all things to take heart respecting the loss of the boy he went to school with. I represented to him that probably that boy never did, within human experience, come out well, when discovered. I urged that I myself had, in later life, turned up several boys whom I went to school with, and none of them had at all answered. I expressed my humble belief that that boy never did answer. I represented that he was a mythic character, a delusion, and a snare. I recounted how, the last time I found him, I found him at a dinner party behind a wall of white cravat, with an inconclusive opinion on every possible subject, and a power of silent boredom absolutely Titanic.

I related how, on the strength of our having been together at "Old Doylance's," he had asked himself to breakfast with me (a social offence of the largest magnitude); how, fanning my weak embers of belief in Doylance's boys, I had let him in; and how, he had proved to be a fearful wanderer about the earth, pursuing the race of Adam with inexplicable notions concerning the currency, and with a proposition that the Bank of England should, on pain of being abolished, instantly strike off and circulate, God knows how many thousand millions of ten-and-sixpenny notes.

The ghost heard me in silence, and with a fixed stare. "Barber!" it apostrophised me when I had finished.

"Barber?" I repeated—for I am not of that profession.

"Condemned," said the ghost, "to shave a constant change of customers—now, me—now, a young man—now, thyself as thou art—now, thy father—now, thy grandfather; condemned, too, to lie down with a skeleton every night, and to rise with it every morning—"

(I shuddered on hearing this dismal announcement.)

"Barber! Pursue me!"

I had felt, even before the words were uttered, that I was under a spell to pursue the phantom. I immediately did so, and was in Master B.'s room no longer.

Most people know what long and fatiguing night journeys had been forced upon the witches who used to confess, and who, no doubt, told the exact truth—particularly as they were always assisted with leading questions, and the Torture was always ready. I asseverate that, during my occupation of Master B.'s room, I was taken by the ghost that haunted it, on expeditions fully as long and wild as any of those. Assuredly, I was presented to no shabby old man with a goat's horns and tail (something between Pan and an old clothesman), holding conventional receptions, as stupid as those of real life and less decent; but, I came upon other things which appeared to me to have more meaning.

Confident that I speak the truth and shall be believed, I declare without hesitation that I followed the ghost, in the first instance on a broom-stick, and afterwards on a rocking-horse. The very smell of the animal's paint—especially when I brought it out, by making him warm—I am ready to swear to. I followed the ghost, afterwards, in a hackney coach; an institution with the peculiar smell of which, the present generation is unacquainted, but to which I am again ready to swear as a combination of stable, dog with the mange, and very old bellows. (In this, I appeal to previous generations to confirm or refute me.) I pursued the phantom, on a headless donkey: at least, upon a donkey who was so interested in the state of his stomach that his head was always down there, investigating it; on ponies, expressly born to kick up behind; on roundabouts and swings, from fairs; in the first cab—another forgotten institution where the fare regularly got into bed, and was tucked up with the driver.

Not to trouble you with a detailed account of all my travels in pursuit of the ghost of Master B., which were longer and more wonderful than those of Sinbad the Sailor, I will confine myself to one experience from which you may judge of many.

I was marvellously changed. I was myself, yet not myself. I was conscious of something within me, which has been the same all through my life, and which I have always recognised under all its phases and varieties as never altering, and yet I was not the I who had gone to bed in Master B.'s room. I had the smoothest of faces and the shortest of legs, and I had taken another creature like myself, also with the smoothest of faces and the shortest of legs, behind a door, and was confiding to him a proposition of the most astounding nature.

This proposition was, that we should have a *Seraglio*.

The other creature assented warmly. He had no notion of respectability, neither had I. It was the custom of the East, it was the way of the good Caliph Haroun Alraschid (let me have the corrupted name again for once, it is so scented with sweet memories!), the usage was highly laudable, and most worthy of imitation. "O, yes! Let us," said the other creature with a jump, "have a *Seraglio*."

It was not because we entertained the faintest doubts of the meritorious character of the Oriental establishment we proposed to import, that we perceived it must be kept a secret from Miss Griffin. It was because we knew Miss Griffin to be bereft of human sympathies, and incapable of appreciating the greatness of the great Haroun. Mystery impenetrably shrouded from Miss Griffin then, let us entrust it to Miss Bule.

We were ten in Miss Griffin's establishment by Hampstead Ponds; eight ladies and two gentlemen. Miss Bule, whom I judge to have attained the ripe age of eight or nine, took the lead in society. I opened the subject to her in the course of the day, and proposed that she should become the Favourite.

Miss Bule, after struggling with the diffidence so natural to, and charming in, her adorable sex, expressed herself as flattered by the idea, but wished to know how it was proposed to provide for Miss Pipson? Miss Bule—who was understood to have vowed towards that young lady, a friendship, halves, and no secrets, until death, on the Church Service and Lessons complete in two volumes with case and lock—Miss Bule said she could not, as the friend of Pipson, disguise from herself, or me, that Pipson was not one of the common.

Now, Miss Pipson, having curly hair and blue eyes (which was my idea of anything mortal and feminine that was called Fair), I promptly replied that I regarded Miss Pipson in the light of a Fair Circassian.

"And what then?" Miss Bule pensively asked.

I replied that she must be inveigled by a Merchant, brought to me veiled, and purchased as a slave.

[The other creature had already fallen into the second male place in the State, and was set apart for Grand *Vizier*. He afterwards resisted this disposal of events, but had his hair pulled until he yielded.]

"Shall I not be jealous?" Miss Bule inquired, casting down her eyes.

"Zobeide, no," I replied; "you will ever be the favourite *Sultana*; the first place in my heart, and on my throne, will be ever yours."

Miss Bule, upon that assurance, consented to propound the idea to her seven beautiful companions. It occurring to me, in the course of the same day, that we knew we could trust a grinning and good-natured soul called Tabby, who was the serving drudge of the house, and had no more figure than one of the beds, and upon whose face there was always more or less black-lead, I slipped into Miss Bule's hand after supper, a little note to that effect; dwelling on the black-lead as being in a manner deposited by the finger of Providence, pointing Tabby out for Mesrour, the celebrated chief of the Blacks of the *Hareem*.

There were difficulties in the formation of the desired institution, as there are in all combinations. The other creature showed himself of a low character, and, when defeated in aspiring to the throne, pretended to have conscientious scruples about prostrating himself before the Caliph; wouldn't call him Commander of the Faithful; spoke of him slightingly and inconsistently as a mere "chap;" said he, the other creature, "wouldn't play"—Play!—and was otherwise coarse and offensive. This meanness of disposition was, however, put down by the general indignation of an united *Seraglio*, and I became blessed in the smiles of eight of the fairest of the daughters of men.

The smiles could only be bestowed when Miss Griffin was looking another way, and only then in a very wary manner, for there was a legend among the followers of the Prophet that she saw with a little round ornament in the middle of the pattern on the back of her shawl. But every day after dinner, for an hour, we were all together, and then the Favourite and the rest of the Royal *Hareem* competed who should most beguile the leisure of the Serene Haroun reposing from the cares of State—which were generally, as in most affairs of State, of an arithmetical character, the Commander of the Faithful being a fearful boggler at a sum.

On these occasions, the devoted Mesrour, chief of the Blacks of the *Hareem*, was always in attendance (Miss Griffin usually ringing for that officer, at the same time, with great vehemence), but never acquitted himself in a manner worthy of his historical reputation. In the first place, his bringing a broom into the Divan of the Caliph, even when Haroun wore on his shoulders the red robe of anger (Miss Pipson's pelisse), though it might be got over for the moment, was never to be quite satisfactorily accounted for. In the second place, his breaking out into grinning exclamations of "Lork you pretties!" was neither Eastern nor respectful. In the third place, when specially instructed to say "*Bismillah*!" he always said "Hallelujah!" This officer, unlike his class, was too good-humoured altogether, kept his mouth open far too wide, expressed approbation to an incongruous extent, and even once—it was on the occasion of the purchase of the Fair Circassian for five hundred thousand purses of gold, and cheap, too—embraced the Slave, the Favourite, and the Caliph, all round. (Parenthetically let me say God bless Mesrour, and may there have been sons and daughters on that tender bosom, softening many a hard day since!)

Miss Griffin was a model of propriety, and I am at a loss to imagine what the feelings of the virtuous woman would have been, if she had known, when she paraded us down the Hampstead Road two and two, that she was walking with a stately step at the head of Polygamy and Mahomedanism. I believe that a mysterious and terrible joy with which the contemplation of Miss Griffin, in this unconscious state, inspired us, and a grim sense prevalent among us that there was a dreadful power in our knowledge of what Miss Griffin (who knew all things that could be learnt out of book) didn't know, were the main-spring of the preservation of our secret. It was wonderfully kept, but was once upon the verge of self-betrayal.

The danger and escape occurred upon a Sunday. We were all ten ranged in a conspicuous part of the gallery at church, with Miss Griffin at our head—as we were every Sunday—advertising the establishment in an unsecular sort of way—when the description of Solomon in his domestic glory happened to be read. The moment that monarch was thus referred to, conscience whispered me, "Thou, too, Haroun!" The officiating minister had a cast in his eye, and it assisted conscience by giving him the appearance of reading personally at me.

A crimson blush, attended by a fearful perspiration, suffused my features. The Grand *Vizier* became more dead than alive, and the whole *Seraglio* reddened as if the sunset of Bagdad shone direct upon their lovely faces. At this portentous time the awful Griffin rose, and balefully surveyed the children of Islam. My own impression was, that Church and State had entered into a conspiracy with Miss Griffin to expose us, and that we should all be put into white sheets, and exhibited in the centre aisle. But, so Westerly—if I may be allowed the expression as opposite to Eastern associations—was Miss Griffin's sense of rectitude, that she merely suspected Apples, and we were saved.

I have called the *Seraglio*, united. Upon the question, solely, whether the Commander of the Faithful durst exercise a right of kissing in that sanctuary of the palace, were its peerless inmates divided. Zobeide asserted a counter-right in the Favourite to scratch, and the fair Circassian put her face, for refuge, into a green baize bag, originally designed for books.

On the other hand, a young antelope of transcendent beauty from the fruitful plains of Camden Town (whence she had been brought, by traders, in the half-yearly caravan that crossed the intermediate desert after the holidays), held more liberal opinions, but stipulated for limiting the benefit of them to that dog, and son of a dog, the Grand *Vizier*--who had no rights, and was not in question. At length, the difficulty was compromised by the installation of a very youthful slave as Deputy. She, raised upon a stool, officially received upon her cheeks the salutes intended by the gracious Haroun for other *Sultana*s, and was privately rewarded from the coffers of the Ladies of the *Hareem*.

And now it was, at the full height of enjoyment of my bliss, that I became heavily troubled. I began to think of my mother, and what she would say to my taking home at Midsummer eight of the most beautiful of the daughters of men, but all unexpected. I thought of the number of beds we made up at our house, of my father's income, and of the baker, and my despondency redoubled. The *Seraglio* and malicious *Vizier*, divining the cause of their Lord's unhappiness, did their utmost to augment it. They professed unbounded fidelity, and declared that they would live and die with him.

Reduced to the utmost wretchedness by these protestations of attachment, I lay awake, for hours at a time, ruminating on my frightful lot. In my despair, I think I might have taken an early opportunity of falling on my knees before Miss Griffin, avowing my resemblance to Solomon, and praying to be dealt with according to the outraged laws of my country, if an unthought-of means of escape had not opened before me.

One day, we were out walking, two and two—on which occasion the *Vizier* had his usual instructions to take note of the boy at the turn-pike, and if he profanely gazed (which he always did) at the beauties of the *Hareem*, to have him bowstrung in the course of the night—and it happened that our hearts were veiled in gloom. An unaccountable action on the part of the antelope had plunged the State into disgrace. That charmer, on the representation that the previous day was her birthday, and that vast treasures had been sent in a hamper for its celebration (both baseless assertions), had secretly but most pressingly invited thirty-five neighbouring princes and princesses to a ball and supper: with a special stipulation that they were "not to be fetched till twelve."

This wandering of the antelope's fancy, led to the surprising arrival at Miss Griffin's door, in divers equipages and under various escorts, of a great company in full dress, who were deposited on the top step in a flush of high expectancy, and who were dismissed in tears. At the beginning of the double knocks attendant on these ceremonies, the antelope had retired to a back attic, and bolted herself in; and at every new arrival, Miss Griffin had gone so much more and more distracted, that at last she had been seen to tear her front.

Ultimate capitulation on the part of the offender, had been followed by solitude in the linen-closet, bread and water and a lecture to all, of vindictive length, in which Miss Griffin had used expressions: Firstly, "I believe you all of you knew of it;" Secondly, "Every one of you is as wicked as another;" Thirdly, "A pack of little wretches."

Under these circumstances, we were walking drearily along; and I especially, with my. Moosulmaun responsibilities heavy on me, was in a very low state of mind; when a strange man accosted Miss Griffin, and, after walking on at her side for a little while and talking with her, looked at me. Supposing him to be a minion of the law, and that my hour was come, I instantly ran away, with the general purpose of making for Egypt.

The whole *Seraglio* cried out, when they saw me making off as fast as my legs would carry me (I had an impression that the first turning on the left, and round by the public-house, would be the shortest way to the Pyramids), Miss Griffin screamed after me, the faithless *Vizier* ran after me, and the boy at the turnpike dodged me into a corner, like a sheep, and cut me off. Nobody scolded me when I was taken and brought back; Miss Griffin only said, with a stunning gentleness, this was very curious! Why had I run away when the gentleman looked at me?

If I had had any breath to answer with, I dare say I should have made no answer; having no breath, I certainly made none. Miss Griffin and the strange man took me between them, and walked me back to the palace in a sort of state; but not at all (as I couldn't help feeling, with astonishment) in culprit state.

When we got there, we went into a room by ourselves, and Miss Griffin called in to her assistance, Mesrour, chief of the dusky guards of the *Hareem*. Mesrour, on being whispered to, began to shed tears.

"Bless you, my precious!" said that officer, turning to me; "your Pa's took bitter bad!"

I asked, with a fluttered heart, "Is he very ill?"

"Lord temper the wind to you, my lamb!" said the good Mesrour, kneeling down, that I might have a comforting shoulder for my head to rest on, "your Pa's dead!"

Haroun Alraschid took to flight at the words; the *Seraglio* vanished; from that moment, I never again saw one of the eight of the fairest of the daughters of men.

I was taken home, and there was Debt at home as well as Death, and we had a sale there. My own little bed was so superciliously looked upon by a Power unknown to me, hazily called "The Trade," that a brass coal-scuttle, a roasting-jack, and a birdcage, were obliged to be put into it to make a Lot of it, and then it went for a song. So I heard mentioned, and I wondered what song, and thought what a dismal song it must have been to sing!

Then, I was sent to a great, cold, bare, school of big boys; where everything to eat and wear was thick and clumpy, without being enough; where everybody, large and small, was cruel; where the boys knew all about the sale, before I got there, and asked me what I had fetched, and who had bought me, and hooted at me, "Going, going, gone!" I never whispered in that wretched place that I had been Haroun, or had had a *Seraglio*: for, I knew that if I mentioned my reverses, I should be so worried, that I should have to drown myself in the muddy pond near the playground, which looked like the beer.

Ah me, ah me! No other ghost has haunted the boy's room, my friends, since I have occupied it, than the ghost of my own childhood, the ghost of my own innocence, the ghost of my own airy belief. Many a time have I pursued the phantom: never with this man's stride of mine to come up with it, never with these man's hands of mine to touch it, never more to this man's heart of mine to hold it in its purity. And here you see me working out, as cheerfully and thankfully as I may, my doom of shaving in the glass a constant change of customers, and of lying down and rising up with the skeleton allotted to me for my mortal companion.

The Queer Client

'It matters little,' said the old man, 'where, or how, I picked up this brief history. If I were to relate it in the order in which it reached me, I should commence in the middle, and when I had arrived at the conclusion, go back for a beginning. It is enough for me to say that some of its circumstances passed before my own eyes; for the remainder I know them to have happened, and there are some persons yet living, who will remember them but too well.

'In the Borough High Street, near St. George's Church, and on the same side of the way, stands, as most people know, the smallest of our debtors' prisons, the Marshalsea. Although in later times it has been a very different place from the sink of filth and dirt it once was, even its improved condition holds out but little temptation to the extravagant, or consolation to the improvident. The condemned felon has as good a yard for air and exercise in Newgate, as the insolvent debtor in the Marshalsea Prison. [Better. But this is past, in a better age, and the prison exists no longer.]

'It may be my fancy, or it may be that I cannot separate the place from the old recollections associated with it, but this part of London I cannot bear. The street is broad, the shops are spacious, the noise of passing vehicles, the footsteps of a perpetual stream of people—all the busy sounds of traffic, resound in it from morn to midnight; but the streets around are mean and close; poverty and debauchery lie festering in the crowded alleys; want and misfortune are pent up in the narrow prison; an air of gloom and dreariness seems, in my eyes at least, to hang about the scene, and to impart to it a squalid and sickly hue.

'Many eyes, that have long since been closed in the grave, have looked round upon that scene lightly enough, when entering the gate of the old Marshalsea Prison for the first time; for despair seldom comes with the first severe shock of misfortune. A man has confidence in untried friends, he remembers the many offers of service so freely made by his boon companions when he wanted them not; he has hope—the hope of happy inexperience—and however he may bend beneath the first shock, it springs up in his bosom, and flourishes there for a brief space, until it droops beneath the blight of disappointment and neglect. How soon have those same eyes, deeply sunken in the head, glared from faces wasted with famine, and sallow from confinement, in days when it was no figure of speech to say that debtors rotted in prison, with no hope of release, and no prospect of liberty! The atrocity in its full extent no longer exists, but there is enough of it left to give rise to occurrences that make the heart bleed.

'Twenty years ago, that pavement was worn with the footsteps of a mother and child, who, day by day, so surely as the morning came, presented themselves at the prison gate; often after a night of restless misery and anxious thoughts, were they there, a full hour too soon, and then the young mother turning meekly away, would lead the child to the old bridge, and raising him in her arms to show him the glistening water, tinted with the light of the morning's sun, and stirring with all the bustling preparations for business and pleasure that the river presented at that early hour, endeavour to interest his thoughts in the objects before him. But she would quickly set him down, and hiding her face in her shawl, give vent to the tears that blinded her; for no expression of interest or amusement lighted up his thin and sickly face.

'His recollections were few enough, but they were all of one kind—all connected with the poverty and misery of his parents. Hour after hour had he sat on his mother's knee, and with childish sympathy watched the tears that stole down her face, and then crept quietly away into some dark corner, and sobbed himself to sleep. The hard realities of the world, with many of its worst privations—hunger and thirst, and cold and want—had all come home to him, from the first dawnings of reason; and though the form of childhood was there, its light heart, its merry laugh, and sparkling eyes were wanting.

'The father and mother looked on upon this, and upon each other, with thoughts of agony they dared not breathe in words. The healthy, strong-made man, who could have borne almost any fatigue of active exertion, was wasting beneath the close confinement and unhealthy atmosphere of a crowded prison. The slight and delicate woman was sinking beneath the combined effects of bodily and mental illness. The child's young heart was breaking.

'Winter came, and with it weeks of cold and heavy rain. The poor girl had removed to a wretched apartment close to the spot of her husband's imprisonment; and though the change had been rendered necessary by their increasing poverty, she was happier now, for she was nearer him. For two months, she and her little companion watched the opening of the gate as usual. One day she failed to come, for the first time. Another morning arrived, and she came alone. The child was dead.

'They little know, who coldly talk of the poor man's bereavements, as a happy release from pain to the departed, and a merciful relief from expense to the survivor—they little know, I say, what the agony of those bereavements is. A silent look of affection and regard when all other eyes are turned coldly away—the consciousness that we possess the sympathy and affection of one being when all others have deserted us—is a hold, a stay, a comfort, in the deepest affliction, which no wealth could purchase, or power bestow.

'The child had sat at his parents' feet for hours together, with his little hands patiently folded in each other, and his thin wan face raised towards them. They had seen him pine away, from day to day; and though his brief existence had been a joyless one, and he was now removed to that peace and rest which, child as he was, he had never known in this world, they were his parents, and his loss sank deep into their souls.

'It was plain to those who looked upon the mother's altered face, that death must soon close the scene of her adversity and trial. Her husband's fellow-prisoners shrank from obtruding on his grief and misery, and left to himself alone, the small room he had previously occupied in common with two companions. She shared it with him; and lingering on without pain, but without hope, her life ebbed slowly away.

'She had fainted one evening in her husband's arms, and he had borne her to the open window, to revive her with the air, when the light of the moon falling full upon her face, showed him a change upon her features, which made him stagger beneath her weight, like a helpless infant.

'"Set me down, George," she said faintly. He did so, and seating himself beside her, covered his face with his hands, and burst into tears.

'"It is very hard to leave you, George," she said; "but it is God's will, and you must bear it for my sake. Oh! How I thank Him for having taken our boy! He is happy, and in heaven now. What would he have done here, without his mother!"

'"You shall not die, Mary, you shall not die;" said the husband, starting up. He paced hurriedly to and fro, striking his head with his clenched fists; then reseating himself beside her, and supporting her in his arms, added more calmly, "Rouse yourself, my dear girl. Pray, pray do. You will revive yet."

'"Never again, George; never again," said the dying woman. "Let them lay me by my poor boy now, but promise me, that if ever you leave this dreadful place, and should grow rich, you will have us removed to some quiet country churchyard, a long, long way off—very far from here—where we can rest in peace. Dear George, promise me you will."

'"I do, I do," said the man, throwing himself passionately on his knees before her. "Speak to me, Mary, another word; one look—but one!"

'He ceased to speak: for the arm that clasped his neck grew stiff and heavy. A deep sigh escaped from the wasted form before him; the lips moved, and a smile played upon the face; but the lips were pallid, and the smile faded into a rigid and ghastly stare. He was alone in the world.

'That night, in the silence and desolation of his miserable room, the wretched man knelt down by the dead body of his wife, and called on God to witness a terrible oath, that from that hour, he devoted himself to revenge her death and that of his child; that thenceforth to the last moment of his life, his whole energies should be directed to this one object; that his revenge should be protracted and terrible; that his hatred should be undying and inextinguishable; and should hunt its object through the world.

'The deepest despair, and passion scarcely human, had made such fierce ravages on his face and form, in that one night, that his companions in misfortune shrank affrighted from him as he passed by. His eyes were bloodshot and heavy, his face a deadly white, and his body bent as if with age. He had bitten his under lip nearly through in the violence of his mental suffering, and the blood which had flowed from the wound had trickled down his chin, and stained his shirt and neckerchief. No tear, or sound of complaint escaped him; but the unsettled look, and disordered haste with which he paced up and down the yard, denoted the fever which was burning within.

'It was necessary that his wife's body should be removed from the prison, without delay. He received the communication with perfect calmness, and acquiesced in its propriety. Nearly all the inmates of the prison had assembled to witness its removal; they fell back on either side when the widower appeared; he walked hurriedly forward, and stationed himself, alone, in a little railed area close to the lodge gate, from whence the crowd, with an instinctive feeling of delicacy, had retired. The rude coffin was borne slowly forward on men's shoulders.

'A dead silence pervaded the throng, broken only by the audible lamentations of the women, and the shuffling steps of the bearers on the stone pavement. They reached the spot where the bereaved husband stood: and stopped. He laid his hand upon the coffin, and mechanically adjusting the pall with which it was covered, motioned them onward. The turnkeys in the prison lobby took off their hats as it passed through, and in another moment the heavy gate closed behind it. He looked vacantly upon the crowd, and fell heavily to the ground.

'Although for many weeks after this, he was watched, night and day, in the wildest ravings of fever, neither the consciousness of his loss, nor the recollection of the vow he had made, ever left him for a moment. Scenes changed before his eyes, place succeeded place, and event followed event, in all the hurry of delirium; but they were all connected in some way with the great object of his mind. He was sailing over a boundless expanse of sea, with a blood-red sky above, and the angry waters, lashed into fury beneath, boiling and eddying up, on every side.

'There was another vessel before them, toiling and labouring in the howling storm; her canvas fluttering in ribbons from the mast, and her deck thronged with figures who were lashed to the sides, over which huge waves every instant burst, sweeping away some devoted creatures into the foaming sea. Onward they bore, amidst the roaring mass of water, with a speed and force which nothing could resist; and striking the stem of the foremost vessel, crushed her beneath their keel. From the huge whirlpool which the sinking wreck occasioned, arose a shriek so loud and shrill—the death-cry of a hundred drowning creatures, blended into one fierce yell—that it rung far above the war-cry of the elements, and echoed, and re–echoed till it seemed to pierce air, sky, and ocean. But what was that—that old gray head that rose above the water's surface, and with looks of agony, and screams for aid, buffeted with the waves!

'One look, and he had sprung from the vessel's side, and with vigorous strokes was swimming towards it. He reached it; he was close upon it. They were HIS features. The old man saw him coming, and vainly strove to elude his grasp. But he clasped him tight, and dragged him beneath the water. Down, down with him, fifty fathoms down; his struggles grew fainter and fainter, until they wholly ceased. He was dead; he had killed him, and had kept his oath.

'He was traversing the scorching sands of a mighty desert, barefoot and alone. The sand choked and blinded him; its fine thin grains entered the very pores of his skin, and irritated him almost to madness. Gigantic masses of the same material, carried forward .by the wind, and shone through by the burning sun, stalked in the distance like pillars of living fire. The bones of men, who had perished in the dreary waste, lay scattered at his feet; a fearful light fell on everything around; so far as the eye could reach, nothing but objects of dread and horror presented themselves. Vainly striving to utter a cry of terror, with his tongue cleaving to his mouth, he rushed madly forward.

'Armed with supernatural strength, he waded through the sand, until, exhausted with fatigue and thirst, he fell senseless on the earth. What fragrant coolness revived him; what gushing sound was that? Water! It was indeed a well; and the clear fresh stream was running at his feet. He drank deeply of it, and throwing his aching limbs upon the bank, sank into a delicious trance. The sound of approaching footsteps roused him. An old gray-headed man tottered forward to slake his burning thirst. It was HE again! He wound his arms round the old man's body, and held him back. He struggled, and shrieked for water—for but one drop of water to save his life! But he held the old man firmly, and watched his agonies with greedy eyes; and when his lifeless head fell forward on his bosom, he rolled the corpse from him with his feet.

'When the fever left him, and consciousness returned, he awoke to find himself rich and free, to hear that the parent who would have let him die in jail—WOULD! Who HAD let those who were far dearer to him than his own existence die of want, and sickness of heart that medicine cannot cure—had been found dead in his bed of down. He had had all the heart to leave his son a beggar, but proud even of his health and strength, had put off the act till it was too late, and now might gnash his teeth in the other world, at the thought of the wealth his remissness had left him.

'He awoke to this, and he awoke to more. To recollect the purpose for which he lived, and to remember that his enemy was his wife's own father—the man who had cast him into prison, and who, when his daughter and her child sued at his feet for mercy, had spurned them from his door. Oh, how he cursed the weakness that prevented him from being up, and active, in his scheme of vengeance! 'He caused himself to be carried from the scene of his loss and misery, and conveyed to a quiet residence on the sea–coast; not in the hope of recovering his peace of mind or happiness, for both were fled for ever; but to restore his prostrate energies, and meditate on his darling object. And here, some evil spirit cast in his way the opportunity for his first, most horrible revenge.

'It was summer-time; and wrapped in his gloomy thoughts, he would issue from his solitary lodgings early in the evening, and wandering along a narrow path beneath the cliffs, to a wild and lonely spot that had struck his fancy in his ramblings, seat himself on some fallen fragment of the rock, and burying his face in his hands, remain there for hours—sometimes until night had completely closed in, and the long shadows of the frowning cliffs above his head cast a thick, black darkness on every object near him.

'He was seated here, one calm evening, in his old position, now and then raising his head to watch the flight of a sea-gull, or carry his eye along the glorious crimson path, which, commencing in the middle of the ocean, seemed to lead to its very verge where the sun was setting, when the profound stillness of the spot was broken by a loud cry for help; he listened, doubtful of his having heard aright, when the cry was repeated with even greater vehemence than before, and, starting to his feet, he hastened in the direction whence it proceeded.

'The tale told itself at once: some scattered garments lay on the beach; a human head was just visible above the waves at a little distance from the shore; and an old man, wringing his hands in agony, was running to and fro, shrieking for assistance. The invalid, whose strength was now sufficiently restored, threw off his coat, and rushed towards the sea, with the intention of plunging in, and dragging the drowning man ashore.

'"Hasten here, Sir, in God's name; help, help, sir, for the love of Heaven. He is my son, Sir, my only son!" said the old man frantically, as he advanced to meet him. "My only son, Sir, and he is dying before his father's eyes!"

'At the first word the old man uttered, the stranger checked himself in his career, and, folding his arms, stood perfectly motionless.

'"Great God!" exclaimed the old man, recoiling, "Heyling!"

'The stranger smiled, and was silent.

'"Heyling!" said the old man wildly; "my boy, Heyling, my dear boy, look, look!" Gasping for breath, the miserable father pointed to the spot where the young man was struggling for life.

'"Hark!" said the old man. "He cries once more. He is alive yet. Heyling, save him, save him!"

'The stranger smiled again, and remained immovable as a statue. '"I have wronged you," shrieked the old man, falling on his knees, and clasping his hands together. "Be revenged; take my all, my life; cast me into the water at your feet, and, if human nature can repress a struggle, I will die, without stirring hand or foot. Do it, Heyling, do it, but save my boy; he is so young, Heyling, so young to die!"

'"Listen," said the stranger, grasping the old man fiercely by the wrist; "I will have life for life, and here is ONE. MY child died, before his father's eyes, a far more agonising and painful death than that young slanderer of his sister's worth is meeting while I speak. You laughed—laughed in your daughter's face, where death had already set his hand—at our sufferings, then. What think you of them now! See there, see there!"

'As the stranger spoke, he pointed to the sea. A faint cry died away upon its surface; the last powerful struggle of the dying man agitated the rippling waves for a few seconds; and the spot where he had gone down into his early grave, was undistinguishable from the surrounding water.

'Three years had elapsed, when a gentleman alighted from a private carriage at the door of a London attorney, then well known as a man of no great nicety in his professional dealings, and requested a private interview on business of importance. Although evidently not past the prime of life, his face was pale, haggard, and dejected; and it did not require the acute perception of the man of business, to discern at a glance, that disease or suffering had done more to work a change in his appearance, than the mere hand of time could have accomplished in twice the period of his whole life.

'"I wish you to undertake some legal business for me," said the stranger.

'The attorney bowed obsequiously, and glanced at a large packet which the gentleman carried in his hand. His visitor observed the look, and proceeded.

'"It is no common business," said he; "nor have these papers reached my hands without long trouble and great expense."

'The attorney cast a still more anxious look at the packet; and his visitor, untying the string that bound it, disclosed a quantity of promissory notes, with copies of deeds, and other documents.

'"Upon these papers," said the client, "the man whose name they bear, has raised, as you will see, large sums of money, for years past. There was a tacit understanding between him and the men into whose hands they originally went—and from whom I have by degrees purchased the whole, for treble and quadruple their nominal value—that these loans should be from time to time renewed, until a given period had elapsed. Such an understanding is nowhere expressed. He has sustained many losses of late; and these obligations accumulating upon him at once, would crush him to the earth."

'"The whole amount is many thousands of pounds," said the attorney, looking over the papers.

'"It is," said the client.

'"What are we to do?" inquired the man of business.

'"Do!" replied the client, with sudden vehemence. "Put every engine of the law in force, every trick that ingenuity can devise and rascality execute; fair means and foul; the open oppression of the law, aided by all the craft of its most ingenious practitioners. I would have him die a harassing and lingering death. Ruin him, seize and sell his lands and goods, drive him from house and home, and drag him forth a beggar in his old age, to die in a common jail."

'"But the costs, my dear Sir, the costs of all this," reasoned the attorney, when he had recovered from his momentary surprise. "If the defendant be a man of straw, who is to pay the costs, Sir?"

'"Name any sum," said the stranger, his hand trembling so violently with excitement, that he could scarcely hold the pen he seized as he spoke—"any sum, and it is yours. Don't be afraid to name it, man. I shall not think it dear, if you gain my object."

'The attorney named a large sum, at hazard, as the advance he should require to secure himself against the possibility of loss; but more with the view of ascertaining how far his client was really disposed to go, than with any idea that he would comply with the demand. The stranger wrote a cheque upon his banker, for the whole amount, and left him.

'The draft was duly honoured, and the attorney, finding that his strange client might be safely relied upon, commenced his work in earnest. For more than two years afterwards, Mr. Heyling would sit whole days together, in the office, poring over the papers as they accumulated, and reading again and again, his eyes gleaming with joy, the letters of remonstrance, the prayers for a little delay, the representations of the certain ruin in which the opposite party must be involved, which poured in, as suit after suit, and process after process, was commenced.

'To all applications for a brief indulgence, there was but one reply—the money must be paid. Land, house, furniture, each in its turn, was taken under some one of the numerous executions which were issued; and the old man himself would have been immured in prison had he not escaped the vigilance of the officers, and fled.

'The implacable animosity of Heyling, so far from being satiated by the success of his persecution, increased a hundredfold with the ruin he inflicted. On being informed of the old man's flight, his fury was unbounded. He gnashed his teeth with rage, tore the hair from his head, and assailed with horrid imprecations the men who had been intrusted with the writ. He was only restored to comparative calmness by repeated assurances of the certainty of discovering the fugitive. Agents were sent in quest of him, in all directions; every stratagem that could be invented was resorted to, for the purpose of discovering his place of retreat; but it was all in vain. Half a year had passed over, and he was still undiscovered.

'At length late one night, Heyling, of whom nothing had been seen for many weeks before, appeared at his attorney's private residence, and sent up word that a gentleman wished to see him instantly. Before the attorney, who had recognised his voice from above stairs, could order the servant to admit him, he had rushed up the staircase, and entered the drawing-room pale and breathless. Having closed the door, to prevent being overheard, he sank into a chair, and said, in a low voice—

'"Hush! I have found him at last."

'"No!" said the attorney. "Well done, my dear sir, well done."

'"He lies concealed in a wretched lodging in Camden Town," said Heyling. "Perhaps it is as well we DID lose sight of him, for he has been living alone there, in the most abject misery, all the time, and he is poor—very poor."

'"Very good," said the attorney. "You will have the caption made tomorrow, of course?"

'"Yes," replied Heyling. "Stay! No! The next day. You are surprised at my wishing to postpone it," he added, with a ghastly smile; "but I had forgotten. The next day is an anniversary in his life: let it be done then."

'"Very good," said the attorney. "Will you write down instructions for the officer?"

'"No; let him meet me here, at eight in the evening, and I will accompany him myself."

'They met on the appointed night, and, hiring a hackney-coach, directed the driver to stop at that corner of the old Pancras Road, at which stands the parish workhouse. By the time they alighted there, it was quite dark; and, proceeding by the dead wall in front of the Veterinary Hospital, they entered a small by-street, which is, or was at that time, called Little College Street, and which, whatever it may be now, was in those days a desolate place enough, surrounded by little else than fields and ditches.

'Having drawn the travelling-cap he had on half over his face, and muffled himself in his cloak, Heyling stopped before the meanest-looking house in the street, and knocked gently at the door. It was at once opened by a woman, who dropped a curtsey of recognition, and Heyling, whispering the officer to remain below, crept gently upstairs, and, opening the door of the front room, entered at once.

'The object of his search and his unrelenting animosity, now a decrepit old man, was seated at a bare deal table, on which stood a miserable candle. He started on the entrance of the stranger, and rose feebly to his feet.

'"What now, what now?" said the old man. "What fresh misery is this? What do you want here?"

'"A word with YOU," replied Heyling. As he spoke, he seated himself at the other end of the table, and, throwing off his cloak and cap, disclosed his features.

'The old man seemed instantly deprived of speech. He fell backward in his chair, and, clasping his hands together, gazed on the apparition with a mingled look of abhorrence and fear.

'"This day six years," said Heyling, "I claimed the life you owed me for my child's. Beside the lifeless form of your daughter, old man, I swore to live a life of revenge. I have never swerved from my purpose for a moment's space; but if I had, one thought of her uncomplaining, suffering look, as she drooped away, or of the starving face of our innocent child, would have nerved me to my task. My first act of requital you well remember: this is my last."

'The old man shivered, and his hands dropped powerless by his side.

'"I leave England tomorrow," said Heyling, after a moment's pause. "Tonight I consign you to the living death to which you devoted her—a hopeless prison—"

'He raised his eyes to the old man's countenance, and paused. He lifted the light to his face, set it gently down, and left the apartment.

'"You had better see to the old man," he said to the woman, as he opened the door, and motioned the officer to follow him into the street. "I think he is ill." The woman closed the door, ran hastily upstairs, and found him lifeless.

'Beneath a plain gravestone, in one of the most peaceful and secluded churchyards in Kent, where wild flowers mingle with the grass, and the soft landscape around forms the fairest spot in the garden of England, lie the bones of the young mother and her gentle child. But the ashes of the father do not mingle with theirs; nor, from that night forward, did the attorney ever gain the remotest clue to the subsequent history of his queer client.'

The Cricket on the Hearth

Chapter 1
Chirp the First

The kettle began it! Don't tell me what Mrs. Peerybingle said. I know better. Mrs. Peerybingle may leave it on record to the end of time that she couldn't say which of them began it; but, I say the kettle did. I ought to know, I hope! The kettle began it, full five minutes by the little waxy-faced Dutch clock in the corner, before the Cricket uttered a chirp.

As if the clock hadn't finished striking, and the convulsive little Haymaker at the top of it, jerking away right and left with a scythe in front of a Moorish Palace, hadn't mowed down half an acre of imaginary grass before the Cricket joined in at all!

Why, I am not naturally positive. Everyone knows that. I wouldn't set my own opinion against the opinion of Mrs. Peerybingle, unless I were quite sure, on any account whatever. Nothing should induce me. But, this is a question of act. And the fact is, that the kettle began it, at least five minutes before the Cricket gave any sign of being in existence. Contradict me, and I'll say ten.

Let me narrate exactly how it happened. I should have proceeded to do so in my very first word, but for this plain consideration—if I am to tell a story I must begin at the beginning; and how is it possible to begin at the beginning, without beginning at the kettle?

It appeared as if there were a sort of match, or trial of skill, you must understand, between the kettle and the Cricket. And this is what led to it, and how it came about.

Mrs. Peerybingle, going out into the raw twilight, and clicking over the wet stones in a pair of pattens that worked innumerable rough impressions of the first proposition in Euclid all about the yard—Mrs. Peerybingle filled the kettle at the water-butt. Presently returning, less the pattens (and a good deal less, for they were tall and Mrs. Peerybingle was but short), she set the kettle on the fire. In doing which she lost her temper, or mislaid it for an instant; for, the water being uncomfortably cold, and in that slippy, slushy, sleety sort of state wherein it seems to penetrate through every kind of substance, patten rings included—had laid hold of Mrs. Peerybingle's toes, and even splashed her legs. And when we rather plume ourselves (with reason too) upon our legs, and keep ourselves particularly neat in point of stockings, we find this, for the moment, hard to bear.

Besides, the kettle was aggravating and obstinate. It wouldn't allow itself to be adjusted on the top bar; it wouldn't hear of accommodating itself kindly to the knobs of coal; it WOULD lean forward with a drunken air, and dribble, a very Idiot of a kettle, on the hearth. It was quarrelsome, and hissed and spluttered morosely at the fire. To sum up all, the lid, resisting Mrs. Peerybingle's fingers, first of all turned topsy-turvy, and then, with an ingenious pertinacity deserving of a better cause, dived sideways in—down to the very bottom of the kettle. And the hull of the Royal George has never made half the monstrous resistance to coming out of the water, which the lid of that kettle employed against Mrs. Peerybingle, before she got it up again.

It looked sullen and pig-headed enough, even then; carrying its handle with an air of defiance, and cocking its spout pertly and mockingly at Mrs. Peerybingle, as if it said, 'I won't boil. Nothing shall induce me!'

But Mrs. Peerybingle, with restored good humour, dusted her chubby little hands against each other, and sat down before the kettle, laughing. Meantime, the jolly blaze uprose and fell, flashing and gleaming on the little Haymaker at the top of the Dutch clock, until one might have thought he stood stock still before the Moorish Palace, and nothing was in motion but the flame.

He was on the move, however; and had his spasms, two to the second, all right and regular. But, his sufferings when the clock was going to strike, were frightful to behold; and, when a Cuckoo looked out of a trap-door in the Palace, and gave note six times, it shook him, each time, like a spectral voice—or like a something wiry, plucking at his legs.

It was not until a violent commotion and a whirring noise among the weights and ropes below him had quite subsided, that this terrified Haymaker became himself again. Nor was he startled without reason; for these rattling, bony skeletons of clocks are very disconcerting in their operation, and I wonder very much how any set of men, but most of all how Dutchmen, can have had a liking to invent them. There is a popular belief that Dutchmen love broad cases and much clothing for their own lower selves; and they might know better than to leave their clocks so very lank and unprotected, surely.

Now it was, you observe, that the kettle began to spend the evening. Now it was, that the kettle, growing mellow and musical, began to have irrepressible gurglings in its throat, and to indulge in short vocal snorts, which it checked in the bud, as if it hadn't quite made up its mind yet, to be good company. Now it was, that after two or three such vain attempts to stifle its convivial sentiments, it threw off all moroseness, all reserve, and burst into a stream of song so cosy and hilarious, as never maudlin nightingale yet formed the least idea of.

So plain too! Bless you, you might have understood it like a book—better than some books you and I could name, perhaps. With its warm breath gushing forth in a light cloud which merrily and gracefully ascended a few feet, then hung about the chimney-corner as its own domestic Heaven, it trolled its song with that strong energy of cheerfulness, that its iron body hummed and stirred upon the fire; and the lid itself, the recently rebellious lid—such is the influence of a bright example—performed a sort of jig, and clattered like a deaf and dumb young cymbal that had never known the use of its twin brother.

That this song of the kettle's was a song of invitation and welcome to somebody out of doors: to somebody at that moment coming on, towards the snug small home and the crisp fire: there is no doubt whatever. Mrs. Peerybingle knew it, perfectly, as she sat musing before the hearth. It's a dark night, sang the kettle, and the rotten leaves are lying by the way; and, above, all is mist and darkness, and, below, all is mire and clay; and there's only one relief in all the sad and murky air; and I don't know that it is one, for it's nothing but a glare; of deep and angry crimson, where the sun and wind together; set a brand upon the clouds for being guilty of such weather; and the widest open country is a long dull streak of black; and there's hoar-frost on the finger-post, and thaw upon the track; and the ice it isn't water, and the water isn't free; and you couldn't say that anything is what it ought to be; but he's coming, coming, coming!—

And here, if you like, the Cricket DID chime in! with a Chirrup, Chirrup, Chirrup of such magnitude, by way of chorus; with a voice so astoundingly disproportionate to its size, as compared with the kettle; (size! you couldn't see it!) that if it had then and there burst itself like an overcharged gun, if it had fallen a victim on the spot, and chirruped its little body into fifty pieces, it would have seemed a natural and inevitable consequence, for which it had expressly laboured.

The kettle had had the last of its solo performance. It persevered with undiminished ardour; but the Cricket took first fiddle and kept it. Good Heaven, how it chirped! Its shrill, sharp, piercing voice resounded through the house, and seemed to twinkle in the outer darkness like a star. There was an indescribable little trill and tremble in it, at its loudest, which suggested its being carried off its legs, and made to leap again, by its own intense enthusiasm. Yet they went very well together, the Cricket and the kettle. The burden of the song was still the same; and louder, louder, louder still, they sang it in their emulation.

The fair little listener—for fair she was, and young: though something of what is called the dumpling shape; but I don't myself object to that—lighted a candle, glanced at the Haymaker on the top of the clock, who was getting in a pretty average crop of minutes; and looked out of the window, where she saw nothing, owing to the darkness, but her own face imaged in the glass. And my opinion is (and so would yours have been), that she might have looked a long way, and seen nothing half so agreeable. When she came back, and sat down in her former seat, the Cricket and the kettle were still keeping it up, with a perfect fury of competition. The kettle's weak side clearly being, that he didn't know when he was beat.

There was all the excitement of a race about it. Chirp, chirp, chirp! Cricket a mile ahead. Hum, hum, hum—m—m! Kettle making play in the distance, like a great top. Chirp, chirp, chirp! Cricket round the corner. Hum, hum, hum—m—m! Kettle sticking to him in his own way; no idea of giving in. Chirp, chirp, chirp! Cricket fresher than ever. Hum, hum, hum—m—m! Kettle slow and steady. Chirp, chirp, chirp! Cricket going in to finish him. Hum, hum, hum—m—m! Kettle not to be finished. Until at last they got so jumbled together, in the hurry-skurry, helter-skelter, of the match, that whether the kettle chirped and the Cricket hummed, or the Cricket chirped and the kettle hummed, or they both chirped and both hummed, it would have taken a clearer head than yours or mine to have decided with anything like certainty. But, of this, there is no doubt: that, the kettle and the Cricket, at one and the same moment, and by some power of amalgamation best known to themselves, sent, each, his fireside song of comfort streaming into a ray of the candle that shone out through the window, and a long way down the lane. And this light, bursting on a certain person who, on the instant, approached towards it through the gloom, expressed the whole thing to him, literally in a twinkling, and cried, 'Welcome home, old fellow! Welcome home, my boy!'

This end attained, the kettle, being dead beat, boiled over, and was taken off the fire. Mrs. Peerybingle then went running to the door, where, what with the wheels of a cart, the tramp of a horse, the voice of a man, the tearing in and out of an excited dog, and the surprising and mysterious appearance of a baby, there was soon the very What's-his-name to pay.

Where the baby came from, or how Mrs. Peerybingle got hold of it in that flash of time, I don't know. But a live baby there was, in Mrs. Peerybingle's arms; and a pretty tolerable amount of pride she seemed to have in it, when she was drawn gently to the fire, by a sturdy figure of a man, much taller and much older than herself, who had to stoop a long way down, to kiss her. But she was worth the trouble. Six foot six, with the lumbago, might have done it.

'Oh goodness, John!' said Mrs. P. 'What a state you are in with the weather!'

He was something the worse for it, undeniably. The thick mist hung in clots upon his eyelashes like candied thaw; and between the fog and fire together, there were rainbows in his very whiskers.

'Why, you see, Dot,' John made answer, slowly, as he unrolled a shawl from about his throat; and warmed his hands; 'it—it an't exactly summer weather. So, no wonder.'

'I wish you wouldn't call me Dot, John. I don't like it,' said Mrs. Peerybingle: pouting in a way that clearly showed she DID like it, very much.

'Why what else are you?' returned John, looking down upon her with a smile, and giving her waist as light a squeeze as his huge hand and arm could give. 'A dot and'—here he glanced at the baby—'a dot and carry—I won't say it, for fear I should spoil it; but I was very near a joke. I don't know as ever I was nearer.'

He was often near to something or other very clever, by his own account: this lumbering, slow, honest John; this John so heavy, but so light of spirit; so rough upon the surface, but so gentle at the core; so dull without, so quick within; so stolid, but so good! Oh Mother Nature, give thy children the true poetry of heart that hid itself in this poor Carrier's breast—he was but a Carrier by the way—and we can bear to have them talking prose, and leading lives of prose; and bear to bless thee for their company!

It was pleasant to see Dot, with her little figure, and her baby in her arms: a very doll of a baby: glancing with a coquettish thoughtfulness at the fire, and inclining her delicate little head just enough on one side to let it rest in an odd, half-natural, half-affected, wholly nestling and agreeable manner, on the great rugged figure of the Carrier. It was pleasant to see him, with his tender awkwardness, endeavouring to adapt his rude support to her slight need, and make his burly middle-age a leaning-staff not inappropriate to her blooming youth. It was pleasant to observe how Tilly Slowboy, waiting in the background for the baby, took special cognizance (though in her earliest teens) of this grouping; and stood with her mouth and eyes wide open, and her head thrust forward, taking it in as if it were air. Nor was it less agreeable to observe how John the Carrier, reference being made by Dot to the aforesaid baby, checked his hand when on the point of touching the infant, as if he thought he might crack it; and bending down, surveyed it from a safe distance, with a kind of puzzled pride, such as an amiable mastiff might be supposed to show, if he found himself, one day, the father of a young canary.

'An't he beautiful, John? Don't he look precious in his sleep?'

'Very precious,' said John. 'Very much so. He generally IS asleep, an't he?'

'Lor, John! Good gracious no!'

'Oh,' said John, pondering. 'I thought his eyes was generally shut. Halloa!'

'Goodness, John, how you startle one!'

'It an't right for him to turn 'em up in that way!' said the astonished Carrier, 'is it? See how he's winking with both of 'em at once! And look at his mouth! Why he's gasping like a gold and silver fish!'

'You don't deserve to be a father, you don't,' said Dot, with all the dignity of an experienced matron. 'But how should you know what little complaints children are troubled with, John! You wouldn't so much as know their names, you stupid fellow.'

And when she had turned the baby over on her left arm, and had slapped its back as a restorative, she pinched her husband's ear, laughing.

'No,' said John, pulling off his outer coat. 'It's very true, Dot. I don't know much about it. I only know that I've been fighting pretty stiffly with the wind tonight. It's been blowing northeast, straight into the cart, the whole way home.'

'Poor old man, so it has!' cried Mrs. Peerybingle, instantly becoming very active. 'Here! Take the precious darling, Tilly, while I make myself of some use. Bless it, I could smother it with kissing it, I could! Hie then, good dog! Hie, Boxer, boy! Only let me make the tea first, John; and then I'll help you with the parcels, like a busy bee. "How doth the little"—and all the rest of it, you know, John. Did you ever learn "how doth the little," when you went to school, John?'

'Not to quite know it,' John returned. 'I was very near it once. But I should only have spoilt it, I dare say.'

'Ha ha,' laughed Dot. She had the blithest little laugh you ever heard. 'What a dear old darling of a dunce you are, John, to be sure!'

Not at all disputing this position, John went out to see that the boy with the lantern, which had been dancing to and fro before the door and window, like a Will of the Wisp, took due care of the horse; who was fatter than you would quite believe, if I gave you his measure, and so old that his birthday was lost in the mists of antiquity. Boxer, feeling that his attentions were due to the family in general, and must be impartially distributed, dashed in and out with bewildering inconstancy; now, describing a circle of short barks round the horse, where he was being rubbed down at the stable-door; now feigning to make savage rushes at his mistress, and facetiously bringing himself to sudden stops; now, eliciting a shriek from Tilly Slowboy, in the low nursing-chair near the fire, by the unexpected application of his moist nose to her countenance; now, exhibiting an obtrusive interest in the baby; now, going round and round upon the hearth, and lying down as if he had established himself for the night;

now, getting up again, and taking that nothing of a fag-end of a tail of his, out into the weather, as if he had just remembered an appointment, and was off, at a round trot, to keep it.

'There! There's the teapot, ready on the hob!' said Dot; as briskly busy as a child at play at keeping house. 'And there's the old knuckle of ham; and there's the butter; and there's the crusty loaf, and all! Here's the clothes-basket for the small parcels, John, if you've got any there—where are you, John?'

'Don't let the dear child fall under the grate, Tilly, whatever you do!'

It may be noted of Miss Slowboy, in spite of her rejecting the caution with some vivacity, that she had a rare and surprising talent for getting this baby into difficulties and had several times imperilled its short life, in a quiet way peculiarly her own. She was of a spare and straight shape, this young lady, insomuch that her garments appeared to be in constant danger of sliding off those sharp pegs, her shoulders, on which they were loosely hung. Her costume was remarkable for the partial development, on all possible occasions, of some flannel vestment of a singular structure; also for affording glimpses, in the region of the back, of a corset, or pair of stays, in colour a dead-green.

Being always in a state of gaping admiration at everything, and absorbed, besides, in the perpetual contemplation of her mistress's perfections and the baby's, Miss Slowboy, in her little errors of judgment, may be said to have done equal honour to her head and to her heart; and though these did less honour to the baby's head, which they were the occasional means of bringing into contact with deal doors, dressers, stair-rails, bed-posts, and other foreign substances, still they were the honest results of Tilly Slowboy's constant astonishment at finding herself so kindly treated, and installed in such a comfortable home. For, the maternal and paternal Slowboy were alike unknown to Fame, and Tilly had been bred by public charity, a foundling; which word, though only differing from fondling by one vowel's length, is very different in meaning, and expresses quite another thing.

To have seen little Mrs. Peerybingle come back with her husband, tugging at the clothes-basket, and making the most strenuous exertions to do nothing at all (for he carried it), would have amused you almost as much as it amused him. It may have entertained the Cricket too, for anything I know; but, certainly, it now began to chirp again, vehemently.

'Heyday!' said John, in his slow way. 'It's merrier than ever, tonight, I think.'

'And it's sure to bring us good fortune, John! It always has done so. To have a Cricket on the Hearth, is the luckiest thing in all the world!'

John looked at her as if he had very nearly got the thought into his head, that she was his Cricket in chief, and he quite agreed with her. But, it was probably one of his narrow escapes, for he said nothing.

'The first time I heard its cheerful little note, John, was on that night when you brought me home—when you brought me to my new home here; its little mistress. Nearly a year ago. You recollect, John?'

O yes. John remembered. I should think so!

'Its chirp was such a welcome to me! It seemed so full of promise and encouragement. It seemed to say, you would be kind and gentle with me, and would not expect (I had a fear of that, John, then) to find an old head on the shoulders of your foolish little wife.'

John thoughtfully patted one of the shoulders, and then the head, as though he would have said No, no; he had had no such expectation; he had been quite content to take them as they were. And really he had reason. They were very comely.

'It spoke the truth, John, when it seemed to say so; for you have ever been, I am sure, the best, the most considerate, the most affectionate of husbands to me. This has been a happy home, John; and I love the Cricket for its sake!'

'Why so do I then,' said the Carrier. 'So do I, Dot.'

'I love it for the many times I have heard it, and the many thoughts its harmless music has given me. Sometimes, in the twilight, when I have felt a little solitary and down-hearted, John—before baby was here to keep me company and make the house gay—when I have thought how lonely you would be if I should die; how lonely I should be if I could know that you had lost me, dear; its Chirp, Chirp, Chirp upon the hearth, has seemed to tell me of another little voice, so sweet, so very dear to me, before whose coming sound my trouble vanished like a dream. And when I used to fear—I did fear once, John, I was very young you know—that ours might prove to be an ill-assorted marriage, I being such a child, and you more like my guardian than my husband; and that you might not, however hard you tried, be able to learn to love me, as you hoped and prayed you might; its Chirp, Chirp, Chirp has cheered me up again, and filled me with new trust and confidence. I was thinking of these things tonight, dear, when I sat expecting you; and I love the Cricket for their sake!'

'And so do I,' repeated John. 'But, Dot? I hope and pray that I might learn to love you? How you talk! I had learnt that, long before I brought you here, to be the Cricket's little mistress, Dot!'

She laid her hand, an instant, on his arm, and looked up at him with an agitated face, as if she would have told him something. Next moment she was down upon her knees before the basket, speaking in a sprightly voice, and busy with the parcels.

'There are not many of them tonight, John, but I saw some goods behind the cart, just now; and though they give more trouble, perhaps, still they pay as well; so we have no reason to grumble, have we? Besides, you have been delivering, I dare say, as you came along?'

'Oh yes,' John said. 'A good many.'

'Why what's this round box? Heart alive, John, it's a wedding-cake!'

'Leave a woman alone to find out that,' said John, admiringly. 'Now a man would never have thought of it. Whereas, it's my belief that if you was to pack a wedding-cake up in a tea-chest, or a turn-up bedstead, or a pickled salmon keg, or any unlikely thing, a woman would be sure to find it out directly. Yes; I called for it at the pastry-cook's.'

'And it weighs I don't know what—whole hundredweights!' cried Dot, making a great demonstration of trying to lift it.

'Whose is it, John? Where is it going?'

'Read the writing on the other side,' said John.

'Why, John! My Goodness, John!'

'Ah! Who'd have thought it!' John returned.

'You never mean to say,' pursued Dot, sitting on the floor and shaking her head at him, 'that it's Gruff and Tackleton the toymaker!'

John nodded.

Mrs. Peerybingle nodded also, fifty times at least. Not in assent—in dumb and pitying amazement; screwing up her lips the while with all their little force (they were never made for screwing up; I am clear of that), and looking the good Carrier through and through, in her abstraction. Miss Slowboy, in the mean time, who had a mechanical power of reproducing scraps of current conversation for the delectation of the baby, with all the sense struck out of them, and all the nouns changed into the plural number, inquired aloud of that young creature, Was it Gruffs and Tackletons the toymakers then, and Would it call at Pastry-cooks for wedding-cakes, and Did its mothers know the boxes when its fathers brought them homes; and so on.

'And that is really to come about!' said Dot. 'Why, she and I were girls at school together, John.'

He might have been thinking of her, or nearly thinking of her, perhaps, as she was in that same school time. He looked upon her with a thoughtful pleasure, but he made no answer.

'And he's as old! As unlike her!—Why, how many years older than you, is Gruff and Tackleton, John?'

'How many more cups of tea shall I drink tonight at one sitting, than Gruff and Tackleton ever took in four, I wonder!' replied John, good-humouredly, as he drew a chair to the round table, and began at the cold ham. 'As to eating, I eat but little; but that little I enjoy, Dot.'

Even this, his usual sentiment at meal times, one of his innocent delusions (for his appetite was always obstinate, and flatly contradicted him), awoke no smile in the face of his little wife, who stood among the parcels, pushing the cake-box slowly from her with her foot, and never once looked, though her eyes were cast down too, upon the dainty shoe she generally was so mindful of. Absorbed in thought, she stood there, heedless alike of the tea and John (although he called to her, and rapped the table with his knife to startle her), until he rose and touched her on the arm; when she looked at him for a moment, and hurried to her place behind the teaboard, laughing at her negligence. But, not as she had laughed before. The manner and the music were quite changed.

The Cricket, too, had stopped. Somehow the room was not so cheerful as it had been. Nothing like it.

'So, these are all the parcels, are they, John?' she said, breaking a long silence, which the honest Carrier had devoted to the practical illustration of one part of his favourite sentiment-certainly enjoying what he ate, if it couldn't be admitted that he ate but little. 'So, these are all the parcels; are they, John?'

'That's all,' said John. 'Why—no—I—' laying down his knife and fork, and taking a long breath. 'I declare—I've clean forgotten the old gentleman!'

'The old gentleman?'

'In the cart,' said John. 'He was asleep, among the straw, the last time I saw him. I've very nearly remembered him, twice, since I came in; but he went out of my head again. Holloa! Yahip there! Rouse up! That's my hearty!'

John said these latter words outside the door, whither he had hurried with the candle in his hand.

Miss Slowboy, conscious of some mysterious reference to The Old Gentleman, and connecting in her mystified imagination certain associations of a religious nature with the phrase, was so disturbed, that hastily rising from the low chair by the fire to seek protection near the skirts of her mistress, and coming into contact as she crossed the doorway with an ancient Stranger, she instinctively made a charge or butt at him with the only offensive instrument within her reach. This instrument happening to be the baby, great commotion and alarm ensued, which the sagacity of Boxer rather tended to increase; for, that good dog, more thoughtful than its master, had, it seemed, been watching the old gentleman in his sleep, lest he should walk off with a few young poplar trees that were tied up behind the cart; and he still attended on him very closely, worrying his gaiters in fact, and making dead sets at the buttons.

'You're such an undeniable good sleeper, sir,' said John, when tranquillity was restored; in the mean time the old gentleman had stood, bareheaded and motionless, in the centre of the room; 'that I have half a mind to ask you where the other six are—only that would be a joke, and I know I should spoil it. Very near though,' murmured the Carrier, with a chuckle; 'very near!'

The Stranger, who had long white hair, good features, singularly bold and well defined for an old man, and dark, bright, penetrating eyes, looked round with a smile, and saluted the Carrier's wife by gravely inclining his head.

His garb was very quaint and odd—a long, long way behind the time. Its hue was brown, all over. In his hand he held a great brown club or walking-stick; and striking this upon the floor, it fell asunder, and became a chair. On which he sat down, quite composedly.

'There!' said the Carrier, turning to his wife. 'That's the way I found him, sitting by the roadside! Upright as a milestone. And almost as deaf.'

'Sitting in the open air, John!'

'In the open air,' replied the Carrier, 'just at dusk. "Carriage Paid," he said; and gave me eighteen pence. Then he got in. And there he is.'

'He's going, John, I think!'

Not at all. He was only going to speak.

'If you please, I was to be left till called for,' said the Stranger, mildly. 'Don't mind me.'

With that, he took a pair of spectacles from one of his large pockets, and a book from another, and leisurely began to read. Making no more of Boxer than if he had been a house lamb!

The Carrier and his wife exchanged a look of perplexity. The Stranger raised his head; and glancing from the latter to the former, said,

'Your daughter, my good friend?'

'Wife,' returned John.

'Niece?' said the Stranger.

'Wife,' roared John.

'Indeed?' observed the Stranger. 'Surely? Very young!'

He quietly turned over, and resumed his reading. But, before he could have read two lines, he again interrupted himself to say:

'Baby, yours?'

John gave him a gigantic nod; equivalent to an answer in the affirmative, delivered through a speaking trumpet.

'Girl?'

'Bo-o-oy!' roared John.

'Also very young, eh?'

Mrs. Peerybingle instantly struck in. 'Two months and three da-ays! Vaccinated just six weeks ago-o! Took very fine-ly! Considered, by the doctor, a remarkably beautiful chi-ild! Equal to the general run of children at five months o-old! Takes notice, in a way quite wonderful! May seem impossible to you, but feels his legs already!'

Here the breathless little mother, who had been shrieking these short sentences into the old man's ear, until her pretty face was crimsoned, held up the Baby before him as a stubborn and triumphant fact; while Tilly Slowboy, with a melodious cry of 'Ketcher, Ketcher'—which sounded like some unknown words, adapted to a popular Sneeze—performed some cow-like gambols round that all unconscious Innocent.

'Hark! He's called for, sure enough,' said John. 'There's somebody at the door. Open it, Tilly.'

Before she could reach it, however, it was opened from without; being a primitive sort of door, with a latch, that anyone could lift if he chose—and a good many people did choose, for all kinds of neighbours liked to have a cheerful word or two with the Carrier, though he was no great talker himself. Being opened, it gave admission to a little, meagre, thoughtful, dingy-faced man, who seemed to have made himself a great-coat from the sack-cloth covering of some old box; for, when he turned to shut the door, and keep the weather out, he disclosed upon the back of that garment, the inscription *G & T* in large black capitals. Also the word *GLASS* in bold characters.

'Good evening, John!' said the little man. 'Good evening, Mum. Good evening, Tilly. Good evening, Unbeknown! How's Baby, Mum? Boxer's pretty well I hope?'

'All thriving, Caleb,' replied Dot. 'I am sure you need only look at the dear child, for one, to know that.'

'And I'm sure I need only look at you for another,' said Caleb.

He didn't look at her though; he had a wandering and thoughtful eye which seemed to be always projecting itself into some other time and place, no matter what he said; a description which will equally apply to his voice.

'Or at John for another,' said Caleb. 'Or at Tilly, as far as that goes. Or certainly at Boxer.'

'Busy just now, Caleb?' asked the Carrier.

'Why, pretty well, John,' he returned, with the distraught air of a man who was casting about for the Philosopher's stone, at least. 'Pretty much so. There's rather a run on Noah's Arks at present. I could have wished to improve upon the Family, but I don't see how it's to be done at the price. It would be a satisfaction to one's mind, to make it clearer which was Shems and Hams, and which was Wives. Flies an't on that scale neither, as compared with elephants you know! Ah! Well! Have you got anything in the parcel line for me, John?'

The Carrier put his hand into a pocket of the coat he had taken off; and brought out, carefully preserved in moss and paper, a tiny flower-pot.

'There it is!' he said, adjusting it with great care. 'Not so much as a leaf damaged. Full of buds!'

Caleb's dull eye brightened, as he took it, and thanked him.

'Dear, Caleb,' said the Carrier. 'Very dear at this season.'

'Never mind that. It would be cheap to me, whatever it cost,' returned the little man. 'Anything else, John?'

'A small box,' replied the Carrier. 'Here you are!'

'"For Caleb Plummer,"' said the little man, spelling out the direction. '"With Cash." With Cash, John? I don't think it's for me.'

'With Care,' returned the Carrier, looking over his shoulder. 'Where do you make out cash?'

'Oh! To be sure!' said Caleb. 'It's all right. With care! Yes, yes; that's mine. It might have been with cash, indeed, if my dear Boy in the Golden South Americas had lived, John. You loved him like a son; didn't you? You needn't say you did. I know, of course. "Caleb Plummer. With care." Yes, yes, it's all right. It's a box of dolls' eyes for my daughter's work. I wish it was her own sight in a box, John.'

'I wish it was, or could be!' cried the Carrier.

'Thank'ee,' said the little man. 'You speak very hearty. To think that she should never see the Dolls—and them a-staring at her, so bold, all day long! That's where it cuts. What's the damage, John?'

'I'll damage you,' said John, 'if you inquire. Dot! Very near?'

'Well! It's like you to say so,' observed the little man. 'It's your kind way. Let me see. I think that's all.'

'I think not,' said the Carrier. 'Try again.'

'Something for our Governor, eh?' said Caleb, after pondering a little while. 'To be sure. That's what I came for; but my head's so running on them Arks and things! He hasn't been here, has he?'

'Not he,' returned the Carrier. 'He's too busy, courting.'

'He's coming round though,' said Caleb; 'for he told me to keep on the near side of the road going home, and it was ten to one he'd take me up. I had better go, by the bye.—You couldn't have the goodness to let me pinch Boxer's tail, Mum, for half a moment, could you?'

'Why, Caleb! What a question!'

'Oh never mind, Mum,' said the little man. 'He mightn't like it perhaps. There's a small order just come in, for barking dogs; and I should wish to go as close to Natur' as I could, for six-pence. That's all. Never mind, Mum.'

It happened opportunely, that Boxer, without receiving the proposed stimulus, began to bark with great zeal. But, as this implied the approach of some new visitor, Caleb, postponing his study from the life to a more convenient season, shouldered the round box, and took a hurried leave. He might have spared himself the trouble, for he met the visitor upon the threshold.

'Oh! You are here, are you? Wait a bit. I'll take you home. John Peerybingle, my service to you. More of my service to your pretty wife. Handsomer every day! Better too, if possible! And younger,' mused the speaker, in a low voice; 'that's the Devil of it!'

'I should be astonished at your paying compliments, Mr. Tackleton,' said Dot, not with the best grace in the world; 'but for your condition.'

'You know all about it then?'

'I have got myself to believe it, somehow,' said Dot.

'After a hard struggle, I suppose?'

'Very.'

Tackleton the Toy-merchant, pretty generally known as Gruff and Tackleton—for that was the firm, though Gruff had been bought out long ago; only leaving his name, and as some said his nature, according to its Dictionary meaning, in the business-Tackleton the Toy-merchant, was a man whose vocation had been quite misunderstood by his Parents and Guardians. If they had made him a Money Lender, or a sharp Attorney, or a Sheriff's Officer, or a Broker, he might have sown his discontented oats in his youth, and, after having had the full run of himself in ill-natured transactions, might have turned out amiable, at last, for the sake of a little freshness and novelty.

But, cramped and chafing in the peaceable pursuit of toy-making, he was a domestic Ogre, who had been living on children all his life, and was their implacable enemy. He despised all toys; wouldn't have bought one for the world; delighted, in his malice, to insinuate grim expressions into the faces of brown-paper farmers who drove pigs to market, bellmen who advertised lost lawyers' consciences, movable old ladies who darned stockings or carved pies; and other like samples of his stock in trade. In appalling masks; hideous, hairy, red-eyed Jacks in Boxes; Vampire Kites; demoniacal Tumblers who wouldn't lie down, and were perpetually flying forward, to stare infants out of countenance; his soul perfectly revelled.

They were his only relief, and safety-valve. He was great in such inventions. Anything suggestive of a Pony-nightmare was delicious to him. He had even lost money (and he took to that toy very kindly) by getting up Goblin slides for magic-lanterns, whereon the Powers of Darkness were depicted as a sort of supernatural shell-fish, with human faces. In intensifying the portraiture of Giants, he had sunk quite a little capital; and, though no painter himself, he could indicate, for the instruction of his artists, with a piece of chalk, a certain furtive leer for the countenances of those monsters, which was safe to destroy the peace of mind of any young gentleman between the ages of six and eleven, for the whole Christmas or Midsummer Vacation.

What he was in toys, he was (as most men are) in other things. You may easily suppose, therefore, that within the great green cape, which reached down to the calves of his legs, there was buttoned up to the chin an uncommonly pleasant fellow; and that he was about as choice a spirit, and as agreeable a companion, as ever stood in a pair of bull-headed-looking boots with mahogany-coloured tops.

Still, Tackleton, the toy-merchant, was going to be married. In spite of all this, he was going to be married. And to a young wife too, a beautiful young wife.

He didn't look much like a bridegroom, as he stood in the Carrier's kitchen, with a twist in his dry face, and a screw in his body, and his hat jerked over the bridge of his nose, and his hands tucked down into the bottoms of his pockets, and his whole sarcastic ill-conditioned self peering out of one little corner of one little eye, like the concentrated essence of any number of ravens. But, a Bridegroom he designed to be.

'In three days' time. Next Thursday. The last day of the first month in the year. That's my wedding-day,' said Tackleton.

Did I mention that he had always one eye wide open, and one eye nearly shut; and that the one eye nearly shut, was always the expressive eye? I don't think I did.

'That's my wedding-day!' said Tackleton, rattling his money.

'Why, it's our wedding-day too,' exclaimed the Carrier.

'Ha ha!' laughed Tackleton. 'Odd! You're just such another couple. Just!'

The indignation of Dot at this presumptuous assertion is not to be described. What next? His imagination would compass the possibility of just such another Baby, perhaps. The man was mad.

'I say! A word with you,' murmured Tackleton, nudging the Carrier with his elbow, and taking him a little apart. 'You'll come to the wedding? We're in the same boat, you know.'

'How in the same boat?' inquired the Carrier.

'A little disparity, you know,' said Tackleton, with another nudge. 'Come and spend an evening with us, beforehand.'

'Why?' demanded John, astonished at this pressing hospitality.

'Why?' returned the other. 'That's a new way of receiving an invitation. Why, for pleasure—sociability, you know, and all that!'

'I thought you were never sociable,' said John, in his plain way.

'Tchah! It's of no use to be anything but free with you, I see,' said Tackleton. 'Why, then, the truth is you have a—what tea-drinking people call a sort of a comfortable appearance together, you and your wife. We know better, you know, but—'

'No, we don't know better,' interposed John. 'What are you talking about?'

'Well! We DON'T know better, then,' said Tackleton. 'We'll agree that we don't. As you like; what does it matter? I was going to say, as you have that sort of appearance, your company will produce a favourable effect on Mrs. Tackleton that will be. And, though I don't think your good lady's very friendly to me, in this matter, still she can't help herself from falling into my views, for there's a compactness and cosiness of appearance about her that always tells, even in an indifferent case. You'll say you'll come?'

'We have arranged to keep our Wedding-Day (as far as that goes) at home,' said John. 'We have made the promise to ourselves these six months. We think, you see, that home—'

'Bah! What's home?' cried Tackleton. 'Four walls and a ceiling! (Why don't you kill that Cricket? I would! I always do. I hate their noise.) There are four walls and a ceiling at my house. Come to me!'

'You kill your Crickets, eh?' said John.

'Scrunch 'em, sir,' returned the other, setting his heel heavily on the floor. 'You'll say you'll come? It's as much your interest as mine, you know, that the women should persuade each other that they're quiet and contented, and couldn't be better off. I know their way. Whatever one woman says, another woman is determined to clinch, always. There's that spirit of emulation among 'em, sir, that if your wife says to my wife, "I'm the happiest woman in the world, and mine's the best husband in the world, and I dote on him," my wife will say the same to yours, or more, and half believe it.'

'Do you mean to say she don't, then?' asked the Carrier.

'Don't!' cried Tackleton, with a short, sharp laugh. 'Don't what?'

The Carrier had some faint idea of adding, 'dote upon you.' But, happening to meet the half-closed eye, as it twinkled upon him over the turned-up collar of the cape, which was within an ace of poking it out, he felt it such an unlikely part and parcel of anything to be doted on, that he substituted, 'that she don't believe it?'

'Ah you dog! You're joking,' said Tackleton.

But the Carrier, though slow to understand the full drift of his meaning, eyed him in such a serious manner, that he was obliged to be a little more explanatory.

'I have the humour,' said Tackleton: holding up the fingers of his left hand, and tapping the forefinger, to imply 'there I am, Tackleton to wit:' 'I have the humour, sir, to marry a young wife, and a pretty wife:' here he rapped his little finger, to express the Bride; not sparingly, but sharply; with a sense of power. 'I'm able to gratify that humour and I do. It's my whim. But—now look there!'

He pointed to where Dot was sitting, thoughtfully, before the fire; leaning her dimpled chin upon her hand, and watching the bright blaze. The Carrier looked at her, and then at him, and then at her, and then at him again.

'She honours and obeys, no doubt, you know,' said Tackleton; 'and that, as I am not a man of sentiment, is quite enough for ME. But do you think there's anything more in it?'

'I think,' observed the Carrier, 'that I should chuck any man out of window, who said there wasn't.'

'Exactly so,' returned the other with an unusual alacrity of assent. 'To be sure! Doubtless you would. Of course. I'm certain of it. Good night. Pleasant dreams!'

The Carrier was puzzled, and made uncomfortable and uncertain, in spite of himself. He couldn't help showing it, in his manner.

'Good night, my dear friend!' said Tackleton, compassionately. 'I'm off. We're exactly alike, in reality, I see. You won't give us tomorrow evening? Well! Next day you go out visiting, I know. I'll meet you there, and bring my wife that is to be. It'll do her good. You're agreeable? Thank'ee. What's that!'

It was a loud cry from the Carrier's wife: a loud, sharp, sudden cry, that made the room ring, like a glass vessel. She had risen from her seat, and stood like one transfixed by terror and surprise. The Stranger had advanced towards the fire to warm himself, and stood within a short stride of her chair. But quite still.

'Dot!' cried the Carrier. 'Mary! Darling! What's the matter?'

They were all about her in a moment. Caleb, who had been dozing on the cake-box, in the first imperfect recovery of his suspended presence of mind, seized Miss Slowboy by the hair of her head, but immediately apologised.

'Mary!' exclaimed the Carrier, supporting her in his arms. 'Are you ill! What is it? Tell me, dear!'

She only answered by beating her hands together, and falling into a wild fit of laughter. Then, sinking from his grasp upon the ground, she covered her face with her apron, and wept bitterly. And then she laughed again, and then she cried again, and then she said how cold it was, and suffered him to lead her to the fire, where she sat down as before. The old man standing, as before, quite still.

'I'm better, John,' she said. 'I'm quite well now—I—'

'John!' But John was on the other side of her. Why turn her face towards the strange old gentleman, as if addressing him! Was her brain wandering?

'Only a fancy, John dear—a kind of shock—a something coming suddenly before my eyes—I don't know what it was. It's quite gone, quite gone.'

'I'm glad it's gone,' muttered Tackleton, turning the expressive eye all round the room. 'I wonder where it's gone, and what it was. Humph! Caleb, come here! Who's that with the grey hair?'

'I don't know, sir,' returned Caleb in a whisper. 'Never see him before, in all my life. A beautiful figure for a nut-cracker; quite a new model. With a screw-jaw opening down into his waistcoat, he'd be lovely.'

'Not ugly enough,' said Tackleton.

'Or for a firebox, either,' observed Caleb, in deep contemplation, 'what a model! Unscrew his head to put the matches in; turn him heels up'ards for the light; and what a firebox for a gentleman's mantel-shelf, just as he stands!'

'Not half ugly enough,' said Tackleton. 'Nothing in him at all! Come! Bring that box! All right now, I hope?'

'Quite gone!' said the little woman, waving him hurriedly away. 'Good night!'

'Good night,' said Tackleton. 'Good night, John Peerybingle! Take care how you carry that box, Caleb. Let it fall, and I'll murder you! Dark as pitch, and weather worse than ever, eh? Good night!'

So, with another sharp look round the room, he went out at the door; followed by Caleb with the wedding-cake on his head.

The Carrier had been so much astounded by his little wife, and so busily engaged in soothing and tending her, that he had scarcely been conscious of the Stranger's presence, until now, when he again stood there, their only guest.

'He don't belong to them, you see,' said John. 'I must give him a hint to go.'

'I beg your pardon, friend,' said the old gentleman, advancing to him; 'the more so, as I fear your wife has not been well; but the Attendant whom my infirmity,' he touched his ears and shook his head, 'renders almost indispensable, not having arrived, I fear there must be some mistake. The bad night which made the shelter of your comfortable cart (may I never have a worse!) so acceptable, is still as bad as ever. Would you, in your kindness, suffer me to rent a bed here?'

'Yes, yes,' cried Dot. 'Yes! Certainly!'

'Oh!' said the Carrier, surprised by the rapidity of this consent.

'Well! I don't object; but, still I'm not quite sure that—'

'Hush!' she interrupted. 'Dear John!'

'Why, he's stone deaf,' urged John.

'I know he is, but—Yes, sir, certainly. Yes! certainly! I'll make him up a bed, directly, John.'

As she hurried off to do it, the flutter of her spirits, and the agitation of her manner, were so strange that the Carrier stood looking after her, quite confounded.

'Did its mothers make it up a Beds then!' cried Miss Slowboy to the Baby; 'and did its hair grow brown and curly, when its caps was lifted off, and frighten it, a precious Pets, a-sitting by the fires!'

With that unaccountable attraction of the mind to trifles, which is often incidental to a state of doubt and confusion, the Carrier as he walked slowly to and fro, found himself mentally repeating even these absurd words, many times. So many times that he got them by heart, and was still conning them over and over, like a lesson, when Tilly, after administering as much friction to the little bald head with her hand as she thought wholesome (according to the practice of nurses), had once more tied the Baby's cap on.

'And frighten it, a precious Pets, a-sitting by the fires. What frightened Dot, I wonder!' mused the Carrier, pacing to and fro.

He scouted, from his heart, the insinuations of the Toy-merchant, and yet they filled him with a vague, indefinite uneasiness. For, Tackleton was quick and sly; and he had that painful sense, himself, of being of slow perception, that a broken hint was always worrying to him. He certainly had no intention in his mind of linking anything that Tackleton had said, with the unusual conduct of his wife, but the two subjects of reflection came into his mind together, and he could not keep them asunder.

The bed was soon made ready; and the visitor, declining all refreshment but a cup of tea, retired. Then, Dot—quite well again, she said, quite well again—arranged the great chair in the chimney-corner for her husband; filled his pipe and gave it him; and took her usual little stool beside him on the hearth.

She always WOULD sit on that little stool. I think she must have had a kind of notion that it was a coaxing, wheedling little stool.

She was, out and out, the very best filler of a pipe, I should say, in the four quarters of the globe. To see her put that chubby little finger in the bowl, and then blow down the pipe to clear the tube, and, when she had done so, affect to think that there was really something in the tube, and blow a dozen times, and hold it to her eye like a telescope, with a most provoking twist in her capital little face, as she looked down it, was quite a brilliant thing. As to the tobacco, she was perfect mistress of the subject; and her lighting of the pipe, with a wisp of paper, when the Carrier had it in his mouth—going so very near his nose, and yet not scorching it—was Art, high Art.

And the Cricket and the kettle, turning up again, acknowledged it! The bright fire, blazing up again, acknowledged it! The little Mower on the clock, in his unheeded work, acknowledged it! The Carrier, in his smoothing forehead and expanding face, acknowledged it, the readiest of all.

And as he soberly and thoughtfully puffed at his old pipe, and as the Dutch clock ticked, and as the red fire gleamed, and as the Cricket chirped; that Genius of his Hearth and Home (for such the Cricket was) came out, in fairy shape, into the room, and summoned many forms of Home about him. Dots of all ages, and all sizes, filled the chamber. Dots who were merry children, running on before him gathering flowers, in the fields; coy Dots, half shrinking from, half yielding to, the pleading of his own rough image; newly-married Dots, alighting at the door, and taking wondering possession of the household keys; motherly little Dots, attended by fictitious Slowboys, bearing babies to be christened; matronly Dots, still young and blooming, watching Dots of daughters, as they danced at rustic balls; fat Dots, encircled and beset by troops of rosy grandchildren; withered Dots, who leaned on sticks, and tottered as they crept along.

Old Carriers too, appeared, with blind old Boxers lying at their feet; and newer carts with younger drivers ('Peerybingle Brothers' on the tilt); and sick old Carriers, tended by the gentlest hands; and graves of dead and gone old Carriers, green in the churchyard. And as the Cricket showed him all these things—he saw them plainly, though his eyes were fixed upon the fire—the Carrier's heart grew light and happy, and he thanked his Household Gods with all his might, and cared no more for Gruff and Tackleton than you do.

But, what was that young figure of a man, which the same Fairy Cricket set so near Her stool, and which remained there, singly and alone? Why did it linger still, so near her, with its arm upon the chimney-piece, ever repeating 'Married! and not to me!'

O Dot! O failing Dot! There is no place for it in all your husband's visions; why has its shadow fallen on his hearth!

Chapter 2

Chirp the second

Caleb Plummer and his Blind Daughter lived all alone by themselves, as the Story-books say—and my blessing, with yours to back it I hope, on the Story-books, for saying anything in this workaday world!—Caleb Plummer and his Blind Daughter lived all alone by themselves, in a little cracked nutshell of a wooden house, which was, in truth, no better than a pimple on the prominent red-brick nose of Gruff and Tackleton. The premises of Gruff and Tackleton were the great feature of the street; but you might have knocked down Caleb Plummer's dwelling with a hammer or two, and carried off the pieces in a cart.

If anyone had done the dwelling-house of Caleb Plummer the honour to miss it after such an inroad, it would have been, no doubt, to commend its demolition as a vast improvement. It stuck to the premises of Gruff and Tackleton, like a barnacle to a ship's keel, or a snail to a door, or a little bunch of toadstools to the stem of a tree.

But, it was the germ from which the full-grown trunk of Gruff and Tackleton had sprung; and, under its crazy roof, the Gruff before last, had, in a small way, made toys for a generation of old boys and girls, who had played with them, and found them out, and broken them, and gone to sleep.

have said that Caleb and his poor Blind Daughter lived here. I should have said that Caleb lived here, and his poor Blind Daughter somewhere else—in an enchanted home of Caleb's furnishing, where scarcity and shabbiness were not, and trouble never entered. Caleb was no sorcerer, but in the only magic art that still remains to us, the magic of devoted, deathless love, Nature had been the mistress of his study; and from her teaching, all the wonder came.

The Blind Girl never knew that ceilings were discoloured, walls blotched and bare of plaster here and there, high crevices unstopped and widening every day, beams mouldering and tending downward. The Blind Girl never knew that iron was rusting, wood rotting, paper peeling off; the size, and shape, and true proportion of the dwelling, withering away. The Blind Girl never knew that ugly shapes of delf and earthenware were on the board; that sorrow and faintheartedness were in the house; that Caleb's scanty hairs were turning greyer and more grey, before her sightless face. The Blind Girl never knew they had a master, cold, exacting, and uninterested—never knew that Tackleton was Tackleton in short; but lived in the belief of an eccentric humorist who loved to have his jest with them, and who, while he was the Guardian Angel of their lives, disdained to hear one word of thankfulness.

And all was Caleb's doing; all the doing of her simple father! But he too had a Cricket on his Hearth; and listening sadly to its music when the motherless Blind Child was very young, that Spirit had inspired him with the thought that even her great deprivation might be almost changed into a blessing, and the girl made happy by these little means. For all the Cricket tribe are potent Spirits, even though the people who hold converse with them do not know it (which is frequently the case); and there are not in the unseen world, voices more gentle and more true, that may be so implicitly relied on, or that are so certain to give none but tenderest counsel, as the Voices in which the Spirits of the Fireside and the Hearth address themselves to human kind.

Caleb and his daughter were at work together in their usual working-room, which served them for their ordinary living-room as well; and a strange place it was. There were houses in it, finished and unfinished, for Dolls of all stations in life. Suburban tenements for Dolls of moderate means; kitchens and single apartments for Dolls of the lower classes; capital town residences for Dolls of high estate. Some of these establishments were already furnished according to estimate, with a view to the convenience of Dolls of limited income; others could be fitted on the most expensive scale, at a moment's notice, from whole shelves of chairs and tables, sofas, bedsteads, and upholstery.

The nobility and gentry, and public in general, for whose accommodation these tenements were designed, lay, here and there, in baskets, staring straight up at the ceiling; but, in denoting their degrees in society, and confining them to their respective stations (which experience shows to be lamentably difficult in real life), the makers of these Dolls had far improved on Nature, who is often froward and perverse; for, they, not resting on such arbitrary marks as satin, cotton-print, and bits of rag, had superadded striking personal differences which allowed of no mistake.

Thus, the Doll-lady of distinction had wax limbs of perfect symmetry; but only she and her compeers. The next grade in the social scale being made of leather, and the next of coarse linen stuff. As to the common-people, they had just so many matches out of tinder-boxes, for their arms and legs, and there they were—established in their sphere at once, beyond the possibility of getting out of it.

There were various other samples of his handicraft, besides Dolls, in Caleb Plummer's room. There were Noah's Arks, in which the Birds and Beasts were an uncommonly tight fit, I assure you; though they could be crammed in, anyhow, at the roof, and rattled and shaken into the smallest compass. By a bold poetical licence, most of these Noah's Arks had knockers on the doors; inconsistent appendages, perhaps, as suggestive of morning callers and a Postman, yet a pleasant finish to the outside of the building. There were scores of melancholy little carts, which, when the wheels went round, performed most doleful music.

Many small fiddles, drums, and other instruments of torture; no end of cannon, shields, swords, spears, and guns. There were little tumblers in red breeches, incessantly swarming up high obstacles of red-tape, and coming down, head first, on the other side; and there were innumerable old gentlemen of respectable, not to say venerable, appearance, insanely flying over horizontal pegs, inserted, for the purpose, in their own street doors. There were beasts of all sorts; horses, in particular, of every breed, from the spotted barrel on four pegs, with a small tippet for a mane, to the thoroughbred rocker on his highest mettle.

As it would have been hard to count the dozens upon dozens of grotesque figures that were ever ready to commit all sorts of absurdities on the turning of a handle, so it would have been no easy task to mention any human folly, vice, or weakness, that had not its type, immediate or remote, in Caleb Plummer's room. And not in an exaggerated form, for very little handles will move men and women to as strange performances, as any Toy was ever made to undertake.

In the midst of all these objects, Caleb and his daughter sat at work. The Blind Girl busy as a Doll's dressmaker; Caleb painting and glazing the four-pair front of a desirable family mansion.

The care imprinted in the lines of Caleb's face, and his absorbed and dreamy manner, which would have sat well on some alchemist or abstruse student, were at first sight an odd contrast to his occupation, and the trivialities about him. But, trivial things, invented and pursued for bread, become very serious matters of fact; and, apart from this consideration, I am not at all prepared to say, myself, that if Caleb had been a Lord Chamberlain, or a Member of Parliament, or a lawyer, or even a great speculator, he would have dealt in toys one whit less whimsical, while I have a very great doubt whether they would have been as harmless.

'So you were out in the rain last night, father, in your beautiful new great-coat,' said Caleb's daughter.

'In my beautiful new great-coat,' answered Caleb, glancing towards a clothes-line in the room, on which the sack-cloth garment previously described, was carefully hung up to dry.

'How glad I am you bought it, father!'

'And of such a tailor, too,' said Caleb. 'Quite a fashionable tailor. It's too good for me.'

The Blind Girl rested from her work, and laughed with delight.

'Too good, father! What can be too good for you?'

'I'm half-ashamed to wear it though,' said Caleb, watching the effect of what he said, upon her brightening face; 'upon my word! When I hear the boys and people say behind me, "Halloa! Here's a swell!" I don't know which way to look. And when the beggar wouldn't go away last night; and when I said I was a very common man, said "No, your Honour! Bless your Honour, don't say that!" I was quite ashamed. I really felt as if I hadn't a right to wear it.'

Happy Blind Girl! How merry she was, in her exultation!

'I see you, father,' she said, clasping her hands, 'as plainly, as if I had the eyes I never want when you are with me. A blue coat—'

'Bright blue,' said Caleb.

'Yes, yes! Bright blue!' exclaimed the girl, turning up her radiant face; 'the colour I can just remember in the blessed sky! You told me it was blue before! A bright blue coat—'

'Made loose to the figure,' suggested Caleb.

'Made loose to the figure!' cried the Blind Girl, laughing heartily; 'and in it, you, dear father, with your merry eye, your smiling face, your free step, and your dark hair—looking so young and handsome!'

'Halloa! Halloa!' said Caleb. 'I shall be vain, presently!'

'I think you are, already,' cried the Blind Girl, pointing at him, in her glee. 'I know you, father! Ha, ha, ha! I've found you out, you see!'

How different the picture in her mind, from Caleb, as he sat observing her! She had spoken of his free step. She was right in that. For years and years, he had never once crossed that threshold at his own slow pace, but with a footfall counterfeited for her ear; and never had he, when his heart was heaviest, forgotten the light tread that was to render hers so cheerful and courageous!

Heaven knows! But I think Caleb's vague bewilderment of manner may have half originated in his having confused himself about himself and everything around him, for the love of his Blind Daughter. How could the little man be otherwise than bewildered, after labouring for so many years to destroy his own identity, and that of all the objects that had any bearing on it!

'There we are,' said Caleb, falling back a pace or two to form the better judgment of his work; 'as near the real thing as sixpenn'orth of halfpence is to sixpence. What a pity that the whole front of the house opens at once! If there was only a staircase in it, now, and regular doors to the rooms to go in at! But that's the worst of my calling, I'm always deluding myself, and swindling myself.'

'You are speaking quite softly. You are not tired, father?'

'Tired!' echoed Caleb, with a great burst of animation, 'what should tire me, Bertha? I was never tired. What does it mean?'

To give the greater force to his words, he checked himself in an involuntary imitation of two half-length stretching and yawning figures on the mantel-shelf, who were represented as in one eternal state of weariness from the waist upwards; and hummed a fragment of a song. It was a *Bacchanalian* song, something about a Sparkling Bowl. He sang it with an assumption of a Devil-may-care voice, that made his face a thousand times more meagre and more thoughtful than ever.

'What! You're singing, are you?' said Tackleton, putting his head in at the door. 'Go it! I can't sing.'

Nobody would have suspected him of it. He hadn't what is generally termed a singing face, by any means.

'I can't afford to sing,' said Tackleton. 'I'm glad YOU CAN. I hope you can afford to work too. Hardly time for both, I should think?'

'If you could only see him, Bertha, how he's winking at me!' whispered Caleb. 'Such a man to joke! you'd think, if you didn't know him, he was in earnest—wouldn't you now?'

The Blind Girl smiled and nodded.

'The bird that can sing and won't sing, must be made to sing, they say,' grumbled Tackleton. 'What about the owl that can't sing, and oughtn't to sing, and will sing; is there anything that

HE should be made to do?'

'The extent to which he's winking at this moment!' whispered Caleb to his daughter. 'O, my gracious!'

'Always merry and light-hearted with us!' cried the smiling Bertha.

'O, you're there, are you?' answered Tackleton. 'Poor Idiot!'

He really did believe she was an Idiot; and he founded the belief, I can't say whether consciously or not, upon her being fond of him.

'Well! and being there,—how are you?' said Tackleton, in his grudging way.

'Oh! well; quite well. And as happy as even you can wish me to be. As happy as you would make the whole world, if you could!'

'Poor Idiot!' muttered Tackleton. 'No gleam of reason. Not a gleam!'

The Blind Girl took his hand and kissed it; held it for a moment in her own two hands; and laid her cheek against it tenderly, before releasing it. There was such unspeakable affection and such fervent gratitude in the act, that Tackleton himself was moved to say, in a milder growl than usual:

'What's the matter now?'

'I stood it close beside my pillow when I went to sleep last night, and remembered it in my dreams. And when the day broke, and the glorious red sun—the RED sun, father?'

'Red in the mornings and the evenings, Bertha,' said poor Caleb, with a woeful glance at his employer.

'When it rose, and the bright light I almost fear to strike myself against in walking, came into the room, I turned the little tree towards it, and blessed Heaven for making things so precious, and blessed you for sending them to cheer me!'

'Bedlam broke loose!' said Tackleton under his breath. 'We shall arrive at the strait-waistcoat and mufflers soon. We're getting on!'

Caleb, with his hands hooked loosely in each other, stared vacantly before him while his daughter spoke, as if he really were uncertain (I believe he was) whether Tackleton had done anything to deserve her thanks, or not. If he could have been a perfectly free agent, at that moment, required, on pain of death, to kick the Toy-merchant, or fall at his feet, according to his merits, I believe it would have been an even chance which course he would have taken. Yet, Caleb knew that with his own hands he had brought the little rose-tree home for her, so carefully, and that with his own lips he had forged the innocent deception which should help to keep her from suspecting how much, how very much, he every day, denied himself, that she might be the happier.

'Bertha!' said Tackleton, assuming, for the nonce, a little cordiality. 'Come here.'

'Oh! I can come straight to you! You needn't guide me!' she rejoined.

'Shall I tell you a secret, Bertha?'

'If you will!' she answered, eagerly.

How bright the darkened face! How adorned with light, the listening head!

'This is the day on which little what's-her-name, the spoilt child, Peerybingle's wife, pays her regular visit to you—makes her fantastic Pic-Nic here; an't it?' said Tackleton, with a strong expression of distaste for the whole concern.

'Yes,' replied Bertha. 'This is the day.'

'I thought so,' said Tackleton. 'I should like to join the party.'

'Do you hear that, father!' cried the Blind Girl in an ecstasy.

'Yes, yes, I hear it,' murmured Caleb, with the fixed look of a sleep-walker; 'but I don't believe it. It's one of my lies, I've no doubt.'

'You see I—I want to bring the Peerybingles a little more into company with May Fielding,' said Tackleton. 'I am going to be married to May.'

'Married!' cried the Blind Girl, starting from him.

'She's such a confounded Idiot,' muttered Tackleton, 'that I was afraid she'd never comprehend me. Ah, Bertha! Married! Church, parson, clerk, beadle, glass-coach, bells, breakfast, bride-cake, favours, marrow-bones, cleavers, and all the rest of the tomfoolery. A wedding, you know; a wedding. Don't you know what a wedding is?'

'I know,' replied the Blind Girl, in a gentle tone. 'I understand!'

'Do you?' muttered Tackleton. 'It's more than I expected. Well! On that account I want to join the party, and to bring May and her mother. I'll send in a little something or other, before the afternoon. A cold leg of mutton, or some comfortable trifle of that sort. You'll expect me?'

'Yes,' she answered.

She had drooped her head, and turned away; and so stood, with her hands crossed, musing.

'I don't think you will,' muttered Tackleton, looking at her; 'for you seem to have forgotten all about it, already. Caleb!'

'I may venture to say I'm here, I suppose,' thought Caleb. 'Sir!'

'Take care she don't forget what I've been saying to her.'

'SHE never forgets,' returned Caleb. 'It's one of the few things she an't clever in.'

'Every man thinks his own geese swans,' observed the Toy-merchant, with a shrug. 'Poor devil!'

Having delivered himself of which remark, with infinite contempt, old Gruff and Tackleton withdrew.

Bertha remained where he had left her, lost in meditation. The gaiety had vanished from her downcast face, and it was very sad. Three or four times she shook her head, as if bewailing some remembrance or some loss; but her sorrowful reflections found no vent in words.

It was not until Caleb had been occupied, some time, in yoking a team of horses to a wagon by the summary process of nailing the harness to the vital parts of their bodies, that she drew near to his working-stool, and sitting down beside him, said:

'Father, I am lonely in the dark. I want my eyes, my patient, willing eyes.'

'Here they are,' said Caleb. 'Always ready. They are more yours than mine, Bertha, any hour in the four-and-twenty. What shall your eyes do for you, dear?'

'Look round the room, father.'

'All right,' said Caleb. 'No sooner said than done, Bertha.'

'Tell me about it.'

'It's much the same as usual,' said Caleb. 'Homely, but very snug. The gay colours on the walls; the bright flowers on the plates and dishes; the shining wood, where there are beams or panels; the general cheerfulness and neatness of the building; make it very pretty.'

Cheerful and neat it was wherever Bertha's hands could busy themselves. But nowhere else, were cheerfulness and neatness possible, in the old crazy shed which Caleb's fancy so transformed.

'You have your working dress on, and are not so gallant as when you wear the handsome coat?' said Bertha, touching him.

'Not quite so gallant,' answered Caleb. 'Pretty brisk though.'

'Father,' said the Blind Girl, drawing close to his side, and stealing one arm round his neck, 'tell me something about May. She is very fair?'

'She is indeed,' said Caleb. And she was indeed. It was quite a rare thing to Caleb, not to have to draw on his invention.

'Her hair is dark,' said Bertha, pensively, 'darker than mine. Her voice is sweet and musical, I know. I have often loved to hear it. Her shape—'

'There's not a Doll's in all the room to equal it,' said Caleb. 'And her eyes!—'

He stopped; for Bertha had drawn closer round his neck, and from the arm that clung about him, came a warning pressure which he understood too well.

He coughed a moment, hammered for a moment, and then fell back upon the song about the sparkling bowl; his infallible resource in all such difficulties.

'Our friend, father, our benefactor. I am never tired, you know, of hearing about him.—Now, was I ever?' she said, hastily.

'Of course not,' answered Caleb, 'and with reason.'

'Ah! With how much reason!' cried the Blind Girl. With such fervency, that Caleb, though his motives were so pure, could not endure to meet her face; but dropped his eyes, as if she could have read in them his innocent deceit.

'Then, tell me again about him, dear father,' said Bertha. 'Many times again! His face is benevolent, kind, and tender. Honest and true, I am sure it is. The manly heart that tries to cloak all favours with a show of roughness and unwillingness, beats in its every look and glance.'

'And makes it noble!' added Caleb, in his quiet desperation.

'And makes it noble!' cried the Blind Girl. 'He is older than May, father.'

'Ye-es,' said Caleb, reluctantly. 'He's a little older than May. But that don't signify.'

'Oh father, yes! To be his patient companion in infirmity and age; to be his gentle nurse in sickness, and his constant friend in suffering and sorrow; to know no weariness in working for his sake; to watch him, tend him, sit beside his bed and talk to him awake, and pray for him asleep; what privileges these would be! What opportunities for proving all her truth and devotion to him! Would she do all this, dear father?

'No doubt of it,' said Caleb.

'I love her, father; I can love her from my soul!' exclaimed the Blind Girl. And saying so, she laid her poor blind face on Caleb's shoulder, and so wept and wept, that he was almost sorry to have brought that tearful happiness upon her.

In the meantime, there had been a pretty sharp commotion at John Peerybingle's, for little Mrs. Peerybingle naturally couldn't think of going anywhere without the Baby; and to get the Baby under weigh took time. Not that there was much of the Baby, speaking of it as a thing of weight and measure, but there was a vast deal to do about and about it, and it all had to be done by easy stages.

For instance, when the Baby was got, by hook and by crook, to a certain point of dressing, and you might have rationally supposed that another touch or two would finish him off, and turn him out a tip-top Baby challenging the world, he was unexpectedly extinguished in a flannel cap, and hustled off to bed; where he simmered (so to speak) between two blankets for the best part of an hour. From this state of inaction he was then recalled, shining very much and roaring violently, to partake of—well? I would rather say, if you'll permit me to speak generally—of a slight repast.

After which, he went to sleep again. Mrs. Peerybingle took advantage of this interval, to make herself as smart in a small way as ever you saw anybody in all your life; and, during the same short truce, Miss Slowboy insinuated herself into a spencer of a fashion so surprising and ingenious, that it had no connection with herself, or anything else in the universe, but was a shrunken, dog's-eared, independent fact, pursuing its lonely course without the least regard to anybody.

By this time, the Baby, being all alive again, was invested, by the united efforts of Mrs. Peerybingle and Miss Slowboy, with a cream-coloured mantle for its body, and a sort of nankeen raised-pie for its head; and so in course of time they all three got down to the door, where the old horse had already taken more than the full value of his day's toll out of the Turnpike Trust, by tearing up the road with his impatient autographs; and whence Boxer might be dimly seen in the remote perspective, standing looking back, and tempting him to come on without orders.

As to a chair, or anything of that kind for helping Mrs. Peerybingle into the cart, you know very little of John, if you think THAT was necessary. Before you could have seen him lift her from the ground, there she was in her place, fresh and rosy, saying, 'John! How CAN you! Think of Tilly!'

If I might be allowed to mention a young lady's legs, on any terms, I would observe of Miss Slowboy's that there was a fatality about them which rendered them singularly liable to be grazed; and that she never effected the smallest ascent or descent, without recording the circumstance upon them with a notch, as Robinson Crusoe marked the days upon his wooden calendar. But as this might be considered ungenteel, I'll think of it.

'John? You've got the Basket with the Veal and Ham-Pie and things, and the bottles of Beer?' said Dot. 'If you haven't, you must turn round again, this very minute.'

'You're a nice little article,' returned the Carrier, 'to be talking about turning round, after keeping me a full quarter of an hour behind my time.'

'I am sorry for it, John,' said Dot in a great bustle, 'but I really could not think of going to Bertha's—I would not do it, John, on any account—without the Veal and Ham-Pie and things, and the bottles of Beer. Way!'

This monosyllable was addressed to the horse, who didn't mind it at all.

'Oh DO way, John!' said Mrs. Peerybingle. 'Please!'

'It'll be time enough to do that,' returned John, 'when I begin to leave things behind me. The basket's here, safe enough.'

'What a hard-hearted monster you must be, John, not to have said so, at once, and save me such a turn! I declared I wouldn't go to Bertha's without the Veal and Ham-Pie and things, and the bottles of Beer, for any money. Regularly once a fortnight ever since we have been married, John, have we made our little Pic-Nic there. If anything was to go wrong with it, I should almost think we were never to be lucky again.'

'It was a kind thought in the first instance,' said the Carrier: 'and I honour you for it, little woman.'

'My dear John,' replied Dot, turning very red, 'don't talk about honouring ME. Good Gracious!'

'By the bye—' observed the Carrier. 'That old gentleman—'

Again so visibly, and instantly embarrassed!

'He's an odd fish,' said the Carrier, looking straight along the road before them. 'I can't make him out. I don't believe there's any harm in him.'

'None at all. I'm—I'm sure there's none at all.'

'Yes,' said the Carrier, with his eyes attracted to her face by the great earnestness of her manner. 'I am glad you feel so certain of it, because it's a confirmation to me. It's curious that he should have taken it into his head to ask leave to go on lodging with us; an't it? Things come about so strangely.'

'So very strangely,' she rejoined in a low voice, scarcely audible.

'However, he's a good-natured old gentleman,' said John, 'and pays as a gentleman, and I think his word is to be relied upon, like a gentleman's. I had quite a long talk with him this morning: he can hear me better already, he says, as he gets more used to my voice. He told me a great deal about himself, and I told him a great deal about myself, and a rare lot of questions he asked me. I gave him information about my having two beats, you know, in my business; one day to the right from our house and back again; another day to the left from our house and back again (for he's a stranger and don't know the names of places about here); and he seemed quite pleased. "Why, then I shall be returning home tonight your way," he says, "when I thought you'd be coming in an exactly opposite direction. That's capital! I may trouble you for another lift perhaps, but I'll engage not to fall so sound asleep again." He WAS sound asleep, surely!—Dot! what are you thinking of?'

'Thinking of, John? I—I was listening to you.'

'O! That's all right!' said the honest Carrier. 'I was afraid, from the look of your face, that I had gone rambling on so long, as to set you thinking about something else. I was very near it, I'll be bound.'

Dot making no reply, they jogged on, for some little time, in silence. But, it was not easy to remain silent very long in John Peerybingle's cart, for everybody on the road had something to say. Though it might only be 'How are you!' and indeed it was very often nothing else, still, to give that back again in the right spirit of cordiality, required, not merely a nod and a smile, but as wholesome an action of the lungs withal, as a long-winded Parliamentary speech. Sometimes, passengers on foot, or horseback, plodded on a little way beside the cart, for the express purpose of having a chat; and then there was a great deal to be said, on both sides.

Then, Boxer gave occasion to more good-natured recognitions of, and by, the Carrier, than half-a-dozen Christians could have done! Everybody knew him, all along the road—especially the fowls and pigs, who when they saw him approaching, with his body all on one side, and his ears pricked up inquisitively, and that knob of a tail making the most of itself in the air, immediately withdrew into remote back settlements, without waiting for the honour of a nearer acquaintance.

He had business everywhere; going down all the turnings, looking into all the wells, bolting in and out of all the cottages, dashing into the midst of all the Dame-Schools, fluttering all the pigeons, magnifying the tails of all the cats, and trotting into the public-houses like a regular customer. Wherever he went, somebody or other might have been heard to cry, 'Halloa! Here's Boxer!' and out came that somebody forthwith, accompanied by at least two or three other somebodies, to give John Peerybingle and his pretty wife, Good Day.

The packages and parcels for the errand cart, were numerous; and there were many stoppages to take them in and give them out, which were not by any means the worst parts of the journey. Some people were so full of expectation about their parcels, and other people were so full of wonder about their parcels, and other people were so full of inexhaustible directions about their parcels, and John had such a lively interest in all the parcels, that it was as good as a play. Likewise, there were articles to carry, which required to be considered and discussed, and in reference to the adjustment and disposition of which, councils had to be holden by the Carrier and the senders: at which Boxer usually assisted, in short fits of the closest attention, and long fits of tearing round and round the assembled sages and barking himself hoarse.

Of all these little incidents, Dot was the amused and open-eyed spectatress from her chair in the cart; and as she sat there, looking on—a charming little portrait framed to admiration by the tilt—there was no lack of nudgings and glancings and whisperings and envyings among the younger men. And this delighted John the Carrier, beyond measure; for he was proud to have his little wife admired, knowing that she didn't mind it—that, if anything, she rather liked it perhaps.

The trip was a little foggy, to be sure, in the January weather; and was raw and cold. But who cared for such trifles? Not Dot, decidedly. Not Tilly Slowboy, for she deemed sitting in a cart, on any terms, to be the highest point of human joys; the crowning circumstance of earthly hopes. Not the Baby, I'll be sworn; for it's not in Baby nature to be warmer or more sound asleep, though its capacity is great in both respects, than that blessed young Peerybingle was, all the way.

You couldn't see very far in the fog, of course; but you could see a great deal! It's astonishing how much you may see, in a thicker fog than that, if you will only take the trouble to look for it. Why, even to sit watching for the Fairy-rings in the fields, and for the patches of hoar-frost still lingering in the shade, near hedges and by trees, was a pleasant occupation: to make no mention of the unexpected shapes in which the trees themselves came starting out of the mist, and glided into it again.

The hedges were tangled and bare, and waved a multitude of blighted garlands in the wind; but there was no discouragement in this. It was agreeable to contemplate; for it made the fireside warmer in possession, and the summer greener in expectancy. The river looked chilly; but it was in motion, and moving at a good pace—which was a great point. The canal was rather slow and torpid; that must be admitted. Never mind. It would freeze the sooner when the frost set fairly in, and then there would be skating, and sliding; and the heavy old barges, frozen up somewhere near a wharf, would smoke their rusty iron chimney pipes all day, and have a lazy time of it.

In one place, there was a great mound of weeds or stubble burning; and they watched the fire, so white in the daytime, flaring through the fog, with only here and there a dash of red in it, until, in consequence, as she observed, of the smoke 'getting up her nose,' Miss Slowboy choked—she could do anything of that sort, on the smallest provocation—and woke the Baby, who wouldn't go to sleep again. But, Boxer, who was in advance some quarter of a mile or so, had already passed the outposts of the town, and gained the corner of the street where Caleb and his daughter lived; and long before they had reached the door, he and the Blind Girl were on the pavement waiting to receive them.

Boxer, by the way, made certain delicate distinctions of his own, in his communication with Bertha, which persuade me fully that he knew her to be blind. He never sought to attract her attention by looking at her, as he often did with other people, but touched her invariably. What experience he could ever have had of blind people or blind dogs, I don't know. He had never lived with a blind master; nor had Mr. Boxer the elder, nor Mrs. Boxer, nor any of his respectable family on either side, ever been visited with blindness, that I am aware of. He may have found it out for himself, perhaps, but he had got hold of it somehow; and therefore he had hold of Bertha too, by the skirt, and kept hold, until Mrs. Peerybingle and the Baby, and Miss Slowboy, and the basket, were all got safely within doors.

May Fielding was already come; and so was her mother—a little querulous chip of an old lady with a peevish face, who, in right of having preserved a waist like a bedpost, was supposed to be a most transcendent figure; and who, in consequence of having once been better off, or of labouring under an impression that she might have been, if something had happened which never did happen, and seemed to have never been particularly likely to come to pass—but it's all the same—was very genteel and patronising indeed. Gruff and Tackleton was also there, doing the agreeable, with the evident sensation of being as perfectly at home, and as unquestionably in his own element, as a fresh young salmon on the top of the Great Pyramid.

'May! My dear old friend!' cried Dot, running up to meet her. 'What a happiness to see you.'

Her old friend was, to the full, as hearty and as glad as she; and it really was, if you'll believe me, quite a pleasant sight to see them embrace. Tackleton was a man of taste beyond all question. May was very pretty.

You know sometimes, when you are used to a pretty face, how, when it comes into contact and comparison with another pretty face, it seems for the moment to be homely and faded, and hardly to deserve the high opinion you have had of it. Now, this was not at all the case, either with Dot or May; for May's face set off Dot's, and Dot's face set off May's, so naturally and agreeably, that, as John Peerybingle was very near saying when he came into the room, they ought to have been born sisters-which was the only improvement you could have suggested.

Tackleton had brought his leg of mutton, and, wonderful to relate, a tart besides—but we don't mind a little dissipation when our brides are in the case. we don't get married every day—and in addition to these dainties, there were the Veal and Ham-Pie, and 'things,' as Mrs. Peerybingle called them; which were chiefly nuts and oranges, and cakes, and such small deer.

When the repast was set forth on the board, flanked by Caleb's contribution, which was a great wooden bowl of smoking potatoes (he was prohibited, by solemn compact, from producing any other viands), Tackleton led his intended mother-in-law to the post of honour. For the better gracing of this place at the high festival, the majestic old soul had adorned herself with a cap, calculated to inspire the thoughtless with sentiments of awe. She also wore her gloves. But let us be genteel, or die!

Caleb sat next his daughter; Dot and her old schoolfellow were side by side; the good Carrier took care of the bottom of the table. Miss Slowboy was isolated, for the time being, from every article of furniture but the chair she sat on, that she might have nothing else to knock the Baby's head against.

As Tilly stared about her at the dolls and toys, they stared at her and at the company. The venerable old gentlemen at the street doors (who were all in full action) showed especial interest in the party, pausing occasionally before leaping, as if they were listening to the conversation, and then plunging wildly over and over, a great many times, without halting for breath—as in a frantic state of delight with the whole proceedings.

Certainly, if these old gentlemen were inclined to have a

fiendish joy in the contemplation of Tackleton's discomfiture, they had good reason to be satisfied. Tackleton couldn't get on at all; and the more cheerful his intended bride became in Dot's society, the less he liked it, though he had brought them together for that purpose. For he was a regular dog in the manger, was Tackleton; and when they laughed and he couldn't, he took it into his head, immediately, that they must be laughing at him.

'Ah, May!' said Dot. 'Dear dear, what changes! To talk of those merry school-days makes one young again.'

'Why, you an't particularly old, at any time; are you?' said Tackleton.

'Look at my sober plodding husband there,' returned Dot. 'He adds twenty years to my age at least. Don't you, John?'

'Forty,' John replied.

'How many YOU'll add to May's, I am sure I don't know,' said Dot, laughing. 'But she can't be much less than a hundred years of age on her next birthday.'

'Ha ha!' laughed Tackleton. Hollow as a drum, that laugh though. And he looked as if he could have twisted Dot's neck, comfortably.

'Dear dear!' said Dot. 'Only to remember how we used to talk, at school, about the husbands we would choose. I don't know how young, and how handsome, and how gay, and how lively, mine was not to be! And as to May's!—Ah dear! I don't know whether to laugh or cry, when I think what silly girls we were.'

May seemed to know which to do; for the colour flushed into her face, and tears stood in her eyes.

'Even the very persons themselves—real live young men—were fixed on sometimes,' said Dot. 'We little thought how things would come about. I never fixed on John I'm sure; I never so much as thought of him. And if I had told you, you were ever to be married to Mr. Tackleton, why you'd have slapped me. Wouldn't you, May?'

Though May didn't say yes, she certainly didn't say no, or express no, by any means.

Tackleton laughed—quite shouted, he laughed so loud. John Peerybingle laughed too, in his ordinary good-natured and contented manner; but his was a mere whisper of a laugh, to Tackleton's.

'You couldn't help yourselves, for all that. You couldn't resist us, you see,' said Tackleton. 'Here we are! Here we are!'

'Where are your gay young bridegrooms now!'

'Some of them are dead,' said Dot; 'and some of them forgotten. Some of them, if they could stand among us at this moment, would not believe we were the same creatures; would not believe that what they saw and heard was real, and we COULD forget them so. No! they would not believe one word of it!'

'Why, Dot!' exclaimed the Carrier. 'Little woman!'

She had spoken with such earnestness and fire, that she stood in need of some recalling to herself, without doubt. Her husband's check was very gentle, for he merely interfered, as he supposed, to shield old Tackleton; but it proved effectual, for she stopped, and said no more. There was an uncommon agitation, even in her silence, which the wary Tackleton, who had brought his half-shut eye to bear upon her, noted closely, and remembered to some purpose too.

May uttered no word, good or bad, but sat quite still, with her eyes cast down, and made no sign of interest in what had passed. The good lady her mother now interposed, observing, in the first instance, that girls were girls, and byegones byegones, and that so long as young people were young and thoughtless, they would probably conduct themselves like young and thoughtless persons: with two or three other positions of a no less sound and incontrovertible character. She then remarked, in a devout spirit, that she thanked Heaven she had always found in her daughter May, a dutiful and obedient child; for which she took no credit to herself, though she had every reason to believe it was entirely owing to herself.

With regard to Mr. Tackleton she said, That he was in a moral point of view an undeniable individual, and That he was in an eligible point of view a son-in-law to be desired, no one in their senses could doubt. (She was very emphatic here.) With regard to the family into which he was so soon about, after some solicitation, to be admitted, she believed Mr. Tackleton knew that, although reduced in purse, it had some pretensions to gentility; and if certain circumstances, not wholly unconnected, she would go so far as to say, with the Indigo Trade, but to which she would not more particularly refer, had happened differently, it might perhaps have been in possession of wealth.

She then remarked that she would not allude to the past, and would not mention that her daughter had for some time rejected the suit of Mr. Tackleton; and that she would not say a great many other things which she did say, at great length. Finally, she delivered it as the general result of her observation and experience, that those marriages in which there was least of what was romantically and sillily called love, were always the happiest; and that she anticipated the greatest possible amount of bliss—not rapturous bliss; but the solid, steady-going article—from the approaching nuptials.

She concluded by informing the company that tomorrow was the day she had lived for, expressly; and that when it was over, she would desire nothing better than to be packed up and disposed of, in any genteel place of burial.

As these remarks were quite unanswerable—which is the happy property of all remarks that are sufficiently wide of the purpose—they changed the current of the conversation, and diverted the general attention to the Veal and Ham-Pie, the cold mutton, the potatoes, and the tart. In order that the bottled beer might not be slighted, John Peerybingle proposed Tomorrow: the Wedding-Day; and called upon them to drink a bumper to it, before he proceeded on his journey.

For you ought to know that he only rested there, and gave the old horse a bait. He had to go some four of five miles farther on; and when he returned in the evening, he called for Dot, and took another rest on his way home. This was the order of the day on all the Pic-Nic occasions, had been, ever since their institution.

There were two persons present, besides the bride and bridegroom elect, who did but indifferent honour to the toast. One of these was Dot, too flushed and discomposed to adapt herself to any small occurrence of the moment; the other, Bertha, who rose up hurriedly, before the rest, and left the table.

'Goodbye!' said stout John Peerybingle, pulling on his dreadnought coat. 'I shall be back at the old time. Goodbye all!'

'Goodbye, John,' returned Caleb.

He seemed to say it by rote, and to wave his hand in the same unconscious manner; for he stood observing Bertha with an anxious wondering face, that never altered its expression.

'Goodbye, young shaver!' said the jolly Carrier, bending down to kiss the child; which Tilly Slowboy, now intent upon her knife and fork, had deposited asleep (and strange to say, without damage) in a little cot of Bertha's furnishing; 'goodbye! Time will come, I suppose, when YOU'LL turn out into the cold, my little friend, and leave your old father to enjoy his pipe and his rheumatics in the chimney-corner; eh? Where's Dot?'

'I'm here, John!' she said, starting.

'Come, come!' returned the Carrier, clapping his sounding hands. 'Where's the pipe?'

'I quite forgot the pipe, John.'

Forgot the pipe! Was such a wonder ever heard of! She! Forgot the pipe!

'I'll—I'll fill it directly. It's soon done.'

But it was not so soon done, either. It lay in the usual place-the Carrier's dreadnought pocket—with the little pouch, her own work, from which she was used to fill it, but her hand shook so, that she entangled it (and yet her hand was small enough to have come out easily, I am sure), and bungled terribly. The filling of the pipe and lighting it, those little offices in which I have commended her discretion, were vilely done, from first to last.

During the whole process, Tackleton stood looking on maliciously with the half-closed eye; which, whenever it met hers-or caught it, for it can hardly be said to have ever met another eye: rather being a kind of trap to snatch it up—augmented her confusion in a most remarkable degree.

'Why, what a clumsy Dot you are, this afternoon!' said John. 'I could have done it better myself, I verify believe!'

With these good-natured words, he strode away, and presently was heard, in company with Boxer, and the old horse, and the cart, making lively music down the road. What time the dreamy Caleb still stood, watching his blind daughter, with the same expression on his face.

'Bertha!' said Caleb, softly. 'What has happened? How changed you are, my darling, in a few hours—since this morning. YOU silent and dull all day! What is it? Tell me!'

'Oh father, father!' cried the Blind Girl, bursting into tears. 'Oh my hard, hard fate!'

Caleb drew his hand across his eyes before he answered her.

'But think how cheerful and how happy you have been, Bertha! How good, and how much loved, by many people.'

'That strikes me to the heart, dear father! Always so mindful of me! Always so kind to me!'

Caleb was very much perplexed to understand her.

'To be—to be blind, Bertha, my poor dear,' he faltered, 'is a great affliction; but—'

'I have never felt it!' cried the Blind Girl. 'I have never felt it, in its fullness. Never! I have sometimes wished that I could see you, or could see him—only once, dear father, only for one little minute—that I might know what it is I treasure up,' she laid her hands upon her breast, 'and hold here! That I might be sure and have it right! And sometimes (but then I was a child) I have wept in my prayers at night, to think that when your images ascended from my heart to Heaven, they might not be the true resemblance of yourselves. But I have never had these feelings long. They have passed away and left me tranquil and contented.'

'And they will again,' said Caleb.

'But, father! Oh my good, gentle father, bear with me, if I am wicked!' said the Blind Girl. 'This is not the sorrow that so weighs me down!'

Her father could not choose but let his moist eyes overflow;

she was so earnest and pathetic, but he did not understand her, yet.

'Bring her to me,' said Bertha. 'I cannot hold it closed and shut within myself. Bring her to me, father!'

She knew he hesitated, and said, 'May. Bring May!'

May heard the mention of her name, and coming quietly towards her, touched her on the arm. The Blind Girl turned immediately, and held her by both hands.

'Look into my face, Dear heart, Sweet heart!' said Bertha. 'Read it with your beautiful eyes, and tell me if the truth is written on it.'

'Dear Bertha, Yes!'

The Blind Girl still, upturning the blank sightless face, down which the tears were coursing fast, addressed her in these words:

'There is not, in my soul, a wish or thought that is not for your good, bright May! There is not, in my soul, a grateful recollection stronger than the deep remembrance which is stored there, of the many many times when, in the full pride of sight and beauty, you have had consideration for Blind Bertha, even when we two were children, or when Bertha was as much a child as ever blindness can be! Every blessing on your head! Light upon your happy course!

'Not the less, my dear May;' and she drew towards her, in a closer grasp; 'not the less, my bird, because, today, the knowledge that you are to be His wife has wrung my heart almost to breaking! Father, May, Mary! oh forgive me that it is so, for the sake of all he has done to relieve the weariness of my dark life: and for the sake of the belief you have in me, when I call Heaven to witness that I could not wish him married to a wife more worthy of his goodness!'

While speaking, she had released May Fielding's hands, and clasped her garments in an attitude of mingled supplication and love. Sinking lower and lower down, as she proceeded in her strange confession, she dropped at last at the feet of her friend, and hid her blind face in the folds of her dress.

'Great Power!' exclaimed her father, smitten at one blow with the truth, 'have I deceived her from the cradle, but to break her heart at last!'

It was well for all of them that Dot, that beaming, useful, busy little Dot—for such she was, whatever faults she had, and however you may learn to hate her, in good time—it was well for all of them, I say, that she was there: or where this would have ended, it were hard to tell. But Dot, recovering her self-possession, interposed, before May could reply, or Caleb say another word.

'Come, come, dear Bertha! come away with me! Give her your arm, May. So! How composed she is, you see, already; and how good it is of her to mind us,' said the cheery little woman, kissing her upon the forehead. 'Come away, dear Bertha. Come! and here's her good father will come with her; won't you, Caleb? To—be—sure!'

Well, well! she was a noble little Dot in such things, and it must have been an obdurate nature that could have withstood her influence. When she had got poor Caleb and his Bertha away, that they might comfort and console each other, as she knew they only could, she presently came bouncing back,—the saying is, as fresh as any daisy; I say fresher—to mount guard over that bridling little piece of consequence in the cap and gloves, and prevent the dear old creature from making discoveries.

'So bring me the precious Baby, Tilly,' said she, drawing a chair to the fire; 'and while I have it in my lap, here's Mrs. Fielding, Tilly, will tell me all about the management of Babies, and put me right in twenty points where I'm as wrong as can be. Won't you, Mrs. Fielding?'

Not even the Welsh Giant, who, according to the popular expression, was so 'slow' as to perform a fatal surgical operation upon himself, in emulation of a juggling-trick achieved by his archenemy at breakfast-time; not even he fell half so readily into the snare prepared for him, as the old lady did into this artful pitfall. The fact of Tackleton having walked out; and furthermore, of two or three people having been talking together at a distance, for two minutes, leaving her to her own resources;

was quite enough to have put her on her dignity, and the bewailment of that mysterious convulsion in the Indigo trade, for four-and-twenty hours.

But this becoming deference to her experience, on the part of the young mother, was so irresistible, that after a short affectation of humility, she began to enlighten her with the best grace in the world; and sitting bolt upright before the wicked Dot, she did, in half an hour, deliver more infallible domestic recipes and precepts, than would (if acted on) have utterly destroyed and done up that Young Peerybingle, though he had been an Infant Samson.

To change the theme, Dot did a little needlework—she carried the contents of a whole workbox in her pocket; however she contrived it, I don't know—then did a little nursing; then a little more needlework; then had a little whispering chat with May, while the old lady dozed; and so in little bits of bustle, which was quite her manner always, found it a very short afternoon.

Then, as it grew dark, and as it was a solemn part of this Institution of the Pic-Nic that she should perform all Bertha's household tasks, she trimmed the fire, and swept the hearth, and set the tea-board out, and drew the curtain, and lighted a candle. Then she played an air or two on a rude kind of harp, which Caleb had contrived for Bertha, and played them very well; for Nature had made her delicate little ear as choice a one for music as it would have been for jewels, if she had had any to wear. By this time it was the established hour for having tea; and Tackleton came back again, to share the meal, and spend the evening.

Caleb and Bertha had returned some time before, and Caleb had sat down to his afternoon's work. But he couldn't settle to it, poor fellow, being anxious and remorseful for his daughter. It was touching to see him sitting idle on his working-stool, regarding her so wistfully, and always saying in his face, 'Have I deceived her from her cradle, but to break her heart!'

When it was night, and tea was done, and Dot had nothing more to do in washing up the cups and saucers; in a word—for

I must come to it, and there is no use in putting it off—when the time drew nigh for expecting the Carrier's return in every sound of distant wheels, her manner changed again, her colour came and went, and she was very restless. Not as good wives are, when listening for their husbands. No, no, no. It was another sort of restlessness from that.

Wheels heard. A horse's feet. The barking of a dog. The gradual approach of all the sounds. The scratching paw of Boxer at the door!

'Whose step is that!' cried Bertha, starting up.

'Whose step?' returned the Carrier, standing in the portal, with his brown face ruddy as a winter berry from the keen night air. 'Why, mine.'

'The other step,' said Bertha. 'The man's tread behind you!'

'She is not to be deceived,' observed the Carrier, laughing. 'Come along, sir. You'll be welcome, never fear!'

He spoke in a loud tone; and as he spoke, the deaf old gentleman entered.

'He's not so much a stranger, that you haven't seen him once, Caleb,' said the Carrier. 'You'll give him house-room till we go?'

'Oh surely, John, and take it as an honour.'

'He's the best company on earth, to talk secrets in,' said John. 'I have reasonable good lungs, but he tries 'em, I can tell you. Sit down, sir. All friends here, and glad to see you!'

When he had imparted this assurance, in a voice that amply corroborated what he had said about his lungs, he added in his natural tone, 'A chair in the chimney-corner, and leave to sit quite silent and look pleasantly about him, is all he cares for. He's easily pleased.'

Bertha had been listening intently. She called Caleb to her side, when he had set the chair, and asked him, in a low voice, to describe their visitor. When he had done so (truly now; with scrupulous fidelity), she moved, for the first time since he had come in, and sighed, and seemed to have no further interest concerning him.

The Carrier was in high spirits, good fellow that he was, and fonder of his little wife than ever.

'A clumsy Dot she was, this afternoon!' he said, encircling her with his rough arm, as she stood, removed from the rest; 'and yet I like her somehow. See yonder, Dot!'

He pointed to the old man. She looked down. I think she trembled.

'He's—ha ha ha!—he's full of admiration for you!' said the Carrier. 'Talked of nothing else, the whole way here. Why, he's a brave old boy. I like him for it!'

'I wish he had had a better subject, John,' she said, with an uneasy glance about the room. At Tackleton especially.

'A better subject!' cried the jovial John. 'There's no such thing. Come, off with the great-coat, off with the thick shawl, off with the heavy wrappers! and a cosy half-hour by the fire! My humble service, Mistress. A game at cribbage, you and I? That's hearty. The cards and board, Dot. And a glass of beer here, if there's any left, small wife!'

His challenge was addressed to the old lady, who accepting it with gracious readiness, they were soon engaged upon the game. At first, the Carrier looked about him sometimes, with a smile, or now and then called Dot to peep over his shoulder at his hand, and advise him on some knotty point. But his adversary being a rigid disciplinarian, and subject to an occasional weakness in respect of pegging more than she was entitled to, required such vigilance on his part, as left him neither eyes nor ears to spare. Thus, his whole attention gradually became absorbed upon the cards; and he thought of nothing else, until a hand upon his shoulder restored him to a consciousness of Tackleton.

'I am sorry to disturb you—but a word, directly.'

'I'm going to deal,' returned the Carrier. 'It's a crisis.'

'It is,' said Tackleton. 'Come here, man!'

There was that in his pale face which made the other rise immediately, and ask him, in a hurry, what the matter was.

'Hush! John Peerybingle,' said Tackleton. 'I am sorry for this. I am indeed. I have been afraid of it. I have suspected it from the first.'

'What is it?' asked the Carrier, with a frightened aspect.

'Hush! I'll show you, if you'll come with me.'

The Carrier accompanied him, without another word. They went across a yard, where the stars were shining, and by a little side-door, into Tackleton's own counting-house, where there was a glass window, commanding the ware-room, which was closed for the night. There was no light in the counting-house itself, but there were lamps in the long narrow ware-room; and consequently the window was bright.

'A moment!' said Tackleton. 'Can you bear to look through that window, do you think?'

'Why not?' returned the Carrier.

'A moment more,' said Tackleton. 'Don't commit any violence. It's of no use. It's dangerous too. You're a strong-made man; and you might do murder before you know it.'

The Carrier looked him in the face, and recoiled a step as if he had been struck. In one stride he was at the window, and he saw—

Oh Shadow on the Hearth! Oh truthful Cricket! Oh perfidious Wife!

He saw her, with the old man—old no longer, but erect and gallant—bearing in his hand the false white hair that had won his way into their desolate and miserable home. He saw her listening to him, as he bent his head to whisper in her ear; and suffering him to clasp her round the waist, as they moved slowly down the dim wooden gallery towards the door by which they had entered it. He saw them stop, and saw her turn—to have the face, the face he loved so, so presented to his view!—and saw her, with her own hands, adjust the lie upon his head, laughing, as she did it, at his unsuspicious nature!

He clenched his strong right hand at first, as if it would have beaten down a lion. But opening it immediately again, he spread it out before the eyes of Tackleton (for he was tender of her, even then), and so, as they passed out, fell down upon a desk, and was as weak as any infant.

He was wrapped up to the chin, and busy with his horse and parcels, when she came into the room, prepared for going home.

'Now, John, dear! Good night, May! Good night, Bertha!'

Could she kiss them? Could she be blithe and cheerful in her parting? Could she venture to reveal her face to them without a blush? Yes. Tackleton observed her closely, and she did all this.

Tilly was hushing the Baby, and she crossed and re-crossed Tackleton, a dozen times, repeating drowsily:

'Did the knowledge that it was to be its wifes, then, wring its hearts almost to breaking; and did its fathers deceive it from its cradles but to break its hearts at last!'

'Now, Tilly, give me the Baby! Goodnight, Mr. Tackleton. Where's John, for goodness' sake?'

'He's going to walk beside the horse's head,' said Tackleton; who helped her to her seat.

'My dear John. Walk? Tonight?'

The muffled figure of her husband made a hasty sign in the affirmative; and the false stranger and the little nurse being in their places, the old horse moved off. Boxer, the unconscious Boxer, running on before, running back, running round and round the cart, and barking as triumphantly and merrily as ever.

When Tackleton had gone off likewise, escorting May and her mother home, poor Caleb sat down by the fire beside his daughter; anxious and remorseful at the core; and still saying in his wistful contemplation of her, 'Have I deceived her from her cradle, but to break her heart at last!'

The toys that had been set in motion for the Baby, had all stopped, and run down, long ago. In the faint light and silence, the imperturbably calm dolls, the agitated rocking-horses with distended eyes and nostrils, the old gentlemen at the street-doors, standing half doubled up upon their failing knees and ankles, the wry-faced nut-crackers, the very Beasts upon their way into the Ark, in twos, like a Boarding School out walking, might have been imagined to be stricken motionless with fantastic wonder, at Dot being false, or Tackleton beloved, under any combination of circumstances.

Chapter 3

Chirp the Third

The Dutch clock in the corner struck Ten, when the Carrier sat down by his fireside. So troubled and grief-worn, that he seemed to scare the Cuckoo, who, having cut his ten melodious announcements as short as possible, plunged back into the Moorish Palace again, and clapped his little door behind him, as if the unwonted spectacle were too much for his feelings.

If the little Haymaker had been armed with the sharpest of scythes, and had cut at every stroke into the Carrier's heart, he never could have gashed and wounded it, as Dot had done.

It was a heart so full of love for her; so bound up and held together by innumerable threads of winning remembrance, spun from the daily working of her many qualities of endearment; it was a heart in which she had enshrined herself so gently and so closely; a heart so single and so earnest in its Truth, so strong in right, so weak in wrong; that it could cherish neither passion nor revenge at first, and had only room to hold the broken image of its Idol.

But, slowly, slowly, as the Carrier sat brooding on his hearth, now cold and dark, other and fiercer thoughts began to rise within him, as an angry wind comes rising in the night. The Stranger was beneath his outraged roof. Three steps would take him to his chamber-door. One blow would beat it in. 'You might do murder before you know it,' Tackleton had said. How could it be murder, if he gave the villain time to grapple with him hand to hand! He was the younger man.

It was an ill-timed thought, bad for the dark mood of his mind. It was an angry thought, goading him to some avenging act, that should change the cheerful house into a haunted place which lonely travellers would dread to pass by night; and where the timid would see shadows struggling in the ruined windows when the moon was dim, and hear wild noises in the stormy weather.

He was the younger man! Yes, yes; some lover who had won

the heart that HE had never touched. Some lover of her early choice, of whom she had thought and dreamed, for whom she had pined and pined, when he had fancied her so happy by his side. O agony to think of it!

She had been above-stairs with the Baby, getting it to bed. As he sat brooding on the hearth, she came close beside him, without his knowledge—in the turning of the rack of his great misery, he lost all other sounds—and put her little stool at his feet. He only knew it, when he felt her hand upon his own, and saw her looking up into his face.

With wonder? No. It was his first impression, and he was fain to look at her again, to set it right. No, not with wonder. With an eager and inquiring look; but not with wonder. At first it was alarmed and serious; then, it changed into a strange, wild, dreadful smile of recognition of his thoughts; then, there was nothing but her clasped hands on her brow, and her bent head, and falling hair.

Though the power of Omnipotence had been his to wield at that moment, he had too much of its diviner property of Mercy in his breast, to have turned one feather's weight of it against her. But he could not bear to see her crouching down upon the little seat where he had often looked on her, with love and pride, so innocent and gay; and, when she rose and left him, sobbing as she went, he felt it a relief to have the vacant place beside him rather than her so long-cherished presence. This in itself was anguish keener than all, reminding him how desolate he was become, and how the great bond of his life was rent asunder.

The more he felt this, and the more he knew he could have better borne to see her lying prematurely dead before him with their little child upon her breast, the higher and the stronger rose his wrath against his enemy. He looked about him for a weapon.

There was a gun, hanging on the wall. He took it down, and moved a pace or two towards the door of the perfidious Stranger's room. He knew the gun was loaded. Some shadowy idea that it was just to shoot this man like a wild beast, seized him, and dilated in his mind until it grew into a monstrous demon in complete possession of him, casting out all milder thoughts and setting up its undivided empire.

That phrase is wrong. Not casting out his milder thoughts, but artfully transforming them. Changing them into scourges to drive him on. Turning water into blood, love into hate, gentleness into blind ferocity. Her image, sorrowing, humbled, but still pleading to his tenderness and mercy with resistless power, never left his mind; but, staying there, it urged him to the door; raised the weapon to his shoulder; fitted and nerved his finger to the trigger; and cried 'Kill him! In his bed!'

He reversed the gun to beat the stock up the door; he already held it lifted in the air; some indistinct design was in his thoughts of calling out to him to fly, for God's sake, by the window—

When, suddenly, the struggling fire illumined the whole chimney with a glow of light; and the Cricket on the Hearth began to Chirp!

No sound he could have heard, no human voice, not even hers, could so have moved and softened him. The artless words in which she had told him of her love for this same Cricket, were once more freshly spoken; her trembling, earnest manner at the moment, was again before him; her pleasant voice—O what a voice it was, for making household music at the fireside of an honest man!—thrilled through and through his better nature, and awoke it into life and action.

He recoiled from the door, like a man walking in his sleep, awakened from a frightful dream; and put the gun aside. Clasping his hands before his face, he then sat down again beside the fire, and found relief in tears.

The Cricket on the Hearth came out into the room, and stood in Fairy shape before him.

'"I love it,"' said the Fairy Voice, repeating what he well remembered, '"for the many times I have heard it, and the many thoughts its harmless music has given me."'

'She said so!' cried the Carrier. 'True!'

'"This has been a happy home, John; and I love the Cricket

for its sake!"'

'It has been, Heaven knows,' returned the Carrier. 'She made it happy, always,—until now.'

'So gracefully sweet-tempered; so domestic, joyful, busy, and light-hearted!' said the Voice.

'Otherwise I never could have loved her as I did,' returned the Carrier.

The Voice, correcting him, said 'do.'

The Carrier repeated 'as I did.' But not firmly. His faltering tongue resisted his control, and would speak in its own way, for itself and him.

The Figure, in an attitude of invocation, raised its hand and said:

'Upon your own hearth—'

'The hearth she has blighted,' interposed the Carrier.

'The hearth she has—how often!—blessed and brightened,' said the Cricket; 'the hearth which, but for her, were only a few stones and bricks and rusty bars, but which has been, through her, the Altar of your Home; on which you have nightly sacrificed some petty passion, selfishness, or care, and offered up the homage of a tranquil mind, a trusting nature, and an overflowing heart; so that the smoke from this poor chimney has gone upward with a better fragrance than the richest incense that is burnt before the richest shrines in all the gaudy temples of this world!—Upon your own hearth; in its quiet sanctuary; surrounded by its gentle influences and associations; hear her! Hear me! Hear everything that speaks the language of your hearth and home!'

'And pleads for her?' inquired the Carrier.

'All things that speak the language of your hearth and home, must plead for her!' returned the Cricket. 'For they speak the truth.'

And while the Carrier, with his head upon his hands, continued to sit meditating in his chair, the Presence stood beside him, suggesting his reflections by its power, and presenting them before him, as in a glass or picture. It was not a solitary Presence. From the hearthstone, from the chimney, from the clock, the pipe, the kettle, and the cradle; from the floor, the walls, the ceiling, and the stairs; from the cart without, and the cupboard within, and the household implements; from everything and every place with which she had ever been familiar, and with which she had ever entwined one recollection of herself in her unhappy husband's mind; Fairies came trooping forth.

Not to stand beside him as the Cricket did, but to busy and bestir themselves. To do all honour to her image. To pull him by the skirts, and point to it when it appeared. To cluster round it, and embrace it, and strew flowers for it to tread on. To try to crown its fair head with their tiny hands. To show that they were fond of it and loved it; and that there was not one ugly, wicked or accusatory creature to claim knowledge of it—none but their playful and approving selves.

His thoughts were constant to her image. It was always there.

She sat plying her needle, before the fire, and singing to herself. Such a blithe, thriving, steady little Dot! The fairy figures turned upon him all at once, by one consent, with one prodigious concentrated stare, and seemed to say, 'Is this the light wife you are mourning for!'

There were sounds of gaiety outside, musical instruments, and noisy tongues, and laughter. A crowd of young merry-makers came pouring in, among whom were May Fielding and a score of pretty girls. Dot was the fairest of them all; as young as any of them too. They came to summon her to join their party. It was a dance. If ever little foot were made for dancing, hers was, surely. But she laughed, and shook her head, and pointed to her cookery on the fire, and her table ready spread: with an exulting defiance that rendered her more charming than she was before.

And so she merrily dismissed them, nodding to her would-be partners, one by one, as they passed, but with a comical indifference, enough to make them go and drown themselves immediately if they were her admirers—and they must have been so, more or less; they couldn't help it. And yet indifference was not her character. O no! For presently, there came a certain Carrier to the door; and bless her what a welcome she bestowed upon him!

Again the staring figures turned upon him all at once, and seemed to say, 'Is this the wife who has forsaken you!'

A shadow fell upon the mirror or the picture: call it what you will. A great shadow of the Stranger, as he first stood underneath their roof; covering its surface, and blotting out all other objects. But the nimble Fairies worked like bees to clear it off again. And Dot again was there. Still bright and beautiful.

Rocking her little Baby in its cradle, singing to it softly, and resting her head upon a shoulder which had its counterpart in the musing figure by which the Fairy Cricket stood.

The night—I mean the real night: not going by Fairy clocks-was wearing now; and in this stage of the Carrier's thoughts, the moon burst out, and shone brightly in the sky. Perhaps some calm and quiet light had risen also, in his mind; and he could think more soberly of what had happened.

Although the shadow of the Stranger fell at intervals upon the glass—always distinct, and big, and thoroughly defined—it never fell so darkly as at first. Whenever it appeared, the Fairies uttered a general cry of consternation, and plied their little arms and legs, with inconceivable activity, to rub it out. And whenever they got at Dot again, and showed her to him once more, bright and beautiful, they cheered in the most inspiring manner.

They never showed her, otherwise than beautiful and bright, for they were Household Spirits to whom falsehood is annihilation; and being so, what Dot was there for them, but the one active, beaming, pleasant little creature who had been the light and sun of the Carrier's Home!

The Fairies were prodigiously excited when they showed her, with the Baby, gossiping among a knot of sage old matrons, and affecting to be wondrous old and matronly herself, and leaning in a staid, demure old way upon her husband's arm, attempting—she! such a bud of a little woman—to convey the idea of having abjured the vanities of the world in general, and of being the sort of person to whom it was no novelty at all to be a mother; yet in the same breath, they showed her, laughing at the Carrier for being awkward, and pulling up his shirt-collar to make him smart, and mincing merrily about that very room to teach him how to dance!

They turned, and stared immensely at him when they showed her with the Blind Girl; for, though she carried cheerfulness and animation with her wheresoever she went, she bore those influences into Caleb Plummer's home, heaped up and running over. The Blind Girl's love for her, and trust in her, and gratitude to her; her own good busy way of setting Bertha's thanks aside; her dexterous little arts for filling up each moment of the visit in doing something useful to the house, and really working hard while feigning to make holiday; her bountiful provision of those standing delicacies, the Veal and Ham-Pie and the bottles of Beer; her radiant little face arriving at the door, and taking leave; the wonderful expression in her whole self, from her neat foot to the crown of her head, of being a part of the establishment—a something necessary to it, which it couldn't be without; all this the Fairies revelled in, and loved her for.

And once again they looked upon him all at once, appealingly, and seemed to say, while some among them nestled in her dress and fondled her, 'Is this the wife who has betrayed your confidence!'

More than once, or twice, or thrice, in the long thoughtful night, they showed her to him sitting on her favourite seat, with her bent head, her hands clasped on her brow, her falling hair. As he had seen her last. And when they found her thus, they neither turned nor looked upon him, but gathered close round her, and comforted and kissed her, and pressed on one another to show sympathy and kindness to her, and forgot him altogether.

Thus the night passed. The moon went down; the stars grew pale; the cold day broke; the sun rose. The Carrier still sat, musing, in the chimney corner. He had sat there, with his head upon his hands, all night. All night the faithful Cricket had been Chirp, Chirp, Chirping on the Hearth. All night he had listened to its voice. All night the household Fairies had been busy with him. All night she had been amiable and blameless in the glass, except when that one shadow fell upon it.

He rose up when it was broad day, and washed and dressed himself. He couldn't go about his customary cheerful avocations—he wanted spirit for them—but it mattered the less, that it was Tackleton's wedding-day, and he had arranged to make his rounds by proxy. He thought to have gone merrily to church with Dot. But such plans were at an end. It was their own wedding-day too. Ah! how little he had looked for such a close to such a year!

The Carrier had expected that Tackleton would pay him an early visit; and he was right. He had not walked to and fro before his own door, many minutes, when he saw the Toy-merchant coming in his chaise along the road. As the chaise drew nearer, he perceived that Tackleton was dressed out sprucely for his marriage, and that he had decorated his horse's head with flowers and favours.

The horse looked much more like a bridegroom than Tackleton, whose half-closed eye was more disagreeably expressive than ever. But the Carrier took little heed of this. His thoughts had other occupation.

'John Peerybingle!' said Tackleton, with an air of condolence. 'My good fellow, how do you find yourself this morning?'

'I have had but a poor night, Master Tackleton,' returned the Carrier, shaking his head: 'for I have been a good deal disturbed in my mind. But it's over now! Can you spare me half an hour or so, for some private talk?'

'I came on purpose,' returned Tackleton, alighting. 'Never mind the horse. He'll stand quiet enough, with the reins over this post, if you'll give him a mouthful of hay.'

The Carrier having brought it from his stable, and set it before him, they turned into the house.

'You are not married before noon,' he said, 'I think?'

'No,' answered Tackleton. 'Plenty of time. Plenty of time.'

When they entered the kitchen, Tilly Slowboy was rapping

at the Stranger's door; which was only removed from it by a few steps. One of her very red eyes (for Tilly had been crying all night long, because her mistress cried) was at the keyhole; and she was knocking very loud; and seemed frightened.

'If you please I can't make nobody hear,' said Tilly, looking round. 'I hope nobody an't gone and been and died if you please!'

This philanthropic wish, Miss Slowboy emphasised with various new raps and kicks at the door; which led to no result whatever.

'Shall I go?' said Tackleton. 'It's curious.'

The Carrier, who had turned his face from the door, signed to him to go if he would.

So Tackleton went to Tilly Slowboy's relief; and he too kicked and knocked; and he too failed to get the least reply. But he thought of trying the handle of the door; and as it opened easily, he peeped in, looked in, went in, and soon came running out again.

'John Peerybingle,' said Tackleton, in his ear. 'I hope there has been nothing—nothing rash in the night?'

The Carrier turned upon him quickly.

'Because he's gone!' said Tackleton; 'and the window's open. I don't see any marks—to be sure it's almost on a level with the garden: but I was afraid there might have been some—some scuffle. Eh?'

He nearly shut up the expressive eye altogether; he looked at him so hard. And he gave his eye, and his face, and his whole person, a sharp twist. As if he would have screwed the truth out of him.

'Make yourself easy,' said the Carrier. 'He went into that room last night, without harm in word or deed from me, and no one has entered it since. He is away of his own free will. I'd go out gladly at that door, and beg my bread from house to house, for life, if I could so change the past that he had never come. But he has come and gone. And I have done with him!'

'Oh!—Well, I think he has got off pretty easy,' said Tackleton, taking a chair.

The sneer was lost upon the Carrier, who sat down too, and shaded his face with his hand, for some little time, before proceeding.

'You showed me last night,' he said at length, 'my wife; my wife that I love; secretly—'

'And tenderly,' insinuated Tackleton.

'Conniving at that man's disguise, and giving him opportunities of meeting her alone. I think there's no sight I wouldn't have rather seen than that. I think there's no man in the world I wouldn't have rather had to show it me.'

'I confess to having had my suspicions always,' said Tackleton. 'And that has made me objectionable here, I know.'

'But as you did show it me,' pursued the Carrier, not minding him; 'and as you saw her, my wife, my wife that I love'—his voice, and eye, and hand, grew steadier and firmer as he repeated these words: evidently in pursuance of a steadfast purpose—'as you saw her at this disadvantage, it is right and just that you should also see with my eyes, and look into my breast, and know what my mind is, upon the subject. For it's settled,' said the Carrier, regarding him attentively. 'And nothing can shake it now.'

Tackleton muttered a few general words of assent, about its being necessary to vindicate something or other; but he was overawed by the manner of his companion. Plain and unpolished as it was, it had a something dignified and noble in it, which nothing but the soul of generous honour dwelling in the man could have imparted.

'I am a plain, rough man,' pursued the Carrier, 'with very little to recommend me. I am not a clever man, as you very well know. I am not a young man. I loved my little Dot, because I had seen her grow up, from a child, in her father's house; because I knew how precious she was; because she had been my life, for years and years. There's many men I can't compare with, who never could have loved my little Dot like me, I think!'

He paused, and softly beat the ground a short time with his foot, before resuming.

'I often thought that though I wasn't good enough for her, I should make her a kind husband, and perhaps know her value better than another; and in this way I reconciled it to myself, and came to think it might be possible that we should be married. And in the end it came about, and we were married.'

'Hah!' said Tackleton, with a significant shake of the head.

'I had studied myself; I had had experience of myself; I knew how much I loved her, and how happy I should be,' pursued the Carrier. 'But I had not—I feel it now—sufficiently considered her.'

'To be sure,' said Tackleton. 'Giddiness, frivolity, fickleness, love of admiration! Not considered! All left out of sight! Hah!'

'You had best not interrupt me,' said the Carrier, with some sternness, 'till you understand me; and you're wide of doing so. If, yesterday, I'd have struck that man down at a blow, who dared to breathe a word against her, today I'd set my foot upon his face, if he was my brother!'

The Toy-merchant gazed at him in astonishment. He went on in a softer tone:

'Did I consider,' said the Carrier, 'that I took her—at her age, and with her beauty—from her young companions, and the many scenes of which she was the ornament; in which she was the brightest little star that ever shone, to shut her up from day to day in my dull house, and keep my tedious company? Did I consider how little suited I was to her sprightly humour, and how wearisome a plodding man like me must be, to one of her quick spirit? Did I consider that it was no merit in me, or claim in me, that I loved her, when everybody must, who knew her? Never. I took advantage of her hopeful nature and her cheerful disposition; and I married her. I wish I never had! For her sake; not for mine!'

The Toy-merchant gazed at him, without winking. Even the half-shut eye was open now.

'Heaven bless her!' said the Carrier, 'for the cheerful constancy with which she tried to keep the knowledge of this from me! And Heaven help me, that, in my slow mind, I have not found it out before! Poor child! Poor Dot! I not to find it out, who have seen her eyes fill with tears, when such a marriage as our own was spoken of! I, who have seen the secret trembling on her lips a hundred times, and never suspected it till last night! Poor girl! That I could ever hope she would be fond of me! That I could ever believe she was!'

'She made a show of it,' said Tackleton. 'She made such a show of it, that to tell you the truth it was the origin of my misgivings.'

And here he asserted the superiority of May Fielding, who certainly made no sort of show of being fond of HIM.

'She has tried,' said the poor Carrier, with greater emotion than he had exhibited yet; 'I only now begin to know how hard she has tried, to be my dutiful and zealous wife. How good she has been; how much she has done; how brave and strong a heart she has; let the happiness I have known under this roof bear witness! It will be some help and comfort to me, when I am here alone.'

'Here alone?' said Tackleton. 'Oh! Then you do mean to take some notice of this?'

'I mean,' returned the Carrier, 'to do her the greatest kindness, and make her the best reparation, in my power. I can release her from the daily pain of an unequal marriage, and the struggle to conceal it. She shall be as free as I can render her.'

'Make HER reparation!' exclaimed Tackleton, twisting and turning his great ears with his hands. 'There must be something wrong here. You didn't say that, of course.'

The Carrier set his grip upon the collar of the Toy-merchant, and shook him like a reed.

'Listen to me!' he said. 'And take care that you hear me right. Listen to me. Do I speak plainly?'

'Very plainly indeed,' answered Tackleton.

'As if I meant it?'

'Very much as if you meant it.'

'I sat upon that hearth, last night, all night,' exclaimed the Carrier. 'On the spot where she has often sat beside me, with her sweet face looking into mine. I called up her whole life, day by day. I had her dear self, in its every passage, in review before me. And upon my soul she is innocent, if there is One to judge the innocent and guilty!'

Staunch Cricket on the Hearth! Loyal household Fairies!

'Passion and distrust have left me!' said the Carrier; 'and nothing but my grief remains. In an unhappy moment some old lover, better suited to her tastes and years than I; forsaken, perhaps, for me, against her will; returned. In an unhappy moment, taken by surprise, and wanting time to think of what she did, she made herself a party to his treachery, by concealing it. Last night she saw him, in the interview we witnessed. It was wrong. But otherwise than this she is innocent if there is truth on earth!'

'If that is your opinion'—Tackleton began.

'So, let her go!' pursued the Carrier. 'Go, with my blessing for the many happy hours she has given me, and my forgiveness for any pang she has caused me. Let her go, and have the peace of mind I wish her! She'll never hate me. She'll learn to like me better, when I'm not a drag upon her, and she wears the chain I have riveted, more lightly. This is the day on which I took her, with so little thought for her enjoyment, from her home. Today she shall return to it, and I will trouble her no more. Her father and mother will be here today—we had made a little plan for keeping it together—and they shall take her home. I can trust her, there, or anywhere. She leaves me without blame, and she will live so I am sure. If I should die—I may perhaps while she is still young; I have lost some courage in a few hours—she'll find that I remembered her, and loved her to the last! This is the end of what you showed me. Now, it's over!'

'O no, John, not over. Do not say it's over yet! Not quite yet. I have heard your noble words. I could not steal away, pretending to be ignorant of what has affected me with such deep gratitude. Do not say it's over, 'till the clock has struck again!'

She had entered shortly after Tackleton, and had remained there. She never looked at Tackleton, but fixed her eyes upon her husband. But she kept away from him, setting as wide a space as possible between them; and though she spoke with most impassioned earnestness, she went no nearer to him even then. How different in this from her old self!

'No hand can make the clock which will strike again for me the hours that are gone,' replied the Carrier, with a faint smile. 'But let it be so, if you will, my dear. It will strike soon. It's of little matter what we say. I'd try to please you in a harder case than that.'

'Well!' muttered Tackleton. 'I must be off, for when the clock strikes again, it'll be necessary for me to be upon my way to church. Good morning, John Peerybingle. I'm sorry to be deprived of the pleasure of your company. Sorry for the loss, and the occasion of it too!'

'I have spoken plainly?' said the Carrier, accompanying him to the door.

'Oh quite!'

'And you'll remember what I have said?'

'Why, if you compel me to make the observation,' said Tackleton, previously taking the precaution of getting into his chaise; 'I must say that it was so very unexpected, that I'm far from being likely to forget it.'

'The better for us both,' returned the Carrier. 'Good bye. I give you joy!'

'I wish I could give it to YOU,' said Tackleton. 'As I can't; thank'ee. Between ourselves, (as I told you before, eh?) I don't much think I shall have the less joy in my married life, because May hasn't been too officious about me, and too demonstrative. Good bye! Take care of yourself.'

The Carrier stood looking after him until he was smaller in the distance than his horse's flowers and favours near at hand; and then, with a deep sigh, went strolling like a restless, broken man, among some neighbouring elms; unwilling to return until the clock was on the eve of striking.

His little wife, being left alone, sobbed piteously; but often dried her eyes and checked herself, to say how good he was, how excellent he was! and once or twice she laughed; so heartily, triumphantly, and incoherently (still crying all the time), that Tilly was quite horrified.

'Ow if you please don't!' said Tilly. 'It's enough to dead and bury the Baby, so it is if you please.'

'Will you bring him sometimes, to see his father, Tilly,' inquired her mistress, drying her eyes; 'when I can't live here, and have gone to my old home?'

'Ow if you please don't!' cried Tilly, throwing back her head, and bursting out into a howl—she looked at the moment uncommonly like Boxer. 'Ow if you please don't! Ow, what has everybody gone and been and done with everybody, making everybody else so wretched! Ow-w-w-w!'

The soft-hearted Slowboy trailed off at this juncture, into such a deplorable howl, the more tremendous from its long suppression, that she must infallibly have awakened the Baby, and frightened him into something serious (probably convulsions), if her eyes had not encountered Caleb Plummer, leading in his daughter. This spectacle restoring her to a sense of the proprieties, she stood for some few moments silent, with her mouth wide open; and then, posting off to the bed on which the Baby lay asleep, danced in a weird, Saint Vitus manner on the floor, and at the same time rummaged with her face and head among the bedclothes, apparently deriving much relief from those extraordinary operations.

'Mary!' said Bertha. 'Not at the marriage!'

'I told her you would not be there, mum,' whispered Caleb. 'I heard as much last night. But bless you,' said the little man, taking her tenderly by both hands, 'I don't care for what they say. I don't believe them. There an't much of me, but that little should be torn to pieces sooner than I'd trust a word against you!'

He put his arms about her and hugged her, as a child might have hugged one of his own dolls.

'Bertha couldn't stay at home this morning,' said Caleb. 'She was afraid, I know, to hear the bells ring, and couldn't trust herself to be so near them on their wedding-day. So we started in good time, and came here. I have been thinking of what I have done,' said Caleb, after a moment's pause; 'I have been blaming myself till I hardly knew what to do or where to turn, for the distress of mind I have caused her; and I've come to the conclusion that I'd better, if you'll stay with me, mum, the while, tell her the truth. You'll stay with me the while?' he inquired, trembling from head to foot. 'I don't know what effect it may have upon her; I don't know what she'll think of me; I don't know that she'll ever care for her poor father afterwards. But it's best for her that she should be undeceived, and I must bear the consequences as I deserve!'

'Mary,' said Bertha, 'where is your hand! Ah! Here it is here it is!' pressing it to her lips, with a smile, and drawing it through her arm. 'I heard them speaking softly among themselves, last night, of some blame against you. They were wrong.'

The Carrier's Wife was silent. Caleb answered for her.

'They were wrong,' he said.

'I knew it!' cried Bertha, proudly. 'I told them so. I scorned to hear a word! Blame HER with justice!' she pressed the hand between her own, and the soft cheek against her face. 'No! I am not so blind as that.'

Her father went on one side of her, while Dot remained upon the other: holding her hand.

'I know you all,' said Bertha, 'better than you think. But none so well as her. Not even you, father. There is nothing half so real and so true about me, as she is. If I could be restored to sight this instant, and not a word were spoken, I could choose her from a crowd! My sister!'

'Bertha, my dear!' said Caleb, 'I have something on my mind I want to tell you, while we three are alone. Hear me kindly! I have a confession to make to you, my darling.'

'A confession, father?'

'I have wandered from the truth and lost myself, my child,' said Caleb, with a pitiable expression in his bewildered face. 'I have wandered from the truth, intending to be kind to you; and have been cruel.'

She turned her wonder-stricken face towards him, and repeated 'Cruel!'

'He accuses himself too strongly, Bertha,' said Dot. 'You'll say so, presently. You'll be the first to tell him so.'

'He cruel to me!' cried Bertha, with a smile of incredulity.

'Not meaning it, my child,' said Caleb. 'But I have been; though I never suspected it, till yesterday. My dear blind daughter, hear me and forgive me! The world you live in, heart of mine, doesn't exist as I have represented it. The eyes you have trusted in, have been false to you.'

She turned her wonder-stricken face towards him still; but drew back, and clung closer to her friend.

'Your road in life was rough, my poor one,' said Caleb, 'and I meant to smooth it for you. I have altered objects, changed the characters of people, invented many things that never have been, to make you happier. I have had concealments from you, put deceptions on you, God forgive me! and surrounded you with fancies.'

'But living people are not fancies!' she said hurriedly, and turning very pale, and still retiring from him. 'You can't change them.'

'I have done so, Bertha,' pleaded Caleb. 'There is one person that you know, my dove—'

'Oh father! why do you say, I know?' she answered, in a term of keen reproach. 'What and whom do I know! I who have no leader! I so miserably blind.'

In the anguish of her heart, she stretched out her hands, as if she were groping her way; then spread them, in a manner most forlorn and sad, upon her face.

'The marriage that takes place today,' said Caleb, 'is with a stern, sordid, grinding man. A hard master to you and me, my dear, for many years. Ugly in his looks, and in his nature. Cold and callous always. Unlike what I have painted him to you in everything, my child. In everything.'

'Oh why,' cried the Blind Girl, tortured, as it seemed, almost beyond endurance, 'why did you ever do this! Why did you ever fill my heart so full, and then come in like Death, and tear away the objects of my love! O Heaven, how blind I am! How helpless and alone!'

Her afflicted father hung his head, and offered no reply but in his penitence and sorrow.

She had been but a short time in this passion of regret, when the Cricket on the Hearth, unheard by all but her, began to chirp. Not merrily, but in a low, faint, sorrowing way. It was so mournful that her tears began to flow; and when the Presence which had been beside the Carrier all night, appeared behind her, pointing to her father, they fell down like rain.

She heard the Cricket-voice more plainly soon, and was conscious, through her blindness, of the Presence hovering about her father.

'Mary,' said the Blind Girl, 'tell me what my home is. What it truly is.'

'It is a poor place, Bertha; very poor and bare indeed. The house will scarcely keep out wind and rain another winter. It is as roughly shielded from the weather, Bertha,' Dot continued in a low, clear voice, 'as your poor father in his sack-cloth coat.'

The Blind Girl, greatly agitated, rose, and led the Carrier's little wife aside.

'Those presents that I took such care of; that came almost at my wish, and were so dearly welcome to me,' she said, trembling; 'where did they come from? Did you send them?'

'No.'

'Who then?'

Dot saw she knew, already, and was silent. The Blind Girl spread her hands before her face again. But in quite another manner now.

'Dear Mary, a moment. One moment? More this way. Speak softly to me. You are true, I know. You'd not deceive me now; would you?'

'No, Bertha, indeed!'

'No, I am sure you would not. You have too much pity for me. Mary, look across the room to where we were just now—to where my father is—my father, so compassionate and loving to me—and tell me what you see.'

'I see,' said Dot, who understood her well, 'an old man sitting in a chair, and leaning sorrowfully on the back, with his face resting on his hand. As if his child should comfort him, Bertha.'

'Yes, yes. She will. Go on.'

'He is an old man, worn with care and work. He is a spare, dejected, thoughtful, grey-haired man. I see him now, despondent and bowed down, and striving against nothing. But, Bertha, I have seen him many times before, and striving hard in many ways for one great sacred object. And I honour his grey head, and bless him!'

The Blind Girl broke away from her; and throwing herself upon her knees before him, took the grey head to her breast.

'It is my sight restored. It is my sight!' she cried. 'I have been blind, and now my eyes are open. I never knew him! To think I might have died, and never truly seen the father who has been so loving to me!'

There were no words for Caleb's emotion.

'There is not a gallant figure on this earth,' exclaimed the Blind Girl, holding him in her embrace, 'that I would love so dearly, and would cherish so devotedly, as this! The greyer, and more worn, the dearer, father! Never let them say I am blind again. There's not a furrow in his face, there's not a hair upon his head, that shall be forgotten in my prayers and thanks to Heaven!'

Caleb managed to articulate 'My Bertha!'

'And in my blindness, I believed him,' said the girl, caressing him with tears of exquisite affection, 'to be so different! And having him beside me, day by day, so mindful of me—always, never dreamed of this!'

'The fresh smart father in the blue coat, Bertha,' said poor Caleb. 'He's gone!'

'Nothing is gone,' she answered. 'Dearest father, no! Everything is here—in you. The father that I loved so well; the father that I never loved enough, and never knew; the benefactor whom I first began to reverence and love, because he had such sympathy for me; All are here in you. Nothing is dead to me. The soul of all that was most dear to me is here—here, with the worn face, and the grey head. And I am NOT blind, father, any longer!'

Dot's whole attention had been concentrated, during this discourse, upon the father and daughter; but looking, now, towards the little Haymaker in the Moorish meadow, she saw that the clock was within a few minutes of striking, and fell, immediately, into a nervous and excited state.

'Father,' said Bertha, hesitating. 'Mary.'

'Yes, my dear,' returned Caleb. 'Here she is.'

'There is no change in HER. You never told me anything of HER that was not true?'

'I should have done it, my dear, I am afraid,' returned Caleb, 'if I could have made her better than she was. But I must have changed her for the worse, if I had changed her at all. Nothing could improve her, Bertha.'

Confident as the Blind Girl had been when she asked the question, her delight and pride in the reply and her renewed embrace of Dot, were charming to behold.

'More changes than you think for, may happen though, my dear,' said Dot. 'Changes for the better, I mean; changes for great joy to some of us. You mustn't let them startle you too much, if any such should ever happen, and affect you? Are those wheels upon the road? You've a quick ear, Bertha. Are they wheels?'

'Yes. Coming very fast.'

'I—I—I know you have a quick ear,' said Dot, placing her hand upon her heart, and evidently talking on, as fast as she could to hide its palpitating state, 'because I have noticed it often, and because you were so quick to find out that strange step last night. Though why you should have said, as I very well recollect you did say, Bertha, "Whose step is that!" and why you should have taken any greater observation of it than of any other step, I don't know. Though as I said just now, there are great changes in the world: great changes: and we can't do better than prepare ourselves to be surprised at hardly anything.'

Caleb wondered what this meant; perceiving that she spoke to him, no less than to his daughter. He saw her, with astonishment, so fluttered and distressed that she could scarcely breathe; and holding to a chair, to save herself from falling.

'They are wheels indeed!' she panted. 'Coming nearer! Nearer! Very close! And now you hear them stopping at the garden-gate! And now you hear a step outside the door—the same step, Bertha, is it not!—and now!'—

She uttered a wild cry of uncontrollable delight; and running up to Caleb put her hands upon his eyes, as a young man rushed into the room, and flinging away his hat into the air, came sweeping down upon them.

'Is it over?' cried Dot.

'Yes!'

'Happily over?'

'Yes!'

'Do you recollect the voice, dear Caleb? Did you ever hear the like of it before?' cried Dot.

'If my boy in the Golden South Americas was alive'—said Caleb, trembling.

'He is alive!' shrieked Dot, removing her hands from his eyes, and clapping them in ecstasy; 'look at him! See where he stands before you, healthy and strong! Your own dear son! Your own dear living, loving brother, Bertha

All honour to the little creature for her transports! All honour to her tears and laughter, when the three were locked in one another's arms! All honour to the heartiness with which she met the sunburnt sailor-fellow, with his dark streaming hair, half-way, and never turned her rosy little mouth aside, but suffered him to kiss it, freely, and to press her to his bounding heart!

And honour to the Cuckoo too—why not!—for bursting out of the trap-door in the Moorish Palace like a house-breaker, and hiccoughing twelve times on the assembled company, as if he had got drunk for joy!

The Carrier, entering, started back. And well he might, to find himself in such good company.

'Look, John!' said Caleb, exultingly, 'look here! My own boy from the Golden South Americas! My own son! Him that you fitted out, and sent away yourself! Him that you were always such a friend to!'

The Carrier advanced to seize him by the hand; but, recoiling, as some feature in his face awakened a remembrance of the Deaf Man in the Cart, said:

'Edward! Was it you?'

'Now tell him all!' cried Dot. 'Tell him all, Edward; and don't spare me, for nothing shall make me spare myself in his eyes, ever again.'

'I was the man,' said Edward.

'And could you steal, disguised, into the house of your old friend?' rejoined the Carrier. 'There was a frank boy once—how many years is it, Caleb, since we heard that he was dead, and had it proved, we thought?—who never would have done that.'

'There was a generous friend of mine, once; more a father to me than a friend;' said Edward, 'who never would have judged me, or any other man, unheard. You were he. So I am certain you will hear me now.'

The Carrier, with a troubled glance at Dot, who still kept far away from him, replied, 'Well! that's but fair. I will.'

'You must know that when I left here, a boy,' said Edward, 'I was in love, and my love was returned. She was a very young girl, who perhaps (you may tell me) didn't know her own mind. But I knew mine, and I had a passion for her.'

'You had!' exclaimed the Carrier. 'You!'

'Indeed I had,' returned the other. 'And she returned it. I have ever since believed she did, and now I am sure she did.'

'Heaven help me!' said the Carrier. 'This is worse than all.'

'Constant to her,' said Edward, 'and returning, full of hope, after many hardships and perils, to redeem my part of our old contract, I heard, twenty miles away, that she was false to me; that she had forgotten me; and had bestowed herself upon another and a richer man. I had no mind to reproach her; but I wished to see her, and to prove beyond dispute that this was true. I hoped she might have been forced into it, against her own desire and recollection. It would be small comfort, but it would be some, I thought, and on I came. That I might have the truth, the real truth; observing freely for myself, and judging for myself, without obstruction on the one hand, or presenting my own influence (if I had any) before her, on the other; I dressed myself unlike myself—you know how; and waited on the road—you know where. You had no suspicion of me; neither had—had she,' pointing to Dot, 'until I whispered in her ear at that fireside, and she so nearly betrayed me.'

'But when she knew that Edward was alive, and had come back,' sobbed Dot, now speaking for herself, as she had burned to do, all through this narrative; 'and when she knew his purpose, she advised him by all means to keep his secret close; for his old friend John Peerybingle was much too open in his nature, and too clumsy in all artifice—being a clumsy man in general,' said Dot, half laughing and half crying—'to keep it for him.

'And when she—that's me, John,' sobbed the little woman—'told him all, and how his sweetheart had believed him to be dead; and how she had at last been over-persuaded by her mother into a marriage which the silly, dear old thing called advantageous; and when she—that's me again, John—told him they were not yet married (though close upon it), and that it would be nothing but a sacrifice if it went on, for there was no love on her side; and when he went nearly mad with joy to hear it; then she—that's me again—said she would go between them, as she had often done before in old times, John, and would sound his sweetheart and be sure that what she—me again, John—said and thought was right. And it was right, John! And they were brought together, John! And they were married, John, an hour ago! And here's the Bride! And Gruff and Tackleton may die a bachelor! And I'm a happy little woman, May, God bless you!'

She was an irresistible little woman, if that be anything to the purpose; and never so completely irresistible as in her present transports. There never were congratulations so endearing and delicious, as those she lavished on herself and on the Bride.

Amid the tumult of emotions in his breast, the honest Carrier had stood, confounded. Flying, now, towards her, Dot stretched out her hand to stop him, and retreated as before.

'No, John, no! Hear all! Don't love me anymore, John, till you've heard every word I have to say. It was wrong to have a secret from you, John. I'm very sorry. I didn't think it any harm, till I came and sat down by you on the little stool last night. But when I knew by what was written in your face, that you had seen me walking in the gallery with Edward, and when I knew what you thought, I felt how giddy and how wrong it was. But oh, dear John, how could you, could you, think so!'

Little woman, how she sobbed again! John Peerybingle would have caught her in his arms. But no; she wouldn't let him.

'Don't love me yet, please, John! Not for a long time yet! When I was sad about this intended marriage, dear, it was because I remembered May and Edward such young lovers; and knew that her heart was far away from Tackleton. You believe that, now. Don't you, John?'

John was going to make another rush at this appeal; but she stopped him again.

'No; keep there, please, John! When I laugh at you, as I sometimes do, John, and call you clumsy and a dear old goose, and names of that sort, it's because I love you, John, so well, and take such pleasure in your ways, and wouldn't see you altered in the least respect to have you made a King tomorrow.'

'Hooroar!' said Caleb with unusual vigour. 'My opinion!'

'And when I speak of people being middle-aged, and steady, John, and pretend that we are a humdrum couple, going on in a jog-trot sort of way, it's only because I'm such a silly little thing, John, that I like, sometimes, to act a kind of Play with Baby, and all that: and make believe.'

She saw that he was coming; and stopped him again. But she was very nearly too late.

'No, don't love me for another minute or two, if you please, John! What I want most to tell you, I have kept to the last. My dear, good, generous John, when we were talking the other night about the Cricket, I had it on my lips to say, that at first I did not love you quite so dearly as I do now; that when I first came home here, I was half afraid I mightn't learn to love you every bit as well as I hoped and prayed I might—being so very young, John! But, dear John, every day and hour I loved you more and more. And if I could have loved you better than I do, the noble words I heard you say this morning, would have made me. But I can't. All the affection that I had (it was a great deal, John) I gave you, as you well deserve, long, long ago, and I have no more left to give. Now, my dear husband, take me to your heart again! That's my home, John; and never, never think of sending me to any other!'

You never will derive so much delight from seeing a glorious little woman in the arms of a third party, as you would have felt if you had seen Dot run into the Carrier's embrace. It was the most complete, unmitigated, soul-fraught little piece of earnestness that ever you beheld in all your days.

You may be sure the Carrier was in a state of perfect rapture; and you may be sure Dot was likewise; and you may be sure they all were, inclusive of Miss Slowboy, who wept copiously for joy, and wishing to include her young charge in the general interchange of congratulations, handed round the Baby to everybody in succession, as if it were something to drink.

But, now, the sound of wheels was heard again outside the door; and somebody exclaimed that Gruff and Tackleton was coming back. Speedily that worthy gentleman appeared, looking warm and flustered.

'Why, what the Devil's this, John Peerybingle!' said Tackleton. 'There's some mistake. I appointed Mrs. Tackleton to meet me at the church, and I'll swear I passed her on the road, on her way here. Oh! here she is! I beg your pardon, sir; I haven't the pleasure of knowing you; but if you can do me the favour to spare this young lady, she has rather a particular engagement this morning.'

'But I can't spare her,' returned Edward. 'I couldn't think of it.'

'What do you mean, you vagabond?' said Tackleton.

'I mean, that as I can make allowance for your being vexed,' returned the other, with a smile, 'I am as deaf to harsh discourse this morning, as I was to all discourse last night.'

The look that Tackleton bestowed upon him, and the start he gave!

'I am sorry, sir,' said Edward, holding out May's left hand, and especially the third finger; 'that the young lady can't accompany you to church; but as she has been there once, this morning, perhaps you'll excuse her.'

Tackleton looked hard at the third finger, and took a little piece of silver-paper, apparently containing a ring, from his waistcoat-pocket.

'Miss Slowboy,' said Tackleton. 'Will you have the kindness to throw that in the fire? Thank'ee.'

'It was a previous engagement, quite an old engagement, that prevented my wife from keeping her appointment with you, I assure you,' said Edward.

'Mr. Tackleton will do me the justice to acknowledge that I revealed it to him faithfully; and that I told him, many times, I never could forget it,' said May, blushing.

'Oh certainly!' said Tackleton. 'Oh to be sure. Oh it's all right. It's quite correct. Mrs. Edward Plummer, I infer?'

'That's the name,' returned the bridegroom.

'Ah, I shouldn't have known you, sir,' said Tackleton, scrutinising his face narrowly, and making a low bow. 'I give you joy, sir!'

'Thank'ee.'

'Mrs. Peerybingle,' said Tackleton, turning suddenly to where she stood with her husband; 'I am sorry. You haven't done me a very great kindness, but, upon my life I am sorry. You are better than I thought you. John Peerybingle, I am sorry. You understand me; that's enough. It's quite correct, ladies and gentlemen all, and perfectly satisfactory. Good morning!'

With these words he carried it off, and carried himself off too: merely stopping at the door, to take the flowers and favours from his horse's head, and to kick that animal once, in the ribs, as a means of informing him that there was a screw loose in his arrangements.

Of course it became a serious duty now, to make such a day of it, as should mark these events for a high Feast and Festival in the Peerybingle Calendar for evermore. Accordingly, Dot went to work to produce such an entertainment, as should reflect undying honour on the house and on everyone concerned; and in a very short space of time, she was up to her dimpled elbows in flour, and whitening the Carrier's coat, every time he came near her, by stopping him to give him a kiss.

That good fellow washed the greens, and peeled the turnips, and broke the plates, and upset iron pots full of cold water on the fire, and made himself useful in all sorts of ways: while a couple of professional assistants, hastily called in from somewhere in the neighbourhood, as on a point of life or death, ran against each other in all the doorways and round all the corners, and everybody tumbled over Tilly Slowboy and the Baby, everywhere. Tilly never came out in such force before.

Her ubiquity was the theme of general admiration. She was a stumbling-block in the passage at five-and-twenty minutes past two; a man-trap in the kitchen at half-past two precisely; and a pitfall in the garret at five-and-twenty minutes to three. The Baby's head was, as it were, a test and touchstone for every description of matter,—animal, vegetable, and mineral. Nothing was in use that day that didn't come, at some time or other, into close acquaintance with it.

Then, there was a great Expedition set on foot to go and find out Mrs. Fielding; and to be dismally penitent to that excellent gentlewoman; and to bring her back, by force, if needful, to be happy and forgiving. And when the Expedition first discovered her, she would listen to no terms at all, but said, an unspeakable number of times, that ever she should have lived to see the day! and couldn't be got to say anything else, except, 'Now carry me to the grave:' which seemed absurd, on account of her not being dead, or anything at all like it. After a time, she lapsed into a state of dreadful calmness, and observed, that when that unfortunate train of circumstances had occurred in the Indigo Trade, she had foreseen that she would be exposed, during her whole life, to every species of insult and contumely; and that she was glad to find it was the case; and begged they wouldn't trouble themselves about her,—for what was she? oh, dear! a nobody!-but would forget that such a being lived, and would take their course in life without her.

From this bitterly sarcastic mood, she passed into an angry one, in which she gave vent to the remarkable expression that the worm would turn if trodden on; and, after that, she yielded to a soft regret, and said, if they had only given her their confidence, what might she not have had it in her power to suggest! Taking advantage of this crisis in her feelings, the Expedition embraced her; and she very soon had her gloves on, and was on her way to John Peerybingle's in a state of unimpeachable gentility; with a paper parcel at her side containing a cap of state, almost as tall, and quite as stiff, as a mitre.

Then, there were Dot's father and mother to come, in another little chaise; and they were behind their time; and fears were entertained; and there was much looking out for them down the road; and Mrs. Fielding always would look in the wrong and morally impossible direction; and being apprised thereof, hoped she might take the liberty of looking where she pleased. At last they came: a chubby little couple, jogging along in a snug and comfortable little way that quite belonged to the Dot family; and Dot and her mother, side by side, were wonderful to see. They were so like each other.

Then, Dot's mother had to renew her acquaintance with May's mother; and May's mother always stood on her gentility; and Dot's mother never stood on anything but her active little feet. And old Dot—so to call Dot's father, I forgot it wasn't his right name, but never mind—took liberties, and shook hands at first sight, and seemed to think a cap but so much starch and muslin, and didn't defer himself at all to the Indigo Trade, but said there was no help for it now; and, in Mrs. Fielding's summing up, was a good-natured kind of man—but coarse, my dear.

I wouldn't have missed Dot, doing the honours in her wedding-gown, my benison on her bright face! for any money. No! nor the good Carrier, so jovial and so ruddy, at the bottom of the table. Nor the brown, fresh sailor-fellow, and his handsome wife. Nor any one among them. To have missed the dinner would have been to miss as jolly and as stout a meal as man need eat; and to have missed the overflowing cups in which they drank The Wedding-Day, would have been the greatest miss of all.

After dinner, Caleb sang the song about the Sparkling Bowl. As I'm a living man, hoping to keep so, for a year or two, he sang it through.

And, by-the-by, a most unlooked-for incident occurred, just as he finished the last verse.

There was a tap at the door; and a man came staggering in, without saying with your leave, or by your leave, with something heavy on his head. Setting this down in the middle of the table, symmetrically in the centre of the nuts and apples, he said:

'Mr. Tackleton's compliments, and as he hasn't got no use for the cake himself, p'raps you'll eat it.'

And with those words, he walked off.

There was some surprise among the company, as you may imagine. Mrs. Fielding, being a lady of infinite discernment, suggested that the cake was poisoned, and related a narrative of a cake, which, within her knowledge, had turned a seminary for young ladies, blue. But she was overruled by acclamation; and the cake was cut by May, with much ceremony and rejoicing.

I don't think anyone had tasted it, when there came another tap at the door, and the same man appeared again, having under his arm a vast brown-paper parcel.

'Mr. Tackleton's compliments, and he's sent a few toys for the Babby. They ain't ugly.'

After the delivery of which expressions, he retired again.

The whole party would have experienced great difficulty in finding words for their astonishment, even if they had had ample time to seek them. But they had none at all; for the messenger had scarcely shut the door behind him, when there came another tap, and Tackleton himself walked in.

'Mrs. Peerybingle!' said the Toy-merchant, hat in hand. 'I'm sorry. I'm more sorry than I was this morning. I have had time to think of it. John Peerybingle! I'm sour by disposition; but I can't help being sweetened, more or less, by coming face to face with such a man as you. Caleb! This unconscious little nurse gave me a broken hint last night, of which I have found the thread. I blush to think how easily I might have bound you and your daughter to me, and what a miserable idiot I was, when I took her for one! Friends, one and all, my house is very lonely tonight. I have not so much as a Cricket on my Hearth. I have scared them all away. Be gracious to me; let me join this happy party!'

He was at home in five minutes. You never saw such a fellow. What HAD he been doing with himself all his life, never to have known, before, his great capacity of being jovial! Or what had the Fairies been doing with him, to have effected such a change!

'John! you won't send me home this evening; will you?' whispered Dot.

He had been very near it though!

There wanted but one living creature to make the party complete; and, in the twinkling of an eye, there he was, very thirsty with hard running, and engaged in hopeless endeavours to squeeze his head into a narrow pitcher. He had gone with the cart to its journey's end, very much disgusted with the absence of his master, and stupendously rebellious to the Deputy. After lingering about the stable for some little time, vainly attempting to incite the old horse to the mutinous act of returning on his own account, he had walked into the tap-room and laid himself down before the fire. But suddenly yielding to the conviction that the Deputy was a humbug, and must be abandoned, he had got up again, turned tail, and come home.

There was a dance in the evening. With which general mention of that recreation, I should have left it alone, if I had not some reason to suppose that it was quite an original dance, and one of a most uncommon figure. It was formed in an odd way; in this way.

Edward, that sailor-fellow—a good free dashing sort of a fellow he was—had been telling them various marvels concerning parrots, and mines, and Mexicans, and gold dust, when all at once he took it in his head to jump up from his seat and propose a dance; for Bertha's harp was there, and she had such a hand upon it as you seldom hear. Dot (sly little piece of affectation when she chose) said her dancing days were over; I think because the Carrier was smoking his pipe, and she liked sitting by him, best. Mrs. Fielding had no choice, of course, but to say HER dancing days were over, after that; and everybody said the same, except May; May was ready.

So, May and Edward got up, amid great applause, to dance alone; and Bertha plays her liveliest tune.

Well! if you'll believe me, they have not been dancing five minutes, when suddenly the Carrier flings his pipe away, takes Dot round the waist, dashes out into the room, and starts off with her, toe and heel, quite wonderfully. Tackleton no sooner sees this, than he skims across to Mrs. Fielding, takes her round the waist, and follows suit. Old Dot no sooner sees this, than up he is, all alive, whisks off Mrs. Dot in the middle of the dance, and is the foremost there. Caleb no sooner sees this, than he clutches Tilly Slowboy by both hands and goes off at score; Miss Slowboy, firm in the belief that diving hotly in among the other couples, and effecting any number of concussions with them, is your only principle of footing it.

Hark! how the Cricket joins the music with its Chirp, Chirp, Chirp; and how the kettle hums!

But what is this! Even as I listen to them, blithely, and turn towards Dot, for one last glimpse of a little figure very pleasant to me, she and the rest have vanished into air, and I am left alone. A Cricket sings upon the Hearth; a broken child's-toy lies upon the ground; and nothing else remains.

The Last Words of the Old Year

This venerable gentleman, christened (in the Church of England) by the names One Thousand Eight Hundred and Fifty, who had attained the great age of three hundred and sixty-five (days), breathed his last, at midnight, on the thirty-first of December, in the presence of his confidential business-agents, the Chief of the Grave Diggers, and the Head Registrar of Births. The melancholy event took place at the residence of the deceased, on the confines of Time; and it is understood that his ashes will rest in the family vault, situated within the quiet precincts of Chronology.

For some weeks, it had been manifest that the venerable gentleman was rapidly sinking. He was well aware of his approaching end, and often predicted that he would expire at twelve at night, as the whole of his ancestors had done. The result proved him to be correct, for he kept his time to the moment.

He had always evinced a talkative disposition, and latterly became extremely garrulous. Occasionally, in the months of November and December, he exclaimed, "No Popery!" with some symptoms of a disordered mind; but, generally speaking, was in the full possession of his faculties, and very sensible.

On the night of his death, being then perfectly collected, he delivered himself in the following terms, to his friends already mentioned, the Chief of the Grave Diggers and the Head Registrar of Births:

"We have done, my friends, a good deal of business together, and you are now about to enter into the service of my successor.

May you give every satisfaction to him and his!

"I have been," said the good old gentleman, penitently, "a Year of Ruin. I have blighted all the farmers, destroyed the land, given the final blow to the Agricultural Interest, and smashed the Country. It is true, I have been a Year of Commercial 'Prosperity, and remarkable for the steadiness of my English Funds, which have never been lower than ninety-four, or higher than ninety-seven and three-quarters. But you will pardon the inconsistencies of a weak old man.

"I had fondly hoped," he pursued, with much feeling, addressing the Chief of the Grave Diggers, "that, before my decease, you would have finally adjusted the turf over the ashes of the Honourable Board of Commissioners of Sewers; the most feeble and incompetent Body that ever did outrage to the common sense of any community, or was ever beheld by any member of my family. But, as this was not to be, I charge you, do your duty by them in the days of my successor!"

The Chief of the Grave Diggers solemnly pledged himself to observe this request. The Abortion of Incapables referred to, had (he said) done much for him, in the way of preserving his business, endangered by the recommendations of the Board of Health; but, regardless of all personal obligations, he thereby undertook to lay them low. Deeper than they were already buried in the contempt of the public, (this he swore upon his spade) he would shovel the earth over their preposterous heads!

The venerable gentleman, whose mind appeared to be relieved of an enormous load, by this promise, stretched out his hand, and tranquilly returned, "Thank you! Bless you!"

"I have been," he said, resuming his last discourse, after a short interval of silent satisfaction, "doomed to witness the sacrifice of many valuable and dear lives, in steamboats, because of the want of the commonest and easiest precautions for the prevention of those legal murders. In the days of my great grandfather, there yet existed an invention called Paddle-box Boats. Can either of you gild the few remaining sands fast running through my glass, with the hope that my great grandson may see its adoption made compulsory on the owners of passenger steam-ships?"

After a despondent pause, the Head Registrar of Births gently observed that, in England, the recognition of any such invention by the legislature—particularly if simple, and of proved necessity—could scarcely be expected under a hundred years. In China, such a result might follow in fifty, but in England (he considered) in not less than a hundred. The venerable invalid replied, "True, true!" and for some minutes appeared faint, but afterwards rallied.

"A stupendous material work;" these were his next words; "has been accomplished in my time. Do I, who have witnessed the opening of the Britannia Bridge across the Menai Straights, and who claim the man who made that bridge for one of my distinguished children, see through the Tube, as through a mighty telescope, the Education of the people coming nearer?"

He sat up in his bed, as he spoke, and a great light seemed to shine from his eyes.

"Do I," he said, "who have been deafened by a whirlwind of sound and fury, consequent on a demand for Secular Education, see *any* Education through the opening years, for those who need it most?"

A film gradually came over his eyes, and he sunk back on his pillow. Presently, directing his weakened glance towards the Head Registrar of Births, he asked that personage:

"How many of those whom Nature brings within your province, in the spot of earth called England, can neither read nor write, in after years?"

The Registrar answered (referring to the last number of the present publication), "about forty-five in every hundred."

"And in my History for the month of May," said the old year with a heavy groan, "I find it written: 'Two little children whose heads scarcely reached the top of the dock, were charged at Bow Street on the seventh, with stealing a loaf out of a baker's shop. They said, in defence, that they were starving, and their appearance showed that they spoke the truth. They were sentenced to be whipped in the House of Correction.' To be whipped! Woe,

woe! Can the State devise no better sentence for its little children! Will it never sentence them to be taught?"

The venerable gentleman became extremely discomposed in his mind, and would have torn his white hair from his head, but for the soothing attentions of his friends.

"In the same month," he observed, when he became more calm, "and within a week, an English Prince was born. Suppose him taken from his Princely home, (Heaven's blessing on it!) cast like these wretched babies on the streets, and sentenced to be left in ignorance, what difference, soon, between him, and the little children sentenced to be whipped? Think of it, Great Queen, and become the Royal Mother of them all!"

The Head Registrar of Births and the Chief of the Grave Diggers, both of whom have great experience of infancy, predestined, (they do not blasphemously suppose, by God, but know, by man) to vice and shame, were greatly overcome by the earnestness of their departing friend.

"I have seen," he presently said, "a project carried into execution for a great assemblage of the peaceful glories of the world. I have seen a wonderful structure, reared in glass, by the energy and skill of a great natural genius, self-improved; worthy descendant of my Saxon ancestors; worthy type of industry and ingenuity triumphant! Which of my children shall behold the Princes, Prelates? Nobles, Merchants, of England, equally united, for another Exhibition—for a great display of England's sins and negligences, to be, by steady contemplation of all eyes, and steady union of all hearts and hands, set right!

"Come hither, my Right Reverend Brother, to whom an English tragedy presented in the theatre is contamination, but who art a bishop, none the less, in right of the translation of Greek Plays; come hither, from a life of Latin Verses and Quantities, and study the Humanities through *these* transparent windows! Wake, Colleges of Oxford, from daydreams of ecclesiastical melodrama, and look in on these realities of the daylight, for the night cometh when no man can work! Listen, my Lords and Gentlemen, to the roar within, so deep, so real, so low down, so incessant and accumulative!

"Not all the reedy pipes of all the shepherds that eternally play one little tune—not twice as many feet of Latin verses as would reach from this globe to the Moon and back—not all the Quantities that are, or ever were, or will be, in the world—Quantities of Prosody, or Law, or State, or Church, or Quantities of anything but work in the right spirit, will quiet it for a second, or clear an inch of space in this dark Exhibition of the bad results of our doings! Where shall we hold it? When shall we open it? What courtier speaks?"

After the foregoing rhapsody, the venerable gentleman became, for a time, much enfeebled; and the Chief of the Grave Diggers took a few minutes' repose.

As the hands of the clock were now rapidly advancing towards the hour which the invalid had predicted would be his last, his attendants considered it expedient to sound him as to his arrangements in connexion with his worldly affairs; both, being in doubt whether these were completed, or, indeed, whether he had anything to leave. The Chief of the Grave Diggers, as the fittest person for such an office, undertook it. He delicately enquired whether his friend and master had any testamentary wishes to express. If so, they should be faithfully observed.

"Thank you," returned the old gentleman, with a smile, for he was once more composed; "I have Something to bequeath to my successor; but not so much (I am happy to say) as I might have had. The Sunday Postage question, thank God, I have got rid of; and the Nepalese Ambassadors are gone home. May they stay there!"

This pious aspiration was responded to, with great favour, by both the attendants.

"I have seen you," said the venerable Testator, addressing the Chief of the Grave Diggers, "lay beneath the ground, a great Statesman and a fallen King of France."

The Chief of the Grave Diggers replied, "It is true."

"I desire," said the Testator, in a distinct voice, "to entail the remembrance of them on my successors forever. Of the statesman, as an Englishman who rejected an adventitious nobility, and composedly knew his own. Of the King, as a great example that the monarch who addresses himself to the meaner passions of humanity, and governs by cunning and corruption, makes his bed of thorns, and sets his throne on shifting sand."

The Head Registrar of Births took a note of the bequest.

"Is there any other wish?" enquired the Chief of the Grave Diggers, observing that his patron closed his eyes.

"I bequeath to my successor," said the ancient gentleman, opening them again, "a vast inheritance of degradation and neglect in England; and I charge him, if he be wise, to get speedily through it. I do hereby give and bequeath to him, also, Ireland. And I admonish him to leave it to his successor in a better condition than he will find it. He can hardly leave it in a worse."

The scratching of the pen used by the Head Registrar of Births, was the only sound that broke the ensuing silence.

"I do give and bequeath to him, likewise," said the Testator, rousing himself by a vigorous effort, "the Court of Chancery. The less he leaves of it to his successor, the better for mankind."

The Head Registrar of Births wrote as expeditiously as possible, for the clock showed that it was within five minutes of midnight.

"Also I do give and bequeath to him," said the Testator, "the costly complications of the English law in general. With which I do hereby couple the same advice."

The Registrar coming to the end of his note, repeated, "The same advice."

"Also, I do give and bequeath to him," said the Testator, "the Window Tax. Also, a general mismanagement of all public expenditure, revenues, and property, in Great Britain and its possessions."

The anxious Registrar, with a glance at the clock, repeated, "And its possessions."

"Also, I do give and bequeath to him," said the Testator, collecting his strength once more, by a surprising effort, "Nicholas

Wiseman and the Pope of Rome."

The two attendants breathlessly enquired together, "With what injunctions?"

"To study well," said the Testator, "the speech of the Dean of Bristol, made at Bristol aforesaid; and to deal with them and the whole vexed question, according to that speech. And I do hereby give and bequeath to my successor, the said speech and the said faithful Dean, as great possessions and good guides. And I wish with all my heart, the said faithful Dean were removed a little farther to the West of England and made Bishop of Exeter!"

With this, the Old Year turned serenely on his side, and breathed his last in peace. Whereon,—

With twelve great shocks of sound,
Was clash'd and hammer'd from a hundred towers
One after one,

the coming of the New Year. He came on, joyfully. The Head Registrar, making, from mere force of habit, an entry of his birth, while the Chief of the Grave Diggers took charge of his predecessor; added these words in Letters of Gold:

May it be a wise and happy year, for all of us!

ALSO FROM LEONAUR

AVAILABLE IN SOFTCOVER OR HARDCOVER WITH DUST JACKET

A JOURNAL OF THE SECOND SIKH WAR by *Daniel A. Sandford*—The Experiences of an Ensign of the 2nd Bengal European Regiment During the Campaign in the Punjab, India, 1848-49.

LAKE'S CAMPAIGNS IN INDIA by *Hugh Pearse*—The Second Anglo Maratha War, 1803-1807. Often neglected by historians and students alike, Lake's Indian campaign was fought against a resourceful and ruthless enemy-almost always superior in numbers to his own forces.

BRITAIN IN AFGHANISTAN 1: THE FIRST AFGHAN WAR 1839-42 by *Archibald Forbes*—Following over a century of the gradual assumption of sovereignty of the Indian Sub-Continent, the British Empire, in the form of the Honourable East India Company, supported by troops of the new Queen Victoria's army, found itself inevitably at the natural boundaries that surround Afghanistan. There it set in motion a series of disastrous events-the first of which was to march into the country at all.

BRITAIN IN AFGHANISTAN 2: THE SECOND AFGHAN WAR 1878-80 by *Archibald Forbes*—This the history of the Second Afghan War-another episode of British military history typified by savagery, massacre, siege and battles.

UP AMONG THE PANDIES by *Vivian Dering Majendie*—An outstanding account of the campaign for the fall of Lucknow. This is a vital book of war as fought by the British Army of the mid-nineteenth century, but in truth it is also an essential book of war that will enthral.

BLOW THE BUGLE, DRAW THE SWORD by *W. H. G. Kingston*—The Wars, Campaigns, Regiments and Soldiers of the British & Indian Armies During the Victorian Era, 1839-1898.

INDIAN MUTINY 150th ANNIVERSARY: A LEONAUR ORIGINAL

MUTINY: 1857 by *James Humphries*—It is now 150 years since the 'Indian Mutiny' burst like an engulfing flame on the British soldiers, their families and the civilians of the Empire in North East India. The Bengal Native army arose in violent rebellion, and the once peaceful countryside became a battleground as Native sepoys and elements of the Indian population massacred their British masters and defeated them in open battle. As the tide turned, a vengeful army of British and loyal Indian troops repressed the insurgency with a savagery that knew no mercy. It was a time of fear and slaughter. James Humphries has drawn together the voices of those dreadful days for this commemorative book.

www.ingramcontent.com/pod-product-compliance
Lightning Source LLC
LaVergne TN
LVHW050921080826
845145LV00001B/164